Forever Treasured

Also by Aimee Martin

The Lake Shores Series

Forever Home

Forever Grateful

Forever Treasured

Aimee Martin

A Lake Shores Series Novel

Mercy Books,

A division of Mercy Pictures

Copyright

ISBN: 978-0-9963063-5-5

FOREVER TREASURED

Published in the United States by Mercy Books,
a division of Mercy Pictures

To all the victims of adultery
Who have found their second chance at love

Acknowledgements

Wow! How is this already book 3 in the Lake Shores Series? It seems like just yesterday when I was hoping and praying you all would love Forever Home, the first in the series. And now we're on the third (and so far, my absolute *favorite*).

First, foremost and biggest thanks... God, The One who has helped me through some rough times and brought me to where I am today.

Thank you to my very own cowboy in a Stetson; the man, the myth, the legend who is always there to answer a question about construction and lend an ear when I'm writing an exciting scene and need his input (or keep his mouth closed if I don't like his criticism). Words will never be enough, mo grádh. Gu siorrádh.

To my three amazing, supportive, kind-hearted children, for loving me and being my own personal cheer squad and always asking, even when you're busy in your little, child lives, how my book was going. I love you all infinity and beyond. I promise to save you each a copy for when you're old enough to read it.

To my editor, Dixie, who I've said before and will say again, is the ninja of all editors. You took a chance on a green, wet-behind-the-ears wannabe and have helped to mold me into something better. Thank you from the bottom of my heart.

To Britney and Lisa.... You two read this book all along with me and the encouragement you gave me kept my own mojo going so I could get it finished. I love you both and can never thank you enough for your enthusiasm and support in this dream of mine.

To my parents, mother in law, and all the rest of my ridiculously large family, thank you all for having faith in me.

And to you... the ones who make this dream possible... the readers. You are all the real rock stars and you all deserve a medal (or at least a cup of coffee... or a glass of wine) for the support you've shown. Thank you for going on this journey with me and for loving my characters as much as I do.

Note From The Author

If you or someone you know has been the victim in an adulterous marriage or relationship, please don't think you are alone. Please don't feel like you have done something wrong. And please, please remember that just because love was lost once, that does not mean you cannot find love again. Seek help if you feel that you are at fault, if you're struggling to move forward, if you're finally moving on and are facing feelings of guilt. Or even if you just need someone to talk to.

For anonymous counsel go to...
http://www.dailystrength.org

If you're not quite ready to seek the help of others (anonymous or not), you can always use your bible. Answers to all your worries and fears are located in those pages in abundance. All scriptures from this book were used from the King James Version, which can be found...
http://www.kingjamesbibleonline.org

Forever Treasured

Prologue

"Thou shalt not commit adultery."
Exodus 20:14

May 15, 2010

Most people think that getting married and having a baby is the happiest time in a woman's life. But in this instance, on this day, they would be wrong.

Allyson Marx was not happy or jumping for joy. She was not anticipating a wedding night full of sweet love and tender kisses and heartfelt whispers of 'I love you.' She *should* be. She *ached* to be. One day.

But no matter how hard she tried, Ally just couldn't muster up the energy she would need to put on that kind of show. Because that is exactly what it would be, a show for the family and friends who had come to express their support for a blossoming love.

She was twenty-two years old, twenty-three next month. She had just moved back to her hometown of Rosy Camp, Montana a week before, after graduating from college at San Diego State University. Ally spent four years getting her degree in public relations and thought she was ready to take on the media world.

Now, she walked down a worn-down, red-carpeted aisle in the old Methodist church her family had attended for many years. She was going to marry a man who had been in her life for five years, a man she had no desire to wed.

The cream-colored wedding dress her mother insisted she wear was stuffy, suffocating with its lace sleeves that stretched from shoulder to fingertip. The material flickered an iridescent white glow on the carpet below her feet from the sun streaming in through the stained glass at the front of the church. The depiction of the downward dove in a multitude of colors gave her no comfort. But it did give Ally the impression that God, Himself, was a party to this farce.

She was not comfortable. The bodice, with its empire waist, was big and billowy with rows and rows of layered tulle that were supposed to make her look like a princess.

All I feel like is a fat, toasted marshmallow.

There were only a select handful of people who sat in the rows of pews that Ally walked past who knew the reason behind the poufy, balloon of a wedding dress. She tried–and failed–to put a smile on her face for those who didn't know the truth, those who thought this was an honest-to-goodness-love match. Ally couldn't help but sigh in resignation that *this* was where her life had ended up.

The layers of material were for the sole purpose of hiding her growing baby bump.

She couldn't blame anyone but herself for being in this situation. She knew the risks. She gave in to pressure and began sleeping with Ben their senior year of high school.

Off they went to college together four years ago and nothing bad ever came from their physical relationship. Neither of them had an inkling that it could. They were so careful. She was not one of those country girls who grew up in small towns, with no goals other than to hunt and procreate.

One night at a frat party, after too much alcohol, and numbed common sense, they threw caution to the wind. *Just this once, nothing will happen, Ben said.* How wrong he was.

If Ally had known that her Daddy was going to make her get married just because she'd gotten pregnant she would've… *What?* Ally thought as she closed in on the alter at the front of the church. *It's not like you'd have hidden it from your parents. Gone and gotten rid of the baby without anyone knowing. Babies are blessings, no matter the circumstances.*

Still, maybe she would have fought harder for the right to stay single and raise the baby alone. Maybe she could have made her parents understand that she didn't need a man in her life to help her raise a baby.

Maybe she could have explained things to them. But she just couldn't find the words to tell them she and Ben had separated. Ally couldn't bring herself to tell them that she had found him in bed with another girl just two weeks after a positive pregnancy test. If she'd only had the nerve to speak up, they might not have insisted on a wedding.

She could have given the baby up for adoption. There were plenty of couples eager and ready to be parents. Couples more prepared to raise a child. She had just begun to find her way in the world. And worse, she was no longer in love with Ben, the man she once thought she would spend the rest of her life with.

You'd have never forgiven yourself if you would have given this baby up and you know it, Allyson Nicole Marx.

That was the absolute truth. Ally would have wondered for the rest of her life if she had made a horrible mistake. She would wonder where the child was, who he–or she–had become. If their life had been a happy one.

So she stepped onto the faded pine dais, took Ben's offered arm and told herself that she would be happy. She *would.* Benjamin Willis had been a good man at one time. He swore he would never cheat on her again. He was respectful, smart and strong. He was tall, handsome with dark brown hair and eyes. Women swooned at his feet when he smiled and those deep dimples appeared. She certainly had.

Once upon a time, anyway.

It didn't matter anymore that she'd fallen out of love with him. There was more to think about now than just her. Ally had to think about the baby growing inside her belly. She should feel privileged to be marrying into one of the most prominent ranch families in the southwest region of Montana.

So why, Ally thought as the minister asked the congregation to bow their heads in prayer, *do I feel like my life is ending, instead of only beginning?*

•••••

January 26, 2015

Aaron Lambert blew out a heavy breath as he walked up the three concrete steps to his house. He took in the yellow glow of the porch light next to the door, at the golden shadow it cast across the black 'Welcome' mat that sat at the threshold. Black, like the night that surrounded him as if it were a coat. Or a shield.

Instead of feeling relief for being home, he felt drained, anxious about facing the woman who waited on him inside. She was probably ready to rip his head off. He glanced at his watch, saw that it was almost ten o'clock and figured he'd better just buck up and prepare for another fight with his wife, something he and Jess seemed to do more and more of lately.

Not seem *to, we fight all the time,* he thought to himself. Ever since Jess brought up the subject of a baby back in August, and he had told her he wasn't ready to take that step yet. Usually multiple times a day. So why should tonight be any different?

He was coming home five hours late.

It didn't matter that the reason he was late was due to an emergency at work. Jess wouldn't care that he and his crew had had to work for over seven hours to put out a fire at the chemical plant he worked at. She would just see it as an excuse, accuse him of doing whatever was in his power to stay away from her and keep from having the same argument yet again and, in her words, "Never think of anyone but himself."

As he unlocked the brushed-nickel handle and walked quietly inside, closed the thin oak door behind him with a faint click, Aaron thought that maybe Jess was right. Maybe he was being selfish and needed to be more open to the idea of having a baby. Which was what she desperately wanted. Again, her words.

Yes, they'd only been married for eighteen months but he was going to be thirty-three this year. Wasn't it time for him to grow up? Take the next step into adulthood and become a father?

I can't. Aaron's shoulders slumped as he tossed his keys on the entry hall table. The same feelings that kept him from giving in to Jessica's requests barreled back into his mind.

His head hung low alongside his shoulders. He just wasn't ready. And he couldn't, in good conscience, say "Sure Jess. Let's have a baby," when he wasn't one hundred percent positive that it was what he wanted. It wouldn't be fair to her or the baby. Not to mention him.

He walked through the living room, noticed the Austin stone fireplace to his left still had embers that burned inside. Their soft crackles broke the silence of the room like Rice Cripsies. Just as he was about to turn the corner and climb the dark stairs that led to the second floor and their master bedroom, he spotted the wine bottle on the ledge in front of the fireplace. But that wasn't what stopped him in his tracks. It was the two wine glasses, remnants of their deep red contents still evident in the bottoms of the clear crystal, which had alarm bells going off in his head.

He slowly turned his face back toward the staircase, strained his tired ears to hear something that sounded out of the ordinary. From down here, it was hard to hear anything that went on upstairs. Add to that his pounding heart that made the blood pool in his ears and all he could focus on was the echo that sounded in his brain. Aaron swallowed past a lump in his throat and started toward the stairs again, slowly walked up them one at a time. *Creeping like a burglar is more like it.* Which was ridiculous considering this was *his* house, but some instinct told him to proceed with caution.

Ten steps later and he stood on the second floor landing. He glanced to the right, saw that it was dark in the open bonus area that looked down over a railing and into the living room, and headed left, down the short hallway that would take him to his bedroom. *Their* bedroom. He paused outside the door. His hand grasped the doorknob so hard his knuckles turned white. With his ear pressed against the cool wood, he listened for a sound. Aaron waited a minute. Then two. When he heard nothing he relaxed his hand and laid his forehead against the door, released the breath he'd been holding.

Get a grip, Aar. She probably just had one of the girls over.

More confident, he turned the knob and started to open the door when he heard what he dreaded. The soft moan that he *knew* came from Jessica. There was another sound, a hard and heavy pant, like a man's, and definitely *not* from his wife. And the unmistakable sounds of a mattress squeaking. Aaron placed his hand flat on the door, pushed gently, and it swung open in slow motion.

Piece by piece, he took in what was in front of him. Large feet encased in white socks, long legs covered in dark hair, the unmistakable barrel chest of a muscular man. Then he saw the body that sat on top of that man. He dragged his gaze up over smooth legs, thin hips and waist, the blonde hair–which Aaron knew would smell like vanilla–that fell in short waves across her neck.

His wife, his Jessica, was having sex with another man. In their house. In their bed.

He fell against the door jam, his body too heavy to hold up anymore. The door swung open the rest of the way, hit the wall hard behind him. The sound broke into the concentration of the two people on the bed less than ten feet away. He watched Jess's back straighten. He heard the deep curse from the man below her. Then two pairs of eyes–one set blue and wide like swimming pools, one set dark and apologetic like a dog who knew he just ate the wrong shoe– turned in his direction.

"What the hell, Jess?"

"Aaron, I… I'm sorry. It just____"

"If you say, "It just happened" I think I might puke."

Jess closed her lips and her mouth turned down at the corners. Tears swam in her eyes. Aaron took in that expression and couldn't help it anymore. He laughed. He laughed so hard that he doubled over, rested his hands against his knees, and let it all out. The ridiculousness of the situation, the worry he had felt at disappointing her again, the way his life turned out. His little brother had just gotten happily married four days ago and here Aaron was, walking in on the woman *he'd* married with another man.

"Aaron," Jess said. "Aaron, what is wrong with you?"

Slowly he stood back up, noticed Jessica and the man had removed themselves from the bed, and he continued to chuckle. The man huddled off in the corner and practically dove into his clothes. She stopped in the middle of the room and tied a blue silk robe around her waist. He looked at that robe, remembered slowly taking it off her on their honeymoon, and the laughter ceased.

"What's wrong with me?" he asked and took a step toward her. His wife backed up until her knees hit the mattress. *Wife... what a crock,* Aaron thought as he advanced until he was almost nose-to-nose with the woman he'd married. *Lord, forgive me.* "What's wrong with me is that I walked in on my wife having sex with another man. What's wrong with me is that the vows my wife spoke to me a year and a half ago were just flushed down the toilet like a dead fish. What's wrong with me is that..." he stopped, scared of what he was about to say, but knowing he had to say it anyway. Air. He needed air. Aaron straightened his spine, took a deep breath and spoke the words he didn't think he'd ever utter in his life. "What's wrong is that I just realized what a sham our marriage was."

"No, it's not like that!" Jess argued. "Just let me explain!"

"There's nothing to explain, Jessica. I want you out of my house."

"This is *our* house, Aaron."

"No," he sighed, "it's not. Not anymore." He turned and headed back to the open door, ready to get the heck out of there. Before he walked away, he spoke to Jess over his shoulder and his words reverberated through the now silent room.

"I want a divorce."

Chapter 1

"To everything there is a season, and a time
to every purpose under the heaven."
Ecclesiastes 3:1

May 15, 2015

"Hey, man… where're ya at?"

Aaron's head snapped up at the sound of his friend Blake Thompson's voice. "I'm here," he answered without conviction and turned his face back down to the scuffed bar top in front of them. He picked at the chipped varnish and prayed his buddy wouldn't ask too many questions tonight.

Normally Aaron wouldn't mind sitting around on a Friday night, ribbing the man to his right while he came up with some smart aleck response about how it should be obvious where he was, since his chair was only two feet from Blake's. But tonight he just wanted to drink his beer and brood.

Aaron had just received the signed divorce papers from his wife. *Ex-wife,* he corrected himself.

One hundred and nine days after he walked in on Jess with another man, their marriage was over. She didn't put up a fight throughout the entire process. Told the judge that she was willing to sign over any rights she might have had, that Aaron could have everything, so long as she was able to walk away and never look back.

The judge had agreed to her request since the house was in Aaron's name, and he'd bought it before they got married. But he had made the stipulation that any furniture and household items acquired during the course of their marriage would have to be divided. Aaron came home from work the next day to find a note on the counter that read simply, **You can have it all.**

After that, it was easy.

Easy... right. What about ending a marriage is easy? Aaron thought and took a big swig off his longneck. What he really wanted was to sit here and get drunk. Newly divorced people did that, right? And wasn't it even accepted? *Not by my mother. She'd kill me if she found out I was sitting around getting wasted and not being the good, Christian man she brought me up to be.*

He wasn't worried about his Mom thinking less of him as a man, or a Christian, for getting a divorce. Adultery was in the bible as one of the very few reasons that divorce wasn't frowned upon. Not to mention the fact that it was an agreement between he and Jessica on the day they'd gotten married. No adultery. No abuse. She broke that agreement, and while some people might have tried to work through it, Aaron knew there'd been no coming back for them. So they'd separated. And he believed, in his heart, that his parents would be okay with it. That they would support him and his reasons for the decision he made.

Problem was, no one in his family knew about the divorce yet. Aaron and Jess had agreed to keep the separation quiet and to tell their families in their own time. He had no clue if his former in-laws knew or not. Didn't know if Jess had told them the truth–that she cheated on him–or if she had made him out to be the bad guy. Truthfully, he didn't care.

All Aaron wanted was to put her out of his mind. And he was going to start by finishing this beer, then ordering another. Blake spoke again as the cool, amber liquid slid down his throat.

"If you're here, then I'm wearing a dress and high heels."

"Lipstick too?"

"Not tonight. It wouldn't fit in my purse."

"That's too bad," Aaron told Blake and turned on his stool to face him, forcing himself to get out of the funk that surrounded him. "I bet you'd look real good with some bright red color painted on your little feminine lips."

Blake laughed and slapped Aaron on the back. "It's about time you got out of your head. I was getting ready to strike up a conversation with old man Winters over there." Blake hiked his thumb behind him to the man with white hair and matching beard–who'd looked that old even when Aaron had been a kid–that slumped over his half-drunk glass of cheap whiskey. "I swear, I think that man has been sitting in that same spot since I moved here back in Ninety-Nine."

Blake had moved to Lake Shores, Texas–the small town of three thousand where Aaron grew up and still lived today– just three years after his high school graduation. Then ten years later, in Oh-Nine, Blake had called and told his friend, Jaxson Mathews, about the ranch that Blake had been working on going up for auction. Jaxson bought it, moved to Texas and kept Blake on as his ranch foreman.

Aaron met both men right here, at The Bar, shortly after Jax got to town. They'd been best friends ever since.

Then Jax ended up marrying Aaron's little sister, Brinley. After his movie-star-of-a-sister had lost her best friend, Annie, in a car accident, and turned her back on her faith, Aaron knew that God had brought Jax into her life at just the right time.

They'd saved each other; that much had been obvious from the start.

And he couldn't have been happier about two of the most important people in his life falling in love and vowing to spend the rest of their lives together.

If Aaron had called Jax, he would have been here tonight. But Jax and Brin had just had a baby less than three months ago, shortly after Aaron had walked in on his *ex*-wife. Aar figured Jax had more important things to do than sit around and stare at him pouting.

He could have called his little brother, too. Alex had just moved back to Lake Shores after spending eight years in the Navy. He worked at Jax's ranch, The Burnt Aggie, as a ranch hand, and would have tomorrow off work. But Alex had just gotten married to a woman he met through Brin, not three months ago. Some California girl named Melanie who moved to their small town to make a life with Alex. Newlyweds didn't want to be interrupted to deal with a man who'd lost hope in the sanctity of marriage. So he'd called Blake instead, knowing the single man was always up for a good time. And usually be counted on for a few laughs, too.

"I think he's been sitting in that same spot since I was born… thirty-two years ago."

Both men laughed as the disc in the jukebox changed from an old George Jones song to something Aaron had never heard before. He listened to it for a second then turned a questioning look to Blake.

"What the heck is this?" he asked because he knew Blake spent more time in here than he did.

"I don't know. Jim's been talking about trying to make the place more welcoming to the younger crowd. So he had his *daughter–*" Blake spit the word out like it left a bad taste in his mouth, "– come in and vamp up the music selections."

Jim was the owner of the place, a bear of a man in his sixties who was always looking for the next best thing for The Bar.

Usually his ideas fell through the cracks, which was exactly what the locals wanted. Change didn't come easily to small towns. Aaron figured the new music was one of Jim's big new ideas and hoped that this one didn't last either. Lake Shores liked their old country tunes, not this slow-paced pop that was playing now.

"You've got to be kidding me. Does Jim really think..." Aaron trailed off as he caught wind of the lyrics. Something about the screaming stopping and a fire burning away. About knowing it's over when there's nothing left to say.

He got up from his stool quickly and the legs squeaked on the floor. He walked over to the jukebox in the back right corner of the building, looked at the name of the band that was playing. Secondhand Serenade. Definitely not someone Aaron had ever heard of before. But he didn't care. He didn't care if Blake thought he was crazy right now. The only thing Aaron could focus on were the words the man and woman sang and how true they rang with his life. Right at this moment.

Because it *was* really over.

What am I supposed to do now? Aaron asked himself as he leaned against the jukebox and listened to the chorus play again. *What's my purpose for being here now that Jess is gone?*

"There you go again," Blake said softly as he stepped up next to Aaron. "Off someplace else. If I'm boring you that much, tell me now and I'll go find a woman to flirt with."

Aaron knew Blake was just trying to make light of the atmosphere again.

But listening to those sung words suddenly put every fear and doubt into the front of his mind. He had no clue what he was supposed to do with his life now.

His job didn't seem important; he had only accepted the position because Jessica's brother offered it and she'd begged him to take it.

His family didn't need him; they were all happy with their spouses. He looked up at Blake, realized he needed to talk to someone. He hoped like hell Blake was the right person.

"I need to tell you something. But you have to promise me this stays between us. For now, at least." Blake's brow crinkled at the seriousness in Aaron's voice. He set his empty beer on a table next to them and crossed his arms over his chest, nodded at Aar to go on. "Jess and I..." he paused, unsure of how to say the words when the situation still felt surreal to him.

He glanced around to make sure none of the other patrons were within earshot. Luckily the place was close to empty since an early Spring cold front blew through this morning and most people were at home, warm with their families. He finally just spit it out. "We got divorced, finalized it yesterday."

Blake's arms fell to the sides of his body, his mouth gaped open and his eyes got wide. Shock. *Yep, that's how I feel, too.*

"When did this… How did you…," Blake stuttered on his words. He took a deep breath and finally settled with, "Does your family know?"

"Not yet. That's why I said this has to stay between us for now."

"Okay. Yeah, no problem." Blake looked around just as Aaron had a minute ago. Aar thought the man looked suddenly uncomfortable before he asked, "Do you wanna talk about it?"

Aaron sighed and he felt the weight lift a little from his shoulders. "Yeah, I do."

"Here?"

"No." Aaron looked around the bar once more and found an empty table in front by the door. "Let's sit over there." He pointed to the table, started over there while Blake kept pace beside him. A waitress came over, asked them if they'd like another beer. Blake told her yes while Aaron said no. After the girl brought the lone beer back and walked off, Aaron turned to Blake and started to talk. "We've been having problems for a few months. Since August, really. She wanted a baby and I told her I wasn't ready. That was the beginning of the end."

"So, what? She divorced you because you didn't want to have kids? That's pretty asinine."

"I divorced her. And no, it wasn't because she wanted kids and I didn't. I do, someday. But not yet. I guess she decided she didn't want to wait around for that day to happen."

Understanding dawned on Blake's face as he sat back in his chair. He tipped the front of his black, felt cowboy hat up and off his forehead a little with the rim of his bottle, held the beer close to his chest while he waited for Aaron to go on.

"I walked in on her with another man. Right after Alex's wedding." Aar gave a short, humorless laugh, shook his head in disbelief yet again at the memory of what he'd seen. "I don't think she was actually trying to get pregnant with some other guy. That's a little too vindictive, even for her. I think she just... crap, I don't know why she did it. Loneliness, maybe. Anger is a possibility. Who knows? But she did it."

"And you couldn't forgive her for that."

"I think I probably could, probably *will*. Someday. But when I saw her and that man, I didn't feel jealous or rage or protective. I was surprised, yeah. But mostly I felt... relief." Aaron huffed out a breath at how good it felt to say those words aloud. He tore at a napkin on the table, watched the tiny pieces of white float to the hard surface like snow as he went on. "It's like somewhere deep down I knew that our marriage wasn't meant to be. But there was so much pressure from her family to get married because we'd been dating for so long that I felt like it was the next logical step. I didn't realize that I was going into it for the wrong reasons. It didn't click until I saw what I saw." He looked up from the napkin to stare at Blake. "I didn't know that my reservations about spending the rest of my life with Jess were based on that gut feeling telling me to not go through with it. At the time, I thought it was nerves so I pushed passed it. And now I'm one of those statistics. One of the "victims" whose spouse strayed, all because I didn't listen to my instincts. I'm such an idiot." This last he whispered and dropped his head into his hands, ran his fingers through his hair to fight back the headache that threatened.

"You're not an idiot," Blake stated. "You're a good person who got duped by someone you trusted. It happens to the best of us."

"Did it happen to you?"

"Something like that." Blake took a quick swig of his beer then said, "My point is that you can't blame yourself and you can't go around with this "woe is me" attitude. It happened. It's over. You need to find a way to move on."

"I don't even know where to start."

"I do."

Aaron waited for Blake to go on. When the man just sat there and said nothing, Aaron finally asked, "Where?"

"Anywhere but here, man. Anywhere but here."

•••••

Allyson sat on a flat rock almost five miles from her family's ranch headquarters. The gray stone was hard and cold underneath her from the drop in the temperature. She shivered, despite the wool parka she wore and two layers of long johns underneath her jeans. A northerner had blown in a couple days ago and made the air colder than the normal mid-fifties for this time of year. Which wasn't unheard of, but she was ready for warmer weather.

Warmer weather meant hunting season was ending for the next four months. It meant she'd have some alone time. It meant she could finally take a break from her Daddy and brother's incessant nagging and just breathe. That's why she was sitting here on this cold rock in the cold temperatures with her breath puffing out in little white clouds of smoke in front of her. Daddy and her little brother, Daniel, never came to this edge of the ranch. It was her territory when it came to guided hunts so they stayed away, Daddy closer to the hunter's bunkhouse next to their home and Danny on the eastern side of the property. She was grateful for their separate divisions. It meant she was able to keep this small pasture on the western edge of the ranch as her own little hideaway.

From where Ally sat, she could just see the top half of Granite Peak rising above low hanging clouds. The setting sun glistened off the snow-capped mountaintop like an iceberg in the ocean. The Peak was almost forty-three miles from Rosy Camp town proper, but the Marx Ranch and Game property–her family's place, known throughout southwest Montana for its trophy black bears and wolves and abundant population of mountain goats–was about fifteen miles west of town. Which made Granite Peak just over twenty miles from where she sat. When there weren't any high-rises and suburbs and God-knows what other manmade objects in the way, like in big cities, you could see forever on the horizon, and twenty-plus miles wasn't so far. At least that's what Ally felt like.

Here she could relax. Here she could inhale the sweet, cool mountain air and exhale all the frustrations of keeping her mouth shut when it came to correcting her little brother every time he acted like he knew more about the ranch than she did. Here she could pretend that her life was normal and happy and healthy instead of covered in disappointment from Daddy and empathy from Momma and regret in herself.

Here, on this cold rock, staring at that mountain miles away, Ally could pretend that she hadn't suffered a miscarriage almost five years ago at twenty-three years old. Just a few months after her impromptu wedding. She could pretend that she hadn't become the black sheep of the family by getting a divorce when she was twenty-five, only a year and a half after she'd lost her baby. She could pretend that she hadn't been perceived as a doormat when everyone discovered she'd been the victim of a straying husband.

Trust in the Lord, and do good.

Ally repeated the verse from Psalms over and over a lot when she was up here. Knowing that she had to trust in the plan that God had for her was the only thing that had given her the courage to leave Ben when she did. And on days like today, when she had no idea *what* God's plan was, and all she wanted to do was crawl into a hole and hide from the world–and her family–those seven words gave her the comfort she needed to remain upright. To stay focused on the bigger picture.

To feel blessed for what she'd been given by discovering Ben's secret when she had. A second chance.

Ally knew it could have been worse when she'd overheard the phone call between her ex-husband and some little hussy just over three years ago. She could have been one of those women that sat around and whined about how horrible it was that her husband had cheated on her. And wonder what she'd done wrong. And ask everyone why hadn't she been enough. But playing the pity-card had never been Ally's strong suit.

If there was one thing her Daddy taught her that she took to heart it was to not take any crap from anyone. To always stand up for what was right. And divorcing that two-timing pig had definitely been right.

So had punching him in the face and breaking his nose.

Ally smiled to herself as she remembered the shocked look on Ben's face that night after she confronted him about the phone call. He had tried to play it off as if she were imagining things at first. But when Ally had stared him down, he finally caved and admitted to having an affair with the Holms girl from town. Who was barely nineteen. Then Ally decked him square in the face and the sound of his nose cracking, followed by his girly squeal, had been enough to make her feel better. She'd shaken out her sore hand, walked out of their house–that was on *his* family's land–and told him to expect a letter from her attorney.

Nine months after that the marriage was over. And now, two and a half years later, Ally was finally starting to feel like herself again. Except for times like today.

Daddy had been hounding her since the sun came up about the last hunters who'd shot a bear in her section a few weeks ago, and how Ally had messed up by not logging it in the record book that night. He didn't care that she fell asleep as soon as she'd walked in the door to her bedroom. Tracking a wounded black bear for six hours tended to wear a person down and that night, Ally had been too exhausted to take a shower. Much less log in a kill.

She had admitted her mistake to Daddy, offered to fix it and even take on a few extra night shifts watching for forest fires (something they did from the beginning of Spring until the end of Fall). And Daddy had been ready to agree. Until Danny came and poked his nose in where it didn't belong and had gotten her father all riled up again, saying that Ally had been irresponsible and should be reprimanded. Danny, who'd still been in diapers when Ally guided her first hunt at seventeen.

Okay, okay... so he was actually ten at that time. He still doesn't have as much experience as me, even if he is twenty-one now.

Danny was a brown-nosing kid, trying to be a man, who stoked their father's ego every chance he got. All because he hoped the ranch would be left to him when their parents retired. And Daddy ate it up like yesterday's buttermilk pie. Had been ever since Ally's older brother died when she was a senior in college. If Danny would stop sucking up and talk to Ally, he would learn that there was no need to try to get on Daddy's good side by making her–the oldest, who should be the beneficiary–look bad. Ally didn't want the ranch.

The only reason she was still here, working for her father, was because she wasn't sure where else to go. Montana was all she knew. If she left, what would she do? Who would she be?

If I left here, Ally thought as she watched the sun sink below the horizon, at the deep orange and purple glow it cast over the land that stretched out in front of her like a royal blanket, *what would my purpose in this life be?*

●●●●●

May 31, 2015

Aaron walked up to his parents' home in Lake Shores, knocked once on the red door and went inside to find his whole family already there for Sunday dinner. Brin sat in the dark brown, leather recliner. Jax hovered right behind her, like a butler who waited for his next command from his boss. Alex and Mel sat on the matching couch on the opposite wall, cuddled together with their hands clasped together.

The perfect picture of devotion.

His Mom, Tina, and Dad, Mitch, stood in the kitchen, Mom with a tiny bundle of pink cradled in her arms like a football. Dad leaned over her shoulder, made faces at baby Sarah and laughed at the gurgles that came from their new grandbaby's mouth. His family looked like a flawless bunch. Unadulterated love radiated from the room like heat from the sun. All except him, who was about to shatter the image like a mirror that had been dropped on a wooden floor with the news of his divorce.

Aaron had purposely waited over two weeks after his night out with Blake. He told himself it was because he needed to make sure the signed papers were filed and that the deed was really and truly finished.

But in reality, Aar knew he'd put it off because he was scared. He took a deep breath, told himself to stop acting like a "Nancy" and face whatever disappointment came his way.

About that time, his Mom looked up from her granddaughter's face, locked eyes with Aaron as he stood in the living room entryway, and smiled.

"Aaron! I'm so glad you're here. Come look, Daddy just had Sarah laughing. It's the sweetest sound you've ever heard."

Aar walked over to his parents, bent and kissed his mother on the cheek and tried to keep the bitterness out of his voice when he said, "I know. I heard it when I walked in. It's definitely sweet."

"Oh what do you know?" his Momma smirked at him. "Where's Jess? She'll appreciate this more than you." Mom craned her neck to the side, looked for a woman that she wouldn't find and turned a questioning look back at Aaron. "Where's Jessica?"

"She's not coming Momma. And before you ask any more questions, I need to tell you something." Aaron turned to face the rest of his family that now looked at him with that same question in their gazes. "All of you."

"Aaron. What's going on, son?" his Dad asked.

"Why don't you and Mom sit down?"

"I don't want to sit down, Aaron. Just spit it out."

"Momma, it'd be better if you just____"

"It will not make a bit of difference whether I'm standing, sitting or lying down in bed. Now tell us what's going on," his mother interrupted.

"It'll be better for me, okay?!" At Aaron's outburst, his parents jerked back as if they'd been slapped. He sighed. "I'm sorry. I don't mean to yell. Please, just sit." He waited until they had taken a seat on the loveseat cattycornered to the couch Alex and Mel sat on before he continued. "Jessica won't be coming for dinner today. Or any other dinner in the future. We... she and I..." Aar stopped and hung his head, the words stuck harder in his throat than they'd been when he talked to Blake.

"Aaron, sweetie?" He looked up at the sound of his Momma's soft voice. "What happened?"

He stared into his mother's deep blue eyes, clear and knowing and so much like his own. Aaron swore he felt like his mother already knew what was coming, but he knew she–all of them–needed to hear the words. He took a deep breath, threw his shoulders back and let the words come as they may.

"Jessica and I got a divorce. It was finalized just over two weeks ago. And before any of you judge, hear me out." He licked his dry lips then said, "I walked in on Jessica having sex with another man. I know some people would work through that, do whatever it took to save their marriage. But when I saw her, I knew in here–" he patted his hand against his chest, right over his heart, "–that there would be no saving ours. I think I always knew we were doomed, but it took *that* moment, that catalyst, for me to see it. For me to know that our marriage was never meant to be. And Momma, even God forgives divorce when it comes about because of adultery. I think, I have to believe, that God has something bigger and better for me. And I hope you feel that way, too. I'm sorry I haven't told any of you before now. I just... I don't know. I was scared. But I can't be scared anymore. I need to move on and I need y'all behind me on this. So, that's it."

He waited for the shocked gasps, the twenty questions. Even a cry of astonishment. But the room remained silent enough to hear a pin drop. One minute turned into two. At the five-minute mark of silence throughout the house, Aaron strongly considered making a break for the front door. Then his mother, God bless her sweet soul, finally spoke.

"That no-good, philandering, promiscuous, little tramp!"

What Aar's speech hadn't been able to do, his mother's one sentence did. The deep gasps from the three other men in the room mixed with the feminine squeals from the two women. Then everyone laughed.

Aaron stared around the room, watched his family find humor in what could have been a very awkward situation, and decided he loved them more than ever. Crazy reactions and all.

"Now, Momma," Brin spoke when she caught her breath. "That was not very Christian-like of you."

"Hmm. Yes, well... Lord, please forgive me," she said as she looked toward Heaven with her hand over her heart. "You know, Aaron, I never thought she was good enough for you anyway. And her family wasn't even from Lake Shores, so that should tell you something."

"Hey, neither am I, Tina," Mel remarked with a grin.

"True. But you're different, Melanie."

"How do you know that, Mom?" This from Alex.

"Call it 'A Mother's Intuition.' We always know when something is right, or wrong, for our children."

"Then why didn't you ever say anything?" Aaron asked her as he sat on the arm of the loveseat beside her. She turned kind eyes up to him. Eyes that were sad when she responded.

"Because sometimes, just like God does for all *His* children, parents have to let their kids make their own mistakes. Free will, learning experiences. Whatever name you put to it, they all mean the same thing. And as your parents, we have to sit by and watch and pray that one day you'll come to your senses. So on the one hand, Aaron, I'm glad you're no longer married to that little____"

"Tina," his Dad warned.

"Fine," she huffed. "To that woman. On the other hand, I'm so sorry that it took such a drastic event for this end to come about."

"It's okay. I understand, I think." And he did. When his mother put it in those terms–about making mistakes and learning from them–Aaron realized that he'd always viewed his marriage as just that. A mistake. He never felt as though his and Jess's union was blessed by God. He thought she was the one when she'd bumped into him while running on the high school track. He'd looked at her and felt something deep in his soul. He knew now it was just hormonal lust. Those feelings never would've been blessed by God. And despite the fact that it made him seem callous, he was glad about it. Because he knew that God had something–some*one*–better for him on the horizon. Someone to stir not only desire, but love. He just needed to be careful not to mix a sugarcoated disaster with a blessing. "Doesn't keep me from feeling a bit like Adam in the garden, though."

"How so?" Jax finally entered the conversation.

"Because I got tricked by the one woman I loved above all others. Or thought I did, anyway. And now I've sinned right along with her."

"Well, lucky for you God is sympathetic and forgiving. Good thing, too, otherwise I never would've ended up with Brin as my wife. Or a beautiful daughter to pass our name on to."

"True. And how did that meeting come about? What did you do to be able to meet Brinley and get married and become a father?" Aar asked his best friend.

Jax gave a short nod and a half smile formed on his mouth. He knew Aaron referred to the fact that after Jax's father died from a tree falling on him during a freak thunderstorm, and Jax blamed himself for it, Jaxson left North Carolina. It was his starting some place new that'd brought about his future.

"I started over," Jax said quietly.

"Yeah. And that's exactly what I have to do."

"What are talking about, Aaron? What do you have to do?" his Dad asked.

"I've got to start over. At least for a while."

"And how are you gonna do that, brother?" Alex probed.

Aaron sighed and looked at each of the faces that stared at him and waited for his answer. He knew this wouldn't last forever. Knew he'd come back home, to Lake Shores. But for now, with a new season upon them, it seemed like the best time. He needed some fresh air. Out of Texas.

Aimee Martin

"I'm leaving Lake Shores."

Chapter 2

"Remember ye not the former things, neither consider the things of old."
Isaiah 43:18

Aaron and Alex sat on the wooden deck at Alex and Mel's new house, stared up at the stars that sparkled down on them like millions of tiny spotlights and each drank a beer in silence.

When the shock of Aaron's confession had worn off, and his mother quit nagging him because she finally realized it was like beating a dead horse–his mind was made up, there would be no changing it–they'd all sat down to a dinner of beef roast, carrots and potatoes.

Aar knew his mother wanted to keep bringing up his declaration of moving. But one look from his father and she would close her mouth, lean over and talk to Brin and Mel instead.

Once the dishes were done, and little Sarah had fallen asleep in her Daddy's arms, Brin and Jax left to get the baby home and in bed. Alex and Mel were not far behind them. Aaron was prepared to tear into Alex for deserting him.

But on the way out, Alex said loud enough for their mother to hear, "Hey, Aar... why don't you come on over to the house with us? Mel got me a new bar-b-que grill. I wanna show it to you and rub it in your face." Their Mom had started to protest, but before she could get her words out, Aaron said that sounded great and told his parents goodbye. He kissed his Mom on the cheek and promised to call her before he made any rash decisions.

Now, an hour later—and still without looking at this supposed new grill—Aaron sat with his little brother and enjoyed the fact that the younger man didn't feel the need to ask a bunch of questions.

He wasn't as angry as he had been a week ago when he'd craved the silence with Blake. But he wasn't exactly at peace, either. He didn't really know how he felt. Just that it wasn't right.

He wasn't whole.

He wanted to wrap his head around it all before he had to explain it to other people.

Aaron brought the bottle up to his mouth, took a small sip and let the cool drink slowly work its way down his throat. Alex chose that moment to talk.

"So was it anybody we knew?"

The beer Aaron just swallowed got stuck and he choked, spit the liquid back up with a loud cough and a glare at this brother.

"What? You don't expect me to be all, "You wanna talk about it? I'm here for you," like some kind of chick, do you?"

Despite his better judgment, Aaron laughed and said, "No, I guess not."

"So... was it?"

Aaron took a deep breath, let it out slow and took another drink before he answered. "No," he said again. "But while we were going through the court proceedings, I overheard a friend of Jess's say that they were still seeing each other, shared a cab to the office every day. That they might be moving into an apartment together up in Houston. So I assume they met at her work." Aaron referred to Domestic Design and Interiors where Jess had worked for the last year.

"Dude works for an interior design company?" Alex asked, one eyebrow cocked way up on his forehead and a grin on his mouth.

"Yeah," Aaron laughed. "In the warehouse department or something. Big guy, muscles for days, meant to intimidate."

"And did he? Intimidate you?"

"Nah. I think he actually seemed apologetic. I never saw him after that night but when we locked eyes over... over Jess's shoulder, I could see the remorse there. I don't think he knew Jess was married."

"Or he was sorry he got caught."

"Maybe."

But Aaron didn't really believe that.

Alex reached over into an ice bucket on the deck in between their chairs, pulled out two more beers and tossed one to Aaron. He took it, twisted the cap and dropped the lid in the bucket with the others.

The silence came again.

But this time, Aaron didn't feel confused. Talking with Alex, even about the man his wife had been unfaithful to him with, calmed him inside. Helped to settle the turmoil of doubt and uncertainty and failure that battled in his brain like a tornado and left only him in the aftermath.

Helped to bring about the quiet. The quiet was easier to deal with than that turmoil. It was easier to make plans and get ready for a future he wasn't entirely certain of when he had a clear mind. It made it easier to accept what he planned for his next step, to follow through despite his hesitancy.

He knew what it was, this step. Wasn't sure why, of all things, *this* was what stuck in his heart and soul.

Just knew that deep down, it was where he was being led to go.

Now he just had to figure out how to get there.

"So what are you gonna do now?" Alex asked.

"Just like I said at our parent's. I'm getting out of Lake Shores."

"Yeah, but not forever. I mean, you'll be coming home once you sow your wild oats, right?"

"I was married, Alex. I don't have any wild oats to sow anymore. Besides, I'm not sure that's what I need right now."

"On the contrary my old brother. I think that's *exactly* what you need."

"Old?" Aar asked with playful irritation. "If I'm old, then that makes me wise, too. And I say no."

"Wise-ass, maybe," Alex laughed then said, "Seriously. You need to get out, find a woman–or two–to have a little fun with, blow off some steam. Then come home and get your life back together."

"You're right about one thing."

"Of course I am."

Aaron ignored the conceited comeback and went on as if Alex hadn't spoken. "I do need to blow off some steam. Try something new for a while. In a new place."

He redirected the conversation away from women and back to him leaving, hoped Alex caught on to the innuendo.

"Okay, I'll bite. What something 'new?' And where?"

"Well," Aar eased into it. "I was thinking that I've always wanted to go up north."

"You mean like New York?"

"No. More northwest."

"Seattle?"

"Nuh-uh."

"Jeez, enough with the juvenile games already. Just spit it out, Aar. Where are you gonna go?" Alex asked, impatience evident.

Aaron looked over, grinned and took a final sip of his beer before he raised the bottle up in a mock salute to his younger brother. And kept his lips sealed.

•••••

June 22, 2015

"Hey, Momma. I'm running to town to pick up the alfalfa order for the horses," Ally called to her mother as she walked down the hallway of their house, came out in the kitchen and found the older woman at the sink washing a head of lettuce. "Do you need anything?"

"No, honey. I think we're good. Actually, wait... I could use a few extra tomatoes for the salad. The ones I got the other day didn't ripen as fast as I thought they would. They're still green."

"Does that mean you're gonna fix some fried green tomatoes?"

"That depends."

Her mother set the lettuce in a stainless colander and turned to face her. The sun shone through the windows at her back and highlighted the thin, silver streaks in her brown hair. Her mother, Suzanne, was short like Ally at barely five-foot. Ally and her mother both had the same hazel eyes and button nose. She was also responsible for passing along that signature chestnut-colored hair to all three of her children.

But the sweet countenance that Suzi–as everyone knew her– was known for must have skipped a generation. Ally, Daniel and their older brother, David (when he'd still been alive) all got their hard-headedness from their father, David Sr.

"Are you going to help me batter and bread them? You know how much work it is."

"Not for you," Ally countered. "You could fry just about anything in your sleep. And still win a tasting contest."

Her mother only smiled and shook her head as she turned back to the sink, picked up a stack of carrots to be peeled. The ever-present radio sat on the windowsill directly above of the sink, a battered and brown permanent object that had been there since Ally was a little girl. She could still remember walking in to find her Grandmamma at the sink, just as Momma was now, preparing food for the family.

When a song by Dolly Parton came on, Suzi leaned up on her tiptoes and turned up the volume. Ally smiled as her Mom hummed along with the lyrics, every now and then singing that one line that she loved so much. *My coat of many colors, my Momma made for me.*

Ally loved hearing her mother sing, listening to her beautiful voice fill a room.

The smile fell from her lips when she remembered why her Mom didn't sing very much anymore. The death of a child kind-of puts a damper on all things happy. Since singing was Suzi's happy place, it mostly went by the wayside ever since that night in early 2010 when David died.

What if I'd been here? Could I have stopped him from going after...

"Try to hurry back so you can help me with those tomatoes."

Her mother's voice broke into the argument Ally had with herself on a daily basis. She shook the thoughts from her head, told her Mom okay, grabbed the keys from the hook next to the back door and walked outside. The cold fronts had finally stopped coming in and left in their wake a warm air that heated Ally's face like a towel fresh from the dryer. She tried to enjoy it while it was here, knowing that a snowstorm could just as easily pass through at any time.

She could smell the sweet but faint aroma of one of her favorite wildflowers, bear grass, trying to bloom with the change in weather. She looked at the small grassy mountain to her right, a hundred yards from the house, and saw the bright magenta that dotted the hillside from the pinkfairies popping out. Ally made a promise to go there this evening and sit amongst those flowers, maybe even bring a small arrangement back for her mother, who never went farther from the house than was absolutely necessary. Not anymore. Not since David.

Not now, Ally, she reminded herself and climbed into the old, black Chevy four-door truck that had seen better days. When she finally got it started on the third try, she put the truck in drive and bumped along the dirt driveway until she reached their county road, hung a left. Five miles and she'd be on Route Seventy-Eight, the way to Rosy Camp. It was a peaceful twenty-minute ride to town and Ally jumped on any chance she had to make the short trip alone.

With the windows rolled down, the wind blew long wisps of hair all around her face. Ally tucked a section behind her ear, listened to the sound of the roaring truck engine, the clank of metal against metal from the crowbar sliding around in the bed of the truck . She wondered, not for the first time, if she had the chance, would she ever be able to actually leave Montana? Despite her arguments to herself a couple weeks ago, she loved it here. Especially this time of year when black bear season was over and new life showed up all over the state. She looked out the windshield, through the dirt blowing in front of her window, and stared at the scenery that had always been her home and thought of the things she loved most. The mountain air. The clear creeks. The endless wildlife.

The freedom.

Would any other place in the world give her the same sense of contentment? Or, the better question, would she ever be able to share it with someone again?

There was that one, Ally thought briefly. *No, no. He was married, Ally. Besides, he was a pompous jerk anyway. Get him out of your head.*

The truth was that she had no interest in men anymore. If there was one good thing that came out of Ben's straying, it was that Ally had opened her eyes, realized she didn't need a significant other to be happy. She could go through this life on her own. *But that's not the truth Allyson.* She hung her head, just for a moment, because her internal argument brought out her genuine reality.

While her faith was strong–Ally didn't think there'd ever be anything to change that–she *had* lost hope that there was someone out there for her. That old adage about there being someone for everyone just didn't apply to her. More and more every day, Ally believed that God had meant for her to be alone in this life. Kind of like Mother Teresa, except she wasn't Catholic.

Ally was just about to turn on the radio to help clear her mind when her cell rang. She pulled it from the front pocket of her blue and pink flannel shirt, glanced at the caller ID. When she saw who it was, she grinned and pulled over to the side of the road, slid her finger across the screen with a flourish to answer the call and brought the phone to her ear.

"If I'd have known all it was gonna take to reconnect with you was to get you married, I'd have auctioned you off a long time ago!"

"Ha. Ha," her best friend, Mel, mocked. "It wouldn't have worked. You didn't have Alex to make the highest bid."

"True," Ally laughed. "I guess we'll just have to be thankful that God brought him to you instead of me interfering. Who knows what you'd have ended up with if I'd have been in charge of the auction block."

"Probably a bear."

"Probably." Ally smiled and leaned her head back against the headrest. "Oh, it's so good to talk to you. How you been, honey? And how's that hottie you married?"

Melanie Moore–*Lambert now*–and Ally had met in college at San Diego State University as freshmen. They'd become close friends during those four years, sharing many classes and a dorm room together and, eventually, in their last semester, an apartment. They'd been inseparable until their senior year. That was when Mel had become distant and Ally had left right after graduation. Of course, Mel didn't know the real reasons for why Ally had packed up and hit the road so soon after turning their tassels. Her friend assumed it had to do with David's death, and Ally never corrected the assumption.

But a few months ago, Mel called Ally out of the blue, told her she was getting married and asked her to be in the wedding. Ally jumped on it, in spite of her father's arguments. Rekindling the friendship that had meant so much to her just a few years ago was the one lifeline Ally clung to in her moments of doubt and loneliness. She knew there was no way she'd ever let her friendship with Melanie get that far out of reach again.

"I'm fantastic. We both are. But if you don't quit talking about how hot my husband is, I'll____"

"You'll what?" Ally interrupted. "Come see me in Montana just to give me a beating? Bring it, sister! Anything to get you out here."

"Oh, I'd love to Allyson. I just can't right now. With Brin just having the baby, Alex has been taking on more responsibility at the ranch so Jax can stay home with his girls. And I… well, I…"

"What is it, Melanie? You're not pregnant already, are you?"

"What? No! Of course not. Not yet, anyway. I hope to be someday but we're, I'm not there yet. What I was going to say is that I'm trying to start up a new business here in Lake Shores and it's taking a lot of my extra time."

"Wow. So you really have turned into a Texas girl for good, then, huh?"

"Yeah, I guess I have."

"So what's this business you're starting?" Ally asked.

"Well, Lake Shores is a small town, you know that. Being from a small town yourself, you understand how it is; the community has the necessities for the town to survive but not much else. And I know that news always spreads fast in places like this but I thought, why not have a way for folks to hear all the news all at once, you know? So… I'm starting a newspaper."

"Look at you! Putting down roots and striking out on your own. You make me so proud."

"Thank you. Wait… are you being sarcastic?"

"Maybe a little," Ally chuckled. "But I am still proud of you. I do have one question. How do you have the capital to start something like that? You haven't worked for Dalton in almost six months. Does Jax really pay that well? Cause if so, I might come down and go to work for him."

"I was very smart with my money. Plus Mr. Evans was more than generous with my bonus."

"That's right. You got a nice ole' sizable handout when you put in your notice. Who does that? Give an employee who's leaving you high and dry a nice chunk of change like they're not disrupting the flow of business."

"Come on, Ally. You know it wasn't like that."

"I know. I'm sorry," Ally apologized sincerely. "Maybe I'm just a little jealous. Wanting the things that I can't have."

"You could always move down here and come to work with me?"

"You mean *for* you?"

"No. I mean *with* me. Oh my gosh, I can't believe I didn't think about this before. We could go into business together. Fifty-Fifty. With your public relations degree, you'd be a huge asset to the paper. What do ya say?"

Ally thought about it. Really thought about it. And while there was a large part of her heart that was shouting, *Yes! Go and go now,* there was also a part telling her to be cautious. Not to jump into a situation she had no control over again. Because the last time she followed through with a plan that she wasn't in control over, her life had ended in a big, fat, ugly divorce. And while she wouldn't be ending a marriage if things went sour, she would lose her friendship and she could not, would not, risk that.

"I don't know, Mel. Let me think about it for a while, okay?"

"Sure, okay. Sorry, I know I kinda threw that on you but it just felt right. No pressure, though. Whatever you decide."

"Thanks for that. So," Ally began, ready to change the subject. "What kind of juicy gossip do y'all have going on down there?"

"Well... I think the biggest has to be about Aaron. You remember him, right? Alex's brother?"

"MmHmm." But he was not someone Ally wanted to think about so while her friend went into some tale about the egotistical man, she zoned out.

She noticed a cloud of dust up in the distance, growing in size the closer it came to where she sat parked on the side of the road. She stared out the front window when she saw the white truck come around the bend in the road, tried to figure out if any of their neighbors–if that's what one called the people who lived three miles away as the crow flies–had gotten a new truck recently. Decided that no, no one had changed vehicles that she knew of.

Ally kept her eyes on that truck, saw it swerve a little to the right and overcorrect to the left. Then it skidded on the dirt road, the front end headed right to Ally's truck. There was so much dirt around them now, Ally couldn't see who was driving if she wanted to.

She quickly threw the truck in reverse, floored the pedal and backed up until she was sure her truck was out of the line of fire. The driver of the white truck slammed on the breaks, caused the bed of the truck to go into a tailspin.

"Idiot," Ally mumbled under her breath.

"Allyson Marx!"

Too late, Ally realized she still had the phone to her mouth with Mel on the other end. "Not you, Mel. Some fool doesn't know how to drive on a dirt road and is about to wreck his truck right in front of me. What are you...!" Ally started to yell at the driver but stopped and lowered her voice back to normal. "Mel, can I call you later? I need to go see if this guy is alright."

"Sure, but... did you hear me? About Aaron?"

"Yeah, yeah. I heard you."

"And you're okay with that?"

"Yeah, sure," she lied. "I'll call you later. Bye, sweetie."

Ally hung up before Mel could respond and flung open her door. She slammed it closed behind her, grabbed the crowbar from the bed of the truck, made her way to the mystery truck that had finally stopped spinning. She walked through clouds of dust and dirt like a bull in a stampede. She was just about as angry, too. She made it to the truck, tapped her crowbar on the driver's side window and stood back, waited for whoever was driving to get out. The door opened and a body fell towards the ground, while coughs and sneezes interrupted the silence.

Finally, the man–and it was definitely a man, judging by the fact that he was at least a foot taller than Ally's five-foot-one-inch frame–stood up, hands held out in front of him like he was afraid Ally was going to hit him with the crowbar. She just might.

"What the hell is the matter with you?!" she yelled. "Don't you know how to drive? You can't go speeding down a county road like that! What if there'd been a herd of our mountain goats on the road, huh? You'd have killed them, most likely. And maybe even yourself, too!"

Ally stopped, took a breath and went right back in to her berating.

"Who are you and what are you…" she trailed off as the cloud around them finally settled. The dust dropped at their feet like tiny, brown raindrops. Her mouth fell open, oblivious to the dirt that drifted in to land on her tongue. Then she narrowed her eyes and growled. Her. A grown woman. Growled like one of the bears their hunters paid to come and shoot.

"You."

"Me."

•••••

He had to admit it, if even only to himself. The look of absolute shock, of confusion (and even that little bit of annoyance and anger, *Okay… a* lot *of annoyance and anger*) had him grinning, despite the crowbar that was clutched in her hand, ready to be swung across his head any moment. He had been unsure of this whole idea of his from the minute he'd left Lake Shores yesterday.

From the five-hour flight to West Yellowstone, Montana via Houston Hobby Airport–thanks to a two-hour layover–to the sleepless night spent in a ratty motel off the Interstate. Then on the hour long drive to Rosy Camp (only to find out that Ally and her family lived another twenty minutes west of town). All that time alone he'd thought, repeatedly, that maybe that feeling he had at the wedding wasn't what he remembered. Or maybe it was just indigestion from too much food.

But now, as he stood face to face with Allyson Marx again–well, her face to his chest, anyway–he knew that this trip had been the right one to make. The knot that had taken up residence in his gut for the last three months loosened, and for the first time since he walked in on his wife, Aaron felt like he could breathe again.

"Aren't you going to say anything? Or are you not done yelling at me yet?"

"What the hell are you doing here?" *So, not done yelling then,* Aar thought as he chuckled. "I'm not laughing. I want an answer. Why. Are. You. Here?"

"I needed a change of scenery."

"Nope. Nuh-uh. Not buying it, so try again."

"I've always wanted to shoot a black bear?" He posed his response as a question.

"There're bears all over the country. Why here?"

"I… Maybe it's just that…" Aaron blew out a rough breath, decided it was too soon to speak the truth just yet, so he changed the subject. "It's nice to see you again, too."

"Too bad those sentiments aren't reciprocated."

Aaron had almost forgotten how smarty her mouth had been. He replayed that spunky attitude in his mind several times the last couple of weeks. His memories hadn't done her justice.

"Can you just cut me a little slack, here? I'm trying to be cordial."

"Yeah, well you weren't very cordial back in January so why should you start now? And you still haven't answered my question. What are doing here?"

Aaron sighed, crossed his arms over his chest and didn't miss the way Ally's eyes followed the movement, stayed focused on his chest for a moment longer than was necessary. When she brought her gaze back up to his, he said, "No joke?" At the shake of her head, he went on. "I needed a break. Away from Texas. And that's the God's honest truth." *Some of it, anyway.* "And I knew you and your family owned a ranch. I have a little experience ranching myself, thanks to my brother-in-law. I thought I'd come see how things were done up here. Maybe see if y'all would hire me on for the summer or something."

"Did you lose your job?"

"No. I quit. Like I said, I needed out of Texas out for a while."

Ally narrowed her eyes on him, the way she had when she first realized it was Aaron that'd climbed out of the truck. Then she mirrored his stance, folded her own arms across her chest, tilted her head to the side as she studied his face. He stood his ground, met her glare for glare. His pride wouldn't let him back down from this tiny, slip of a woman.

But after a few minutes of silence, he had to force himself not to fidget. She had one heck of a death stare, this woman. Just when he was about to say forget it, hop back in the truck and head in the direction he'd come, Ally spoke.

"Okay. Now that I believe. Where's your wife?" she asked as she leaned around him, looked in the direction of his rental truck for another person.

"She's not here."

Ally raised a questioning eyebrow to him. In answer to her unspoken query, he brought up his left hand, now devoid of a wedding band (as long as the white skin from a tan line didn't count).

And finally, that got a reaction other than anger out of Ally. Her eyes widened, both arms fell to her sides. Her mouth opened and closed several times like a fish out of water. A speechless Allyson. Now that was a novelty. At least, it seemed so from the little interaction he'd had with her.

"Ally?" he spoke softly. "Ally, you gonna say anything? Or just sit there and stare at me like I've got a third eye or something?"

"I'm sure it's something much more dangerous than a third eye," she finally retorted. "And no, I'm not just going to sit here and stare. I have better manners than that." Aaron snorted. Ally ignored it and kept on with a sigh. "Come on. You can stay in the bunkhouse at the ranch until you figure out where you're going." She turned and headed back to her own rig and Aaron wondered if her hips always had that sexy sway to them or if it was more pronounced right now, for him.

He shook his head and tried to clear the foreign thought from his mind. *You shouldn't be thinking like that, Aar. You just got divorced. This is what people refer to as "The rebound" and you do* not *need to be sucked up into a situation like that.*

"Follow me," she yelled, right before she slammed her door and started up the engine.

"I plan to," he murmured to himself–against his better judgment–smiled and climbed into the truck.

Chapter 3

*"Therefore came I forth to meet thee, diligently to
seek thy face, and I have found thee."*
Proverbs 7:15

"What in the world is that man doing here? How am I
supposed to work knowing that he's just across the yard?
And what happened with his wife? And why, *why*, does the
fact that he's no longer married make me go all weak in the
knees?"

Ally asked the questions aloud even though no one was in
the truck with her to answer them. She wasn't even sure she
wanted answers. Especially that last one. But she hoped that
if she ran through all the possible scenarios to herself, she
wouldn't feel inclined to ask him. Aaron. She didn't need to
get to know him better or spend any more time around him
than necessary. She needed to get him out of Rosy Camp, out
of Montana. And fast.

She pulled through the cattle gate at the ranch, hopped out of the truck with her hand in the air to tell Aaron to stop and held the gate open. He pulled through, stopped right behind where she'd left her Chevy. He rolled the window down as she walked past. She tried to ignore it but then he asked, "So this is your place?"

Ally huffed out a breath, turned and looked at the stranger in her driveway. Because he was a stranger. The only thing she knew about him was that he was Alex's brother, he was apparently now divorced, and he was a jerk.

"No. It's my *family's* place. Has been for years."

She gave him no chance to ask any more questions and instead, walked away quickly, jumped back into her rig and pulled up the driveway. She took the gravel drive that wound around the backside of the house, past the barn where the horses were and the chicken coop housing their three dozen, buff-colored Brahma chickens. The drive curved around one of the pens set up for branding and stopped at the bunkhouse set up for hunters, half a mile from the main house. Ally threw the truck in park, shut off the engine and hopped out. Again. She waited by the hood while Aaron got out of his own vehicle and made his way over to her. Then she turned, headed for the house without a word. She heard him jogging on the gravel to catch up but didn't bother slowing down.

When they made it to the front door, Ally opened the place up, swept her arm past her in a show of manners. "After you," she said through a clenched jaw.

Aaron stepped up to the doorway but didn't walk inside. Instead, he stayed right there next to her, stared at her with that stupid grin on his face. She sighed and crossed her arms over her chest, annoyed with his haughty attitude.

"What?"

"Nothing. Just waiting for a little hospitality is all."

"I am being hospitable. If I wasn't, I'd have sent your butt back the way you came. Now, would like a place to stay for the night or not?"

"Yes, I would."

"Fine." And she walked in ahead of him since it was obvious he wasn't going to enter before her. "This is our hunter's bunkhouse. Living room, breakfast nook, kitchen," she said as she indicated each section of the open space on the ground floor. "There are two bedrooms separated by a bathroom back there–" she pointed to the open doors at the back of the house, "–and upstairs there're another three bedrooms and a bathroom." She tilted her chin up toward the second story landing that boasted four closed doors along the walkway. "Luckily it's empty right now. We don't have anyone scheduled to come out for a few weeks so you have the place to yourself. *Not* that you'll be staying that long."

Ally stopped talking, turned and froze. Aaron leaned against the banister next to the staircase on the left side of the house. The pale cedar post made the skin showing at his throat seem much tanner than normal, almost the color of honey. He tucked his hands into his back pockets and his chest puffed out with the action. Ally could see the defined muscle of his shoulders through the cotton, the way his pecs pushed against the flimsy charcoal, long-sleeved t-shirt he had on as if they were trying to find a way to escape. But it wasn't a bulky muscle like he enjoyed working out more than his next meal. His strength was more subtle, more toned and refined but in no way less noticeable. Nor less enticing. She turned her face to the side to avoid being caught staring, knew he'd seen her anyway when she heard him chuckle.

He wasn't this happy when I first met him. I think I liked him angry and rude better. Maybe then I wouldn't be the angry and bitter one. Ally sighed. *This is not you, Allyson. Stop acting like a child.*

She forced herself to relax, removed the scowl from her face and looked back at the man who stood five feet from her. She would not resort to immature tactics the way he had back in January. She would not let him be the one to dictate how she acted. Or reacted. She'd never be a doormat again.

More determined, Ally looked into his eyes and tried not to sound so irritated when she asked, "How long *are* you planning on staying?" He only shrugged his shoulders, which made Ally notice the way they strained against that shirt again. "Are you not talking now?" Still nothing, just that grin that made his eyes crinkle the corners. "Oh good grief, this is ridiculous! There are sheets and towels in the linen closet under the stairs. Make yourself at home. I have errands to run. I'll come and check on you later this afternoon."

And with that, she stormed out of the house. She might have slammed the door a little harder than was necessary but she didn't have time to dwell on it. She had hay to pick up.

•••••

Aaron watched Ally walk swiftly out of the house, at the way those hips sashayed from side to side. He decided then that no, she hadn't done it for him, as he'd thought earlier on the county road. *So... just her natural sway. I could get used to watching that.* He frowned when the thought of watching her popped into his head again. But that frown quickly turned into a smile when the door slammed and the pictures on the walls rattled with the force of it. She was a spitfire, alright. Just like Alex had warned him. And he couldn't wait to see more of it.

He pushed off the banister he'd leaned against, walked around the bunkhouse for a closer look since Ally hadn't given him much time to take the space in. He admired the dark chocolate, leather sofa and loveseat, their overstuffed cushions that would make for a perfect afternoon nap. There was a large flat screen T.V. mounted on one wall, a dark gray brick fireplace on the wall cattycornered to it. The multi-colored braided rug on the floor was round and huge. It took up the entire space designated for the living room.

Aaron roamed into the kitchen, ran his hand along the concrete countertop, appreciated the look when matched with the open cabinets. And they were open. No doors, just shelving that boasted plates, bowls, mugs–all in a hodgepodge of designs and colors. By the front of the house, there was a round oak table, complete with four matching chairs and a vase of some kind of pinkish-purplish flower. Aaron didn't even pretend to know what kind of flower it was.

He headed to the back of the house to check out the bedrooms. One was made up for multiple people to sleep in with two sets of twin-sized bunk beds. The other room Aar guessed was meant to be like the master of the place, with a king sized, four-poster bed. He walked over to it, sat down on the mattress and gave a little bounce. It felt like a pillow-top, didn't squeak and sat high enough off the ground that he wouldn't have to crawl off it in the mornings. There was a large bay window on the west wall with a chest of drawers right next to it. The light from outside lit up the room and not a speck of dust could be seen anywhere. He walked over to the window, saw the view of a grassy mountain off in the distance. Farther back from that, a large mountain peak rose behind that grassy hill. It was only the tip of the mountain; Aar knew it must be miles away. But he felt like he could reach out and touch it, the sky was so open. He decided that this was the room he'd take for now and took a pass on checking out the upstairs.

The downstairs bathroom was nothing fancy but it did have a walk-in, brick shower that matched the fireplace. A bench was built into the wall in the corner of the shower and on it sat an array of shampoos and soaps. It seemed that Ally and her family were quite the hosts. With nothing left to do but get settled in, Aaron walked out to his rental, grabbed his suitcase from the backseat. On his way back in the front door, his phone rang. He set the bag down by the table, pulled the phone free from his front pocket and answered without looking to see who it was. "Yeah?"

"Hey, man. You make it to Rosy Camp alright?" Alex asked on the other end of the line.

"Hey, brother. Yeah, I made it. Didn't know I was gonna have to drive another twenty minutes just to get to Ally's place, but I'm here. Getting ready to get unpacked in the hunter's cabin."

"So she's letting you stay, huh?"

"Of course. Why wouldn't she?"

"Oh, I don't know. Maybe because you were so nasty to her the first–and only, I might add–time that you met her. It wouldn't have surprised me if she slammed the door in your face."

"She couldn't. We met up on the side of the road about five minutes from her family's ranch. She did look like she was gonna hit me with a crowbar, though." Alex laughed and Aaron went on. "She'll come around."

"Aar... I gotta ask. Are you sure about this? I mean, you just got divorced. Maybe you should take the time to be alone, you know? Do what you told me you were going to and just work on the ranch for a while, then come home."

"This from the man who told me I needed to find a woman to spend some time with?"

"That was before I knew you had your sights set on my wife's best friend. She's important to Mel, which means she's important to me. I don't want anything to come between them," Alex said solemnly.

"I know. It won't. And yes, I'm sure. I don't know why, but I am. More so than I've been about anything for a long time. It's not as if I'm hopping into a relationship with the woman. I'm just going to hang out here for a while, hopefully work, and then it'll be back to Lake Shores for me. And like I said… She'll come around," he repeated.

"Alright, then I'll support you. But if you screw things up, you're on your own."

"I won't screw it up. I have faith."

"Yeah, well, just remember that when Ally starts trying to push you away. She's not one to lie down and follow commands."

"Will do. I'll check in with y'all in a few days, okay?"

"Sounds good. Talk to ya later. And remember not to make this whole thing like some sort of business arrangement. Have some fun while you're there," Alex said and hung up.

Aaron tossed his phone on the table, picked up his suitcase, headed back to the master bedroom. An hour later, he finished putting the last of his clothes away. Just as he slid his suitcase under the bed, he heard the front door open. He walked out of the room with a smile, expected to see Ally standing in the front room. Instead, he came face to face with a man.

A very large man.

A worn down, dirty cowboy hat put his face in shadow and made it difficult to see who the man was. A red and black flannel shirt mostly covered his upper body, his hairy forearms the only thing exposed. The man's broad shoulders took up most of the doorway and his head almost came to the top of the seven-foot frame. Long legs were covered in a pair of work-roughened jeans and the biggest set of steel-toe boots Aaron had ever seen covered the man's boat-like feet.

At six-foot-two, Aaron rarely felt small. But one look at this burly stranger had him feeling like a midget. He swallowed past a lump in his throat, forced himself to straighten his back and asked, "Can I help you?"

"Who are you and what are you doing in my bunkhouse?"

"I was told the place was unoccupied for the next several weeks and that I was able to use it as I saw fit." Not exactly a lie, but more exaggerated than the truth. "So I guess I should be asking you… What are *you* doing in *my* bunkhouse?"

The big man took a few menacing steps into the room and Aaron was not ashamed to admit that he took those same steps back. If cartoons were real, he'd bet there'd be smoke blowing out of the man's ears right about now. As it was, the man's face had definitely turned a darker shade than normal and ventured on a deep red.

"Listen here, you little twerp. I don't know who____"

"Daddy!" Ally's voice drifted in behind the man.

Daddy? Aaron thought to himself. *Ah, crap. You just mouthed off to the father of the woman who basically holds your imminent future in her hands. Smooth move, Aar. Real smooth.*

"What are you doing here? You were supposed to be out in the east fields with Danny." Ally came around the big man, stopped right beside him.

The man kept his eyes on Aaron but slung his beefy arm around Ally's shoulders when she reached him.

"Hey Punkin'," he said and pulled Ally in close to his side. "We were out there. Got finished tagging the new stock early so I thought I'd come see if you wanted a hand in town. Then I saw the strange truck in the drive here, so I popped on in to find out who was at the hunter's cabin. You still haven't told me who you are," he stated to Aaron.

"Calm down, Daddy." Ally rubbed a hand over her father's chest and walked out from under his arm, right up to Aaron. She placed that same hand on his shoulder, gave him a smirk that said she enjoyed his discomfort and turned back to face her Dad. "This is Aaron Lambert, Mel's new brother-in-law. He came out for a visit. Just got in a little over an hour ago so I haven't had a chance to introduce him to anyone yet."

"I was unaware that you'd invited anyone out to the ranch while you were down in Texas. Five months ago."

Aaron felt the sweat start to build up around his neck and under his arms. If this man was trying to intimidate Aaron, he was doing a damned fine job. Add in the fact that he hadn't *exactly* been invited, and his nerves were barely hanging on by a thread. Not knowing how Ally would answer that question, he pulled his eyes off the older man and looked down at her. She stared back at him and at any other time, Aaron might have gotten lost in those beautiful hazel eyes. Tried to pick out where the greens and yellows and browns met while they all swirled together like a kaleidoscope. But right now, he couldn't. He didn't want to be thrown out on his butt. Not before he'd had a chance to do what he came for.

Something in his own eyes must have shown his pleading and desperation. Ally sighed, gave him a smile and turned back to the man on the other side of the room who waited for an explanation.

"I'm sorry, Daddy. I guess things just got so busy after the Winter hunting season that I forgot. Anyway, like I said, this is Aaron. He's never been to Montana before and asked back in January if he could come for a visit sometime. I told him sure, just to wait til after bear season was over. Since it ended a little over a month ago, we're in the clear for now. We don't have any hunters booked until September–" *September? She said they had bookings in a few weeks.* "–so I told Aaron that this would be the best time to come up. Really, Daddy. Everything's fine."

"If you say so, Punkin'." But the man didn't look convinced.

Aaron knew he'd meet her parents while he was here. When his feelings of viewing this trip as just that–a trip– waned, and the other feelings came out (the ones that said this trip was something more), he'd planned to woo her mother. And to get on her Dad's good side by talking about hunting. He had not planned to start off like this. With her Dad looking at him as if he was some sort of criminal.

He knew what his own father had expected when a man wanted to date his sister so, with that in mind, Aaron shook off the uneasiness and walked right up to Ally's Dad.

"Mr. Marx, my name is Aaron Lambert. It's nice to meet you." He held out his hand, waited for the man to take it. With a wary eye, he finally did and the grip he bestowed on Aaron was harder than necessary. More intimidation, Aar guessed.

But this time, he didn't let himself back down.

"I hope my coming here isn't an inconvenience. I'd really like the opportunity to see this beautiful part of the country and more of your family's ranch. I'd actually talked to Ally about seeing if there was a summer job opening, since I have some ranching experience. But if this isn't a good time, I'd be happy to reschedule. Maybe when you'd be available to show me around as well."

The older man studied Aaron with a suspicious eye for a full minute before he finally told him, "No. Now would be fine. Whatever my daughter's offered you by way of hospitality, consider it done."

"Actually, sir, we haven't had a chance to get around to the formalities yet since I just got in a little over an hour ago."

"Allyson." He threw a scolding glance over to his daughter and she had the good grace to look a little ashamed.

"Sorry, Daddy. I'll get right on that."

"No need. You," he looked back at Aaron, "come on over to the main house for supper. We'll go over all the rules that guests get when they come to stay at Marx Ranch and Game. Then we'll talk about that work."

"Yes sir, Mr. Marx."

"And..." the man paused, blew out a breath and said, "You can call me Big Dave. But don't abuse the privilege."

"Yes sir. Big Dave," Aar corrected when the man shot him a look similar to the one he'd given Ally a second ago.

With a nod to Aaron and Ally, Big Dave turned and left the house. His hulking frame bounded down the gravel drive and hopped into a red pickup truck with far more ease than Aaron would have thought possible for a man his size.

When he drove off, clouds of dust settled in his wake. Aaron turned back to Ally.

She had a hip propped up on a barstool next to the kitchen counter and held on to the concrete as if to keep herself seated. But she stood up, bent at the waist and laughed loudly as soon as Aaron shut the front door.

Right then, the sun poured in from the window by the kitchen sink. The glow formed a circle around the top of Ally's bent head and Aaron swore that it looked like a halo. *Is this a disaster or a blessing?*

He decided that in his heart, he already knew the answer to that. But he needed to be cautious. To get to know her better.

And to see if, maybe, the feelings he'd had since he met her at his brother's wedding weren't just one sided on his part. To see if Ally had that same, unshakeable urge to get to know him, too.

•••••

Ally tried to hold it in. Really she did. But the look of shock and dread that was on Aaron's face when she walked around her father and saw him had been so evident–and so unmitigated–that she couldn't help it. She laughed. And laughed. And laughed until she thought her lungs would explode and her heart would burst out of her chest.

She never heard his footsteps on the concrete floor. But when his shoes came into her line of sight where she was hunched over, she stood up quickly. And banged her elbow on the counter to her right. "Ow," she exclaimed, rubbed the spot that now throbbed.

"Awe… did you hit your funny bone?"

"It's not funny."

"Yeah, well, neither was laughing at my expense. You could have warned me about your Dad."

"Warned you? Number one, when have I had the time? You haven't been here very long, remember? And number two, what, exactly, did you want a warning about?"

"I don't know. Maybe the fact that he's part bear himself? Jeez, no wonder you all are known to have so many bears in this part of the country. Look at what you're housing as humans!"

"Hey! My Daddy may resemble a bear. But inside he's just a big teddy bear."

"Yeah. Tell that to my aching hand that he just about squeezed off when he shook it."

Ally snorted, chuckled some more and said, "Sorry. He's just territorial, I guess."

"Like a bear."

"Gah, what is it with you Texans obsessing over bears? First Mel, now you. It's like you think that's all us Montanans deal with. There's more to us than just bears, you know."

"Wait, what? What about Mel?" Aaron asked, confusion written all over his face.

"Never mind," Ally mumbled. She walked over to the fridge, pulled out a bag of frozen peas and held it to her sore elbow. She turned back to Aaron, tried to figure out why he brought out the worst in her. No matter how good her intentions, one wrong look or word from him and her manners and good sense seemed to go by the wayside and she wouldn't listen to reason. Like Lot's wife. Ally decided then to just stop sinking to his level. She walked back to him, held out her hand (albeit at an awkward angle since she had the makeshift icepack on it) and said, "Truce."

Then he smiled. *Oh, that smile is gonna get me in trouble.*

"Truce," he agreed and reached out, clasped his fingers around Ally's and squeezed.

The jolt that emanated from where their skin touched surprised her. It felt warm and fuzzy and addicting all at once, like she'd been zapped with an electric wand. And liked it. Why had she never noticed that feeling before? Then she realized this was the first time they'd ever actually touched. She jerked her hand out of his grasp with a small gasp, noticed the look on his face matched hers.

His mouth was open a little, like he struggled to get in enough oxygen. His breathing was faster than normal. And his eyes, a deep blue that could rival any Caribbean sea, stared right through hers. She felt that stare in her soul, didn't welcome the way it made her feel like she'd been flayed open like a fish, and looked down to break the spell.

But his fingers tipped her chin back up and she jerked away, tried to block out the warmth that wanted to spread from there, as well.

"You felt it, too," he whispered into the quiet room. "What was that?"

There was a gruff awe in his voice. Ally had never heard anything so honest and sensual at the same time.

Instead of answering, Ally presented a question of her own. One that had plagued her since she first met up with him in the middle of the road. One that she swore she'd keep to herself when he hadn't been forthcoming, but found that she desperately needed the answer to. She kept her gaze on his face, looked for signs of any untruth as she asked, "Why did you come here, Aaron?"

He brought his hand back up to her face, cradled her cheek gently. Ally jumped but didn't jerk out of his hold. She stared at his face while he stared at his hand on her skin. She watched the pulse beat in his throat, fast and hard. She watched as he took a deep breath, licked his lips. Then his free hand moved, cupped the other cheek so that his hands caged in her face and Ally was forced to look directly into his eyes.

"I came to find you, Allyson."

Aimee Martin

Chapter 4

*"Know ye not that they which run in a race run all,
but one receiveth the prize? So run, that ye may
obtain."*
I Corinthians 9:24

"Wh-What do you mean, "You came to find me"? I
thought you just needed to get out of Texas for a while.
That's what you said. Right?"

Ally's whispered words brought Aaron out of the dreamy
haze. The one where all he could see was her eyes and her
lips and that golden halo surrounding her hair. He dropped
his hands from her face—*I don't even remember putting them
up there*—and took a step back. Distance. That's what he
needed. Distance to get his priorities right, to keep his head
on straight and not off in the clouds like some sort of
lovesick romantic. That's not what this trip to Montana was
about. Was it?

No. He was here for a break from Texas, as she'd just reminded him. For a break from the memories that surrounded him at every corner in his house. To clear his mind, not get it muddied up again with feelings he wasn't even sure were real or just some illusion brought on by a lack of sleep.

But there was something there. What had he just said to himself? That it felt right in his heart? To follow through but to take things slowly.

The thoughts were still there, even though he tried to replace them with the ones that said acting on a gut feeling with no supportive argument was ridiculous. That bouncing back into a relationship right after a divorce would be a very bad idea. Not that a relationship was even what was going on right now.

Those thoughts though, they lingered in the back of his mind like a morning fog and told him to stop fighting it.

To not fight *this*.

That what he'd felt when his hands had been on Ally's face wasn't some sort of cruel trick or misguided attempt at a rebound. There was a pounding in his chest, like someone was knocking on his heart saying, "Hello! Wake up! This is real!"

Just when he believed that the confusion in his life had settled, these conflicting emotions tugged on him. Aaron did not know what the right choice was.

Lord, please don't let me be fooled again, he prayed.

"I did. Say that I was here to get out of Texas for a while, I mean. I'm not sure why I said that other stuff. I'm sorry. I haven't had much sleep the last few days."

"I don't need an apology. I need an explanation." Ally's chest heaved, her eyes darted back and forth between his as she searched for an answer that he knew she wouldn't find. "Why did you say that?"

"I just told you, Ally. I'm not sure. Can we just leave it at that for now?"

"No, no I don't think we can. Listen, if you have some sick little plan in that arrogant head of yours… If you think you can show up here and sweep me off my feet and right into bed, you've got another think coming. I'm not that kind of woman."

"That's not why I'm____" Aaron started to defend himself but she cut him off.

"And even if I was, it definitely wouldn't happen with someone like you. I'm not interested in you that way."

"Oh, really?" he asked, incredulous. Aaron didn't know why but at that moment, he had the urge to prove her wrong. He took a step back in her direction, grinned to himself when she took a step away. He advanced again and her breathing sped up even more than before. He got right in front of her, caged her in between his body and the kitchen counter, but didn't touch her. For his own sanity as well as her space.

"Then tell me why you're about to hyperventilate from breathing so fast? Why is your pulse thundering just as hard as mine from me standing so close to you?" He bent his head so that their eyes were in line together. "Why is your skin flushed with red at the thought of me putting my hands back on you? Why do your lips automatically open like they're calling to mine for a kiss? You might not be that kind of woman, Allyson Marx. And that suits me just fine since I'm not looking for another promiscuous woman. Been there, done that. But don't lie to me, or yourself, by saying that you wouldn't be interested. We both know that's not true. Given the right time, the right circumstances, *both* of us would be ready to take that leap."

Aaron never even saw her hand move.

One minute, she stood stock still in front of him with her arms by her sides. The next, her hand sailed through the air, whizzed past his ear like a bee and connected with his cheek.

●●●●●

Ally's hand flew to her open mouth. *Oh God,* she thought, mortified. *What did I do that for?* But she didn't need an answer from God. She already knew why she'd hit him.

It was because everything he had said was true. She *was* panting and she could feel her heart pounding. She felt her skin grow hot as if she'd sat in the sun for too long. And she did feel, Lord help her, like calling to his lips and begging him to kiss her. Ally had slapped Aaron because he made her face the reality of their current situation.

She wanted him. But she didn't *want* to want him. Did she?

Before she could answer herself, Ally watched Aaron bring his head back around to face her. There was an angry handprint on his left cheek where her hand had connected with his skin. Her palm still tingled from the impact. She'd slapped him a lot harder than she had intended. Actually, she hadn't intended to hit him at all. It just happened. And she felt horrible and childish because of it.

"I'm so sorry. I didn't mean to do that," she said, her voice quavering.

Aaron opened his mouth, worked his jaw around in a circle before replying, "That was a heck of a whack. Did your Daddy teach you to do that?" Ally scrunched her nose and her eyebrows fell low on her forehead as confusion took over her remorse. Aaron laughed and then said, "You don't need to apologize. I was out of line. I'm the one who's sorry."

"But I hit you."

"Yeah, but I provoked you."

"Not on purpose," she argued. Then she saw the sheepish grin on his face, the way he ducked his face down a little to try to hide it. "You said all that on purpose? Were you trying to get me to hit you? What are you, a masochist?"

"Yes, I said it all on purpose. No, I wasn't trying to get you to hit me. I didn't know you had that much feistiness in you. And I am definitely not a masochist. However," he began as he rubbed his cheek where Ally's handprint had begun to fade. He stepped up close to Ally again with a calculating gleam in his eyes and said, "I would be more than happy to take any pain for the chance to stay this close to you. Tell me… What's it gonna take to sweep you off your feet and carry you upstai____" he broke off and laughed when Ally shoved him in the shoulder, pushed him out of her personal space.

But she still laughed right along with him.

"Don't be a jerk," she said through her smile. "Okay, I get it. Point made and understood. How about that truce?"

"I think we're way past that, don't you?"

"We should be. But we also seem to bring out the worst in each other."

"Then I guess we'll have to work on fixing that. 'Course, if this has been your worst, I'm not sure I could keep up with your best."

"What do you mean?"

"Your witty comebacks keep me on my toes and make me want to pull you into my arms. I can only imagine how much more clever they'll be when you're not focused on anger. And how much harder it'll be for me to be around you without wanting to kiss you."

"Well… I guess you'd better invest in a set of earmuffs then. And practice some restraint."

She headed for the front door, turned to look at him over her shoulder when she stood in the doorway and asked, "You wanna take a look around?"

His smile grew until his eyes crinkled at the corners and Ally knew that grin was her answer. She didn't wait for words, just turned and walked out the door, down the two wooden steps and headed for the road. He caught up with her as she passed the two trucks in the driveway. She saw out of the corner of her eye when he almost reached down to grab her hand, but put his hands in his pockets instead. She didn't know if she was relieved or disappointed, but chose not to dwell on it.

"So where are you taking me?"

"I thought I'd show you the grounds. The ones we can get to on foot, at least."

"Technically you can get anywhere on foot."

"True, but you won't want to walk to some of the places I'll show you the next few days. There's some rough country out here." She glanced askance at him. "Even if you did want to, I'm not sure a city boy like you could handle it."

"City boy? You do realize that I live in a place with a population of three thousand people, right? That's not what most consider a "city." It's a town, relatively small and only a few hundred bigger than your Rosy Camp."

"But still bigger, nonetheless. Ergo, city boy."

"Whatever you say, pumpkin."

"Hey, no way. That's my Daddy's nickname for me and you're not allowed to use it."

"Okay, cupcake." Ally stopped walking, put her hands on her hips and tapped her toe in the dirt. Aaron stopped too and turned back to look at her, took in her position and chuckled. She didn't think it was funny. "Sweet cheeks? Sugar pie?"

"Oh my gosh," she exclaimed and threw her hands up in the air. "Will you just stop it?!"

"Nope. Not as long as you're gonna call me city boy. So, do you want to go back to regular names?"

Ally huffed but couldn't keep in her giggle. "Fine," she said and started walking again. "No more nicknames."

They walked in silence for a bit, small rocks kicked up under their feet as they strolled down the drive toward the chicken coop. Ally took the time to sneak a few peaks at Aaron.

He was tall. Then, most people were when they stood next to her petite frame. And his muscles were definitely evident under that shirt, as she had seen at the house. She noticed again that his build wasn't bulky, and appreciated the natural look. The ridges in his forearms were tanned, sleek, and they flexed when he put his hands in his pockets. His biceps and shoulders curved around the bones with a masculine grace that spoke more of good genes than artificial creation. His long legs were covered in jeans, but Ally could still see the indentions from his solid thighs when they strained against the denim. His neck, like his forearms, was tanned, and the curve of his Adam's apple stood out like a focal point that needed to be touched. His jaw was firm, the arc from his chin to his ear covered in a light brown stubble. Ally had the desire to see if that stubble was prickly like a cactus or soft like a blanket. She wanted to see what it felt like under her fingertips, her cheek. Her mouth.

She jerked her head back around, forced herself to not look at him anymore. It was obvious her thoughts sunk to the level of a hormonal teenager when she stared at him for too long. To become enamored with a man that got on her nerves the majority of the time they spent together was not a smart move. The last thing she needed was to get all googly-eyed over a man who was probably just like Ben and wanted to hit on any woman he saw.

Be cordial. Keep your distance. Maintain a platonic understanding.

Her pep talk did little to alleviate the way her heart pounded in her chest when she looked at him and Ally prayed that Aaron wouldn't be able to tell.

When they made it to the coop, Ally crossed her arms on top of the chicken wire, laid her chin on her hands. Aaron mimicked the pose next to her. She watched the claws of the birds. They dug in the dirt, immediately followed with their beaks as they pecked at the freshly tilled ground and searched for worms and insects to snack on. One of the larger chickens pecked at a runt, their squawks loud in the silence of the afternoon.

"What did she do that for?" Aaron asked.

"You don't know?"

"No. We never had chickens growing up. My experience on a ranch is mainly with cattle. Not poultry."

"Huh."

"What's that supposed to mean?"

"Nothing. I guess I just thought it would've been obvious."

"Well it's not. So, you care to enlighten me as to why you have cannibal chickens?"

"They're not cannibals. She wasn't trying to eat the smaller one. She was putting her in her place. Have you ever heard of "hen pecking" or a "pecking order"?" Ally glanced over at Aaron, saw his nod while he continued to watch the birds, and went on. "Well this is where it comes from. That large one, we call her Big Momma because she's the biggest of the bunch. If one of the others gets in her space, or acts out of line, she'll peck them. Straighten them out because she's at the top of the____"

"Pecking order," Aaron finished her sentence. "Right. That makes sense."

"Of course it does, city boy." Aaron cut her a look from the side and started to say something but Ally spoke back up before he could. "Sorry. I know; no more nicknames. But you kinda walked right into that one. I mean, it's more common sense than knowing about ranching."

"Alright. I'll give you that." He turned to the side, his left arm hooked over the top of the wire and cracked a grin at Ally. "Not that I'm not enjoying looking at your birds hen peck, but what else have you got out here? Anything more exciting than flying feathers? Or is this all you feel comfortable with? Being a woman and all."

"That sounded like a challenge, Mr. Lambert." He only shrugged his shoulders so she said, "Okay, then. Come on. I'll show how much more exciting I can be."

She didn't wait for a response, just took off at a trot and headed for the barn. He caught up with her after she ran through the gate of the holding pen, right before she reached the open barn door, grabbed her hand and pulled her back into his chest. They both breathed fast, Ally's more from excitement than exertion when he leaned down and whispered in her ear, "If you wanna race, make it fair. But I'll warn you now... I'll catch you every time."

That's what scares me, Ally thought.

•••••

Aaron dropped Ally's hand, stepped away from the heat of her body. He felt as if he'd been burned, right on the chest, where he'd pressed up against Ally's back.

His hand reached up of its own accord, rubbed across his chest where he was sure her scent would linger for the rest of the day. Not some overly sickly-sweet scent like vanilla–his ex-wife's favorite–but something more clean, and no less heady.

Honeysuckle, he thought to himself. *She smells like summer rain and honeysuckle.*

He cleared his throat and waited for her to walk into the barn. She stood still for a minute, her back still to Aaron. He was about to walk around her, make the first move toward the stables, when she took a deep breath and then a step.

Her back was ramrod straight, her head high. Her long chestnut hair was piled in a bun on the top of her head. Several long strands had slipped free and flowed around the sides of her face and neck. Aaron swallowed past the lump in his throat when he thought of how close he'd been to placing his lips at that same spot, right below her ear. And because he was a glutton for punishment, Aar let his eyes travel down the length of her back, to her hips. He dropped his chin to his chest, forced a breath into his lungs. *Stop doing that, Aar. It's not right.*

But no matter what his arguments for keeping his distance from Ally were, his brain quit working as soon as he was around her and something else took over. Instinct, maybe. His heart possibly. Corny as it sounded, he felt like he *had* to be close to her. To keep a hand on her, because she might disappear on him if he didn't.

He was saved from his fearful contemplations when they walked under a low-hanging oak beam and into the heart of the barn. There were eight stalls, four on each side, separated by a dirt pathway in the middle. On the wall straight in front of them, past the stalls, was an open door. Aaron saw a couple of saddles on stands along with reins and halters hanging on the wall. The tack room.

Half of the stalls were empty, the other half taken up by four horses. Ally walked right up to a big bay gelding who stood well over fifteen hands high. He stuck his head over the wooden rail, nose down as she rubbed in between in his ears. Her face lit up with a smile when the horse's mouth nudged at her hand.

"This is Fury," Ally told Aaron. "And he's a spoiled little bugger, aren't ya boy?" she crooned and then to Aaron, "He's looking for sugar cubes. I might have gotten him hooked on them when he was just a colt. Now every time he sees me, he's looking for the sweets." She kept her eyes on the horse but said to him over her shoulder, "Come on, introduce yourself." When Aaron still didn't make a move to join her at the stall's gate, she turned and looked at him. "Quit acting like a shy, little school girl and get over here. He won't bite."

Aaron walked over to where Ally stood, reached his hand out to let the horse sniff him. When he nudged Aar's hand, too, he laughed, reached up to rub where Ally was.

"He's a good looking guy. Is he yours?"

"I ride him more than any of the others. He's fast and strong, confident on any terrain. He took more to me than my brother or Dad. So yeah, I____" her words were cut off by a loud neigh from the stall next to Fury's. "That's Trixie, our only paint. She's a young mare, only five. Still a little green and not quite used to strangers," Ally explained. With her right hand still on Fury's nose, she turned to face Aaron, put her free hand on her cocked out hip then said, "Is he exciting enough for you?"

"We're just petting him."

"That's what you think." And she walked off toward the tack room. Aaron stayed rooted to his spot until she came back with arms full. A bucket with various supplies was hooked over her left arm. A blanket and bridle rested on top of the bucket handle. And on her right arm was a saddle. She hefted her arm up, laid the saddle on the rail, the blanket on top. The bridle she placed on the hook next to the gate and then handed the bucket to Aaron. "Here you go."

He took it with a wary hand, eyed it speculatively and looked to Ally with a question. "What do you want me to do with this?"

"Get him ready. We're going out." Then she turned and headed back to the room, returned with armloads of the same equipment and stopped at the stall next to his. She held on to her own bucket, walked into the stall slowly, talked softy to Trixie where the mare waited in the back corner. The horse's hind leg muscles twitched as Ally walked closer, still using that soft voice as if the horse were a baby. The paint whinnied, blew a breath out of her mouth.

"Ally, are you sure that one's safe? She seems a little high strung."

"She's good," Ally promised, reached out a hand to the horse. "She just needs a little coaxing every now and then. She's got spirit."

Like you, Aaron thought but didn't say out loud. When the horse finally let Ally pet her head and leaned into Ally's touch a little, Aaron let out a breath. Satisfied that she was safe, he walked into Fury's stall. It had been a few years since he'd saddled a horse. When he told Ally that he had experience on a ranch, he hadn't pointed out that most of the time he was on one of the four-wheelers. While Aaron wasn't completely ignorant of horses, he wasn't as adept at the ins and outs of the animals as his brother-in-law, Jax.

He set the bucket down and grabbed the brush and comb, ran them across the horse's strong back and under his belly, watched dust fly off his coat like a cloud of pale brown smoke. When Aaron was satisfied Fury was clean, he put the brush down, took the bridle off the hook, set it into place and let the reins hang loose across the horse's neck. He picked up the blanket off the rail and settled in the middle of the horse's back. He grabbed the saddle, which was heavier than it looked (Ally had easily carried it), slung it over the top of his bay and centered it. Then he stood back, eyed the two straps that hung down the opposite side of the horse's belly and tried to remember which one to buckle first.

"Strap the girth into place first, then the cinch," came Ally's voice from behind him. He turned and froze when he saw her. She held the reins of Trixie in her right hand, clearly quicker at saddling a horse to ride than he was. The horse sidestepped a little then stilled when Ally held firm on the reins. But her command over the animal wasn't what made Aaron stop and stare.

She'd let her hair down and a straw cowboy hat covered her brown hair that fell in waves down her shoulders. Like a silken curtain that hid her graceful neck from his view. She had a small grin on her face and his gaze was drawn to her lips. Plump and pink and begging to be kissed. Her eyes, and all the colors that swirled around in them, danced in happiness. It was obvious she loved this part of the ranch and her enthusiasm at getting out on the horses was infectious. Aaron couldn't wait to get out there, too. He was looking forward to racing with her down to that grassy mountain he'd seen.

"Sorry. But you looked like you could use a little guidance."

"Don't apologize. You're right." He turned back to Fury, grabbed the front strap and buckled it snugly into place. He reached for the cinch and said to Ally over his shoulder, "Was it that obvious that I was stuck?"

"Well, you were looking at the thing like it was a Rubik's Cube and you didn't know which row to turn first. Make sure that cinch is tight so the saddle doesn't move when you're riding." He did as she told and when he stood up and grabbed the reins, Ally opened the gate for him. "Come on, city boy. You wanted a race. So let's go see what ya got."

Aaron let the "city boy" comment go, decided that she used it more as a term of endearment than an insult. As they walked their animals to the opening of the barn, out of the pen and to the gate that opened to the vast ranch before them, Ally stopped. She opened the gate, walked Trixie through and Aaron followed. Then she mounted her horse and Aaron admired the way her jeans stretched tight over her hips, at the feminine strength he noticed in her thighs when she settled herself in the saddle. His eyes roamed up her waist, past her chest quickly, landed on her face that looked down at him. Only she didn't seem offended that he'd been blatantly staring. It was like her whole demeanor and attitude changed as soon as she'd walked into the barn with the horses. Aaron liked it, this confidence and lack of bashfulness.

He lifted himself up onto Fury, took a second to get his bearings being this high off the ground again. When he felt secure, he looked over at Ally, gave a short nod of his head. She smiled, her cheeks flushed with excitement.

"Welcome to my neck of the woods, Mr. Lambert." She took off at a gallop and headed straight for that mountain.

He knew right then–as he watched Ally race off ahead of him, knowing that he would follow–that he had to put his doubts aside. He'd never win the prize if he didn't try, right?

Aaron kicked his heels into Fury's side and took off after her, ready for the game.

Aimee Martin

Chapter 5

"For jealousy is the rage of a man: therefore he will
not spare in the day of vengeance."
Proverbs 6:34

He watched them through the scope of his rifle a couple
hundred yards away from where he lay on his belly, hidden
by the overhanging branches of a large group of Douglas fir
trees. Their fallen needles cushioned the ground underneath
him, with a few that poked through the thin material of his
camouflaged shirt, making it hard to stay focused on the task
at hand. Reconnaissance. That's all this was about.

He had no intention of putting the weapon to use. But
watching the man and woman ride off side-by-side, looking
calm and happy and *intimate*, had his index finger itching to
reach out for the trigger.

It wasn't jealousy he was feeling. That would imply that
he was envious of the man being with the woman right now.

And he couldn't be envious of something that belonged to him. Because she did. Belong to him. So he reigned in his irritation at their momentary togetherness.

Not now, he scolded himself and lifted his face away from the special Leupold scope he'd ordered for just this occasion. He laid the Remington Model Seven Hundred with its own camo sleeve covering on his backpack beside him, stroked the cool barrel as if it was a lover. *Soon, but not yet.*

Opting for the set of binoculars that didn't give him untimely urges, he searched the distance until he found them again, just as they came up to the small mountain that was no more than a hundred yards from the house, two hundred from him.

He watched them dismount from their horses, watched the woman run toward the small incline, laughing as she looked back over her shoulder. His body jerked in anger when he saw the man tackle her, knocking her onto a pile of pinkfairies, coming down hard on top of her.

If he kisses her, I won't be able to hold back.

His hands tightened around the binoculars, his knuckles cracking and turning white with his grip, while he waited with bated breath to see if his worst nightmare was going to come to fruition or not. He released a pent up breath when the man rolled over to his side, lying next to her instead of on top of her. Still too close for his liking; but at least he wasn't kissing her.

Those kisses belonged to *him*. Not some interloper.

And it was about damned time that the woman learned that, once and for all.

Before his blood pressure could rise any more, he stuffed the binoculars back into his pack, slung it around his shoulders. He stood up to a crouch, ran his hand over the needles so they didn't look like they'd been laid on. With one last glance at the man and woman, he turned, crawled out of the woods. Leaving nothing but silent rage in his wake.

Aimee Martin

Chapter 6

*"And Jacob kissed Rachel, and lifted up his voice,
and wept."*
Genesis 29:11

Ally hadn't felt this much energy in years, if ever at all.

When she had taken off on Trixie from the barn, she headed for the grassy mountain where the pinkfairies were. She knew it would only be a matter of time before Aaron and Fury caught up to her. That bay gelding could outrun almost any horse in their stable and be barely winded at the end. That's why she'd named him Fury, because he ran with a vengeance.

If Aaron had even the slightest amount of riding experience–and she could tell he did when she glanced back and saw him bent low over the horse's neck, the reins laid forward to give the horse his head–then he would catch her in no time.

No sooner had she faced forward again, spurred her boots into the sides of Trixie to get her horse to ratchet it up another notch, did she hear the thundering hoof beats of Fury. She mimicked Aaron's pose and laid low, pushed her paint faster. Aaron pulled up almost even with her, reached out to try to grab onto her reins. She laughed and a loud "No way!" fell from her lips. She sidestepped to the left, tried to keep Aaron out of reach and stay in front of him all at the same time. But the sideways movement gave him a headfirst advantage.

Aaron sped ahead of Ally. Normally she'd do whatever she could to catch him and be the first to the mountain. Her competitive nature would never let her knowingly lose. But as he passed, she noticed the look of his muscled back twisting and flexing under his shirt. At the way his butt sat up on the saddle a little, with just enough room for her hand to squeeze in between the space. Ally swallowed past the need to do that and see if his rear was as firm as it looked.

It's unladylike, Ally. Not to mention stupid.

So instead, she reigned in Trixie, slowed down not only her mare's hankering to go fast, but her own craving for Aaron, too.

They reached the mountainside with Aaron just a fraction ahead of her. Ally hopped off Trixie quick, decided that since she couldn't beat him to the mountain, she'd beat him to the top, and raced to the edge of the hill. She spared only the briefest of laughing glimpses behind her as she climbed.

Right as she started up the incline, a pair of strong arms wrapped around her middle, knocked her off balance. Then they both fell, Ally's face set to take the brunt of the fall. Aaron placed one hand out at the last second and half turned them so that they she landed on his arm and not the hard ground underneath. With the wind knocked out of her, she couldn't do anything but wheeze and cough as she laughed. He was right there with her and the sound of his deep laugh in her ear and the feel of his hard body lying on top of her made goose bumps rise all over her skin.

Then she wasn't laughing any more. She panted, her breath puffing out in fast spurts as it mingled with his directly above her. She stared up into his blue eyes, very aware of his left arm curled under her back and the hand on that same arm squeezing her shoulder, as if he couldn't decide if he wanted to push her away or pull her closer. *Let it be the latter,* Ally thought. He moved his face closer to Ally's, his lips parted. She couldn't help it. She closed her eyes and waited for the touch of his mouth as the atmosphere around her got warmer.

Cool mountain air replaced that warmth. She opened her eyes to see that Aaron had plopped down beside her, his right arm thrown over his eyes. Ally decided then– remembering her debate on whether she should be disappointed or relieved when he didn't grab hold of her hand, earlier on their walk–that she was definitely disappointed. And she wasn't going to hide that from herself anymore. She did want to feel her pulse speed up just because he'd gotten closer to her. She wanted to feel her skin warm with excitement when he put his hands on her face. And she desperately wanted to feel his open mouth against hers.

Just because she didn't trust that men could be monogamous didn't mean she couldn't have a little fun, did it? Besides, it would only be a kiss.

She propped up on her elbow, ready to lean in and make the first move. But his words stopped her.

"Forgive me."

"Forgive you?" she asked, her brow furrowed at his whispered plea. "For wha..." her question died in her throat when Aaron sat up quickly, moved so that his arms imprisoned her, chest pressed close to her own, and forced her to lie back down on the ground behind her. She reached up and grasped onto his arms to keep from falling too hard. Her fingers automatically wrapped around his biceps. The muscles twitched under her palms; she held on tighter. His eyes searched her face and Ally swore she could feel each pass of his gaze as if it were a caress. From her eyes to her cheeks to her mouth and throat and back up to her eyes, she shivered as she imagined his mouth taking the same path.

She felt her pulse speed up as her skin flushed. And, God help her, her lips did part and beckon for Aaron to join them with his. All the reactions that he'd claimed were there, she felt as clear as the cool flowers and grass underneath her.

Then he leaned down, ran the tip of his nose on a barely-there trail from her ear to the corner of her mouth, and stopped when his lips were only an inch from hers.

"For this."

Then *he* kissed *her*.

•••••

What the heck are you doing, Aar? This isn't right. It's too soon. She doesn't even like you. You're gonna get your face slapped again.

No matter what arguments he ran through in his mind, Aaron couldn't pull away from Ally's mouth. Not even when he anticipated another sharp slap.

Aaron had wondered earlier, back at the bunkhouse when he'd goaded her, if her lips would be soft and surrendering to his. Or if they'd be hard and unyielding, unwilling to let him give them both what they wanted. He was so glad that he'd decided to find out. Because soft, they were. And perfect. The way her full lower lip fit against the seam of his mouth. The dampness that made it easier to slide his lips over hers. Her taste seeped into his brain and made all other thoughts–everything that didn't revolve around Ally and her mouth–fly out of his mind.

He hadn't planned to kiss her. At least not yet.

Ally looked over her shoulder and laughed at him as she ran, almost as if she was taunting him, teasing him to catch her. So he did. When they fell to the ground, the feel of her little feminine frame beneath him made him tremble with desire. He was a man. Men weren't supposed to tremble.

But he had.

Aaron had forced himself to lie back, take away the temptation. But all that had done was allow her unique honeysuckle scent to waft into his face by the breeze that blew in from the west. In that instant, with her scent and the feel of her body still imprinted on his own, he knew he had to have her. God, how he wanted to kiss her.

Now, he clamped his mouth shut, determined to lock his tongue inside and not scare Ally–or himself–with something they weren't ready for. But the more he slid his lips against hers–the more he tilted his head to kiss her harder so that she knew it was *him* that was in control–the more that stupid appendage inside his mouth tried to push its way out, as if it had a mind of its own. As if it would do anything to mingle with hers.

He tore his mouth away, rested his forehead against hers so he couldn't see her lips. Maybe if he didn't look at them, he could resist the urge to claim them completely. He closed his eyes and held in a moan when she ran the tips of her fingers through the hair at his temples. That soft touch soon turned into something firmer when she grasped those same hairs and pulled so that he was forced to lift up and look at her. Her hazel eyes swam with emotions and Aaron couldn't pick out which one was prominent. Surprise, desire and definitely irritation. If he wasn't mistaken, he thought he saw a little mischief in there, too.

"Do you make a habit of going around throwing women onto the ground and kissing them senseless?"

He couldn't help the smile that crept onto his lips. "You call that being kissed senseless?" he countered and added, "Seems like I've got a lot to teach you, then."

"Don't even think about it."

"Are you gonna slap me again if I do?"

Ally had the good grace not to lie. "No," she whispered. "But that doesn't mean it's a good idea."

Aaron agreed. For now, anyway. So he leaned down and placed a small peck on her button nose and rolled off her. He pulled his legs up, wrapped his arms around his knees and looked toward the pasture they just rode across. The length of a football field. That's all it had taken for him to go from *thinking* it was a mistake to get involved with Ally, to *knowing* that it was exactly what he wanted. If he were honest with himself, part of him thought it was exactly what he needed, too.

There is a fine line between wanting something and needing it. Aaron had to decide what this attraction to Ally was, because wanting faded with time. That much was obvious with his marriage. He'd wanted Jessica in the beginning and look where that had gotten him. However need, that was something else altogether. Some needs lasted forever. He didn't think he'd ever needed Jess like this. What he was feeling with Ally was different, more intense, more shattering.

Aaron thought about a scripture his mother used to quote to him all the time when he was growing up, from the book of *Matthew*, about God knowing what you need even before you ask Him. Was that what this was all about? Had God brought him to Montana, pushed him to come here, to be with Ally, because He'd known she was what Aaron needed?

He watched the knee high grass in the field bend sideways with the breeze, the tips of the blades reaching down to the ground as if they needed to be connected in a full circle, with a complete link, not just from the roots. He realized the truth behind his musings about Jess. They had never needed each other in every aspect of their lives, the way a husband and wife should. He hadn't needed Jessica to fulfill him as a man. She sure hadn't needed him to make her feel like a woman; not if that other guy was any indication.

What he wanted was some kind of indication his life was going in the direction God intended. He had learned the hard way that veering off God's path for him left him lost and broken. He could not let that happen again. This almost instantaneous rush of emotions confused him, but there was no mistaking his attraction to this beautiful woman.

The faint touch of a cool, small hand on his forearm brought Aaron back to the present. Ally sat up, too. Her hat had fallen off her head when they landed on the ground and her long hair blew in the wind. It was lovely, like streams of cinnamon colored silk in the sunlight. With her round, innocent eyes and cute, pert nose, she looked like an adorable little imp. *My own little Elf,* Aaron thought. He noticed that the look of mischief had vanished, replaced with uncertainty and maybe a little embarrassment. Then it was gone and she frowned.

"That's a serious expression you've got going on there." She tilted her head to the side, studied him a minute. "Want to talk about what's giving you premature wrinkles?"

"What? I'm not getting wrinkles. I'm only thirty-two."

"Yeah, well you're gonna look fifty-two if you don't get rid of that scowl on your forehead. Kissing me couldn't have been *that* bad. I realize that might not have been the kiss of the century, but you didn't exactly give me much notice. I'd have prepped a little more had I known it was coming."

"And take away the element of surprise? Never," he said and chuckled at her droll way of looking at the world. Then he ran his thumb along her bottom lip and said, "And I could never be disappointed with a kiss from you. It was perfect."

"How very sappy and romantic of you. But you haven't seen me at my best, yet."

"Yet? Interesting choice of words. Maybe we should try again?" He waggled his eyebrows at her and she giggled, placed her hand on his chest to hold him back.

"Some other time, Romeo."

"Alright." He stood up, dusted the flower petals from his pants, turned and helped Ally stand. He bent over and picked up her hat, placed it on her head, admired the smile that graced her lips when he tucked a few stray strands of hair behind her ears. "Then take me somewhere that I won't be tempted."

"You got it," she answered and walked over to the horses that grazed just a few yards away. She mounted Trixie, waited while he got up on Fury. Then she turned and headed back toward the barn at a slow clip. Aaron stayed beside her as they rode, tried to think of something to say to break the silence, but couldn't come up with anything. But he enjoyed the fact that it wasn't uncomfortable or strained.

It was safe. It was peaceful. He smiled to himself as he recognized that it was *exactly* what he wanted. And needed.

•••••

Ally was in trouble.

From the minute he'd laid his mouth across hers, and she'd felt that undeniable urge, Ally just knew that she was in serious, knee deep trouble. While they cantered back toward the barn, Ally tried to justify her reaction when Aaron had kissed her.

It was pheromones.

It was a natural response between a man and a woman.

It had been three years since she'd been kissed.

But except for the last one—because she *hadn't* been kissed since she'd gotten divorced from Ben—they were all lies. The truth of the matter, the reason she'd responded so eagerly, was because it was Aaron. It was *his* chest that had felt like a safe weight on top of her. It was *his* woodsy cologne that hung in her nose and tempted her to search for the place on his body where it was the strongest. It was *his* lips that had fit against hers so smoothly, so perfectly, that it was as if they were made to mold together.

And that had scared her.

So when he had lifted his mouth from hers, Ally had reverted to her go-to attitude to try and hide the way she'd really felt. Sarcastic, overconfident, funny. And it worked, distracted him enough that he didn't notice the way her body trembled. She was a grown woman who'd been through a lot in this life. She had no business trembling.

Except for when he kisses you, Allyson. There's no stopping that.

And the part that worried her most was that she couldn't wait to do it again.

They pulled up to the fencing surrounding the barn right as dusk started to set in. Ally hopped off Trixie and walked the mare into the pens. Aaron followed suit, pulled Fury right alongside them. He paused at the barn entrance and looked at Ally, opened his mouth to say something then closed it without a word, only a small smile. Since Ally wasn't sure she wanted to know what he planned to say, she returned his smile and walked into the building. She guided Trixie to her stall and began unsaddling her, listened as he repeated her process in the stall next to them. After both the horses had been brushed and hosed off to cool down, Aaron took the tack to put up. Ally gave each of the horses a good helping of alfalfa and a coffee can full of oats, filled their troughs with fresh water.

She stood outside the stalls, her arms hooked over Fury's gate, when Aaron walked up beside her. They watched her big buddy eat in silence for a minute before she felt his hand on her back, silently getting her attention. She laid her head sideways on her arms, looked over at him while he kept his eyes forward, on Fury. She waited for him to speak and when he finally did, it was with a smile and a crinkled brow, like he couldn't decide whether what he was about to say was good or bad.

"Thank you for the ride. I had a great time."

"You don't appear so sure of that." At this he looked over at her. "You're scowling."

"Sorry," he said and visibly relaxed his forehead. "I'm just surprised that I had that much fun. It has been a long time."

"Since you had fun? Or since you were on a horse?"

"Both."

Ally grinned at him, gave her head a little nod up and down. "You're welcome," she whispered into the quiet barn.

Then their quiet was interrupted by the sound of a radio being turned on, loud static from an AM station at first, followed by the skipping sounds that come when trying to find a better signal. Aaron tensed at the intrusion and he scanned the area, searched for the source. Ally didn't move; she knew that there was no one in the world who was less harmful than the person who'd turned on the radio.

Aaron's posture relaxed when the music drifted through the barn to where they stood. As the strands from George Strait's song *All My Exes Live In Texas* came on, they both laughed. "That's the truth," Aaron said, "But I'd be happy if she was gone by the time I made it back there. As big as Texas is, it seems it's not big enough to avoid running into people you'd just as soon never see again."

It was on the tip of her tongue to ask what had happened between Aaron and his ex-wife when the little old man in overalls, white t-shirt and straw hat came around the corner from the stairs that led to the loft. Aaron automatically moved to stand in front of her, like a piece of armor, his guard right back up. Ally smiled at the overprotective stance, debated on whether or not to come right out and tell Aaron who the "mystery man" was. Then decided she wanted to see how this little scenario would play out first.

The newcomer had his head down, a brush in his hand swiping back and forth over a boot to try to clean off the dirt. He stopped by a bale of hay outside one of the empty stalls, plopped down heavily on it, set the clean boot on the ground. Then he took off the other boot and went to work on it, oblivious to the other two people in the barn with him.

Ally could see the side of Aaron's face and his expression was a mixture of confusion and guarded curiosity. When the old man finally looked up and noticed them, he jumped up off the bale of hay and Aaron's body flexed in response.

"What are you doing in here?" the old man asked her, his voice raspy from years of yelling at horses.

"We've been here," Aaron responded. "Who are you? What do you want?"

Ally had to roll her lips together to keep from laughing and her shoulders shook with the effort from it. The man narrowed his eyes at Aaron as if he'd just noticed there was a visitor in the barn. Then he turned his gaze back to Ally, head tilted to the side, exasperation evident on his face. He sighed. "Allyson Marx. I asked you a question. You were supposed to be at the house for dinner thirty minutes ago. Your Momma is gonna think I had something to do with your being late. Are you trying to get me fired?"

Aaron turned his head, looked at Ally over his shoulder with a question in his eyes. She couldn't hold it in anymore. She laughed so hard that she snorted. She covered her mouth and nose, embarrassed by the outburst, but still laughed. Aaron raised an eyebrow, waited for an explanation. It was several minutes before Ally was in control enough to talk.

"Aaron, this is Jerry. Jerry Allen, meet Aaron Lambert." She turned and looked at Jerry. "And you couldn't get fired from this place if you wanted to. So quit acting like some put-out teenager."

"So you know him?" Aaron asked and crossed his arms over his chest. Ally kept her eyes on his face, the memory of those strong arms encircling her–and how she longed for them to do so again–still too fresh in her mind.

"Since I was a baby. Jerry here is our stable master and horse trainer."

"Stable master?" Ally nodded her head at Aaron's question. "What is this, the nineteenth century? Do people still use stable masters?"

"I prefer that than head stable boy," Jerry piped in. "I haven't been a boy in many years. And since I'm older than every person on this ranch, they humor me."

"Right. Sorry." Aaron walked over and shook the elder man's hand. "It's nice to meet you Jerry. I apologize if I came across as____"

"As a grandiose bodyguard?" Aaron laughed at Jerry's blunt description and Jerry continued. "It's no problem. I'd have been sorely disappointed if someone wasn't defensive of my girl over there." He tilted his head in Ally's direction and she smiled at him.

"Jerry's like the grandfather I never had," she explained to Aaron.

"What is it with you not warning me when the men in your life sneak up on us?" Ally only shrugged her shoulders to Aaron's inquiry. "I swear, I think you're trying to get me killed for being disrespectful to my elders. Are there any other men I need to be prepared to run into?"

"Just Danny, my little brother."

"Yeah and he's hardly a man." This from Jerry.

"Okay, then," Aaron said and turned, walked back to where Ally still stood next to Fury's stall. "But you're going to explain that it's *your* fault we're late to dinner. I've already started off on a shaky foot with your father. He doesn't need any more ammo to be judgmental of me. Not to mention the poor first impression this is bound to have on your mother."

"Then we'd better hurry, huh?"

"Lead the way." He swept his arm out in front of him. Ally stepped away from the gate, gave a wave to Jerry, walked out of the barn to head to the house.

And ignored the flutter in her belly when Aaron placed his warm hand on the small of her back.

Chapter 7

"Be not forgetful to entertain strangers: for thereby some have entertained angels unawares."
Hebrews 13:2

Aaron stopped when they reached the back porch of the big ranch house and fought down the urge to lean over and throw up. Nerves ran rampant in his gut, making him feel even more hollow than he already was. What was he so nervous about? It's not like he was meeting the parents of a girlfriend.

But you kissed her.

True. But that didn't make Ally his girlfriend. When you reached a certain age, terms like boyfriend and girlfriend no longer applied. You simply dated. And if you were serious, you became exclusive. Period. He wasn't dating Ally. Sure, they'd shared a kiss. But that didn't mean anything more than the heat of the moment had gotten the better of him.

What did mean something–and probably contributed to the nausea in his stomach right now–was how much he wanted to kiss her again. If it had been nothing more than a passing moment, he wouldn't ache to have another one just like it. Over and over. He wouldn't remember the way she had felt pressed underneath him, a perfect fit. He wouldn't have to clench his fists to keep from reaching for her, to run his fingers through her hair just to have her honeysuckle and rain scent engulf him and calm his nerves.

That was what made this whole evening worrisome. Because no matter what reasoning he tried to maintain, he knew how obvious it would be to her parents that he was interested in Ally as more than an employer or friend. Would they turn him out? Make him leave Rosy Camp and Montana and get as far away from their daughter as possible? Or would they welcome him with cautious permissibility?

"Hey, why'd you stop? We're already late, you know." Ally's voice brought his gaze up to where she stood on the ten-foot wide porch that ran around the entire perimeter of the house. Her hand rested on the screen doorknob, paused in the process of opening it and walking inside. She narrowed her eyes at him, dropped her hand and walked back to where he stood at the bottom of the stairs. "What's the matter?"

"I'm nervous," Aaron admitted. "What if your Mom doesn't like me? Or your Dad decides he made a mistake earlier and uses his beefy arms to throw me out of the house?"

"You should be more concerned with the fact that you being late isn't a good impression for someone wanting a job. Not how my mother views you."

"Not. Helping."

"Sorry."

"Yeah, sure you are." He took a deep breath, let it out slowly. "I feel like I'm going to get an immediate X on my forehead because I'm bringing *you* home late."

"Aaron, this isn't high school. I'm a grown woman. The only reason I'm here, living under their roof at all, is because I haven't decided where I want to go. What I want to do. They know that and they get that me coming home to dinner with them every night is temporary. They won't be mad. They'll understand because they're happy they have this time at all." Aaron gave her a skeptical look. Ally raised her eyes to the ceiling of the porch, gave a frustrated sigh before looking back at him. "How about this. I promise that if Daddy tries to throw you out, I'll stand in the way. He'd never toss you on your butt if he thought I might get hurt in the process. And as for Momma, she loves everyone. Just don't bring up David and the night should be fine."

"David?" Aaron asked, curious if this was a past boyfriend. *There's that stupid word again.* Only in this instance, thinking this guy was some significant other from Ally's past had jealousy rearing its ugly head. Aaron didn't want to think about any other boyfriends Ally had before. He only wanted to think about being hers now.

"My older brother." He breathed a sigh of relief and she turned, walked back to the screen door and waited for Aaron to come up beside her.

"Okay. Can I ask why?"

She looked sideways at him and there were tears in her eyes. Aaron hated it, hated they he felt as if *he'd* been the one to put them there, even though he had no idea where the tears had come from. He reached up, ran the tip of his finger along her cheek to catch the one drop that fell.

"Because he's dead."

That was not what Aaron had expected. He opened his mouth to ask what had happened, but Ally spoke again.

"Don't ask. Not tonight, okay?" He nodded his agreement and she went on. "Take your boots off." She glanced down and noticed that he was actually wearing tennis shoes, looked back up at him with a grin. "We're going to fix that issue tomorrow."

She pulled open the door and walked inside before he had a chance to explain that he had boots, just hadn't had a chance to change into them before she'd taken him to the barn. He toed off his sneakers, snuck in the door before it had a chance to slam closed. Ally stood at a deep copper sink in what Aaron assumed was a mudroom. Large, eighteen-inch ceramic tiles covered the open space and their dark brown color hid any dirt that might get tracked in. A stainless washer and dryer took up one wall and a row of pine shelves sat opposite, stocked with towels and laundry supplies. Next to the shelves was a row of cabinets, names written on the doors and–if Aaron wasn't mistaken when he glanced at the open door that had Ally's name on it–a change of clothes. Ally turned, grabbed a towel from the shelf, saw Aaron staring at the setup.

"Momma likes to keep extra clothes in here for when the weather is bad. She does not, under any circumstances, allow us in her house after a snow or rain storm until we've showered and changed."

Aaron's gaze circled around the room and there, in the corner by the door they'd just come in through, was a copper tub that matched the sink, a shower head perched directly above it and a shower curtain circling the back half, waiting to be closed for use. He turned back to Ally, a sly smile on his face that he couldn't get rid of if he wanted to, the image of Ally freshly showered now stamped on his brain.

She laughed, tossed her towel at his chest and said, "Not today, city boy. Wash up and I'll take you in to meet her."

He did as he was told and hung the towel on a hook next to the sink. When he turned back to Ally, she had pulled her hair back up and it lay in a mess of endearing curls on the top of her head. Her exposed neck looked graceful, enticing him more than the smells coming from the kitchen. He walked to where she stood and tilted her chin up to look at him. By the expression in her eyes, she was thinking the same thing he was.

But she had enough sense to stop him.

"Not now, Aaron." Feeling reprimanded in the most understanding of ways, he took a step back, dropped his hand from her face. "Daddy might not throw you out for being late to dinner," she began and turned to walk through the sliding wooden door that separated the mud room from the kitchen, "but he will if he catches you making moves on his daughter. So you'd better keep your hands to yourself."

"Easier said than done," he mumbled under his breath and, even though he felt like he was walking into the lion's den, followed her inside.

•••••

Ally strolled into the kitchen, acted much more carefree and unaffected than she really felt. The truth was she was just as nervous as Aaron claimed to be. Even though Daddy had invited him to dinner under the impression that this was a possible employment opportunity for the younger man, she was afraid there'd be a sign that blazed above their heads that said, "Aaron and Ally, kissing in a tree."

Daddy would be too engrossed in questioning Aaron–and eating his dinner–to take notice. She hoped, anyway. But her mother, who was more astute than anyone Ally knew, would hone in on that sign, analyze it, then egg it on in the most offhand of ways to try and get Ally to step out of the protective shell she'd erected around herself since the divorce.

She wasn't ready for that kind of meddling. She didn't even know if what had happened with Aaron on the mountainside was the start of something between them, or just a fluke. She didn't know because she hadn't been involved with a man since Ben. He'd been the *only* man Ally had ever been involved with. She didn't know how to read the signs that Aaron put off.

But you do know, she thought to herself. *If the way he looked at you in the mudroom is any indication, Aaron will be trying to kiss you again before the end of the night.* And that both excited her and terrified her. Because she did want to come out of her shell, just a little, like a baby chick first hatching, to see if there was anything scary in this new world with Aaron in it. If it was safe and okay to trust him. Or if he'd end up exactly like her ex had been, like most men were. Lying, cheating fools.

She decided that the only way she'd be able to find out, was if her Mom didn't know anything yet and no had chance to interfere. So she schooled her expression, walked up to stove where her mother stood and kissed the older woman on the cheek.

"Hey Momma," she began. "Sorry we're late. It was completely my fault and I'm supposed to make sure you know it so you don't get a bad impression on our new guest." She turned back to look at Aaron who stood just inside the doorway. His mouth hung wide open, eyes bugged out of his head. She held in a laugh at his look of disbelief.

"Why did you say that?" Aaron mouthed to her and she shrugged her shoulders at him with a wink, turned back to the stove with a hand on her Mom's elbow. Ally pulled her away from the stove, marched her right up to Aaron.

"Momma, this is Aaron Lambert. He's Mel's new brother-in-law. He came out here to see if he could get a job for the summer and Daddy invited him for dinner so they could talk about it."

"Yes, I heard," her Mom said and studied Aaron with her maternal eye. Then a smile broke out on her face and Aaron visibly released a pent up breath. "Hi Aaron. I'm Suzanne."

"Very nice to meet you, Suzanne." He held out a hand to shake and her Momma pulled Aaron in for a big hug.

"Please, call me Suzi." She released him and set him away from her, held on to his upper arms as she openly looked him over. "You are a handsome one, aren't you?" she asked and went on without waiting for an answer, oblivious to the blush that crept up on Aaron's neck. Ally made a mental note to tease him about that later. "Just look at those eyes, Ally. So blue they'd blend in with our famous Montana sky. And don't you worry about being late. We're used to it around here with my daughter."

"Hey," Ally protested. "I'm not always late."

"You are when you get out there on those horses. Which is just about every day. Now, stop arguing with me and go make sure the table is set while I have a word with our guest."

"Yes ma'am."

Ally took a few steps backwards, shrugged once again at Aaron and headed into the dining room. She heard her mother's first question about Aaron's upbringing and knew that he was about to get the Suzanne Marx Inquisition. Ally hadn't lied when she'd told Aaron that her mother liked everyone.

She just forgot to mention that Momma would want a full history lesson first.

Ten minutes later Ally, Aaron and both of her parents sat at the long rectangle, oak dining room table. Daddy said a prayer and blessed the food, then Momma passed around dishes. Ally took the plate of roasted venison, forked a slice onto her plate and passed it to Aaron. After they had their helpings of fried potatoes and salad, they all ate in silence for a few minutes before Daddy started in on Aaron. Ally kept her head down, shoveled food into her mouth and tried to become invisible so she wouldn't be brought into the conversation. Aaron would have to hold his own against her Dad or he'd never stand a chance working here for the summer.

"So, Aaron," her father started. "What do you do when you're not traveling to a new state, looking for a new job, with a bunch of people you don't know?"

"Well, sir, I used to work at the chemical plant down in Lake Shores. In fire safety."

"Used to?"

"Yes, sir. I decided I needed a change of pace. That job wasn't what I wanted for my life anymore."

"And what makes you think you'd be a good fit here?"

"Because before that I dilly-dallied on my brother-in-law's ranch, helped him out with everything from rounding to branding to fixing fence posts. Plus I grew up with summer jobs on ranches back when I was a kid and had to handle the more menial roles. So I've got the experience you're looking for."

"That sounds like an answer I'd *want* to hear."

"Isn't that helpful in this case?"

"Not if it ain't true."

Ally heard Aaron gulp from beside her before she felt him sit up tall in his chair as he replied.

"Since it is true, I guess we're good then, right?"

Ally looked at her father from underneath her lashes, tried to gauge his reaction to Aaron's response.

The older man studied the younger man with an air of surprise, curiosity and appreciation. Ally knew her father respected the fact that Aaron hadn't backed down and waited for the approval she knew would come by the look in his eyes.

"Alright, then," Daddy said. "You start tomorrow. Seven a.m. at the barn. We'll saddle up and head out to the east fields. Don't' be late."

Aaron relaxed beside her, smiled at her father and said, "Yes, sir. Thank you, Big Dave."

"You're welcome," he stated. "Now... what are your intentions with my daughter?"

•••••

Aaron's fork froze halfway to his mouth and his hand shook so bad he thought his venison was going to fall off the silverware. He cut his eyes to the side, caught Ally's stare and pleaded with his eyes for her to help him. All she did was sit back and wipe her mouth with her napkin, pick up her glass of tea and hold it in front of her mouth. He knew she hid a smile behind that glass. But she kept her mouth closed.

"Well... Um... You see, Big Dave, I..." Everything Aaron started to say sounded dumb in his own ears and he stuttered on his words. *But look how well it had gone when you'd manned up and spoken to Big Dave like someone who wasn't easily cowered.* With that thought in mind, Aaron met the other man's gaze head on. And even though he hadn't spoken about this with Ally, he figured it'd serve her right to find out like this. Payback for not coming to his aid.

"Mr. Marx, I'm not going to lie to you. I enjoy being around your daughter. I admire her dedication to family and faith. Her sense of humor and spirit____"

"Spirit? Is that what you call it?" Big Dave interrupted.

"David. Hush, now. Let the man finish." Suzi smiled in Aaron's direction and he went on.

"Yes, her spirit. They are both incredibly charming. And, to be honest, when I look at Allyson..." he paused, set his eyes on the woman he spoke about–and took a little pride in the shocked look on her face–then said, "I think she's the most beautiful woman I've ever seen. And with your permission, sir," he looked back at Big Dave, straight in the eye, "I'd like the chance to take her out on a date. Get to know her a little better."

Ally's head swung back and forth as she looked from Aaron to her father and back at Aaron again, her brow furrowed at his declaration.

He only spared her a quick glance, kept his eyes on her father while he waited for his answer. The older man sat back in his chair, steepled his fingers in front of his face while he studied Aaron.

Finally, after several excruciatingly long minutes, Big Dave brought his hands back down to his lap, a small grin on his mouth as he said, "Alright. But let's see how you do on the range, first."

"Doesn't anybody want to know what I____" Ally started in but Aaron cut her off.

"Deal."

July 23, 2015

It had been a month since Aaron showed up in Rosy Camp. A month since he started work for Big Dave at the ranch. Thirty of the hardest laboring, back-breaking days of his adult life. And he'd loved every minute of it.

When he'd shown up at the barn the morning after dinner with Ally's parents, Aar had expected to do just as her Dad had said; to saddle up and head to those fields he'd talked about. Big Dave had other plans. Aaron had mucked the stalls, given four of the horses a bath and played tool retriever to the farrier who'd come out to shod all eight of their horses. Dave had looked on from the corner of the barn, those big arms of his crossed over his chest while he watched every job he'd assigned Aaron take place. But Aaron never complained, just took each task with ease because this was what he'd signed up for.

Fury was the last horse to get new shoes and once that was finished, Big Dave finally told Aaron to saddle up so they could head out. When they'd made it to the east fields, the work that followed made what Aar had done in the barn seem like child's play.

They spent half the day chasing down a herd of mountain goats to get as close to an accurate count as possible, in preparation for the upcoming hunting season. After a quick thirty-minute lunch break, they'd headed to the far eastern side of the property to run the six-foot high fence line, looking for downed posts, holes or weak spots in the metal mesh.

By the time Big Dave had called it quits for the day, Aaron had passed on the offer of dinner at the ranch house and fallen in to an exhausted sleep at the bunkhouse, every muscle in his tired body aching. Only to rise bright and early the next morning and start the whole process over again, shodding the horses being the only task left out.

He hadn't seen Ally much in the last month, either, with the exception being the three nights he had gone to dinner at the house, and the handful of times she'd come to check on him at the cabin. When he'd invited her in for a cup of coffee, she'd only shaken her head and walked off, giving the excuse that until her Daddy gave the okay, they'd better keep their distance.

He realized he hadn't been as inconspicuous as he'd thought about looking around for her out in the pastures when Dave finally told him that Ally was making her own runs on the western side of the property with her own crew. Aaron's shoulders had slumped with the news, which Big Dave laughed heartily at. Then he clapped Aaron on the back, almost knocking him off Fury, and told him to stop acting like a lovesick puppy, that they had work to do.

Then two nights ago, as Aaron was brushing down Fury and Big Dave was brushing down his own horse–a massive dapple grey gelding named Tuff who made Fury look like a Shetland pony–the older man had finally given his permission for Aaron to take Ally out.

"But if you hurt her," he'd warned, "I know plenty of places to bury a body in my mountains." When Aaron had tried to laugh off the threat, Big Dave had only reiterated,

"I'm serious, boy. She's been through enough. So if all you're looking for is a piece of tail, you need to pack and leave now."

That had sobered Aar up. With a seriousness he'd felt deep in his bones, he'd told Dave, "I won't hurt her. You have my word."

Today was the day Aaron would finally take Ally out, away from prying eyes, someplace where the two of them could talk and get to know each other. Today was, hopefully, the day Aar would find out if Ally had any of the same feelings he felt for her that grew stronger every day, despite not seeing her much.

Today was the day he'd kiss her again.

He'd enlisted the help of Suzi–who had announced after dinner that first night that she was on "Team Aaron" all the way–and as he walked out to the barn (where Dave had said Ally was), he swung the picnic basket back and forth in his hand and imagined how Ally would look when he found her. Would her hair be up in that bun she seemed to prefer? Or would it flow down her back, that cute little cowboy hat perched on her head? Would she be in jeans and a ranch shirt? A tank-top? For his sake, he hoped it wasn't the latter.

He stepped into the dimly lit interior of the barn, spied the object of his thoughts in the last stall on the right, brushing down a horse he'd only encountered that first day when it had been shoed. Ginger, if he remembered correctly. A palomino filly who Jerry had been trying to saddle break for a couple weeks. Like Trixie, Ginger was a little wild and difficult from what he'd observed before, but hadn't given it much consideration since Ally seemed to favor Trixie now that he'd kind of taken over Fury.

But when Aar saw Ally in the stall with her, watched her lay the brush down and gently settle a blanket in the center of the horse's back, he straightened in worry and alarm. *Surely she's not going to get on that horse now, is she?* Then she placed a saddle on top of the blanket and he knew that, yes, she did plan on riding that filly. With no one around to help her if she got into trouble.

He dropped the picnic basket on the ground and stormed over to them. Ginger tried to rear up on Ally at his rushed gait in their direction, but she held the horse firm. Aaron slowed his steps, spoke softly to Ally when he reached the gate to the stall. "What are you doing, Ally?"

She jerked and looked back, surprised to see him, he guessed. Then she squared her shoulders and said, "I'm getting ready to ride Ginger. What does it look like I'm doing?"

"Being an idiot." She gasped at his statement and he continued. "Don't act all surprised. I bet Jerry will agree with me." Aaron looked around the barn, saw no sign of the older man. "Where is your stable master, anyway?"

Ally ducked her head, sheepish with her answer. "He's off for the day. Went to town to spend the afternoon with his granddaughter."

"Uh-huh. And what would he say if he were here, saw you about to mount that horse there?" She didn't answer, only scowled at him. "That's what I thought. Come on, now. Get that saddle off her before you do something stupid. Like try to ride her, get thrown off and get yourself killed."

"You're not my father. You can't just march in here and tell me what to do, city boy." She made to turn around, back to the horse and what she'd been doing. He reached over the stall, grabbed a hold of her hand and tugged her to him. The thin, two-inch wide slatted gate was the only thing that separated them.

"You're right. I can't tell you what to do. But I can ask nicely. Will you please come out of this stall and get the idea of riding this horse out of your head?" Her eyes stayed narrowed at him so he pushed some more. "Pretty please?" Now she pursed her lips, like she was holding in a smile. "With a cherry on top?" Finally, she laughed and Aaron relaxed for the first time since he'd walked in here.

"That's so juvenile. I haven't heard anyone say that since I was twelve," she said as she turned around, removed the saddle from Ginger's back, set it and the blanket on the stall railing.

"Maybe it is. But it worked, didn't it?"

"Maybe." But she walked out of the stall, stood directly in front of Aar with her hands on her hips. "Now what am I supposed to do with my day off since you put an end to my fun?"

Aaron smiled at her, reached for her hand again. With her tiny fingers engulfed in his much bigger ones, he pulled her backwards to where he'd dropped the basket. He picked it up, held it out for her to see.

"How about a date?"

Chapter 8

"Every man shall kiss his lips that giveth a right answer."
Proverbs 24:26

Ally breathed through the tingles that raced up her arm and forced herself not to show any outward sign that the feel of Aaron's hand holding her own was both terrifying and thrilling.

Good grief, Ally. It's just his hand. Calm down.

But she couldn't. Not when the calluses on his palm rasped against her skin and made goose bumps rise on her whole body.

She prayed he wouldn't notice.

"A date, huh? That's awfully presumptuous of you to come in here, already expecting me to say yes."

"Not presumptuous. Optimistic." He tilted his head, lowered his legs so that he was at eye level with Ally. She could get lost in those eyes. Paul Newman eyes. "So what do you say?" he asked.

"Okay." He grinned at her answer; but, before he got too excited, she threw down some ground rules. "But no kissing." At this he frowned, his lips turned down at the corners like a sad clown. "At least not unless I give you permission."

He gave a short nod in acceptance. "Alright. Anything else?"

"No roaming hands."

"Awe. I suppose next you're gonna tell me I can't throw you over my shoulder and cart you off to the closest bedroom, either."

"Darn straight. And…" she stopped, knowing she had to make sure this last request was agreed upon. Because she just wasn't ready to go there, yet. "You have to promise me that you won't ask about my older brother David. The one that passed away. I can't… it's just not something I can talk about right now, okay?"

"Okay, you got it." She sighed in relief and walked outside to the large silver Quonset hut on the right side of the barn. When they reached the doors, she pulled the chain, raised the sliding door until a variety of equipment was revealed inside. Aaron whistled when he saw the contents. "Now this is what I call a man cave," he said absently as he took in the six-seater ATV, the three four-wheelers, the industrial sized tractor and the old Seventy-Nine Jeep Cj5.

The last is where Ally headed and she climbed into the cab. Aaron ambled slower over to the car, set the picnic basket in the back seat and ran his hands along the hunter green roll bar. Ally watched the way his fingers skirted across the metal with reverence and wondered what it would feel like if his hands moved over her arms, her back and neck, the same way. She saw the way his eyes roamed over the well-worn, black leather interior and remembered how it felt to have his gaze travel over her like a warm caress.

And when he finally sat down on the seat, his bicep bulged as he hung on to the roll bar above his head. She wanted to run her fingers along that muscle, watch it twitch under her touch, and follow it with a kiss. *What would his skin...*

Aaron cleared his throat and her thoughts were cut off. *Thank You God for small mercies.*

"Are you done ogling me, yet?"

She cut her eyes up to his, gave him a sour look and said, "I was not ogling you."

"Whatever you say," he laughed. She started up the old Jeep, threw it into reverse and backed out of the hut. When she put the car in drive, maneuvered down the old dirt trail that headed west toward her territory, and would take them where she wanted to go, he added, "But just so you know, I wouldn't mind if you did. Not one bit."

"Well it's a moot point since I *wasn't*." He only laughed again and she rolled her eyes.

"So where are you taking us?"

"Down to the crick."

"The what?"

"The crick. There's a little shed down there with a few poles. I thought we could eat whatever it is you've got in that basket back there and maybe throw a line out. Momma would love some fresh trout for dinner." When Aaron remained silent beside her, she glanced at him, saw a stupid grin on his face. "What?"

"You mean creek." He said it as a statement rather than a question.

"That's what I said. Crick. Kind of like a river, only smaller. And this one comes off the Missouri so it's well stocked."

"And they say Texans have a strange accent."

"Watch it, city boy." Again with that laugh. It wouldn't bother Ally so much if it weren't deep and throaty and didn't skirt across the space between them as if that laugh wanted to reach out and touch her. "Don't make me send you back home to your Texan family."

"You couldn't even if you wanted to," he said and went on before she could think of a justified argument. "Come on, Elf. Show me what you got out here."

Elf, she thought to herself. *Where the heck did* that *come from?* But she didn't dwell on it. Instead, she floored the gas, determined to give Aaron the ride of his life down the mountains.

Thirty minutes later, Ally pulled the Jeep to a stop beside the creek, shut off the engine and turned to her passenger. His knuckles were white from his death grip on the roll bar and glove box. His lips were pressed tightly together. And his breathing was downright erratic. Now it was her turn to do the laughing. At the sound, Aaron turned his head, stared hard at her.

"I take back what I said earlier."

"What's that?"

"You're not just going to get yourself killed by riding a filly that's not ready. You're going to kill us *both* just by being in the driver's seat. Be it horse, car, or any other contraption that can be steered."

"Hey, I resent that."

"No you don't." He climbed out of the Jeep, grabbed the picnic basket from the backseat. "I do believe that was your intention all along."

"Yes, well…" she broke off as she started to climb out of the Jeep herself, only to be stopped when Aaron stood directly in front of her. He'd set the basket down and placed his hands on either side of her–one on the steering wheel, the other on the headrest of her seat–and effectively caged her in.

"You owe me, now."

"No I don____"

"Yes, you do," he cut her off and never gave her a chance to protest before he brought his mouth down to hers.

Her hand flew to his chest. She'd intended to push him away. But the way he kissed her–hard, insistent, unrestrained–had her clutching the fabric instead. Had her pulling him close instead of farther away, like she should.

What's he doing to me?

•••••

What's she doing to me? Aaron thought as he pressed his lips against Ally's. She caused all his promises–the ones she'd made him make–to go out the window, along with his manners and good sense and levelheadedness. She made his blood boil. He had the desire to throttle her for driving recklessly and taking risks with her life. But, on the other hand, he wanted to kiss her into surrender.

Because it all made sense to him now. He was through worrying about the length of time it'd been since his divorce. He was through wondering if other people would see his actions and feelings as hasty. He knew what was real in his mind and heart. And no matter how much Ally fought it, this–what was going on between them–was undeniable and meaningful and it mattered. If he had to fight her every step of the way to make her recognize it too, then so be it.

But this, kissing her so hard he might bruise her, was not the way.

He tore his mouth from hers, panting as he stared at her. Slightly swollen lips, half-lidded eyes that hid their beautiful array of colors, flushed cheeks. No, she was definitely not as unaffected as she tried to act. He was ready to make sure she knew that he was in this all the way. And that he wasn't going to give up easily.

Aaron had a vision of Jacob from the Bible, slaving away for seven years–and then another seven after that–just to be with the woman he loved. Aar might not love Ally, but he cared about her. Deeply. And he couldn't deny it any more than she could. He vowed to stick around for as long as it took for Ally to admit those same feelings. Because he knew they were there. He *knew* it. But she struggled with them, and Aaron felt it had to do with whatever had happened in her past that Big Dave had warned him about. Something that made it too hard to trust her instincts now.

It seemed that was something they had in common, not trusting instincts. Because there was a small part of his brain that said he couldn't really trust Ally either, despite the deep impulses that told him to move forward with her. That little devil on his shoulder that fought for a place in his mind said she'd end up being just like Jess, unable to remain committed to one man. Or that maybe he just wasn't man enough to keep her happy. Aar fought those dark thoughts, forced his mind to focus on the here and now and what he *knew* was going on with them. He believed God had planned it.

Time to fight the good fight… just like Saint Paul said.

"Don't ever do that again." He waited for her to argue. When she kept her mouth closed, he went on. "Don't be so careless with your life. Don't take such unnecessary risks. And do not put yourself in danger, anywhere, anytime."

"What makes you think you can make demands of me like that?" she whispered, her voice shaky, her breathing still a little wild. But her eyes never left his face.

Aaron smiled, leaned close to her ear and spoke softly. "Because I'm not done with you yet. Not by a long shot." Her breath hitched when he placed his lips right below her ear. It was just the briefest of touches, but it was enough. For both of them. He stood upright, pulled her with him so she was tucked up against his side and threw his arm over her shoulders. "Now come on, Elf. Take me to the water."

They walked the short distance to the creek and Ally's arms remained by her sides. She held her body stiff as a board, despite Aaron's arm slung across her shoulders. She stopped when they reached a small gassy patch of land. It was devoid of the white flowers that looked like buttercups that surrounded the rest of the area. Aar figured this grassy spot must see a lot of traffic to keep the flowers from growing.

He leaned down to set the basket on the ground and she took the opportunity to slip out from under his arm.

"I come here a lot to think," Ally said quietly, confirming his speculation from a moment ago. She stared past the creek's narrow crossing to the other side, where more of the white flowers grew. "It's peaceful, far enough away from the ranch that I don't have to worry about anyone intruding. But close enough that if trouble comes along, help isn't too far away."

"What do you think about?" he asked and turned to look at her. Her hair blew in the breeze and covered most of her face from his view. But her mouth he saw, and she rolled her lips inward, refrained from answering.

Instead, she turned to him and said, "Want to grab a couple poles from the shed?" She hiked her chin in the direction behind him and Aaron half-turned and saw the small building that looked more like an outhouse several yards away. He turned back to ask her if she'd rather eat first–and to see if he could get her to answer his question–but she'd already walked down to the water's edge.

He sighed, decided there'd be plenty of time to delve into her secrets later, and went to grab a couple fishing poles. When he stood next to Ally again he handed her a rod. She took it and gave him a sly smile.

"Do you know how to use one of these, city boy?"

"Of course. I'm hurt that you'd even think otherwise."

"Really? Well, most people know how to throw a line out. The real test is whether or not you can actually catch anything."

"That sounds like a challenge." He dug in the moist dirt at his feet, found what he was looking for and stood back up, stuck the large mayfly's body on his hook. "Care to make a wager on who'll catch the biggest fish?" She narrowed her eyes at him but smiled anyway as she squatted down, dug around for her own insect. When she found what she wanted, she stood up tall, kept her eyes on him as she pierced the fly on her own hook. He appreciated that she wasn't so girly about it.

"You're on. If I win, you have to clean the fish." He smirked, raised an eyebrow at the ridiculous prize she chose. *Does she really think that's that big of a concession for me?* "And-" she continued, "-you have to keep your mouth shut about me riding Ginger." Now that seemed more fitting. Of course she'd throw in something dangerous. He sighed, shook his head, but agreed nonetheless.

"Okay. But if I win____"

"Which you won't."

"If I win," he went on as if she hadn't spoken, "then I get to kiss you."

"You've already done that."

"Anytime. Anywhere. However I want to." She opened her mouth, no doubt to object, but he placed his clean hand on her lips and stopped her. "I'm conceding to not make a stink about you riding that wild filly. I don't think I'm asking for much in return."

She huffed, moved her face away and Aaron let his hand fall back to his side. "Point made. Fine," she complied. "But that doesn't mean I have to like it."

"Whatever you say, Elf."

There was no more talking. They both cast out into the water and remained silent, waited for the fish to bite. Ally had the first hit, a small bass that wasn't worth the work it'd take to clean. "And besides," she said, "we're fishing for trout."

Twenty minutes into the contest, Aaron finally had his first bite. He set the hook, reeled in slow and steady. As the fish came into view, its beige body covered in charcoal-colored spots and the telltale fuscia stripe along its side, Aaron knew he had one that would be hard to beat. He pulled the fish onto shore, reached down and held its body while he removed the hook from its mouth. Ally squinted her eyes at him, tossed him the basket that would hold the fish until they made it back to the ranch house. But she never said a word, just kept her eyes on the water's surface.

"Really? You're not gonna comment on how big my guy here is?" She cut her eyes at him but still didn't say anything. "Come on, I figure he's got to be at least three and a half, maybe four pounds." Still nothing. "And probably close to two feet long." Now she looked over at him.

"Are you always this preoccupied with size?"

He grinned, wiggled his eyebrows in her direction and gave her a wink. "I am when being able to kiss you is on the table."

"Typical male. Well, don't get too cocky. The day's still young. And these are *my* waters, you know."

But try as she might for the rest of the day, Ally never could catch a trout that matched the size of Aaron's, despite the other three keepers she'd reeled in. "I think I should be the winner since I caught more fish. That means I've got more weight and length in total."

"Nuh-uh. That was not the bet. The bet was who could catch the biggest. Not the most." Aar had long since set his pole down and rested with his legs stretched out in front of him while he leaned back against a large boulder. He crossed his hands behind his head and smiled at her. "Besides, the only reason you caught more was because I quit trying. It was obvious you weren't going to get one bigger than mine."

"You don't know that. And since you quit fishing, I think that counts as a forfeit."

"It's only a forfeit if one person concedes that the other person out fished them. Since I have the biggest catch in that basket, I definitely do not concede."

"Yes, but____"

"Quit trying to back out of the bet, Elf. What's the matter? Are you not woman enough to own up to the fact that you lost? Or is it that you can't face the punishments from losing?"

He waited, knew that ribbing her pride would get him the reaction that he wanted.

He didn't have to wait long.

Ally tossed her pole on the ground, stood up quickly. She stomped over to where he sat on the ground, looked down at him through irritated eyes. "I always face my punishments," she said right before she leaned down and brought her lips to his.

Her sudden kiss took Aaron by surprise, but only for a moment. The next instant, he pulled her down to his lap. He laid one hand across her cheek, his thumb tight against her jaw to hold her steady. She tried, weak as it is was, to get off his lap. Aaron wrapped his free arm around her back and she sunk into his embrace, gave herself over to his hold. So he squeezed her tighter against his chest.

And never intended to let her go.

•••••

Ally couldn't believe she'd actually done it. She couldn't believe she'd been the one to make the move and kiss *him*. Sure, it wasn't the first time and he had been the one to kiss her first in the other instances.

But just because they'd already kissed didn't mean it was okay for her to take the lead whenever she felt like it, did it?

She didn't even care what the answer was. All she knew was one minute he was goading her, teasing her for losing. Then the next minute, she'd decided to show him that she wasn't a coward. That she was willing to own up to her end of the bargain. And what better way to do that than to be the one to kiss him, instead of waiting around for him to decide when and where and how?

Except she hadn't considered the consequences of her actions. She hadn't planned on being pulled down onto his lap. She hadn't expected to feel safe and secure in his arms rather than suffocated and stuck. She hadn't figured that what was supposed to be a punishment for losing the bet, would actually feel like a reward.

But most of all, she hadn't thought that being in Aaron's arms, cocooned from the outside world, would make her doubt all her previous opinions of men. That her views of the opposite sex all being selfish and licentious and incapable of monogamy were actually wrong. At least where this one was concerned. Because somehow Ally knew, deep down, that Aaron wasn't the kind of man to treat his woman like a doormat. He wouldn't be one to stray behind her back. He would be honest and upfront and deal with the results head-on.

And that was important to her. Honesty, fidelity, dependability. They all mattered. Just like Aaron did. Ally couldn't lie to herself anymore. She cared about him. More than she probably should, but her heart didn't care what her mind argued. The more time she spent with him, the more he kissed her, the more she felt herself softening. She felt her tower crumble underneath her, breaking apart so she fell directly into his arms.

Like now.

Ally was acutely aware of the way Aaron's large hand spanned almost the width of her back, the way it slid around to the other side to curl against her hip and hold her in place. She felt every callous on his hand when he ran his palm down her cheek to rest against her throat, right against her beating pulse. And she shivered when she felt the tip of his tongue lightly touch her lips, seeking entrance.

She jerked back, momentarily shocked, but not scared.

He wrapped his hand around the back of her neck, pulled her back to him. "Not yet, Allyson," he murmured as his lips connected with hers again. "Just a little more."

This time, when he sought entry again, she let him in.

And fell against his chest at the warmth that seeped through her body and made her feel like a wet noodle.

The way Aaron kissed her, the sensations he aroused inside her chest, made her feel cherished, fragile. Feminine. All things she wasn't used to out here in Big Sky Country where she was looked upon as "one of the guys." And all things that she realized she'd missed.

His tongue lightly skated across hers before retreating and then advancing again, a little farther. Slow and calm, he kissed her with reverence instead of quick necessity, like Ben used to. His hands behind her neck and on her side squeezed, kept her tight against him. She wrapped her own arms around his shoulders, ran her fingers along the muscles that tightened in his back. He tilted his head the other direction and Ally turned on his lap, searched for a way to deepen the kiss.

Their chests lay against each other and Ally could feel the pounding of his heart next to her own. She couldn't tell whose was harder, only that they beat in time, as if they sought a connection of their own.

The thought made her restless; it had been so long since she'd felt the desire to connect with anyone. And now, in this moment, all she wanted was more.

But Aaron pulled away.

"Wha... why did you stop?" she asked, breathless. She felt him chuckle and thought she heard him mumble, something about rules going out the window. But she couldn't be sure since the blood pounding in her ears made everything around them sound like a distant echo.

He laid his forehead on her chest, wrapped both arms around her back. His heavy breath puffed out against her shirt and the material grew warm against her already heated skin.

Then he raised his head, just enough so that his chin rested where his forehead had just vacated. He looked into her eyes and the vulnerability Ally saw there made her own breath catch. Something made this man–this strong, virile, assertive man–seem so insecure right now.

Maybe you've got more in common than you first thought, Ally.

"Because I needed you to... I can't..." he stopped, laid his head back down. His arms tightened around her, held her as if he were afraid she would run off. She lifted her hand from his back, ran her fingers down the side of his face until he looked up at her again. She focused on his eyes, tried to get him to see her sincerity.

"You what, Aar? What is it?"

He smiled slightly at her, just the corners of his mouth lifted. "That's the first time you've ever called me that."

"What?"

"Aar. It's a nickname only my family ever uses."

"I'm sorry. It just slipped out. I won't say it again."

"No, don't apologize. I like the way it sounds coming off your lips." Ally blushed a little as visions of her lips on his just a minute ago flooded her mind. "I was going to say that I need you to be truthful with me. I need a real, honest answer." He paused and said, "I need you to tell me if what's going on between us is just a fleeting moment for you. Or if this is something more."

Ally thought about it. She hadn't imagined that anything would come from his being here, in Montana. But now that this had started, whatever it was, Ally knew she wouldn't be able to ignore it. She'd never be able to climb back in her tower and pretend that Aaron hadn't shaken her world in the most unexpected way. But at the same time the most amazing way.

She'd never forgive herself for not living the life God had set before her. And that included Aaron. So she let go of her reservations and gave him the truth from her heart.

"More."

Aimee Martin

Chapter 9

*"For nothing is secret, that shall not be made
manifest; neither any thing hid, that shall not
be known and come abroad."*
Luke 8:17

Aaron reclined on the blanket he'd laid out that he found
from the back seat of the Jeep. He and Ally were still out by
the creek, the fish cleaned and resting comfortably in a
Ziploc bag surrounded by ice (thanks to the small ice chest
Suzi had packed in the picnic basket). The contents of the
basket were spread out beside them, remnants of sandwiches,
fresh fruit and vegetables, cheese and crackers drawing in
ants who searched for a meal. But he didn't pay any attention
to the small pests.

He had Ally in his arms. And it was wonderful.

Laying the way he was–his big body using up most of the
blanket–she'd had no choice but to cuddle up next to him, her

head on his bicep while she stared out at the creek. Dragonflies swooped down to the water, searched for smaller bugs for dinner. A largemouth bass jumped up from beneath the surface, caught one of the flying insects for its own meal. The sun was just beginning to set and a deep purple glow mixed with the dark red of the fading sun, caught on the glittering water and reflected the image like a mirror.

He held his head up on his hand–Ally's head nestled in that crook of his shoulder–with the other stretched across her stomach where he ran his fingers lightly across the skin exposed between her shirt and jeans. Goosebumps rose under his touch and he laid his hand flat to warm her skin.

"Maybe we should head back," he leaned down and whispered in her ear. "It's getting late. And you're cold."

"Not yet. I don't want this moment to end."

"It doesn't have to." She turned her gaze from the creek to look up at him, a question in her eyes. Aar brought his hand up from where it rested against her belly, stroked her cheek softly.

"This moment, Ally. We can make it last longer than tonight. We can make it last as long as you want."

"And what about you, Aaron? How long do you want it to last?"

"For as long as you'll let it." She gave a short laugh, a small puff of air fell from her lips as she turned back to the water and his hand fell from her face. "You don't believe me."

"I'm not sure what to believe. What to trust in."

He laid his hand across her heart, felt it speed up under his touch. Ally tilted her head down, stared at the contact but didn't look back at him. "Trust what's in here, Ally. Nothing else."

"That's a lot easier said than done." She brought her hand up, rested it on the back of Aaron's and linked their fingers together. "Do you ever feel that sometimes your past can dictate your future? I mean, that it can change how you used to view the world? And not necessarily for the best?"

"Yes," he said. "I do. But this, this *is* for the best Allyson."

"It's so sudden though. It's too soon to know that, isn't it?"

Aaron brought their linked hands up to her face, held on to her chin and turned her face to his. He leaned down, kissed her once on the lips. "Not for me. But I'll be certain enough for the both of us if I have to."

"What if it's not enough?" The doubt in her voice set him on edge. He didn't know what he'd have to do to get her to see that he was sincere. Aaron didn't make promises lightly, and he didn't take kindly to people not taking him for his word. He needed to get to the root of her issues so he'd know how to tackle them. *But you're not sharing your issues with her, either, Aar.*

True. But maybe if he could get her to open up, then he could open up, too. There was only one way to find out.

"What happened, Ally?"

"What do you mean?"

"I mean why did your Dad warn me about hurting you, tell me you'd been through enough in this life?"

"I don't know what you're talking about."

"I think you do. And I think you're scared to tell me because you're afraid I'm gonna judge you. I also think you don't like people to see any weaknesses in you. So you hide behind that cocky attitude." She scowled up at him, rolled her lips inward in anger. "See? Right there. You've got some quick comeback on the tip of your tongue that turns cutting in the blink of an eye. How about instead of running from the past, you embrace it. That's the only way to move forward."

"Says the man who ran to Montana when he was fresh from a divorce?"

"Touché," he conceded. "Let's make a deal. I'll show you mine if you show me yours."

"Are we talking about something else, now? That was quick."

"Weaknesses, smarty-pants. I'll show you mine when you show me yours."

"Why do I have to go first?"

"Because you're the one still trying to hide from them."

She huffed and her eyebrows dropped low on her forehead. "Daddy should have kept his mouth shut," she mumbled under her breath as she sat up, tucked her legs against her chest. She wrapped her arms around her shins, rested her chin on her knees.

Aaron stayed where he was, hoped that if he continued lying down she wouldn't feel threatened and clam up before she even got started. Several minutes passed, the only sounds around them the crickets chirping as they woke up and the splashes in the water from the few fish who hadn't gone to ground for the night. The first stars twinkled out around them, one bright and glittering directly above Ally's head as if it were a light bulb blinking an idea in her mind. He waited, watched her swallow a few times as she gained her courage.

She began to talk.

•••••

"You're not the only one who's been divorced." Ally heard Aaron suck in a breath, figured she just shocked him with that little opening statement. *Good*, she thought. *Maybe the best way to find out his true feelings is to keep him on his toes.* "Yeah. See, I've been divorced for almost three years now. My ex, Benjamin—he's from here, from Rosy Camp—we started dating at the beginning of our senior year of high school. Typical love story; he was captain of the football team and I was head cheerleader. Then we both got accepted into San Diego State University, went off together in Oh-Six. We were on top of the world at eighteen. That old song and dance about high school sweethearts who stay together for the rest of their lives? Yeah, that was us. Or so I thought.

"We were each other's firsts." Ally stole a glance at Aaron. "At… everything. I didn't think it was a big deal because I just knew in my heart that we'd be together forever. But we were still safe about it. All the way through college until our senior year. Safe, every time, except for one. And that one time was all it took."

Ally saw Aaron move from the corner of her eye. She turned, rested her cheek against her knees while she watched him sit up. He didn't make a move to come to her, just sat those two feet away with his elbows hooked around his own knees. His brow furrowed while he looked at her. She waited for him to just say, "Forget this!" and walk away.

Or call her every dirty name in the book for getting pregnant out of wedlock. But he didn't. Just sat there and waited for her to continue.

So she did.

"When I told him I was pregnant, he asked if it was his. I should have known then and there that something wasn't right. That *we* weren't right. But I was so shocked at that positive test that nothing else seemed to sink in. Not until much, much later. Then when I called Momma and told her, she and Daddy said I had no choice in the matter. That Ben and I would have to get married, ASAP, to keep the mouths from running. Small town gossip. You know how that goes."

"Yeah," he spoke quietly.

Ally smiled over at him, happy he'd entered the conversation. Even if it was only one word.

FOREVER TREASURED

"As soon as we graduated, Ben and I came home to Rosy Camp. His family owns one of the larger ranches in this area. Their place is about fifteen miles east of town proper. Anyway, our mothers threw together a very impromptu wedding ceremony as soon as we'd gotten home. And a little over a week after we'd moved back, I was a married woman. Just like that. Ben and I moved into a cabin on his family's place and started playing house."

"What happened, Allyson?"

She didn't need him to clarify. She knew he wondered where the baby was. After all, that was the whole reason she'd just given him for why she'd gotten married in the first place.

"I miscarried at four months."

"Oh, Elf. I'm so sorry." She shook her head, dismissing his apology. "No, really. I didn't know. We don't have to talk about this. We can wait."

"No, you were right. Best to get it out in the open sooner than later, right?"

"Yeah, but____"

"No buts. It's ok." She reached over, grabbed onto Aaron's hand but kept her seat. With her fingers gripped tightly in his, Ally went on. "A couple weeks after I found out I was pregnant, I found Ben in bed with another girl. Some sorority hussy, I don't even know who she was. I told him I was done, that I'd raise the baby alone. He begged me to give him another chance, promised he'd never do it again. I didn't want to. Then when I told my parents about the pregnancy, they put their two cents in. Said we had to get married to save the family name. In this area, a good name means the difference between a prosperous hunting season and a weak one. They didn't know about his straying. And when I weighed their reasoning, I knew it made sense, so I didn't see the point in sharing that indiscretion with them.

"For the first little while after the miscarriage, things were alright between Ben and me. He was very attentive, played the doting husband to a tee. He even said that he'd agree to try again as soon as the doctor gave the okay. We might not have planned on getting pregnant when I did, but, during those four months, I grew to love that baby so much. And it destroyed me when I lost him. So it took almost a year before *I* was ready to try again. At first, I didn't think anything about the amount of time it seemed to take. I'd heard that it could be several months after coming off birth control.

"But one month turned into two. The next thing I knew it'd been six months and still nothing. I started to worry that maybe something had happened when I'd miscarried. Something that made me getting pregnant again harder, maybe impossible. I came home from the ranch early one day to talk to Ben about scheduling an appointment to get tested, see if anything was wrong. When I walked in the door, I heard him in the back bedroom. Our bedroom. I stopped outside the door and, even though I knew it was wrong, listened in on his phone conversation. Turned out not to be such a bad thing after all. I heard him, that voice that had spoken words of love to me for years, saying the same things to someone else. Talking about all the pleasure he'd give her, just as soon as he could get away for the night.

"I was shocked. But I think what threw me over the edge was when he said something to the effect of "It'll be better than every other time." That was it for me, cause it told me that whatever, whoever, he'd been with, it was obviously an ongoing thing. And I was done." Ally stopped talking, took a deep breath and released it slowly.

Well, there it all is. Let's see where he goes from here.

Aaron gave their linked hands a little shake. "So what did you do?" She looked over at him and a sly smile crept onto her lips. Ally couldn't hold in the laugh that bubbled up. Aaron tilted his head, his eyes searched hers and a smile of his own graced his face.

"Ally, Ally, Ally. You did something bad didn't you?"

"Depends on your definition of bad." He just raised an eyebrow, waited for her to tell him. So she did. "I walked in when he was going on and on about a very explicit plan. He froze midsentence when he saw me, hung up the phone quick and tossed it on the bed. Then he had the audacity to tell me I hadn't actually heard anything, that I was imagining everything. He finally caved, admitted to sleeping around with the girl from the next town over. And she *was* a girl, barely nineteen at the time."

"You're rambling."

"I am not. I'm telling you the story."

"No, you're avoiding answering my question. About you doing something bad."

"Do you want to hear this or not?" she asked him, her own eyes narrowed at him for good measure. He gave an affirmative nod and she said, "Alright, then. Stop interrupting. So-" she turned back to watch the water glisten under the moonlight that had come out, "-when he admitted to everything, I took it all in. I turned my back on him, paced our bedroom slowly, and just absorbed what he'd said, very quietly. Then he started in on those same old promises I'd heard before. The ones from college. That was my boiling over point. I stopped mid-step, turned to face him and he was right on my heels. I remember taking that one second to look at his face, a face that I used to find handsome as sin. And in that one second, I saw everything I despised in this world. Liars, cheats, people who used their looks and money to get them whatever they wanted in life. In that one second, I saw exactly the type of man Ben was. A philandering, immoral, lying scumbag who thought he'd always be at the top of the totem pole because of his looks and his family's name. So in that one moment, I did the only thing that I knew would bring his arrogance down several notches.

"I punched him in the face and broke his nose."

Ally waited, didn't dare look over at Aaron after she'd just admitted that she decided to play Rocky Balboa and punch somebody. The sensible part of her brain said that he'd understand. But the part that still let Ben's taunts telling her she was too much like a man for a man to love her, unsettled her and caused insecurity to rear its ugly head. And it was hard to push down. Because she didn't want that to be the way Aaron looked at her. She wanted him to see her as feminine, graceful.

She wanted him to see her as a woman. All woman.

When several minutes passed and he hadn't said anything, she sucked in a deep breath for courage and finally looked at him. His bright blue eyes were wide, his very kissable lips pursed. And his shoulders shook. Then his mouth burst into a huge grin and a booming chuckle escaped his lips. He fell backwards onto the blanket, held onto his stomach while shouts of laughter floated into the night air, blended in with the breeze that blew across the creek.

His laughter was infectious and Ally found herself giggling along with him. Then her girly giggles turned into hoots and hollers as she replayed (for the hundredth time) the way Ben had looked with blood spurting from his nose.

At that moment, with Ben's "perfect face" sporting a very less-than-perfect, crooked nose, Ally hadn't been able to find the desire to ask for forgiveness from God for acting out of spite.

Later–much later, months after the divorce–she had sought forgiveness. And she believed God had given it to her.

But that didn't change the fact that she still took satisfaction from her memories of that day.

"I can't decide if I'm upset that I wasn't there to defend your honor, or proud that you handled that situation like a real woman." *Real woman,* Ally thought to herself. *He doesn't think I was manly for punching a guy. He thinks I handled it like a woman.* That alone gave Ally hope. For Aaron and for their future. Wherever that future may lead. "But honestly..." he stopped, took a deep breath in between laughing fits, "I think it's the latter." He rolled over onto his side, propped his head onto his bent elbow again and looked at her, his blue eyes flashing with something that Ally swore looked a lot like pride and longing. "I wish I could have been there to see it."

"It was messy."

"Good." Ally shook her head, tried to get her own laughs under control. "I'm serious. It's good. For you and for his broken nose. No one deserves to be put through that. Infidelity causes a lot more emotional problems than people realize, in my opinion. And I think it's fantastic that instead of lying down and taking that type of abuse–because it *is* abuse–you stood up for yourself. In that moment, you took your life by the horns and led it where you felt you deserved to go. Luckily for me, it led you right here."

She eyed him from her place a couple feet away, her eyes small slits as she said, "Except my actions didn't lead me here. I was already here. In Montana."

"Yeah, but you weren't available. Now you are."

"So are you."

"Yes." That was it. That's all he said.

Ally probed him some more. "Well... now it's your chance to tell me what led *you* here."

"Turnabout is fair play, I guess. And we did have a deal."

"Darn right we did."

"Okay, okay," he said and held his hands up in an act of surrender.

He sat up, leaned his back against a large rock that rimmed the outer edge of the blanket. He bent his legs at the knees, leaving a small space between them, and held out his arms to Ally. She crawled over to him, settled her body in between his legs with her back against his chest. Aaron wrapped his arms around her waist, pulled her tighter against him and Ally felt his heartbeat against her spine. But it wasn't fast and erratic, as she'd assumed it would be when nerves came into play. It was slow and steady and it comforted her.

"Don't get your panties in a wad."

Ally tried to pull out of his grasp but Aaron held her firm. She still scolded him, even if she couldn't see his face. "You did not just say that."

"Yes, I did. Now be quiet and let me tell you why I'm here."

•••••

Aar knew he needed to talk, to tell Ally what had happened with him and Jess. Especially now that he knew what had happened with her marriage.

We're the same.

That had been his first thought when she'd told him she'd been the victim of a straying spouse, too. With the exception of the pregnancy, of course. His second thought had been the now unfailing belief that God had brought them together, brought him here, for such a time as this.

"My Mom used to tell me when I was a teenager that someone who'd been cheated on would never cheat on someone else."

"Because you know how it feels," Ally agreed softly.

"Yeah." He leaned down, pressed a quick kiss to the top of her head, closed his eyes for a second as he inhaled her sweet, honeysuckle scent. "Anytime I was in a serious relationship–which, granted, there weren't many before I got married; I was too focused on having fun–the thought of straying never even crossed my mind. Old school, I guess.

"But when I walked in on my wife with another man, that gut-wrenching pain I felt, the betrayal, pretty much guaranteed that I would never be that person. I could never put someone I loved, or even just cared about, through that kind of hurt. Especially when it's so much easier to just call things off, you know?" Ally had stiffened a little in Aaron's arms when he'd admitted to his wife's infidelity, but she never spoke a word. Just listened.

"That's what happened to my marriage, and it's not so different from yours, right? I came home late one night from work, back in January. And when I walked into my bedroom, I saw my wife having sex with some guy. And it was just as I said a minute ago, gut-wrenching. But only for a minute. Then it was like I was outside my body, watching the whole scene while I floated on the ceiling. I saw them. I saw myself, an outsider in my own home. I saw the absurdity of our entire life together. And I lost it, in a way.

"I was so shocked at first that I lost my balance, fell back against the door. That's when the two of them stopped being so involved with each other and finally noticed that I was there. Jess–my ex-wife–started in on the apologies and as I took in the whole scenario, I think I went a little crazy. I started laughing so hard that I couldn't breathe. Even while the two of them were trying to get clothes on, I still laughed. It wasn't until I saw her put on a robe from our honeymoon that I stopped. Seeing that silk on her was like a slap in the face. A bucket of cold water. A kick in the pants."

"Okay, I get it. Enough with the clichés. You were hysterically upset and then you sobered up quickly," Ally stopped him from coming up with any more silly expressions. "Get on with it."

"Don't be impatient."

"Don't get sidetracked."

"I'm not."

"Yes, you are. Do you need some ADD medicine?"

"No," he said. "But if you don't stop insinuating that something is wrong with me, you'll be sorry."

"Then you need to stop acting like something is wrong with you," she countered. "And how exactly will I be sorry?"

Instead of answering, Aaron brought his hands from where they rested against her belly, wrapped his fingers around her sides. Then he tickled her. She laughed and yelled and pleaded with him to stop but Aaron just kept right on at it. His fingers moved quickly, up and down and around her ribcage, glued to her body despite her feeble attempts to get away from him. Which probably weren't actually feeble, but the sheer size difference between them didn't allow her to stand a chance.

"Are you sorry yet?" he asked, still tickling.

"No, never!" So he went after her harder, tickling more and more until she panted and begged in between breaths for him to stop. She'd scooted down so much in her struggles that she was practically on her back. Her shirt rose up on her stomach so Aaron moved his attack there, his fingers frantic and rough against her soft skin. Her eyes were sealed tightly shut, her tantalizing mouth curled up into something between a smile and a grimace. Her cheeks flushed a bright pink with every bit of exertion she put forth. She looked beautifully uninhibited and he was tempted to show mercy, just so he could sit still and stare at her.

But as he brushed against her hipbone, Ally just about came unglued. *Ah... so that's the sweet spot.* His previous thoughts of pity now gone, Aar dug his fingers into the skin just below her hip and laughed at the squeals that came from her mouth before she finally admitted defeat. "Alright, alright. Yes... I'm sorry. I swear..." she paused, sucked in a breath because Aaron refused to let up on her until she finished the words. "I'll never do it... again. Just please... please stop tickling me. I can't... take it anymore." Aaron eased off slightly, but not all the way, his fingers lightly grazing her skin now and, he guessed (by the way she continued to struggle) still wreaking havoc. "I'll do anything!"

"Anything?" he asked as he finally relaxed his hands, let his palms lay against her bare belly. He stared at their skin, loved the way hers was pale and toned, like an ivory board, next to his own darker hide. He worked his gaze up, past her chest and graceful neck, landed on her lips. He watched them move, breathless, when she answered.

"Yes."

Slowly, he brought his mouth down and hovered right above hers as the anticipation built. They both knew what he wanted. To kiss her. But he wanted to make her wait. To make her want it as much as he did. Because right now–*Hell*, he thought to himself, *for the rest of my life*–kissing Ally became as vital as taking his next breath.

Just before he was ready to seal the two of them together in a way as old as time, she spoke again, still breathless but more frisky than before. "You're making me feel like Kirsten

Dunst in Spiderman. Should we wait and continue this when it's raining?"

Aaron jerked his head back a fraction, couldn't figure out if she was kidding or not. He caught her cute, little giggle-snort just in time. "Oh, you..." he stopped before he had a chance to finish his thought and instead, wrapped one fist around her hair and his other around the material bunched above her waist, held her still for him.

And fastened his lips to hers as if his life depended on it.

Chapter 10

"But every man is tempted, when he is drawn away of his own lust, and enticed."
James 1:14

"That sonofa..." he cut off, realized that if he spoke too loudly, they'd hear him. And they couldn't know he was watching them. Not yet. It was still too soon. It took everything in his power to keep from running the short distance to them and jerking that piece of crap up and off of his woman and taking care of the other man once and for all. Then to discipline her, show her that he would not tolerate her going around and spreading her legs for any man that happened by.

"You don't know that they've done that yet," he whispered to himself, hoping his voice blended in with the crickets chirping and that they wouldn't catch him on the other side of the creek. He'd taken a chance, getting this close. But when dusk came and they'd shown no signs of leaving, he knew his scope wouldn't do any good. Not when he'd left his night vision cap at home. So he belly-crawled to the edge of the creek, huddled behind an aspen tree, and watched as they kissed and laughed and kissed some more.

He figured even if they hadn't actually done the deed, it was only a matter of time. And he had to stop them before it came to that. Because there was no way he could be with her if she let that man, that *Texan*, touch her. She'd be tainted and he'd probably have to take care of her, too. What a waste that would be.

All this time, prepping for just the right moment, only to have it come crashing down because she wouldn't wait for him. Yes, it would be a waste, but if he found out that she'd been spoiled, so be it. It would pain him to do so, but he would not hesitate to take that direction.

Because that's what he did.

He followed through.

It had taken him years to get to the point where he was now, the point where he'd be able to bring to a head the plan he'd formulated when he'd first seen her, the one that would be accomplished when she was his and no one else's. He'd thought he'd had her before, but she'd proven harder to tame than he'd given her credit for. So he was going to have to reevaluate and redesign his plan, perfect it until he was certain the time was right. He'd allowed her to play the solitary woman for long enough.

Even though this other guy being here, encroaching on his territory, on his woman, caused a little bit of a hiccup, it was nothing he couldn't handle. He already had his alternate plan thought out, ready to set in motion. It was time to begin taking the steps to make it happen, time to get started so he could have her before the end of the year. Because this was a marathon, not a sprint, and he had to take his time to make sure everything was done right.

His index finger on his right hand began to itch, desperate to pull the trigger of the rifle that lay beside him, never too far out of reach. Despite his earlier arguments to himself about it being too soon, he knew that he couldn't hold off. The longer he did, the more restless he would become. And restlessness meant agitation, which led to mistakes. He couldn't have that; he needed to have a clear head.

He'd waited long enough.

Aimee Martin

Chapter 11

"Wherefore receive ye one another, as Christ also received us to the glory of God."
Romans 15:7

August 21, 2015

Ally never realized how true that old saying of "Time flies when you're having fun" was until she started having fun again.

It had almost been two months since Aaron came to Montana and started working at the ranch. Almost two months since he changed the way she felt about men and relationships and everything that came with the two. She'd gone from never caring if she ever dated again, to not knowing what she did before she and Aaron were together. *At least, I* think *we're together.* They hadn't actually put a name to what they were.

But ever since that trip to the creek, Aaron and Ally had been nearly inseparable. She'd almost forgotten how fun and free it could feel when two people were in those early stages of a relationship. The endless kisses goodnight, glimpses of longing from across the room, butterflies that went haywire from a soft caress. And the look in a man's eyes that said he'd do anything for just one more moment.

It wasn't just Aaron who gave those looks, either. Ally knew that every time he took her face in his hands, every time he brought his lips to hers, she looked at him the same way.

Because she felt it, too. She felt that stirring in her heart and soul that called out to him. That begged for that same moment, the one that never ended and had infinite possibilities.

Of course, then there were those other times, the ones where all she wanted to do was throttle him because he would get too protective or too bossy. And sometimes, too indifferent. Those were the times that hurt, but she understood them. She knew that that indifference came from a place of self-preservation. She battled them, too. That's what came with being the victim of a wandering spouse, the constant worry that you wouldn't be enough. That you wouldn't be able to hold onto them, no matter how hard you tried.

That the trust you put into another person was futile. Everyone disappoints.

During those times, she would stare at him, try to see into his mind to know where he stood with her, with *them*. They both fought their insecurities. But Ally felt that maybe, just maybe, Aaron's were stronger. Even though he'd been the one to make the first move, he'd also been the one to go through a divorce most recently. It was during those times when Ally would doubt herself and question whether getting involved with a man fresh from a divorce was a smart idea.

She didn't want to be a rebound girl. She wanted to be a forever girl.

But do I want that with Aaron? she asked herself as she led Fury out of the barn, past the gates and into the pasture that opened before them like a football field. Yellow and white flowers dotted the grass and broke through the tall, green strands like the little munchkins from the Wizard of Oz coming out to play. She pulled her gelding to a stop, placed her foot in the stirrup and swung her free leg over the horse's strong back. She laid the reins along the side of his neck, turned him toward the west and kicked her heels into his sides.

As Fury took off, gained speed with each push off from his hind legs, and the wind blew across Ally's face, she decided to let the question hang in the air. There was no rush in what they were or where they were going or what they expected from the other person. She didn't need to be in a hurry to find out how he felt. She wasn't even sure how *she* felt. For now, they were just having fun and enjoying one another. For now, they were exploring who they were as a man and woman, as two people who were attracted to each other. Nothing more, nothing less.

And for now, that was enough.

Ally and Fury were at the edge of the pasture in a few short minutes and she reined him in quickly, just before they reached the tree line. She ducked under the low branch of a Ponderosa pine, raised her right hand up to hold the pesky limb away from her face, before she let it fall behind her. The thick twig swooshed as it bounced back into place and it was loud in the quietness that surrounded her. They wound down the narrow trail, and fresh mud from the rain this morning kicked up in Fury's wake.

When they reached the fork in the trail, Ally stopped and hopped off her horse's back. She stood there for a few minutes, stared down the right of the Y that would take her to the creek where she and Aaron had fished that first date (and many more times since then).

Then with a sigh that spoke more of her need to be alone than the fact that she'd ridden off–without telling anyone–she turned Fury to the left, headed to the small pasture that held her favorite flat rock.

She admitted silently, some thirty minutes later, that coming this far from the house on horseback, by herself, might not have been the smartest decision. But she hadn't known at the time this was where she'd end up. She'd just needed to get away to process what she'd seen. To try to figure out what it meant for her future, for her family's future.

She had watched the way her Daddy looked at Aaron as he chopped wood for the storage building in preparation for the coming Winter (because out here, you could never be too prepared). Ally recognized in her father's eyes the pride and respect he granted the younger man, even if Aaron hadn't paid attention. She had seen that same look a thousand times over the years, but not once since David died. Until now. Until Aaron. Her mother walked out of the house with a smile on her face, a tray loaded with glasses and a pitcher of lemonade balanced on her left hand. Daddy took the tray from her and set it down on an upturned log, then threw his big arm around her small shoulders and bent to kiss her loudly on the cheek. She giggled–Suzi Marx, a grown woman, giggling–and Aaron had looked up from his work. They must have called him over because he plunged the axe into the log and walked to where they stood ten feet away.

Aaron poured a glass of the cool drink and guzzled it down. Ally knew it was extra sweet, just the way Daddy liked it. Then her mother picked up the corner of the apron she wore and wiped away something from Aaron's angular jaw that Ally had kissed so many times over the last weeks. She didn't know if it was lemonade, sweat, or a combination of the two. It didn't matter. What mattered was that when she'd seen it from her hidden spot behind the open barn door, her heart flipped a little on the inside. Was Aaron replacing

David in her parent's eyes? Was he doing the same thing to her?

Ally plopped down on the flat rock, Fury's reins held loosely in her hands, and watched the sun stretch over Granite Peak. A muggy fog floated across the tip of the peak from the humidity left in the rain's wake. As the sun rose higher in the sky, the shadows on the mountain were replaced with a pale yellow light, and she pondered what she knew was the hardest question of all.

Was *she* willing to let the memory of her older brother go–let the shadows fade–just so she could take the chance to make new memories with Aaron?

•••••

Aaron laughed at the older couple in front of him, at the way Suzi swatted her husband's hands away, at the way Big Dave used his left hand as a distraction only to wrap his right around her back and playfully grip her slender hips. Then pull her to him for a loud kiss. It was obvious the two were deeply in love. That kind of love lasted an eternity. It was the kind that would never waver no matter what obstacles life through at them. And it was definitely *not* the kind of love he'd had with Jess.

But maybe with Ally.

He shook that thought away before it had a chance to take root in his mind. Love wasn't what he and Ally were about.

They were just two young and single people enjoying life and, for the moment, each other. *That's a load of crap and you know it, Aar.*

Okay, so that was true. They weren't just about fun, but it wasn't love. To be honest, Aaron wasn't sure he'd ever be able to trust giving his love and heart to another woman again. Jess may have just ruined him for any future relationships. And yet, even as he thought that, there was a small, niggling part of his brain that said, "It wouldn't be like that with Ally. She's one to trust." Problem was, it was a lot easier to listen to the former, to believe that there could never be a chance for them. If he didn't have to take a chance, he didn't have to worry about having his heart broken again.

Over the last two months, with the more time he spent with Ally, Aaron could feel his guard shifting. He'd admitted to himself some time ago that he believed God sent him here for a reason. But he'd fought the voice telling him that it was because they were meant to be together forever. He blocked that out and instead tried to convince himself that God brought him here so they could help each other. And that help had an expiration date. Aaron clung to that expiration date as if it were a lifeline and tried not to get swept away on the sea of emotions that rolled through his heart and mind every time he was with Ally. He tried, with all that he had, to sway his traitorous heart away from thoughts of "forever" and back into "temporary" territory.

But it seemed like the more he wrestled with those thoughts, the more insistent they were. The more he fought, the more those feelings worked their way inside his soul. And they'd quickly taken up residence, dug their feet in for the long haul, just like one of the oak trees back home in Lake Shores that seemed to grow the strongest roots.

Last month, when he and Ally had both confessed the details of their failed marriages, they'd turned a corner on how they felt, how they acted with each other. She still snipped at him, used her silver tongue to bring his ego down a few notches whenever he, in her words, "Went all caveman on her." But underneath those purpose-driven remarks, Aaron could sense the fondness in her tone. He recognized the appreciation she felt at his need to protect her, but was too damn proud to admit to.

And he fed off it. Protected her even more, because he knew she loved it. Even if she never owned up to it. He loved protecting her, whether from herself, or others. He enjoyed being the one to look out for her. But more than that, he *wanted* things between them to be that way. He wanted her. Any way he could get her.

"Have y'all seen Ally around?" he asked her parents as the thoughts of her and *them* made him realize he hadn't heard from her since this morning over breakfast. Big Dave tore his gaze away from Suzi, a scowl fixed on his face and directed right at Aaron. Aar smirked at him; he knew by now that Dave was all bark and no bite.

"Boy, didn't anyone ever tell you it's rude to interrupt a man and his wife when they're kissing?"

"Oh, David, stop that." Suzi swatted Big Dave on his chest as she cut her eyes sideways at him, then turned to look at Aaron. "I saw her walk off inside the barn right after I brought the lemonade out here. Go on and check in there."

"That's okay. I need to finish with this wood first. I'll find her when I'm done."

Aaron turned back to the log, yanked the axe out and poised it above his shoulder, ready to get back to work. He heard Suzi's quiet voice and then a heavy sigh, presumably from Big Dave. Then a large hand wrapped around the handle of the axe, jerking it from his grip so hard that Aaron lost his balance and stumbled back a few steps. Dave snickered, which earned him another reprimand from Suzi. The older man ducked his head, mumbled an apology to her and turned to offer the same apology to Aaron. It still amazed him that this mountain of a man could be brought to his knees with one look from his little wife.

"You've done good, today. Why don't you take the rest of the afternoon off, see if you can find Allyson? Maybe you two can catch some more of that fish for dinner."

"Only if you're gonna eat it grilled, David. You know what the doctor said about your cholesterol, which means no more fried foods. Not until we get it down."

"But____"

"No buts. Grilled fish, or none at all."

"Fine," he sighed and turned back to Aaron again. "If you can't find her in the barn, and Fury is missing, go on and saddle up Tuff."

"Are you going to look for her?" Aaron asked.

"No. You are."

"But Tuff is your horse."

"Yeah, and he's also the only chance you've got at finding her when she's on that bay of hers. But if you bring him back with one hair out of place-" Big Dave warned, "-I'll make you regret it."

Aaron was too shocked at first to say anything. Dave was almost as protective over his horse as he was of his 'Punkin'. The fact that he just offered the animal to Aaron was a huge show of trust. He prayed he wouldn't give the older man a reason to regret it as he held his hand out and said, "Thank you, sir. It's an honor, and one I'll not take for granted." Big Dave grunted and nodded his head in approval, then turned around and headed back to the house with Suzi, her small hands still swatting his away as he tried to grope her backside. Aaron shook his head and laughed, then turned around himself and jogged over to the barn, eager to find his Elf.

Jerry helped him saddle up Tuff, even though he was skeptical at first that Dave had actually given Aaron permission to ride the dapple gray gelding. Once the horse was ready to go, Aaron led him out of the barn, Jerry in step beside him. Aar asked him if he had any idea where Ally was, to which Jerry replied, "Probably out daydreaming at the Peak."

"Care to tell me where that is?"

Jerry eyed him over the neck of the horse, pushed his hat up and off his forehead, and chewed on his wrinkled lip for a minute. Even though Aaron seemed to have won the hearts of Ally's parents, Jerry was a tougher nut to crack. Uncomfortable with that all-knowing stare, Aar looked down at the stirrups, adjusted them to fit his height when the other man finally said, "Take a left at the fork in the trail and ride on for about half an hour. You can't miss it."

"What trail?" Aaron lifted his head and asked.

But Jerry had already headed back toward the barn, his stiff gait more pronounced as he made his way through the mud.

He knew that Ally spent the majority of the time on the western side of the property, and he knew there was a fork in the road that led them to the creek. On the assumption that that was the trail Jerry referred to, Aaron hopped up on Tuff and took off in that direction, hoped that his guess was right. The left side of the trail was slimmer than the right side and Aaron had to get off his horse, walk him through the dips and curves around several types of large pines and junipers. The vegetation was so think at times that he feared he might have chosen wrong.

And more than once he thought he'd have to leave his horse–Dave's horse–tethered to a tree to keep up his search.

Then, he noticed another set of hoof prints in the mud along with a small set of boot tracks next to them. Aaron took them as a sign that he was on the right path. The trek was slow going, but he finally saw a clearing through a break in the trees not more than twenty yards ahead of him. It had been almost an hour since he'd left Jerry at the barn.

Half an hour my butt, he thought to himself as he ducked under a thick Spruce tree and out into a small clearing. He stopped and held his breath, eagerly stamped the image before him into his mind so he could call upon it any time he wanted to envision perfection.

Ally sat on a flat rock in the middle of the clearing, her jean-covered legs bent and her chin on her knees. The pale blue and white top she wore floated down her body, clung to every dip and curve and showcased just how much of a woman she was. Her straw cowboy hat sat beside her and her long tawny hair blew down her back and around the sides of her face, a pale-brown curtain that hid her beautiful imp features from his view.

Fury stood a few feet away, content to nibble on grass. Ally kissed at the animal and he lifted his head and walked to her. He bent his head next to hers and Ally wrapped a hand under his neck, laid her fingers across his jaw and stroked his hair softly. Aaron knew how delicate those hands were, how they could ignite his blood when she bestowed those gentle caresses upon him. The thought of her doing it had his heart beating faster even now.

FOREVER TREASURED

The sun streaked through the clouds overhead and golden beams surrounded her like a blanket of light, as if God Himself were reaching out to touch her.

He wasn't sure how long he stood there, immobile as he stared at her. Could have been minutes or several hours. And he would have stood there even longer had she not moved. As if she sensed him, Ally turned her head, spotted him at the opening of the clearing. She didn't jerk in surprise as he'd suspected she would. She only stared right back at him, a look of shy desire in her big, brown eyes.

"You found me," she whispered, her words floating across the small distance that separated them. They pulled him toward her like a drowning man searching for land.

His feet moved of their own accord, walked in slow steps until he stood next to her rock. He looked down at the beautiful woman before him and reached down to run the back of his knuckles across her cheek. She closed her eyes, sucked in a breath and released it slowly as she reopened her eyes and stared into his. And that's when he saw it, the worry that mixed with the desire. *What are you worried about, sweet Ally?* he thought but didn't ask.

Instead, he crouched down on his haunches so they were at eye level with each other. His turned his hand over and tightened his grip around her jaw, just enough to bring her closer to him. Their mouths were so close together that Aaron could feel her breath as it mixed with his own. "I'll always find you, Elf. There's no place you can run that would keep me from getting to you." His mouth was just a hairsbreadth away from hers now and he could feel the softness of her lips against his as she spoke.

"Is that so?" He only nodded his head, the friction between their mouths making him want to shut her up and kiss her. Now. Hard, so she wouldn't be able to smart off to him any longer. He wanted to accept the precious gift God had given him in the form of this beautiful woman sitting in front of him. And as long as she was talking, he couldn't.

"Why would you do that?" she asked, her voice barely above a whisper. Aaron let go of Tuff's reins and brought his now-free hand up to hold onto the other side of her face, kept her still while he answered.

"Because you're mine."

•••••

Ally never stood a chance. As soon as Aaron had uttered the words against her lips, she felt her heart leap, literally jump in her chest. It pounded against her ribs like it was trying to reach out to him, hold onto him. If there was any doubt as to how she felt before, he'd just crushed those uncertainties with three little words.

She was in love with him.

She barely had time to register her admission before he pressed his lips to hers, hard and insistent, as if he wanted to seal them together forever.

And that's exactly what I want.

But she wouldn't tell him. Couldn't. Not yet. She didn't want to give him any reason to tuck tail and run. She wanted to bask in these feelings–as scary as they were–for just a little bit longer before she had to worry about what he would say or do or feel. Before she had to worry that he might leave.

Her thoughts fled as Aaron tilted her head, his hands strong and warm on her face. Then he deepened the kiss, stroked his tongue against hers almost nervously, as if he were seeking permission. She gave it willingly, wrapped her arms around his neck and held on tight, pulled him closer to her so that he *knew* she wanted what he gave. Wanted him.

Then she was moving, her back lowered to the flat rock she sat on, landing with a gentle thud. Aaron came down on top of her, one hand out to the side as he held himself up so as not to crush her. She pulled him harder, wanted to feel the heavy weight of him like a blanket that would keep her warm in the cool nights. He complied, the air whooshing out of his mouth as their upper bodies came into contact. He rested on his forearms, bent his elbows beside her face and held on to her hair. She ran her hands up his back, under his shirt and across the firm muscles that twitched beneath her palms and his hands tightened in those long strands. The tug on her hair was somehow comforting, like a reminder that he was here with her and wasn't letting go.

Ally relished that sensation.

Aaron tore his mouth from hers, lifted his head just a little and stared down at her with heated eyes. His pupils were dilated, the black almost taking over the bright blue that she so loved to look into. He breathed heavily through his nose, his mouth closed and lips wet. The angles of his jaw were firm and Ally saw when the muscles clenched, like he was struggling with some inner debate.

She took the decision away from him, raised her head from the rock and kissed along his neck. Ally placed tender little pecks right above the hem of his t-shirt and then up, up, up to his Adam's apple. She gave a longer kiss there and felt him swallow beneath her lips. Aaron shuddered, his hands tightening again as he tilted her head back and attacked her mouth like a starving man. She held on tighter, desperate to stay in this moment, to stay wrapped up in his arms for as long as she could.

Ally felt the heat of his body on top of hers, his lips sliding against hers and the fluttering of his heart next to hers. Separately, they meant nothing. But together, together they let loose feelings of wild abandon. Ally thought there might be a future for them. She wanted to grasp onto it, to make him feel, too.

She wanted to be *Aaron's* forever girl.

As he glided his mouth down the side of her neck, past her pounding pulse and landed on the hollow of her throat, he gave a small lick there. Ally knew she was ruined for any other man. She knew that no one would ever compare to

Aaron and the way he made her feel. How could any other man make her see the world with such passion and love? Aaron made everything seem brighter with vivid colors reflecting all around them like a prism. And they were at the center of it, basking in its light. She knew right then that there would never be anyone else. If he never felt the same way, then she would go to her grave with these memories, reliving them on cold and lonely nights.

But if he did feel the same way, she would spend every night for the rest of their lives showing him just how much he meant to her. And how much she loved him. Because with every pass of his lips across her heated skin, she already felt that love–the love that was fresh and new and uncharted– grow into something she wasn't sure her heart could contain. Ally didn't want to contain it. She wanted to let it out, scream it from the rooftops and savor the warmth that her love for Aaron gave her.

Her thoughts faded when she felt Aaron's fingers trail down her neck, past her chest and land on her waist. His rough palm rasped against her tender flesh as he worked his way behind her, pulling her to him with pressure on her lower back. *I can't get any closer,* she thought, *but I'd give anything to try.*

That was the only thing that scared her. She'd been burned so badly by Ben. She didn't want to give herself to a man if he had no intention of sticking around, being faithful and putting as much into a relationship as she did.

She might not love often. But when she did, she loved with all her being. Ally placed one hand on his chest and gave a weak push.

Aaron sat up immediately, took one look into her eyes and closed his own as he let out a heavy breath. "I'm so sorry, Elf. I didn't mean for that to happen."

"It's okay, Aar. Don't apologize. Nothing happened that I didn't want to."

"Yeah, but I should have been stronger."

Ally gave a gentle squeeze to the muscles on his chest and back, enjoyed the flexing of his toned body for a second before she said, "Feels like you're plenty strong to me."

Aaron gave a short laugh and said, "You know what I mean."

"Yes, I do. And again, don't be sorry. I'm not. Just the opposite in fact." He gave her a quizzical look so she went on. "I'm grateful for you, for what we have. But Aaron, I can't get involved with another man like I did with Ben. It would break me. And as much as I… like you… I can't let anything or anyone break me. Ever again." It took everything Ally had in her to keep from saying "love" but she managed, chose to hold in that four letter word as her own secret until she knew the time was right.

"I'd never do that, Allyson. You mean too much to me."

"Do I? Really?" He gave a slow nod and she took a deep breath. "Then wait for me. Wait for us. For the right time. Because now isn't it. Not yet."

"Not now doesn't mean never." He said it more as a statement than a question. Ally took comfort from that. It wasn't a promise or a declaration of love. But it was enough of an assurance to her that he felt there'd be more tomorrows for them, too.

"No, not never. Just for right now. "

Aaron bent down, rested his forehead against hers and gave a small peck to her mouth. Then he sat up quickly, pulling her with him. With a smile on his lips and a twinkle in his eyes he said, "I've got all the time in the world, my beautiful Elf. I'm not going anywhere."

Aimee Martin

Chapter 12

"Whereas ye know not what shall be on the morrow. For what is your life? It is even a vapour, that appeareth for a little time, and then vanisheth away."
James 4:14

Aaron ran his fingers lightly down the side of Ally's face, brushed a few wayward strands of hair behind her ear, bent and kissed the high arch of her cheek. She sighed against his face and he smiled, lips still pressed to her soft skin.

They stayed on that flat rock even though it seemed their need for privacy was over.

For now.

He didn't want to go back to the ranch yet. Out here, away from prying eyes and eavesdropping ears, he felt more open with her, more willing to show her the parts of himself that he normally kept bottled up.

Those parts were for him and Ally and no one else. He didn't want to share them, or her, with anyone. He wanted to hide these precious moments and keep them protected from the rest of the world, like a caterpillar hiding itself in her cocoon.

He wrapped his arms tighter around her, looked into her hazel eyes. The green was more pronounced now with the bright grass around them glittering like emeralds from this morning's rain. They didn't speak a word, just stared at each other. With Ally curled up against his chest, her fingers tracing the outlines of his pecs through his shirt, he realized that protecting her was exactly what he was doing now. And he never wanted to stop.

Aaron wasn't sure when Ally had become so important to him. He didn't know when his feelings had crossed from the territory of curious desire to one based more on an honest connection with real emotions. But they had. He knew it the second she'd put her hand on his chest and asked him to wait for the right time. With any other woman, at any other time, he'd have used that as his escape. After what had happened with Jess, he never planned to give a woman that much power over him again.

With Ally, Aar knew that there'd be no escaping. No matter what control he thought he had, he admitted to himself that she held more. Ally had woven her way into his heart, burrowed into the creases of his soul like a little bunny searching for a warm shelter. Aaron tightened his hold around the woman in his arms and vowed to himself that he would be her shelter. For as long as she'd have him.

Aaron turned his face, laid his cheek down on the crown of Ally's head as he looked out at the endless horizon in front of them, with mountains and blue sky as far as the eye could see. Here, away from the hustle and bustle of a city–even small towns like Lake Shores and Rosy Camp–the sounds and sights of the world were so much clearer.

A small group of mountain chickadees nestled into the pines surrounding them, their melodic chirps loud in the quiet air. A flock of Canadian geese flew overhead, the telltale patches on either side of their beaks stark white against the black of their bodies. A black-tailed prairie dog scurried across the edge of the field and headed to the shelter of a burrow just inside the tree line. Three young pups followed closely behind, their short legs moving quickly to keep up with their mother.

Aaron watched the mother, the way she stood just outside the domed mound, waiting as each of her babies ran inside before following them to safety. And he wondered what it would be like to see Ally as a mother with children of her own. He smiled and shook his head at the mental image that thought created. She'd be protective, her firecracker attitude more than enough to keep strangers at bay. But Ally was shrewd, too. She wouldn't try to handle a dangerous situation on her own. She wouldn't hesitate to ask for help if she thought her kids were in jeopardy.

As proud as she was at times, Ally had common sense and a whole lot of faith. And Aaron knew she would never let her pride overtake those two things. *Does she have faith in us?* he wondered. *Or was she just spewing nonsense before to get me to back off?*

Aaron was afraid of getting involved with a lying and manipulating woman like Jess. His ex-wife didn't start out that way. His mind flashed a caution sign but his heart knew better. Ally wasn't manipulative. She was honest and wore her feelings on her sleeve. Her outlook on life and what others thought of her was a "love it or leave it" one. He didn't know if he was ready to love it. But he definitely didn't want to leave it.

"What are you thinking about?" she whispered. He raised his head, tilted his chin down to look into Ally's face. Her eyes were worried and questioning and her lips turned down at the corners. When he hesitated—because, really, how was he supposed to explain that he'd been thinking of her as a mother?—she added, "You got really still and your heart started beating fast. I just wondered what was going on in your head to make that happen."

He opened his mouth to answer, found he still couldn't come up with a logical response that didn't sound outlandish, closed his mouth again and gave his head a little shake. Ally's shoulders slumped as she attempted a smile.

"It's okay. You don't have to tell me." She tried to sound reassuring but Aar sensed the disappointment in her voice, in the way it quivered a little. She turned her face back to the openness around them, but not quick enough for Aaron to miss the look of hurt in her eyes.

He reached down and grasped her chin between his forefinger and thumb, turned her face back to him. He swallowed thickly past a lump in his throat and, with a fortifying breath, said, "I was thinking of you. Of how remarkable it would be to see you as a mother, because I know how protective and loving you'd be." Her mouth opened, Aaron guessed in surprise. He lowered his head, kissed her gently, and gave a quick swipe of his tongue against her open lips. And because in this instance it just felt *right*, he added, "I'm wondering what it would be like if you were the mother of my babies and what it would be like raising a family with you."

•••••

Ally had not expected a declaration like that from Aaron. She didn't think there was anything he could say that would have thrown her off balance, at least not any more than she'd been when she realized she was in love with him. But that admission rocked her.

After everything that had happened when she lost her baby, and the events that followed with Ben, Ally hadn't given much thought to what it would be like to be a mother. She believed that she'd had her chance, and it had been taken away from her. Not that she was angry with God for it. He had His reasons and she had to believe in them, have faith in Him when everything else seemed out of her control. And she did.

Since her divorce, Ally didn't think there would be a second chance for love and happiness and *babies*. She wasn't sure she wanted to try again. There were no guarantees in life. A child could be ripped out of your arms in an instant. She lived through the devastation her parents suffered when David died. They were all still grieving. She didn't know such pain existed until she lost her baby. Even though it tore her heart out it could not have equaled the pain her parents felt. She loved and lost a child she really didn't know. But her mother and father buried the boy they'd raised for twenty-five years. Could she risk the uncertainty of life? Until Aaron showed up in Montana, her answer would have been a resounding no.

Despite their rocky start, he'd worked his way into her heart and already proven those first two wrong. Because she *was* in love and she *was* happy. She cherished those emotions that had seemed out of reach for so long. Did that mean motherhood was in her future now, too? Ally had buried that desire deep within her.

But now that Aaron had brought it up? Having a baby–having *his* baby–didn't seem like such a far-off hope.

Is that a hope I can put my faith in? she wondered, and then forced the notion out of her head. What was she thinking? She hadn't even told him how she felt. She didn't even know if he felt the same way.

There was a difference in optimism and realism. And while she could be hopeful, optimistic, about a future with Aaron, she had to be realistic, too. Planning for a life and a family with a man who she knew was gun-shy about commitment could only hurt them both. She had to stick to her plans to keep these feelings to herself. She had to let Aaron be the one to move this relationship forward, much as it pained her to sit back and play follower.

Ally realized she'd stayed silent after his confession, licked her dry lips and forced a small smile, tried to lighten the situation. "Don't you think you're jumping the gun a little bit?"

"Don't you think you're taking it a little too literally?"

"How am I supposed to take it when you say something like that?" Ally sounded defensive, she knew it, and that's not at all how she thought this conversation would go when she tried for humor.

"I thought you'd take it…" he paused, released a heavy breath, dropped his head and closed his eyes. Then in a softer voice, "I don't know how I thought you'd take it. Honestly, I didn't really think at all. It just came out. I'm sorry."

"No, I'm sorry. I didn't mean to sound prissy." She laid her palm across his cheek and angled his face back to hers, waited until he opened his eyes to go on. "I guess my attempt to lighten the mood didn't exactly go as planned."

"I guess my attempt at a sweet declaration didn't go as planned, either. Now that I think about it, it kinda came across as pushy and obsessive. Not really the mood I was going for there."

"No," Ally laughed, "not really. So we *both* went about this whole conversation wrong. How about we-" her suggestion to "start over" died in her throat when Aaron's stomach grumbled so loudly, Ally swore she could feel the rumbling in her own body. She laughed harder when Aaron gave her a sheepish look and shrugged. "How about we go get you some dinner?"

Aaron looked around and arched his brows. He noticed that the sun was starting to set. "Do you think we'll make it back before dark?"

"Are you afraid of the dark?"

"My little brother used to love that show," he said and then with a smirk aimed at her, "And no, I'm not. I was just wondering if the horses could handle that trail."

Ally hopped up from Aaron's lap, walked over to where they'd tethered the horses to a juniper tree and untied their reins, handing Tuff's set to Aaron. "Don't worry. Fury and I will protect you." Then she swung onto her gelding's back and with a quick look behind her to make sure he was ready, Ally took off at a steady clip through the trees. With Aaron hot on her tail, Ally headed home.

With less light, it took longer to make it back to the barn. The thirty-minute trip turned into forty-five. As Ally and

Aaron pulled their horses to a stop at the gate, dismounted and walked inside the fenced-area, her stomach was rumbling as much as Aaron's had. But before they could head to the house for dinner, they had to take care of the horses.

Jerry's radio played quietly from the loft when they entered the barn, and soft strains from a country song lilted through the darkness. Ally smiled, taking comfort from the sound of music that always made her feel like she was home.

She led Fury into his stall and unsaddled him, placed the gear on the stall gate and brushed him down with a currycomb to loosen up the dirt stuck to his coat. Then she worked him over with the dandy and body brushes, laughing as he turned his neck to lay his head on her shoulder. "Yeah, you like that, don't ya, boy?" she purred to her horse.

When she finished, she gave him a rubdown with her hand, stroked his mane and placed a kiss to his nose. With one last pat to the side of his neck, she turned to head out of the stall and found Aaron watching her.

He leaned against the bales of hay on the wall opposite her, his legs crossed at the ankles and elbows perched on the alfalfa behind him. The way his upper body balanced on the grass had his shoulders straining against his shirt, emphasizing the muscles beneath the white cotton. His forearms looked tanned in the dim light and Ally traced the sinewy lines with her eyes as she worked her gaze down to his trim hips.

He was still lean, but since he'd started working here he'd packed on more muscle and the difference was noticeable everywhere, especially in the way his jeans clung to his long legs. Ally remembered the way it felt to have those legs on either side of hers on that first trip to the mountainside that first day. She wondered what it would feel like now, to be surrounded by the strength encased in that faded denim.

While she gawked at those powerful limbs, they moved. Ally jumped, flushed at the fact that she'd been caught staring at him. Again. Instead of looking up at Aaron, she kept her eyes down, watched his dirt-covered boots slowly walk to where she stood. She focused on the stitching of those boots, too embarrassed to look at the man wearing them.

He took the option away from her when he lifted her chin up with his hand. She saw the grin on his face and wanted to wipe it off. But the only way that came to mind was to kiss him. Given that she'd just been ogling him, she figured that would only give him more ammunition. So she bit her lip and held her tongue, instead.

"Like what you see, Elf?"

"No," she lied.

"Are you sure? I'd be happy to walk back over there so you could get another look. Just to be positive."

"Oh, get off your high horse____"

"I already did," he interrupted and jerked his chin in the direction of Tuff's stall. Ally turned, saw that Aaron had already taken care of Daddy's pride and joy. "Quicker than you, too, I might add."

"Smartass," she mumbled under her breath. He chuckled in response, the sound rich in her ears.

Until the song changed.

Aaron stopped laughing, quickly ran to the ladder that led to the loft and climbed just enough rungs so he could reach the radio. He turned up the volume–Ally heard the unmistakable sound of an acoustical guitar–and was back in front of her before she could ask what he was doing.

"Dance with me."

"What? Here?"

"Why not here? No one's around. It's just you and me and the horses. And I don't think they'll tell anybody."

"Smartass," she said again and then, cocked her head. "Okay."

He grinned at her acceptance, took her hands and led her into the middle of the barn. With one hand firmly on her lower back, he pulled her closer to his chest, grabbed her right hand with his free one. He spun them in a slow circle, his palm warm on her back through her shirt. His cobalt eyes shimmered under the low-hanging chandelier that was nothing more than an old, wrought-iron wagon wheel with three light bulbs.

He hummed along with the tune of the song, then sang the lyrics quietly as they began. The deep tone of his voice resonated in her chest, warmed her body from the inside out.

She listened to the singers, heard the voice of Ray Charles mix with that of Willie Nelson. Two seemingly different artists and yet, their voices blended like a well-oiled machine. "I've never heard this song before."

"Not surprising," Aaron said. "You weren't even born yet. You're just like a little baby, missing out on all the good music."

"Watch it old man."

"Old?"

"Older than me. By five years, too. Do I need to go find you a walker to finish the dance with? Or do you think you can keep up?" Instead of answering, he spun her out quickly then right back into his chest. Two more times he performed the little jig before he responded.

"Don't tempt me when it comes to dancing. I'll outlast you all night long."

"Just this kind?" she teased, earned a low growl from Aaron. He ducked his head, nipped the side of her neck and followed it with a sweet kiss.

"Maybe someday you'll find out. If God's plans are anything like mine."

Ally's breath caught at the underlying promise in his voice.

Don't think about it, Ally. Not right now. Just don't think about it. But her warning did little to stop her imaginings, now that he'd planted that seed. So instead, she focused back on the music.

"What's the song about?" she asked when he lifted his head and looked down into her eyes.

"It's a love story. Probably one of the greatest love stories ever written for a song."

"Tell me about it?" He released her hand, wrapped his arms around her back and held her tight. Ally wound her arms around his neck, toyed with the hair at the nape of his neck while she rested her cheek against his shoulder. Aaron set his chin down, pressing it into the curve of her neck and shoulder. When he spoke, his breath tickled and had her heart racing while goose bumps spread over her skin.

"It's about a man and woman who are deeply in love. They're in Mexico and they've been on the run from the law. They heard these Texas lawmen coming for them, and the man asks his woman to pray for him."

"Why?"

"Because there was no way he was going back to Texas in handcuffs. So he stood off with the lawmen, and they killed him."

"How sad. Why not just go with them? Fight for his freedom in a court?"

Aaron lifted his head, looked down into Ally's eyes. She knew they were wide in disbelief and she waited to hear what happened next. "Because he'd rather die than be taken to prison. Was it right? No, but that's not the saddest part."

"I'm not sure it could get much worse," she whispered into the quiet barn, the soft music their only interruption.

"When the man was shot, the woman stood there, saw the whole thing happen. She saw the lawmen with rifles pointed at her, and she saw her love lying dead at her feet. She knew she couldn't live without him. Didn't want to even contemplate a future without the love of her life. So she bent down and picked the gun up, asked for forgiveness from God, and pointed the empty gun at the lawmen."

"They killed her, too," Ally gasped.

Aaron tightened his hold on her as her eyes filled with tears and the scene of the song played out between them as if it were real. She could feel the woman's pain at being alone as if it were *her* pain.

"They did."

"How horrible."

"A bit morbid for the dance floor but, in a crazy way it's a little romantic. Don't you think? Loving someone so much that you'd rather die too, than to live without them. Kinda has that Romeo and Juliette thing going on. Can you imagine it?"

Yes, she thought to herself but didn't say aloud. *I can, with you.* She nodded her head and licked her dry lips, swallowed past a lump in her throat.

Aaron brought his hands up and cupped her face, ran his thumbs across her cheekbones to wipe away the tears that had fallen.

But when he bent and kissed her–so softly it made her heart ache–the tears came again and slipped between their lips. The salty moisture, mixed with the sweet taste of Aaron, made her brain a jumble of feelings. The fright, the confusion, the love. She didn't know which to hold onto.

So she held onto him, instead.

She grasped his head in her hands and deepened the kiss, their lips sealed so tightly together that there was no way for even air to move between them. Aaron's hands fell from her face, skimmed down her sides and wrapped around her lower back. He bent at the knees and then Ally was flying as he lifted her into the air so they were at eye level. Her lids were tightly closed to block out the world around them. Still she kissed him, not willing to break their contact for even a second.

But he pulled back and a small whimper fell from her lips. She opened her eyes, found his bright and intense as he stared back at her. There was a mix of emotions swirling in those deep blue depths, a tender torment at the forefront. His brow furrowed and he swallowed. His Adam's apple bobbed and Ally wanted to kiss him there again. But the look in his eyes held her back, until he finally spoke.

"Tell me you feel it, too, Elf?"

•••••

She didn't answer him and Aaron held his breath while he waited for either denial or confirmation. He didn't care at this point what her answer was. He just needed to know if these feelings were one-sided. Did Ally share them? Was it too much to hope for that this thing they had between them could move forward, grow stronger?

He needed to know that if he put his heart on the line, it would be worth it.

When he first showed up in Montana, he had no idea something like this would happen. He didn't know if anything would come out of the strange connection he'd felt with Ally. He wasn't sure when he left for Montana if the road he had taken was his own idea, God's or even the devil whispering in his ear. But the more time he spent with her, the more he realized how right this was. She was right. They were right. And now, as he held her in his arms and put their future in her hands, he knew it'd been God all along. He didn't know what would happen tomorrow or next week or next year. Life on earth was precious and short-lived. He wanted to enjoy it for all it was worth. And he wanted to emjoy it with Ally.

My God, he thought while she remained silent. *I'm in love with her.*

Before he had a chance to wrestle with that new development, she spoke.

"Yes," she breathed. "I feel it. The question is… what do we do with it?"

Aaron slowly set her feet back on the ground, kept a hand on her back and brought his other up to cradle her angelic face. "We nurture it and protect it and watch it grow."

"I'm scared, Aaron."

"Me, too. My God, Allyson, I'm terrified. But we're in this together, right?" She nodded her head in his hand. "Then we'll protect each other. We only have this one life. Let's live it to the fullest."

"Okay."

He had no more words. Aaron didn't know if he could speak them even if he did. Instead, he bent and kissed her again, just once. Then he reached behind his neck, took her hands down from where they gripped him tightly. He walked backwards, pulled her until she followed him out of the barn. When they reached the doorway, they both stopped. Aaron looked up at the sky, at the millions of stars that twinkled above them. He watched as a shooting star flashed across the darkness and disappeared into the heavens. And he took it as a sign that he and Ally were right on track, right where they were supposed to be, reaching for their own Heaven here on Earth.

He looked down at Ally, saw she'd seen the same star. And when she brought her gaze back to his, her face lit up and her eyes glittered just like the stars overhead. He knew, right then, that it everything was going to be alright.

"Let's go eat," he said. "I'm starved."

She smiled at him and they headed toward the main house. Aaron threw his arm over her shoulders and pulled her in close to his side while they walked. He never intended to let her go.

Until the shot rang out beside them.

Aimee Martin

Chapter 13

"LORD, how are they increased that trouble me!
many are they that rise up against me."
Psalms 3:1

She wasn't sure what had just happened.

One minute she'd been wrapped up in Aaron's arms, headed to the house to grab some supper. The next, they heard a shot ring through the air. The retort was almost deafening despite the fact that it had likely originated from around a hundred yards away.

Aaron reacted with lightning speed. He shoved Ally to the ground and threw himself on top of her, knocking the wind out of her with the force of his weight. Ally was terrified and as soon as she caught her breath, she opened her mouth and tried to scream. He had to know she was scared and that he was hurting her.

But, he obviously didn't think about that now.

He covered her head with his arms, her mouth with a hand and told her to be quiet.

They stayed like that, huddled on the ground with Aaron acting as a human shield, for what seemed an eternity. But was probably no more than five minutes. They both listened intently. Everything was still and quiet. Whatever danger they sensed seemed to have passed.

Finally, Aaron whispered harshly in her ear, "What the hell was that?" She tried to answer but couldn't get enough air into her lungs, not with his weight still awkwardly pushing down on her upper body and his hand still covering her mouth. When she didn't say anything right away, he raised his head an inch and looked down into her face. "Ally, are you okay? You're not hit, are you? No. No, no, no. Please tell me you didn't get hit."

"Can't… breathe…" she finally managed to mutter from beneath his fingers, in between short gasps.

"Oh, thank God. You scared me Elf," he sighed and rested his forehead against hers, his heartbeat erratic against her chest. Ally loved the feel of his body covering her, but this was hardly the time for a tender moment. She managed to wiggle her hands free just enough to give Aaron's shoulders a little push and pull his hand away from her mouth. "Still… can't breathe… Aaron."

"Crap! I'm sorry." They both stood and he said, "Here," then quickly pulled them deeper into the darkness, out of sight. He placed his trembling hands on either side of her face and Ally took her first deep breath since her back hit the ground, savored the sweet feeling of fresh air in her lungs. Then she brought her hands to rest on those arms, wrapped her fingers around his biceps and gave them a gentle squeeze. "Better?" She only nodded. "Now I'm gonna ask again. What the hell was that?"

"A gun shot," she said matter of factly. "Guess somebody wants you gone."

He scowled and she swore she heard a low growl come from his throat. His expression frightened her a bit so she amended, "I'm really not sure. Shouldn't be any hunters out at night, so that's not it. And that was too close to have come from someone else's property."

"Could it have been your Dad or brother? Maybe Jerry? Kids out spot lighting?"

Ally was already shaking her head no even before he'd finished asking. "No. Daddy's always at the house for supper. And Danny went up to Billings for the weekend to spend some time with his girlfriend. There aren't any kids nearby and if there were, they know there's no game that close to the buildings."

"I didn't know he had a girlfriend." Aaron said and Ally thought how strange his remark was after they had almost been killed. *Nerves,* she mused.

She was puzzled by his demeanor but then again, she wasn't exactly thinking straight either. "Um…Yeah. Her name's Nicole and they've been together since they were freshmen in high school. Ever since she went off to college, he tries to get up there as often as possible. He's hoping she'll want to come back here after she graduates in a year, start a life with him. But I don't think that'll happen. Not after she's experienced life outside of Rosy Camp."

"You did."

"It's not the same thing. There were extenuating circumstances."

"Yeah, I know. The baby and Ben."

"Among other things."

"Does that have anything to do with your older brother? The one who died?"

Ally rolled her lips inward, kept the trembling at bay, but just barely. "Yes," she admitted. "Some of it."

"Are you gonna tell me about it?"

"Right now? When someone just shot at us?"

Her reminder brought out his protectiveness again. His body tensed as he remembered what they were up against and he scanned the open fields that surrounded them. But the darkness had descended on them like a heavy blanket and thwarted any chance they might have had to spot a trespasser.

With his brows lowered and a few lines wrinkling the space between them, he said, "No. We need to get out of here. We're sitting ducks as soon as the moonlight hits us." He looked around slowly one more time, glanced up at the sky and said, "That's going to be any minute now. Come on.

Let's get back to the house and try to figure out what the heck is going on. And Ally, I'm sorry for throwing you down like that. I was trying to keep you safe."

"Who's going to keep me safe from you?" she asked.

They stood still and she looked up into his face, lightly traced the angle of his jaw with her fingertips. He closed his eyes at the touch, laid his palm over hers and held her hand still on his cheek.

Without opening his eyes he asked, "Is that what you want, to be protected from me?"

"No," she answered quietly and he opened his eyes. She tried to show him with her gaze that she meant it but added, "Not in the least, but warn me before you jump on me again. My side is killing me. And no, I'm not hurt. Just a little bruised."

He shuddered and released a heavy breath. She understood. They could have been seriously hurt.

They could have been killed.

Aaron was still trembling.

"God help me, Allyson," he half whispered, half moaned. "I just found you, I can't lose you. I… I don't think I'll ever be able to let you go."

She went up on her tiptoes, brushed her lips across his for the briefest of seconds, whispered against his mouth, "I'm counting on it."

•••••

Aaron wasn't sure what he was more afraid of at the moment. The fact that someone had just fired a gun at them. Or that he'd admitted to never being able to let Ally go, which in his book might as well have been a marriage proposal.

As he kissed her, wrapped his arms around her back and pulled her tight against his body, he knew that he wasn't actually afraid of what he'd said. He meant it with his whole heart. And the thought of spending the rest of his life with the beautiful, little imp in his arms wasn't such a daunting image after all. It gave him a peace in his soul that he had hadn't felt in a long time.

He almost broke the kiss and laughed at the dichotomy. He was no longer trembling with fear, but with the depth of his feelings for her.

What kind of idiot is peaceful after dodging a bullet? And you've never felt anything remotely close to this before.

And that was true. Even before his marriage fell apart, Aaron had been restless, like he was about to crawl out of his skin at a moment's notice. He hadn't felt settled or happy. He hadn't felt like he belonged.

He hadn't felt loved.

But with Ally, he did feel those things. Every single one of them. And Aaron knew he would do whatever it took to make sure that he kept on feeling them. To make sure that nothing jeopardized what he and Ally had together. Because this–her and *them*–was special.

Then stop wasting time out here where you're both vulnerable and get her inside, Aaron!

The reprimand only he heard broke the spell, brought his mind back to the present. They were standing out in the open. Someone could still be out there waiting for the moonlight to fall on them and give him a second shot.

"Let's go," he said and pulled her hand, walked quickly until they reached the mudroom of the main house.

He didn't realize he'd held his breath until he had Ally safely inside–the door locked behind them–and he released a heavy sigh, his lungs on fire from the lack of oxygen. He removed his boots and set them in the corner with the six other pairs that rested there, turned and held Ally's hand while she took off hers and placed them right next to his.

"You know we have to tell your parents about this, right?"

"I'm pretty sure they already know we've been seeing each other. Daddy gave you his permission, remember?"

Man, Aaron loved her smart mouth. But this was neither the time nor the place for that mouth to make light of the situation. Irritated, he glowered at her until she relented.

"Yes, I know we need to tell them. But don't you think we should wait until tomorrow? Once it's daylight we can go see if we can find any tracks, find out who did it. Then we can disclose this to them."

"No, Elf. We need to tell them tonight. As much as I'd love nothing more than to be the one to protect you, I'm also man enough to admit that I'm out of my element here. But your Dad isn't. He could be a big help to us in trying to figure out what's going on."

"I know. You're right. It's just..." she trailed off and turned her face to the side. Aaron walked to her, placed his hands on her shoulders, waited. She didn't look back at him when she spoke. "It's just that I don't want to worry them unnecessarily."

"Someone just shot at us, baby. I think we're past that. This is definitely a necessity." She jerked her head back and Aaron prepared for a fight. He didn't expect the shock on her face. "What?"

"You just called me baby."

"Okay."

"You've never called me that before."

"Well then I'll make sure to never do it again."

"No!" she said. "I... I liked it. You can call me that whenever you want."

Aaron squeezed her shoulders and smiled down at her. "Alright, then. I will." He ran his hands up from her shoulders, rested them on the smooth skin of her exposed neck. His thumbs traced the veins on either side of her throat and he savored the feel of her life's blood. He'd come close to losing her and it had scared him more than he wanted to admit. But here, in this quiet room on the side of the house, with no one else around, he knew his fear for what it'd really been. All encompassing. Debilitating. He never wanted to feel it again.

Instead of focusing on what he could have lost, he focused on the fact that she was still here in his arms. His little Elf. He looked into her eyes in the dim light from the single bulb that burned overhead. The yellow glow brought out the brown in her irises and the glossy coating that made them seem as if they were swimming was more noticeable. Aaron had a feeling that her barely there tears had nothing to do with what they'd just gone through. He didn't know why. A gut feeling, maybe.

But somehow, he saw her fear for what it was as well as he recognized his own. He understood she was afraid to tell her parents. They had already lost so much. What would it do to them to learn they could have lost her too? Aaron took a deep breath. It was time to broach the subject he knew Ally was reluctant to share with him. But, in light of the previous half hour's events, it was time he learned the truth.

"What happened, Ally?" he asked. She gave him a quizzical look and he explained. "With your brother. What happened to David?"

She pulled away from Aaron and paced the small space. Aaron leaned against the sink, crossed his ankles and rested his hands behind him. And waited. She had her arms crossed over her middle, her right thumb pulled up as she bit her nail. He had never seen her do that before. Ally was a bundle of exposed nerves. Several minutes passed while she wore a hole in the floor and still he waited her out, knew she'd speak when she was ready.

"Have you ever regretted not being there for someone you loved?" she asked suddenly as her feet moved quickly across the tile. "I mean, has something bad ever happened to someone you loved and you weren't there for them and you thought that if you just had been, then none of the bad stuff would have taken place? Or that you could have prevented it somehow?" Now she stopped, just for a second, and stared at him from the other side of the room. "Well?"

Aaron thought about it. But being put on the spot like that, with her impatience showing from across the room, he had a hard time thinking of a time. He shook his head no, and Ally have a short nod as if that was the answer she expected and resumed her worried steps.

"Well, I have. With David. And there's not a day that goes by that I don't think about what went down with him and think to myself that if only I'd been here, none of it would have transpired." Now she stopped and stared out the oval window on the door, the beveled glass distorting the stars that shone brightly outside. "If I'd been here, he'd still be alive."

Aaron stayed where he was but spoke from across the short distance, "How did he die, Elf?"

"Police report said it was a suicide. But my parents and I never believed that. David wouldn't have done that. He wouldn't have taken the coward's way out. He had so much to live for. Daddy was grooming him to take over the ranch and that's exactly what David had wanted. He couldn't wait until the day the Marx Ranch and Game place would be his to run. We'd talked about it often when I called from college. About how things were finally falling into place for both of us. This was before I got pregnant," she added as she gave Aaron a sideways glance and then returned her gaze to the outside.

He held his breath, swallowed thickly against the pain he felt for Ally and her family. To lose someone so young was hard in and of itself. But to lose someone like that, whether it was suicide or not, had to have been unbearable. Aar knew how much responsibility Ally took for her family and this ranch. That would have broken her. And yet, here she was, resilient and beautiful and standing tall, not willing to let the horrors of life beat her down. He'd never admired her more than he did right then, hearing what life had thrown at her and knowing the strength it took for her to keep going.

It was what brought them together.

"Supposedly, there was a forty-five automatic next to his body," she said, "along with a note that said something about him not being happy anymore and wanting this life to just be over. Aside from the fact that we all *knew* he wasn't unhappy, that gun was the biggest clue. David didn't own a forty-five. None of us did."

"Did y'all tell the police that?"

"Yes. And they said that just because we didn't know about it didn't mean he hadn't gone and purchased one without our knowledge. We told them he wouldn't have just upped and bought a gun without telling us. That's not the way our family works. We're close. We look out for one another. And when it comes to firearms, Daddy is very strict. From early ages, he taught us about gun safety. That they are not toys and that we must always assume they're loaded. And that we are never, ever, to leave this house without telling someone where we're going and what firearms are going with us.

"The sheriff said that a depressed person wouldn't be inclined to share that information. Not when suicide was on their minds. We fought with them for over a year on the outcome but they closed the case despite our constant arguments. Said they had no reason to believe anything other than where the evidence pointed. His fingerprints were on the gun. He'd left a note. To them, it was an open-and-shut case."

"What about gunshot residue? Did they test for that?"

"This isn't CSI New York. We're a small town. We don't have that kind of testing available. When the sheriff feels it's necessary, he'll send off the proper requests, of course. But again, they said there was no evidence to dispute the obvious. Eventually they just quit answering our calls. They even threatened to file harassment charges on Momma if she wouldn't quit coming up there and, in their words, "Continue to beat a dead horse. The case is closed and that's the end of it." Their insensitivity broke Momma's spirit even more than David's death already had."

"So what did you do?" Aar asked.

"The only thing we could. We dropped it, even though it broke all of our hearts to do so, just like Momma's. We forced ourselves to move on." Ally turned to look at Aaron now and he wanted nothing more than to take her in his arms, kiss her and tell her everything would be okay. "But we've never stopped believing that they were wrong. David... that wasn't him."

"What do you think happened to him?"

Ally took a deep breath, hunched her shoulders and shivered a little, like she was cold from just thinking about her brother and his death.

"I think he was murdered."

Aaron couldn't stay still any longer. Even though he'd been afraid that that was where she was headed with her story, hearing the words come out of her mouth–her normally loud and proud voice that was now small and quiet as a mouse–broke the wall he'd put up around himself. He unfolded his body from its resting place against the sink and walked to her.

She eyed him with wariness as if he were a snake getting ready to strike. When he reached her, he held out his arms, waited for her to move the rest of the way.

She fell into his embrace and he released a breath as he wrapped his arms around her. Her shoulders shook and he heard a quiet sob. Aaron just squeezed her tighter and let her have her moment. He turned his face, laid his cheek flat on the top of her head, rocked her slowly back and forth. He hoped it was comforting. He kept an arm around her shoulders, brought the other down to rub circles on her lower back, and just let her cry. *Dear God, was someone trying to kill her too?*

"Someday," she whispered, her words muffled against his chest, "I'll find out what really happened. Somehow, I'll find out who killed him and why. I don't know when or how or who'll help me. But I will, Aaron. If it's the last thing I do."

"I'll help you, Allyson. Anytime, anywhere. Whatever you need, I'll be here for you."

"Do you promise?"

He stopped rocking them, tilted her chin up so she could see the sincerity in his eyes. "I promise. I'm here, baby. I'm in this for the long haul." And he meant it, with all of his heart.

"I am too, Aaron."

He closed his eyes, bent his head and brushed his lips across hers in the briefest of kisses, just to let her know that he *was* here, physically and figuratively. She took a deep breath and straightened her spine. Resolve took the place of her vulnerability. She inhaled deeply, let her breath out slowly.

"All right. Let's go tell my parents what's going on."

"I'm right behind you."

"No," she said and took his hand, pulled him to walk next to her. "Your place is right here, beside me."

•••••

Please, Lord, Ally prayed silently as she led Aaron through the kitchen and headed in the direction of the dining room, *please don't let my heart get broken again. Please don't let Aaron turn out like Ben, a liar and a cheat. I can't take that kind of pain again.*

Ally didn't understand how Aaron had become so important to her in such a short amount of time. How their relationship had become something so important, so vital to her.

But it had, and he was more necessary to her life than the air she breathed. She'd do anything to keep from losing this, to keep from losing him.

Telling him about her brother David had been a step in the direction of full disclosure, and that was something Ally felt was imperative to give a relationship a fighting chance. As much as it had hurt to bring up those memories, to dredge through the past, she knew when he'd asked that she had to tell him. So she had relayed the events of her brother's death.

The shock at hearing her brother was dead seemed as fresh as if it had happened yesterday. The overpowering grief, knowing in her heart someone had taken his life. Ally didn't care what the police report said. Her brother did not kill himself. If she had been here, maybe she could have saved him. Guilt tore her apart. She hadn't been there for him. It crushed her heart and ruptured her soul.

Then Aaron had held her and promised that he'd be here with her, that he'd help her find out what happened to David, and all the pain eased. It left her heart and was replaced by a quiet sense of peace. He did that to her. Made her feel as if all was right in the world. That as long as his arms were around her, nothing could touch them.

A thought niggled in the back of Ally's mind, the one about there being a calm before the storm. But she pushed it away. For the better part of three years she'd focused on too much of the bad in life. Now, with Aaron by her side, she was determined to keep her eyes on the good and the happy.

She meant to take her blessings to heart. And the man next to her was the most precious one.

As they rounded the corner and stepped into the room where her parents already sat, she paused, noticed the handful of tapered, white candles lit in the center of the table. Their clean linen scent filled the room and mingled with the smell of Momma's homemade spaghetti sauce. Ally felt like she'd walked into an old Sicilian home rather than their ranch house in the mountains of Montana.

Her Daddy sat at the head of the table, an elbow on the arm of his chair as he leaned over toward her mother. The older woman met him in the middle, a smile on her lips more radiant than Ally had seen in a long time. The wrinkles around her mouth spoke of how much she had aged since David's death. Ally had a brief moment of hesitation and thought maybe telling them what had just gone on outside might not be the best idea after all. She turned her head to say something to Aaron but he shook his head no before she had a chance to get the words out.

"No, Elf. We have to tell them. Good girl," he said when Ally nodded her head, albeit a bit reluctantly. "Go on. I'm right here."

With her hand held firmly in Aaron's grasp, Ally walked to the table right as Daddy placed a kiss to Momma's waiting mouth. Aaron squeezed her hand, gave her support. She squeezed back and cleared her throat. Her parents pulled swiftly back from each other like they were a couple of toddlers caught with their hands in the cookie jar.

"Took you two long enough," her father grumbled. He straightened in his chair, scowled and his mouth turned down at the corners. Ally knew he saw the worried look on her face and Aaron's protective stance when he paused and asked, "What's going on?"

Her mother looked up, saw the same thing Daddy did and sat up in her chair, her embarrassment long gone. "Allyson, honey," she said when they continued to stand there, "what's wrong? You two look like you've seen a ghost."

It was right then that Ally figured out why she was so worried about disclosing the gunshots. She was thinking more of David and connecting dots she hadn't seen before now. She was afraid David's murder and the gunshots were connected. Was it a stretch? Maybe, but she wasn't sure she believed in those types of coincidences. What were the chances that two different people wanted to kill her brother and then her and Aaron?

Slim to none. Those are the chances.

"I kinda feel like I have, Momma."

"Sit down and tell us what's going on."

Aaron started to do as he was told but stopped when Ally held her place, one hand on the back of the chair and the other still wrapped up in Aaron's.

"I'd rather stand for the time being," she said and then added, "We need to tell y'all about something. And you're probably not going to like it."

Daddy stood up suddenly and his chair fell backwards, landed with a loud smack on the wooden floor. "Did he hurt you, Punkin'?" He pointed an accusatory finger at Aaron then nodded towards him, "You didn't get her pregnant, did you?"

"What? No! No, Daddy, that's not what's going on."

She held tight to Aaron's hand when she felt him start to take a step back. She couldn't blame him. Her father could be quite intimidating.

"Aaron has been a gentleman to me since the beginning. This is not about us. Well, it is but not like *that*. Please, sit back down."

She waited while her father righted his chair and with a look of warning at Aaron, sat back down.

"I… I think…" she stumbled over her words.

Aaron released her hand, wrapped his arm around her shoulders. He bent down and placed a soft kiss to her cheek, then whispered in her ear, "It's okay. I'm here. We're in this together."

Despite her earlier self-protests about being a grown woman who could take care of herself, she was worried. She did not want to go through this alone. As much as it might have pained her once upon a time to admit that she wanted the security of a man, Ally no longer felt that way. The safety she felt in Aaron's embrace was something she wanted to hold onto and trust in, especially when she had to tell her parents someone had just taken a shot at her.

So she nodded against his head, took a deep breath and gathered strength from his words.

"We think someone just tried to kill us."

Aimee Martin

Chapter 14

"Hatred stirreth up strifes: but love covereth all sins."
Proverbs 10:12

Crap! Aaron thought as he watched Suzi slide from her chair. He let go of Ally and reached out to break her fall, but his reaction time was slow. Her mother landed with a loud thud on the hardwood floor and her petite body gave a small bounce. Suzi fainted and was out cold. She landed near a floor vent and the air conditioner blew directly onto her closed eyes. Aaron knelt beside her and placed his hands on either side of the older woman's head, held her in one place in case she'd broken something and looked accusingly at Big Dave, ready to ask why he had done nothing to stop his wife's fall.

But Dave stared at Ally, a look of pure anger and vengeance on his weathered face. The man's thick, meaty hands clenched into tight fists, his knuckles bleach white as they strained against an invisible adversary. His neck turned a darker shade of red. His son was already dead and now someone had just tried to shoot his daughter. Aaron noticed something else there, too. Dave swallowed slowly, inconspicuously. His large body gave an almost imperceptible shudder, so small that had he not been two feet away, Aaron probably wouldn't have seen it. Dave's knees were shaking under the table. He was too shook up to keep himself calm. Aaron saw fear in his eyes, despite the fact that the man tried hard to hide it.

Suzi moaned and moved a little in his arms and Aaron turned his attention back to her, kept her still as she opened her eyes and peered up at him in confusion.

"Aaron, what are you doing? Why am I on the floor? Stop that!" she scolded and slapped at his hands when Aaron tried to open her eyes wider to inspect her pupils. Then, like a morning fog clearing with the day, the confusion evaporated and she remembered. Her eyes widened and looked glassy as tears tried to form. "Tell me it was just a bad dream, Aaron," she whispered through trembling lips. "Tell me I didn't really hear what I think I heard."

"I'm sorry, Suzi. I can't do that. Wait," he protested when she tried to get up. "You might have broken something. You probably shouldn't move yet."

"I'm fine."

"But____"

"Young man, I know my own body," she interrupted. "Nothing is broken or fractured or sprained. Not unless you count my heart and soul. Only God can help me with those. I might be a little sore tomorrow, but that's nothing I can't handle. Now help me up!"

"Yes ma'am." Aaron helped Suzi into a sitting position, slowly stood her up with his hands beneath her elbows, guided her over to the table and waited to release her until she was seated in the chair. "Okay. Ally," he called. She had a look of anguish on her face as she stared back at them from behind the chair, "why don't you come on in and sit down, tell your parents what happened."

Ally nodded her head, her bottom lip clenched between her teeth and sat down at the table. Aaron walked to the other side and sat down in a chair next to her and took her hand in his. He ran his fingers along her palm and when she turned her head to look at him, offered her a smile of encouragement. She gave another slight nod and with a deep breath, began to speak.

"Aaron and I were walking from the barn and we stopped for a bit to look at the stars. We talked for a few minutes and we… kissed." Aaron noticed the flush that rose on Ally's cheeks. "Then Aaron put his arm around my shoulders and we started walking again. That's when a gun shot fired out of nowhere." Suzi gasped and Aaron thought he heard her mutter something that sounded an awful lot like "Not again," but he wasn't sure.

Big Dave finally moved, leaned forward to place his elbows on the table and rested his chin on his folded hands. He was serious and all about business now. Aaron knew he'd made the right call when he'd convinced Ally to tell them tonight.

"We both went to the ground and stayed there, stock-still and real quiet. After several minutes, Aaron dragged me into the shadows and when it was pretty clear that it was over, we beat it back to the house."

"Which direction did they come from?" Dave asked Aaron but Ally answered before he had a chance to.

"Far west."

"How far?"

"A hundred yards, give or take a dozen."

Big Dave nodded his head as if he knew exactly where the shooter had found cover. Then, "Alright, we'll head out at first light. See what we can find over there. I do have one question, though."

"What's that, Daddy?"

"Not for you Punkin'." He turned his face and glowered at Aaron. Aaron wasn't afraid of the big man anymore but he saw the underlying fury on Big Dave's face, knew it was directed at the shooter, and thanked God that *he* wasn't the one who'd have to tangle with that wrath. "Did you protect my baby out there?"

"Yes, Dadd____" Ally tried to answer but her Dad cut her off, still focused on Aaron.

"Not. You. Allyson. I asked Aaron, and I'll ask again. Did you protect my baby?"

"Yes sir. I covered her body with mine so that if any bullets found their way to us, I'd be the one hit. I protected her with my life, sir. And I'd do it again in a heartbeat."

"Good," was all Dave said before he rose from the table and stalked off to his bedroom.

•••••

Ally prided herself on being strong and capable. Independent. But she was scared and wasn't too arrogant to admit it. She had a terrible feeling about what had taken place outside not more than an hour ago. She could not shake the feeling that somehow it was connected to David's death. *But who would want to kill me?* she thought as she headed to her bedroom with Aaron right behind her. They reached the door before she had a chance to come up with an answer and she vowed that she would put it out of her mind for the night. Her nerves were shot and she needed to try to get some rest.

Things would be clearer after a night's sleep.

She reached out to grab the brass doorknob but stopped before turning it. Instead, Ally laid her forehead against the cool cedar door. She released a shaky breath and closed her eyes as the events played through her mind like an old time movie reel. When her mind got to the scene where Aaron had laid his own body over hers, the air shifted behind her and his hands landed on the door on either side of her head. He was so close that she could feel his body heat through their clothes.

One minute Ally was trembling but as soon as she felt his warm body, her shaking ceased. She felt warm and safe. Aaron removed his right hand from the door, placed his palm flat against her stomach and pulled her closer to him. He bent his head, nuzzled the side of her neck for the briefest of seconds before he laid his lips gently on her skin, kissed her softly.

Ally felt cherished.

"I'll never let anything happen to you, Allyson," he whispered into the quiet, dark hallway. "I promise."

Emotion clogged her throat and she could only nod in response. He removed his other hand from the door, wrapped that arm across her chest and pulled her even tighter into him.

Ally brought her hands up, laid them on the arm that held her upper body, relished the strength she felt just beneath his skin. She looked down and watched her hands as she stroked along his forearms and took pleasure when goose bumps rose on his skin.

"Is it bad," she asked, "that with everything that's going on right now, all I really want is for you to just hold me… kiss me… lo…" she broke off, realized she had only barely kept herself from asking him to *love* her.

"No." Aaron turned her to face him, wrapped his arms around her lower back and held her tight in his embrace. "Because I want the same thing, baby. I want to hold you through the night. I want to wake up with you in my arms. I want to keep you close to me, make sure that you're real."

Ally laid her hand across his cheek and rubbed along the light brown whiskers that had grown longer since he'd last shaved. "I am real, Aaron."

"I want... I need to feel your heart next to mine. Because I swear, Ally... I think mine will stop beating without yours."

Ally's breath hitched at his tender words. She wanted to take comfort in them. She really did.

But, she knew better than anyone that just because a man was good at reciting some floral retort, didn't mean he meant what he said. She'd promised herself never to move forward with a man the way she had with Ben unless she knew it was the real thing. A forever thing. As strong as her feelings were for Aaron, she couldn't, wouldn't move to the next phase of their relationship without a guarantee. Some might think that made her a cynical prude, Ally thought of it as smart and responsible. An unprotected heart was an easy thing to break.

"Aaron, I can't go to bed with you. I won't give up that part of myself again. Not like I did with Ben. The consequences just aren't worth it to me. I care for you. So much. But I'm not going to just hand over my body to you and hope that you don't stomp on it on your way out the door."

He stared at her through narrowed eyes, his brow furrowed and his lips turned down into a frown. Then he laughed. Ally quickly covered his mouth with her hand to silence him but he just kept at it. His eyes glistened as she kept his mouth covered, and small laugh lines popped out on the corners of his eyelids. After a minute, Aaron took a deep breath under her palm and Ally slowly, carefully, removed her hand.

"Are you finished?" she asked. Aaron nodded and she went on. "Would you like to tell me what was so darn funny?" He shook his head no. "Why not?" Ally asked, puzzled.

"Because you wouldn't understand."

"Try me."

Aaron tilted his head to the side, watched her with a small smile still on his lips and that gleam that made his eyes shine like the deepest sapphires. Finally, he told her, "I don't want to go to bed with you, Ally." She sucked in a quick breath and worried that maybe she had read him wrong this whole time. "Wait, that didn't come out right," he corrected quickly when he felt her try to pull away, tightened his hold so she couldn't move. Ally stopped fighting, bit the inside of her cheek to keep from smarting off to him. Instead she raised her eyebrows, gave him the chance to redeem himself.

"Of course I *want* to go to bed with you. But I won't. Because in the choice between your body and your love, I'll choose your love every time."

"Who said you had my love?"

"You didn't have to. It's mine."

"It is not."

"Is too."

"No it isn't."

"Yes it is."

"It is not!"

"I am not going to play this game with you, Allyson."

"Why? Are you afraid of a little snot stew?" she asked and they both laughed, taken back to that ridiculous game so many kids play during childhood. "Ugh. I never even liked playing that as a kid when David or Danny would try to goad me into it. I always thought it was so gross, talking about snot in stew." She shuddered over-exaggeratingly and Aaron chuckled again. She wrapped her arms around his shoulders, linked her fingers behind his neck and said, "Sorry. You can continue now."

"Thank you, O Mighty Queen of Permission."

"You're welcome." Aaron cut his eyes, trying to look formidable but she saw the smile he fought off and knew he wasn't mad.

"My point, Elf, is that the physical will come later. Hopefully. And if not, that's okay, too. Because that's not what matters to me. And that's not what I meant when I said I wanted to hold you and wake up with you and feel you next to me. What I meant was *literally* that. I want to hold you. Just as I am now, only throughout the night. Nothing more, nothing less. No," he said and placed a finger on Ally's lips when she tried to talk. Ally nipped at the finger but he didn't budge. "Let me finish. I know that's not exactly in the realm of possibility. We're in your parent's house, number one, and that would be extremely disrespectful. Number two, I wouldn't put either one of us in that position, where we might cross a line neither of us would be able to back out of. And number three, some things are worth waiting for. And I do believe, my beautiful Elf, that you're at the top of that list."

Ally grabbed his hand and kissed each of his other fingers before placing his palm on her chest right over her heart. She felt it pick up speed under his touch. Ally savored her reaction, the speed at which her heart told her how much the man in front of her meant to her.

"Thank you, Aaron," she whispered and then, even though she had no idea how he felt, and just because it was pointless to hold back the truth, added, "And I do."

He grinned, slowly, until a dimple she had never noticed before dinted his left cheek.

"You do what, baby?"

She leaned forward, kissed that cute dimple and whispered in his ear, "I do love you."

Aaron growled low in his throat and grabbed her hair, tipped her head back and attacked her mouth. It was a kiss of possession, and it made Ally weak. She stretched on tiptoes and held on tighter around his neck. When he ran his tongue along the seam of her lips, Ally let him in, kissed him back, as ravenous for him as he was for her.

She didn't want it to end. She didn't want them to end.

Aaron pulled back and laid his forehead against hers, his breathing erratic and heavy. And she knew her breathing matched his. Ally admitted to herself that this night needed to end. Their emotions were running so high that it would be easy to let things get out of hand, Ally wanted no regrets. *Actually, I think he has more will power than you do, Allyson. So call it quits for the night... before it's too late.*

"I think that's my cue."

"Yeah." His voice was hoarse and he cleared his throat. Then, "I'll meet you at the barn at first light."

As soon as she agreed, Aaron reached behind her, turned the knob and opened the door. With a gentle shove, he pushed her back into her room.

Even though he had not responded in kind, Ally saw the level of his devotion on his face. The adoring eyes, the irresistible smile, the glow that radiated from every surface of his skin.

No, he had not said the words, but she knew Aaron loved her. She felt it. For now, that was enough. She leaned against the door, used the heavy cedar to hold her body upright as he walked backwards away from her.

"Good night, Elf."

"Good night." He winked once, turned, and hurried down the hall. When she heard the mudroom door close a few minutes later, she shut her own door, plopped down on her bed with arms and legs sprawled out like a spread eagle, and quickly fell asleep.

•••••

September 6, 2015

Aaron brushed down Fury after a long day spent out with Danny tending to the mountain goats they had just tagged in preparation for their release into the wild. He thought about everything that had happened over the last two weeks.

The morning after the gun fire, he and Ally met Big Dave at the barn. Despite the protests from all the men involved in her life and a friend of Dave's named Jack, they all saddled up and headed west, Ally included. Aaron had assumed they would canter down the trail he and Ally often took to the creek.

But Big Dave had other plans.

There was another trail, one Aaron had not noticed before, about fifty yards south of the one he and Ally used. The pines and cedars were so thick, Aaron was grateful Dave had thought to bring a machete to cut the troublesome branches away. Even still, there had been more than one occasion when they had to dismount and walk the trail on foot.

Dave had spent most of the seven hours they searched with his boots on the ground, regardless of the times the rest of them were on their horses, as he'd inspected tracks and limbs. Two or three times, Dave squatted and ran a surprisingly gentle hand across a bed of leaves. Then he would look in direction of Jack and Ally and give a slight nod.

Aaron knew that look meant someone had definitely been out there.

And not someone who was supposed to be.

Even though they had worked through lunch and supper, with the sun quickly setting in the distance, their search had turned up no evidence. They had headed back to the barn and Dave had issued a warning. No one goes out alone, no one goes out unarmed, and no one–especially Ally–was to be out past dark unless they were in a truck. Ally had put up a fight and then smarted off to her old man, saying he might as well put her under house arrest.

Aaron chuckled at the memory as he finished with his gelding's hindquarters and recalled that Big Dave had threatened to do just that if he caught her breaking that rule. Of course, then he had brought Aaron into their argument and told her he would have Aar help tie her to the bed if she put up too much of a fight. Aaron had grinned over at Ally, winked at her when her father's back was turned. That was the end of her arguing, much to Aar's disappointment. He enjoyed watching her act like a spitfire.

Once Aaron had Ally safely tucked inside her bedroom that night, he'd gone back to the bunkhouse and, despite the fact that it was after midnight, made a phone call he never thought he would have to make.

•••••

August 23, 2015

Aaron walked into the kitchen of the bunkhouse, grabbed a beer from the fridge and plopped down at the small table in the breakfast nook. He twisted off the top, took a long swig and let the cool liquid work its way down his throat while he stared at his cell phone. He really didn't want to make the call, but he had a feeling they were now in over their heads here. A deep twisting in his gut told him this whole situation with the shooting was more than they could handle alone.

They needed help.

With a deep sigh, he picked up his phone, punched in the number he knew by heart. His brother picked up on the third ring.

"What?" Alex sounded grumpy, maybe been sleepy.

"Hey, man. I didn't wake you, did I?"

"Aaron?" he asked. "What the hell are you doing calling me at… almost two o'clock in the morning?"

"It's only twelve-forty-five."

"No, you're an hour behind me. Ergo, it's closer to two for me. Hold on," he said and Aaron could hear the soft voice of his sister-in-law in the background. After a minute, Alex came back on the line. "This had better be good. You're taking me away from my wife."

"Well, I don't know how good it is. But it is important." He tried not to sound grim.

Alex knew him too well and the tone of Aaron's voice alarmed him. This was not going to be a pleasant conversation.

"Alright Aaron, I'm all ears. Tell me what's wrong."

"I need the number of that guy that helped you and Mel out in California. The private investigator."

"What's going on, brother?"

"Nothing. I just need it, okay?"

"No, no it's not okay. And I'm not giving you squat until you tell me what's going on."

Aaron sighed again, took another drink from his beer. Then, "Fine. Last night, actually two nights ago, I guess. Anyway, Ally and I were headed to her house to grab some dinner with her parents when someone took a shot at us."

The words had barely left his mouth when Alex shouted, "What?" Then, in a much quieter voice, he asked, "What do you mean someone took a shot at you? Did you see who it was?"

"No. It was dark out. We couldn't see anything. But we formed a little search party this morning and spent the better part of the day out there looking for any sign of who it was. Big Dave–that's Ally's Dad–he didn't find anything other than a few traces that someone *was* out in the woods.

Nothing concrete. And I thought, maybe, that your P.I. friend could help us out."

"He's an investigator, Aaron. I'm not one-hundred percent certain how he runs his business, but I'm pretty sure he at least needs a name so he knows *who* to investigate."

"Yeah, I know. Call me optimistic, but I'm hoping that maybe, with as small a town as Rosy Camp is, that he might be able to find out something. Look, I know it's probably a long shot, but I'm willing to try anything if it means I can keep Ally safe."

"How are things between you, two?"

Aaron paused, debated on how much he should tell his little brother. Alex already thought he was crazy coming to Montana to spend time with a girl he barely knew. But he remembered how quickly Alex had fallen for Mel and knew his brother would understand, if anyone could.

At least, he hoped so.

"They're good," he said at length. "Really good. She loves me."

Alex whistled low and chuckled. "And what about you? Do you feel the same?"

"I think so."

"You think? Look, you either love her, or you don't."

"I know that. I just… I'm waiting until I *know*. It wouldn't be fair to either of us if I told her I love her when I don't know for certain that I do. I don't want my heart broken again."

"You sound like a pansy."

"Shut up," Aar told Alex. "If you'd been through what I went through with Jess, you'd understand."

There was a pause on the other end of the line.

"I *do* understand. Really. And I don't blame you one bit. But remember what I said when you first got out there. If you don't think you're gonna eventually feel the same way for Ally that she does you, don't string her along. It wouldn't be right."

"I hear ya. And I do care about her, Alex. A lot. Getting involved so deeply scares me. But right now, my main concern is that her life is in danger." Aaron stood from the table, walked to the windows at the front of the house and stared into the blackness outside.

The night was so dark, he couldn't even make out the outline of the barn a few hundred yards away. Somewhere out there was a man who wanted to hurt Ally. Aaron swore he'd never let that happen.

"I'll do whatever it takes to keep her safe, Alex. With or without anyone's help."

"Alright, brother. You got a pen?" Alex asked then gave Aar the information he needed.

Everything from Ted Wilson's name and number to his email and mailing addresses. Aaron thanked his little brother for the info and right before they got off the phone, Alex added, "Promise me you'll call if you need any help up there."

Aaron hesitated. Alex would be here in a heartbeat if he asked him to come. He couldn't see the sense in Alex stepping into the line of fire, not yet anyway. He sighed and finally said. "I promise, and I mean it. If I can't handle things, I'll call in the cavalry. And thanks, Alex. I appreciate it."

"No thanks necessary, man. Keep me updated on what's going on. I'll be on the next flight out as soon as you give the word."

"Will do. Give my sister-in-law a kiss for me."

"With pleasure."

"And that's my queue to hang up. Later, Alex."

Aaron finished his beer, tossed the bottle in the trash and headed to his bedroom. He put his phone on the charger. Holding the little piece of paper in his hand, he debated whether he should call the P.I. immediately, but decided against it. Confiding in Alex was one thing, but he didn't really know this guy, Ted. He would give himself some time to decide how to approach him.

After brushing his teeth and stripping down to his boxers, he pulled the curtains closed on the windows and climbed into bed. Even though is body was exhausted, his mind was racing.

As he began to doze off, he pictured Ally, the way she'd looked at him as they stood in the hallway the night of the shooting. Her hazel eyes had sparkled in the low light and he swore he could still feel her emotions. He tried to focus on the good things that had recently come into his life rather than a faceless enemy.

Despite all that had taken place over the last forty-eight hours, he went to sleep with a smile on his face, content in the knowledge that Ally loved him.

•••••

September 6, 2015

Aaron dropped Fury's brush when he heard the tack room's door slam closed.

He shook himself out of the memories from two weeks ago—and his phone call with Alex—and peered over the gate to see who had joined him in the barn.

Jerry ambled out of the small room, saw Aaron in the stall and headed in his direction.

Aar stooped, picked up the brush and set it back in the bucket right as the older man reached him and hooked his arms over the top of the gate.

Jerry stood in stoic silence. Aaron finished with the horse, gave the big gelding a pat on the neck, then turned to the old stable master.

He knew the question was coming even before the words had left Jerry's mouth.

"Y'all find who fired the shot yet?"

"No, not yet."

"You planning on keeping up the search?" Aaron wasn't sure so he shrugged and Jerry went on. "What if there's another incident? What do you figure on doing then?"

"If there's something on your mind, Jerry, just ask. Don't play this runaround game. It doesn't suit you."

"Alright. I wanna know what you plan on doin' with my girl if she's in danger. You just gonna leave her to the fate of some unseen enemy? Or are you gonna get her out of here? Someplace safe."

"I'd love nothing more than to take Ally away, keep her locked up in some hotel room until this–whatever this is–blows over. Just like her Dad wanted. But you know as well as I do that she'd never go for that. She's not the type of woman to go cower in a corner at the first sign of trouble. She's going to want to fight."

"Yeah, I know. Girl ain't got the good sense God gave her."

"I don't know about that." Aaron said. "Just because she wants to face a threat head-on doesn't make her foolish. That shows guts, determination. Ally's strong willed. I can't see her backing down from a fight. She can take whatever life throws at her and..." Aaron stopped, realized he'd been about say how Ally wasn't afraid to love with everything she had. And that wasn't for him to share.

As far as he knew, no one else was aware of just how he and Ally felt about each other. For now, it needed to stay that way.

Jerry nodded his head and smiled, and Aaron noticed the man was missing a few teeth. But it wasn't the gaps in his mouth that drew his attention. A twinkle in the old man's eye let Aaron know he wasn't fooling anybody.

"What?" he asked Jerry, who shook his head, his grin broadening. "What's that look for? What are you so happy about?"

"Boy, if you can't figure it out on your own, then I'm darn sure not going to be the one to fill you in."

"Figure out wh..." he broke off when he felt the short hairs on the back of his neck stand on end. He knew he was being watched.

Aaron turned his head and spotted Ally standing in the doorway of the barn.

She leaned a hip on the wood and stuck her hands in her back pockets. The sun sunk behind her, cast a long shadow in front of her body and made her pale blue shirt seem darker, like the color of her jeans. Her straw cowboy hat rode low in her head, but not enough to block the way her eyes crinkled in the corners when she smiled at him. Suddenly arguing with Jerry didn't seem so important.

"We'll finish this later, old man," he said quietly and opened the stall gate, closed it softly behind him and walked over to Ally.

Aaron slid his hands in the holes her bent arms had formed, cupped his fingers together behind her back, pulled her close. He bent his head to kiss her and right as his lips touched Ally's, everything else was blocked out. Including Jerry's parting words.

"No, son. We won't."

Chapter 15

"Where no counsel is, the people fall: but in the
multitude of counsellers there is safety."
Proverbs 11:14

September 8, 2015

Ted Wilson sat at his desk in his office in Los Angeles, California, tapped out his last email of the day with a date and time to meet a client. It was the type of meeting he never enjoyed having, to deal with the type of surveillance his team never enjoyed being a part of.

But he reminded himself, just as he did his team of five, that sometimes they just had to take the "cheating spouse" cases to pay the bills.

"They can't all be high-profile, top secret, guns-a-blazing missions," he murmured to no one in particular as he hit send and closed down his laptop.

He reached up and squeezed the bridge of his nose between his index finger and thumb, massaged the tension headache that always worked its way down his face from his forehead.

Just as he was getting the pain to ease, his cell phone blared from beside his computer and the pain sharply reconnected as quick as he'd gotten it to go away. He sighed, lowered his hand, picked up his phone.

He squinted his eyes at the number he didn't recognize and sat up slowly as he got that feeling in the base of his spine. The one that said something big was about to go down and he needed to be on alert.

Warily, he answered the phone. "Yeah."

"Uh... Ted? I mean... Mr. Wilson?"

"Who's asking?"

"My name's Aaron. Aaron Lambert. I met you at my brother Alex's wedding to Melanie." Ted's unease relaxed a little, but his senses were still piqued. "I was hoping you'd be able to help me out with a problem."

"Depends on what your problem is. I'm not some man who's keen on charity cases."

"No!" Aaron spouted out quickly. "No, I know you're not. And it's not charity. I'd like to pay you."

"Let's stop beating around the bush here. Pay me for what?"

"Well, you see sir, I'm in Montana and my... girlfriend...?" he stopped as if he were expecting Ted to give him the answer. Ted remained silent. "Yeah, my girlfriend. She and I were shot at the other day."

"Sounds like a job for the police, not an old retired marine like me."

"There's only a small sheriff's department here. The problem is that this is hunting country and since, technically, we don't have any evidence, there's not a lot they can do."

"If you don't have any evidence, why are you so certain someone shot at you?"

"Because there weren't any hunters out that night and the shot was too close to have come from another property."

"That's it?" Ted asked, still not convinced that there was a problem.

"No. I feel it in my gut, Mr. Wilson. I know that's not enough for some people. And if you feel the same way, I'll hang up right now and never bother you again. You have my word. But somehow I don't peg you as the type of person to take that kind of intuition at face value."

Ted was quiet as he mulled over what the other man had said.

Aaron was right.

There were too many memories to count where a gut feeling had saved Ted's life when he'd been in Desert Storm. Not to mention all the times that same intuition had helped him solve a case. He knew better than anyone how important it was to follow those hunches. For him, Aaron's gut was enough.

"Alright, you have my attention Aaron. Why don't you start from the beginning?"

Chapter 16

"A man's heart deviseth his way: but the Lord
directeth his steps."
Proverbs 16:9

Ally walked into the bunkhouse without bothering to knock and shut the door quietly behind her. She stood for a minute, listened for any sign of Aaron. When she didn't hear anything, she assumed he was in the shower getting ready for their date tonight, and headed into the kitchen. She opened the fridge, saw a few beers and bottles of water along with a block of cheese and lunch meat. She grabbed the cheese and two beers, set them on the counter. She plucked a box of crackers from the shelf next to the refrigerator and got to work slicing the cheese.

As she laid the cheese and crackers on the cutting board and twisted off a cap to one of the beers, she heard Aaron's voice. She smiled, thought he was talking to her. But as she listened closer, she heard him say the name "Ted" several times. She set the beer down, tiptoed to the bedroom where he'd been staying, listened at the cracked door for a minute. When he spoke about the incident a couple weeks ago, she gave up eavesdropping–*Momma always said that was a nasty habit*–and pushed open the door.

Aaron stood on the other side of the room, faced the windows that looked out into the pasture with his cell phone pressed to his ear. When the door hit the wall he paused, looked over his shoulder at Ally. She saw a mix of emotions in his eyes. Surprise, worry. And if she wasn't mistaken, a little guilt, too. He smiled at her but it didn't reach his eyes.

She crossed her arms over her chest and cocked an eyebrow, intent to wait for him to get off the phone. At her stance, Aaron's shoulders slumped and he made no pretense of hiding what he'd been talking about. He watched her while he continued to relay the information about the shooting, the search, and something about feelings in the pit of his stomach.

Ally couldn't decide if she was angry that he felt the need to spread their business to God knew whom, or if she was relieved that he'd taken some sort of initiative. Probably both.

Plus, as she watched his mouth move, listened to the deep timbre of his voice when he spoke, she felt something else. A stirring in her own gut that had her craving the feel of his lips on her and the vibration of his voice against her skin. She swallowed thickly and sat down on the bed as she continued to wait, her knees too weak to hold her up when those feelings of wanting coursed through her.

"Yes," Aaron was saying, "that's right. Yeah, about an hour. Okay. That sounds great." He paused, listened while he stared at Ally and she tore her eyes away from him, focused on the wall across from her and picked out the tiny white daisies in the picture of a Montanan landscape in a dark brown, wooden frame. "I really appreciate this, Ted," Aaron said. "Truly. Okay, just give me a call when you're getting close and I'll come find you. Yeah. See you soon."

He ended the call and Ally heard him set the cell down on the nightstand next to the bed. She kept her gaze averted until he stood directly in her line of sight and blocked her view of the framed picture.

So instead, she stared at his shirt, a blue so dark it was almost black. And Ally knew if she were to look into his eyes, they would be darker, too. Like midnight pools instead of their normal cobalt.

But after several minutes of silence, Aaron took the option away from her.

He reached under her chin and tilted her face up so she had no choice but to look at him. And his damned beautiful eyes that searched hers with a pleading that was as plain as the nose on her face. *Pleading for what?* she wondered.

"Are you mad?" he finally asked.

"What do I have to be mad about, Aaron?"

"I called a friend, asked for his help in finding out who's after us." She nodded her head because she'd suspected as much. "I'm sorry I didn't bring it up to you. Or your Dad. But... I'm worried that we're in over our heads here, Ally. And I felt... I really believe that we could use some professional expertise."

"Who did you call?"

"Ted Wilson. I got his number from my brother. He helped Alex and Mel out a while back with____"

"I know who he is," Ally cut Aaron off, "and I know what he did." She paused, licked her lips and took a deep breath. "And I'm not mad, because I think you're right. But next time, don't make those kinds of decisions without me. Without at least asking for my input."

"Would you have argued with me if I'd have brought it up to you?"

"Probably. But," she said when he tried to talk, "I would have eventually agreed. I may be headstrong, but I'm not stupid."

"I never said you were. I just wanna keep you safe, baby."

Ally felt her anger fade. She really loved it when he called her that. And, though she'd never admit it, she loved "elf" more. Even if she didn't know where it came from.

"I know that, Aaron. Who's going to keep you safe, though?"

He squatted down on his haunches, cupped her cheeks in his warm hands. "We'll keep each other safe. Okay?"

"Okay," she whispered then said, "Are you gonna kiss me now?"

"Do you want me to?" Ally nodded silently and his hands tightened on her face. "Then it'd be my pleasure."

Aaron wasted no time, just dove right in and attacked Ally's mouth. The force took her off guard and she fell back on the bed. Aaron followed her, lay down beside her and kissed her almost feverishly, like it might be the last time they would ever be connected like this. She wrapped her arms around his shoulders, slipped her fingers under the seam of his sleeves, lightly traced the sinew of his biceps. They flexed and quivered under her touch and she smiled into their kiss. Aaron broke off, stared down at her with a devious look in his eyes.

"You think that's funny, huh?" Again, she nodded without a word. "We'll see about that," he said and moved back to her lips.

But right before he touched her waiting mouth, he turned his head, kissed a trail from her ear to her throat. Ally's eyes rolled back before they fluttered closed and her grip tightened on his arms. When he gave a gentle lick to her pounding pulse, her hands fell from Aaron and landed with a soft thud on the bed. She arched her neck, ached to have him continue his sweet assault.

She felt his hands slide down her face, past her neck and chest and settle on her sides. Her eyes popped open and she looked down, saw his open eyes watching her as he kissed her neck and licked her throat. Then he winked at her. Right as his hands curled around her ribcage and he tickled her.

Ally bucked her upper body, tried to dispel his weight so she could escape. But he was too big and too strong and she was too weak when she started laughing. His hold tightened on her sides and his fingers deftly moved harder and faster, tickled with an enthusiasm that Ally just knew bordered on sick pleasure. She laughed so hard she cried and her tears blurred his image, made it seem like there were two Aarons with two sets of lips on her neck and two tongues driving her crazy.

"Please, stop!"

He lifted his head slightly but kept his hands on their mark, never stopped their attack on her ribs. "Still think it's funny, Elf?"

"No! No," she sucked in a quick breath, "it's not funny. I swear, I won't laugh anymore. Just please, stop tickling me."

He didn't stop, not yet. And Ally was taken back to another time just like this one, barely six weeks ago, when she and Aaron had fished and shared stories of their pasts and made a connection that had led them here, with her loving him more and more every day.

Suddenly it didn't tickle anymore, not as she thought about how much it was true. How much she loved him. How much she desperately wanted his love in return.

Aaron must have sensed her change. He stopped tickling, lifted his head and stared at her. Worry made his brow furrow and his lips turn down into a slight frown. "What's wrong? I didn't hurt you, did I?"

"No. Not yet." The crease between his eyebrows deepened so Ally went on. "And you won't, as long as you don't break my heart."

"Never, baby. I promise."

"Don't write checks you can't cash, Aaron."

"I'm not. Honestly."

"Then how can you make a promise like that? When you have no idea what you might feel tomorrow or next week or next year?"

"Because I love you."

•••••

He hadn't planned to say it.

He hadn't planned to mean it.

But he did.

On both counts.

Aaron loved her.

He knew the truth behind his words as soon as they'd left his mouth. Knew that his heart had spoken the truth. He knew that his path, this path with Ally, was all God's doing, and he couldn't be more grateful. But Ally must not have believed them.

As soon as he said it, she froze, held her breath, then whispered a barely there, "What?"

"I love you, Allyson." He took a deep breath, gave a small laugh at the way his heart felt fuller from saying it again. So he told her once more. "I love you."

Ally closed her eyes and a tear rolled from the corner of her eyelid. Aaron bent forward, kissed the salty droplet away. Gave small pecks to each of her closed eyes, to her pert, little nose. He kissed her cheeks, rosy and flushed from laughing. When she opened her eyes and looked at him, joy evident in the sage-green depths with flecks of gold flickering in her glossy irises, he kept his gaze connected with hers as he kissed her lips. Once, only once, before he sat back up, held his weight up with his hands on either side of her head. Ally beamed up at him and he released a breath he hadn't realized he'd held.

"I love you, too." He rested his forehead against hers, too caught up in emotion to think of any romantic words to say. "So much, Aaron." He ran his hands absently through her long brown hair, so dark in the now-dim room it was almost the color of hickory.

They stayed like that–with Aar running his fingers through her hair and Ally running hers up and down his spine–until the sun had fully set and the bedroom was cast in utter darkness.

As the day ended, Aaron couldn't wait to start the next one. For the last few weeks, he'd been so caught up in Ally's safety and who was after them that he hadn't paid attention to just how much his feelings for her had grown.

But now that he knew, he wanted to spend every waking moment–and every sleeping moment–exploring and treasuring and nurturing their love until it was an unbreakable entity all on its own.

You sound like a freakin' woman, Aar. He did, but he didn't care.

Never, not even with Jess, had Aaron ever felt something so raw and untamed yet flawless and serene at the same time. Never had he felt something so blessed by God, that he'd be a fool to ignore it. To not cherish it for the gift it was.

He made a promise for the second time that night–to himself and to God–right then, to never take for granted what had been laid before him in the form of this beautiful, strong and spirited imp of a woman.

And that included not taking for granted what their bodies had been made for by God. The longer they laid here, on his bed, the more he realized how much he wanted her. And he couldn't, wouldn't, undervalue their virtue. Despite the fact that they'd both been married, this time, with each other, they were starting over. And that meant protecting every aspect of their relationship. Including the parts that hadn't come to fruition yet.

With reluctance, he lifted himself away from her warm body and stood up, held his hands out for her. She took them, her small fingers curled around his palms, and he pulled her up from the bed. "Let me walk you back to the house."

"What about our date?"

He looked out the windows at the stars and moon that shone bright against an inky sky, looked back at Ally with a raised eyebrow. "I'm pretty sure we missed our chance. Plus it's dark out and your Dad is already going to be pissed at me for bringing you home at this time. I'll make it up to you, though. I promise."

"Another promise?"

"Yep," he admitted. "I'm full of them."

"You're full of something."

"Watch it, Elf." He backed away from her, headed through the door and into the living room with Ally right behind him.

"Oh, I am. Very closely." He peeked over his shoulder, caught her staring at his butt.

"You're making me feel objectified."

"Oh, schnookems," she teased, "does the big, strong man not like a little attention?"

Aaron stopped abruptly and Ally ran into his back. He turned around, caught her up in his arms and lifted her off the floor so they were at eye level. He squeezed her tight and she squealed. "Does the beautiful, little woman not like being manhandled?" She scowled at him.

"Little. Woman?"

"Yeah. *My* little woman."

"And don't you forget it."

"Never," he said. "Now let's get you home."

September 12, 2015

Aaron hadn't forgotten about his promise to make up for his and Ally's lost date the other day. But they'd been so busy hauling hay and fixing fences this week in preparation for a coming storm that he hadn't been able to keep that promise.

Until today.

Finally, after four days, he and Ally would pick up where they'd left off that night in the bunkhouse. He was on his way to the main house to pick her up and head into Rosy Camp town proper, for a real date. Not that he didn't thoroughly enjoy riding horseback all over their ranch, but he wanted to do this right. And that started with Big Dave.

Aar knocked on the front door–strange in and of itself because he'd gotten so used to using the mudroom door–and stood back into yellow glow of the porch light. He watched the moths fly into the glass surrounding the light, spotted a few lightening bugs out of the corner of his eye, their green-yellow tails bright in the darkness. An owl called somewhere in the distance, its hoot loud with the silent night.

Aar was just about to knock again when Dave answered a minute later. He glowered down at Aaron with his burly arms crossed over his chest.

"What do you want?"

"I'm here to take your daughter out on a date, sir."

"And just who gave you permission to do that?"

"I did," came a small voice from behind Dave. Suzi walked around her big husband, smiled up at Aaron. "David, invite the boy in and stop acting like some overprotective bear." Aaron laughed, remembered the time he'd compared the older man to the same animal, but stopped as soon as Dave cut his eyes in Aar's direction. But he couldn't hold in the snort when Dave growled at him. Suzi, not intimidated by her spouse in the least, grabbed Aaron's arm and guided him inside. "Ally will be out in just a minute. Would you like a glass of iced tea? A beer?"

"Don't be giving that boy alcohol when he's gonna be driving around my Punkin'!" came Big Dave's booming voice from the entry hall behind them.

"Nothing for me Suzi. But thank you."

They walked into the great room and sat down, Aaron and Suzi on the cream-colored leather sofa and Big Dave on his matching recliner. A sheepskin rug took up most of the floor, hiding the dark brown, original wooden floors underneath. A mix of animal heads hung from three of the walls. Everything from mountain goats to several types of deer to foxes. And yes, there was a bear head over the large pine mantle.

Despite the summer season, the temperature had dropped outside to the mid-forties and Dave had started a small fire. Which wasn't actually small, but seemed that way in the oversized, Montana Gold River Rock fireplace. The burning embers crackled and popped in the quiet room.

Once upon a time, Aaron might have been nervous about sitting here, with his girlfriend's parents, while he waited on said girlfriend to make her appearance. But now he knew these people, the Marxes. He respected them. He felt like he belonged. And that made any sense of uneasiness fly out the window.

"So where are you two headed tonight?" Dave asked at he took a swig from his mug of coffee, steam from the hot drink floating over his hand.

"We're going into town to grab some dinner at the Rosy Camp Steakhouse," Aaron told them. "And I thought maybe we'd go for a walk around town or head to the movies."

"I'm not sure that's a good idea. What with all the hoopla that's been happening around here."

"David, nothing has gone on since that first night. I'm sure everything is fine. Let these two have a nice evening without having to worry about anything. Or anyone," she added when Dave tried to talk. Dave frowned, not liking his wife's decision, but chose not to argue with her. She nodded her head once, satisfied with his agreement. Then to Aaron, "I am going to ask you one thing, Aaron."

"Anything Mrs. Marx. Suzi," he amended when she shook her finger at him for using her formal name.

"That storm that's headed our way is supposed to be a big one. Really big. Please be careful out there tonight. And ignore my husband, but if it looks like you two are going to get caught in it, I'd just as sure rather you stay at the motel in town than try to drive back here." Aaron tilted his head to the side, took a breath and opened his mouth to argue. But he was cut off before he could make his case. From Big Dave.

"She's right, son. Much as I hate to admit it. I'd rather you two just skip this "date" business altogether. But even I can admit that you've earned a night away. So just... well, like Suzi said, be careful."

Aaron's gaze bounced between the husband and wife for a minute as he processed what they'd said. It wasn't that they basically just gave him permission to spend the night with their daughter. If it came down to it, he and Ally would get separate rooms at the inn. What had him feeling confused in the most unexpected–but wonderful–way, was how they worried not only for their daughter's safety, but his too. He knew how much of a leap of faith they were taking in handing over their daughter's well-being to him in the midst of what had taken place several weeks ago. And he realized how much it meant to *him* to be included in the Marx family, to be thought of as one of them. To be cared about as if he were their own son, not a guest.

Aaron knew right then that he wanted to always feel like this with Ally's family. And he wanted her to feel the same way with his.

Holy crap, Aaron thought as the revelation hit. *Am I actually thinking what I'm thinking?*

He paused his internal debate when he heard footsteps down the hall. He looked up and watched as Ally made her way into the room and over to the back of the couch. He stood when she reached him, ran his appreciative gaze up and down her body, not quite believing his eyes.

Her long hair was down and curled around her shoulders and back. The locks framed her face that was normally free of much makeup. But tonight, she had on a layer of golden shadow that brought out the honey in her eyes, and her thick black lashes lowered when she caught him staring. Her lips glistened with a dark pink gloss and he wanted so badly to kiss her and see if her lips tasted like the raspberries they looked like. She wore a long blue dress with spaghetti straps, her toned shoulders on display for the world to see. The material looked soft and had a faint shimmer when the light hit it, like the finest silk. On her feet, she wore a pair of wedge black sandals that crisscrossed up her ankles and gave her an added four inches of height. Of course, even with the extra boost, she was still a good eight inches shorter than Aaron.

He slowly brought his eyes back up her body until he connected with hers. *Yes, I most definitely was thinking of spending the rest of my life with her.* He wanted to reach out and stroke her face. But he balled his hands into fists instead, afraid he might take it too far with that private confession still floating around in his head and heart. When he tried to talk, his voice cracked and Ally smiled. Aaron cleared his throat and finally managed, "You look beautiful."

Ally's grin grew and she stepped around the couch until she stood directly in front of him. She ran her hand lightly down the navy, button-down shirt Aaron wore, took his hand in hers. "You're not so bad yourself, handsome."

"You trying to sweet talk me into a steak dinner?"

"Is it working?"

"Might be."

"Then yes, I am."

"Well okay. Shall we?"

He held out his arm, bent at the elbow, and waited for Ally to place her hand in the crook. She did and he led them to the front door. He heard footsteps following them but was too caught up in Ally to look behind him or care.

But the big hand on his arm stopped him before he and Ally made it out the door. He looked over his shoulder, turned completely around when he saw Dave and Suzi had both followed them.

"You remember what I said," Ally's Dad reiterated.

"Yes sir."

"And have a good time." This from Suzi. Ally let go of Aaron's hand, leaned forward and gave her Mom a hug. The older woman whispered something in Ally's ear but it was too quiet for him or Dave to hear. Dave gave a little scowl in Aaron's direction when Ally giggled and Aar just shrugged his shoulders. Suzi released her hold on Ally, pushed her back toward Aaron and added, "Be safe," for the second time that night, and Dave closed the front door.

"Well, what do ya say, Elf? Would you like to go have dinner with me tonight?"

"I'd love nothing more."

"Except me."

"Not necessarily," she joked as they reached the truck. Aaron opened the passenger door, held her hand while she hopped up inside. "I'll let you know after I eat the steak."

•••••

Ally and Aaron pulled up in front of the Rosy Camp Steakhouse just after seven o'clock. He made her wait while he got out of the truck and walked around to open her door. The feminist in her wanted to protest. But the conservative roots that coursed through her veins–thanks in large part to her Momma and Grandmamma–had her smiling graciously, blushing even, at his thoughtfulness and chivalrous conduct.

They walked into the restaurant and waited while the hostess–a cute little brunette named Samantha who Ally used to babysit–went to check for an empty table.

Aaron looked around the space while they stood there, took in the high ceiling covered in a rusted corrugated tin and the matching tin on all the walls. The floors were just concrete, but they'd been stained the color of sandstone and polished to a high shine and reflected the white glow of the chandeliers that hung from the ceiling every fifteen feet. Booths with black and brown leather seats lined the sides of the restaurant and tables with either four or six chairs were scattered all over the rest of the space. Inside, it looked like an old barn or metal building rather than a four-star steakhouse.

Which was one of the reasons that Ally loved it so much. Aside from hunting season–when every restaurant and spare room in town were occupied–the place usually stayed empty. Like now. There were probably only about a dozen other patrons in the room and they were all locals. Which was both a blessing and a curse.

She enjoyed the lack of loudmouth weekenders, but knew that there'd be calls and questions about who her new "guy" was. Not that she was embarrassed by Aaron; she just didn't want to share him yet. Didn't want to share what they had with the rest of the county.

Maybe not ever.

When Samantha returned, they followed her to the back of the restaurant. As they weaved their way through the tables, Aaron's hand possessively on her lower back, Ally listened to the strands of a Vince Gill song on the speakers from the ceiling. And when he said *Just look at us*, she felt like everyone in the place was doing just that. When they reached a booth in the back corner, with half of the table shrouded in darkness, Ally thanked Samantha and slid onto the cool leather. Aaron sat down right beside her, slung his arm over the top of the booth and curled his hand around Ally's shoulders. They faced the rest of the restaurant, and neither of them could miss the curious glances and stares they got from the rest of the people.

"Ten bucks says your Momma gets at least ten calls tomorrow," Aaron whispered in her ear.

"Twenty says it's at least double that," Ally countered and turned her face to him. Which put her lips right at his, an incidence too sweet to pass up.

So she kissed him, right there on his full and wet lips, while all the people in the restaurant looked on. She didn't linger, but stayed locked onto his mouth long enough to give a quick swipe of her tongue across his lower lip. He sucked in a breath and she backed away. His eyes widened at her boldness and she said with a smirk, "What? Might as well give 'em something to talk about."

"Well in that case..." he broke off as he slid his hand under the table, a wicked grin on his face. She slapped his hand away and laughed.

"I said something to *talk* about, not something to have a heart attack over."

"Fine."

Just then, their waiter showed up and took their order. They both had the ribeye, cooked medium-rare, with sides of au gratin potatoes and salads. Aaron ordered a bottle of Shiraz to go with their steaks. Fifteen minutes later, they sat in a comfortable silence and ate. Ally stopped, took a sip of her wine and watched Aaron demolish his steak. He glanced up, saw her staring.

"What?"

"Nothing. Just wondering when the last time you ate was."

"Ha. Ha. I'm hungry, that's all. And I'm a man. You put a steak in front of me, I'm gonna eat."

"You have to be a man to eat a steak?"

"No. But I'm not sure I'd trust any man who doesn't enjoy a good cut of beef like this. And it is good. Really good," he said and cut off another huge bite.

"Does that surprise you?"

"No," he answered. "Maybe a little. I didn't expect to get a steak that you could cut with a fork in a small town like Rosy Camp."

"We're just full of surprises."

At that he stopped, laid his fork down, reached over and grabbed onto her hand. He gave her fingers a squeeze and with a smile in his eyes, said, "Yes. And you're the best one."

"Don't be such a romantic. It's weird."

"Not sweet?" She shook her head no, even though the answer was most definitely yes. He leaned closer to her, brought his free hand up and ran his thumb over her lower lip. Then he brought his thumb to his mouth and licked something off. "You had a little wine left there."

"Well we can't have that." She ran her tongue along her lower lip even though she knew there wasn't any wine left. And just as she'd hoped, she got a rise out of Aaron. His gaze zeroed in on her mouth, his chest heaved with a sudden breath. "Wouldn't want any of it to go to waste," she whispered.

"I'm not hungry anymore," Aaron admitted. "You ready to leave?"

"Yes."

He quickly flagged down their waiter and asked for the bill. After he'd paid, he rose from the booth, held out a hand for Ally. She took it and let him help her up. They stood there, chest to chest, and she felt all the eyes that had forgotten about them as they ate come back to rest on them, again. Without warning, Aaron wrapped his arm around her back, dipped her low and kissed her hard.

Horrified at what the people–*her* people–would say, Ally tried to push him off and stand back up. But he held her firm and, lowered as she was, she had no strength to fight him off. She finally gave up and wrapped her arms around his shoulders, squeezed tight to the muscles that flexed beneath her palms.

Might as well make this worth it, she thought and tilted her head, kissed Aaron deeper, let her tongue dance with his. Ally smiled at the catcalls that came from everyone that surrounded them. Aaron lifted his head and stared down at her, a twinkle in his bright blue eyes.

"Mission accomplished."

"What mission?"

"The one where I win the game. Don't even act like that's not what you were doing," he said when she'd opened her mouth to protest. She grinned up at him because he was right. Then, "And now, everyone in Rosy Camp will know that we're together. And that you're off limits."

"Awfully possessive, don't you think?" He stood up straight, brought Ally with him and kept his hand firmly on her back, close to him. She rested her hands on his chest and he gently cupped her cheek, gave her one last parting peck on the tip of her nose.

"Of you? Always."

Chapter 17

"Eye for eye, tooth for tooth, hand for hand, foote
for foote."
Exodus 21:24

Aaron kept his arm wrapped around Ally's shoulders as they walked from the restaurant and out to the truck. He lifted his face and smelled the air, could almost taste the rain that he knew was headed their way. He hoped they'd left with enough time to make it back to the ranch. As much as he wanted to make their date last a little longer, he knew they were out of time.

"I think we need to head back."

Ally looked up into the dark night too, no doubt seeing the same clouds zoom through the sky that he saw. "I think you're right. That storm is coming fast." She looked back at him and smiled. "Thank you for a wonderful date. Even if it is getting short."

"You're welcome. Thank you for coming with me."

"Hm… stay at home and listen to Daddy snore in his recliner, or go on a hot date with a hot man… wasn't a very tough decision."

"I don't know whether to be offended that you decided I was a better choice than your Dad, or happy at the fact that you just called me hot."

"Oh please. You know you're good looking. What, with your toned body and sexy muscles-" she ran her hands down his arms and across his belly that clenched in response to her touch, "-to your beautiful blue eyes-" she leaned forward and lightly touched her lips to his closed lids, "-to that perfect mouth that borders on sinful." He smiled and she ran her index finger across his lower lip. "Don't act like it's some sort of surprise. Modesty doesn't become you."

"Sure it does," he argued. "You just said it yourself. I'm hot. And I think that includes the times when I'm not afraid to show a little humility."

"Humility. Is that what they're calling overconfidence these days?"

"I'm not *over*confident. " He wrapped his hands around her waist, curled his fingers against her hipbones. They almost reached all the way around her, she was so petite. And he loved it.

Loved her.

"I'm just the right amount. Especially when you give me every reason to believe that you like it." Now he walked his fingers up her back, slipped his hands under her curtain of hair, skimmed the skin of her neck.

"What makes you so sure that I like that?" she asked, breathless.

He lowered his head and spoke softly in her ear. "Because you're breathing faster, and your heart's pounding, and you just licked your lips, dying for me to kiss you."

"Then do it, already."

So he went in, slowly, seductively, intent to draw the anticipation out. He felt her breath on his mouth when he was only a hairsbreadth away. He heard her heart hammering away in her chest. *Or maybe that's my heart.* He wasn't sure and he didn't care. He moved in all the way and right as he began to lay his lips on hers, he felt it.

The first raindrop.

"Crap," he muttered and broke away, quickly opened the door and practically shoved Ally inside while he ignored her squeal. He ran around the hood of the truck and got inside just as the skies opened up and the downpour began. "So much for trying to get out of here before the storm hit."

"Yeah," she agreed and leaned forward to look out windshield. Despite his quickness, large drops of rain had fallen on her face and hair. The dampness sparkled in the truck's interior light, made her look just like the ethereal fairy he imagined her to be.

His throat tightened at the emotion that swelled in his chest when he looked at her. Love, yes. Protectiveness, most definitely. But there was something else, too. Something more transcendent than just the feelings of the heart. As he looked at Allyson, he knew it was his *soul* that had become fulfilled. The other half to his being, just like Adam and Eve.

"I thought we'd have more time to make it back before it got this bad." She looked over at him then said, "I'm afraid this might be too rough to drive in, Aaron. I think my parents might have been right. We probably need to find a place to hunker down in until this storm passes. At least enough so we can see more than ten feet in front of us." When he didn't say anything, just continued to stare at her, she added with a frown, "Are you okay?"

"Yes."

"Are you sure?"

"Yes."

She sighed, apparently exasperated at his one-word answers. "Then why are you staring at me like that?"

"Because you're beautiful."

She pulled down the visor and looked at her reflection. She ran a finger underneath her eyes, showed him the black mascara that had run down her cheeks. "My makeup is gone. It looks like I've been crying for days. My hair is a mess," she ran a hand through her damp and tangled locks, "and my dress is probably ruined." Aaron used all his willpower to not look down at her dress. He just knew the silky material would be translucent now that it was wet, and there were some things a man couldn't control when confronted with an attractive woman's body. "*Beautiful* is not the word I would use to describe myself right now."

"Okay," he countered, "stunning, then. Gorgeous. Breathtaking." She cut him off before he could go on.

"Alright, alright, Casanova. You made your point."

"Not yet, I haven't."

"Then why don't you go ahead and make it so we can figure out where we're going to stay for the next little while."

"I love you." Ally lost some of her bravado at those three words that Aaron enjoyed saying more and more every day.

"I love you, too, Aar."

"Really?" She nodded her head. "Good." Now her brow furrowed in confusion.

"Why is that good?"

"Just hear me out before you say anything, okay?"

He waited until she agreed. Then he turned in his seat so he faced her, reached across the truck and took her hands in his. They were cool from the rain and he watched as he rubbed them together in between his to warm them. Really, he was just buying himself time. *Man up, Aaron.* He took a deep breath and looked back up into her eyes that regarded him curiously. He felt like his silence made her nervous so he quit lollygagging and finally just spit it out.

"I love you. A lot. I mean…. I love you more than I thought would be possible. Not for me, not again. And I want you… I need you… crap, I'm screwing this up." He closed his eyes, ran a hand over his forehead. Her fingers wrapped around his and brought his hand down. The look on her face wasn't confused anymore. Or nervous. It was compassionate, loving and hopeful. When she curled their hands together, brought them to her lips and gave the connection a tender kiss, he wasn't nervous anymore, either.

"After Jess, I wasn't sure I'd ever be able to love someone again. I definitely didn't think I'd ever want to put my faith and trust in another woman. But God has a funny way of bringing two people together, doesn't He? And I think, I believe that's what He's done here. With us. I know He brought us together so we could heal each other. So we could learn from each other." He pulled his hand free from hers, cupped her cheek, ran his thumb along her jawline and held her still as he moved closer to her.

"So we could love each other. I believe God has given us a second chance, Allyson. A chance to forget the past and what was done to us, just like it says in Isaiah, and to focus on the here and now and what He's put right in front of us. For me, that's you. I want to focus on you and what we have together."

He wiped away a few tears that fell from the corners of her eyes. "I want to focus on our future. I know this isn't ideal or even normal. But since when have we have been a normal couple, you know? I think it's the abnormal relationship we have, the spiffs and the sarcasm and the love that shines through it all, that makes this, *us*, so special. And I don't ever want to lose it. If that means doing something out-of-the-ordinary, then I'll choose that road every time. Because you'll be at the end of it, waiting.

"Allyson Marx, will you marry me?"

•••••

Even though when Aaron started talking and floundered on his words she'd had an idea of where he was going, the question still took Ally off guard.

Maybe because, like him, she hadn't planned to ever get married again. She hadn't planned to be so willing to give her heart to someone else. After Ben, she'd never wanted to face the hurt and humiliation and anger she'd faced with him. So she figured she'd stay single the rest of her life and take the chance of that happening out of the picture.

Then Aaron had strolled into her picture, and the colors went from dark and dreary to bright and full of life. And now that she'd been reintroduced to the beauty of the world, she didn't want to go back into the dark. She wanted to bask in the light with him and she wanted to do it forever.

But there was one problem.

"Aaron..." she paused and bit her lip, afraid of how he'd react. When his shoulders sunk and his face dropped like a deflated balloon, her fear disappeared. She couldn't let him sit there, two feet from her, and think that she didn't feel the same way. "Of course I want to marry you. But there is a small... issue." Now he tilted his head to the side, confusion on his face. Until the light bulb went off. He blew out a heavy breath with a small laugh and shook his head.

"I know," he said. "I know I need to ask your father. And I will, I promise. I'd actually thought about it earlier this evening. Then you walked into the room and all I could focus on was you. It was like I had tunnel mind____"

"You mean tunnel vision?" she interrupted.

"No, I meant tunnel mind. It wasn't just that you were all I could *see*. You were all I could focus on or think about. Every part of me tuned into you and all other thoughts and feelings went by the wayside. When you walked into that room, you were all there was."

"Awe, Aaron. That's probably the sweetest thing anyone has ever said to me."

"Don't get used to it. I'm bound to make you mad and say the wrong thing and mess up. A lot. But always remember that my heart is in the right place. My heart is with you." He got a mischievous look in his eye and smirked. Ally waited to hear what was about to come out of his mouth with a mixture of suspicion and happy anticipation. "So I guess… if I do something wrong, it could technically be *your* fault, since you have my heart."

She scowled at him but he saw right through her mock anger. "Don't even think about putting your faults on me, buddy."

"How about if I put something else on you?" He wiggled his eyebrows for added effect.

"Don't go putting the cart before the horse, either."

"I'm not. And I won't."

"I know."

"So."

"So," she repeated, purposefully playing coy. She knew what he wanted, but he was going to have to work for it. It didn't take long.

"You're gonna make me ask again, aren't you?" She smiled at him, nodded her head. "Okay, I will. But," he added when she started to talk, "not before I have a chance to talk your Dad. If we're going to do this, we're going to do it right."

Now it was her turn to look a little deflated. She thought he was going ask her again. Now, not later. "Al-right," she said slowly. "Are you going to tell me when you plan on talking to him?" He shook his head no. "Why?" He didn't answer, only tapped his forefinger on the side of his nose. "Fine, keep your secrets," she huffed. To which he laughed. *Laughed!*

Instead of adding fuel to the fire that he brewed inside her, she turned to face the windshield again, crossed her arms over her chest for emphasis. Apparently, that was even funnier because his laugh just got louder. Much as she wanted to maintain her air of irritation, she had to admit that his booming laugh echoing off the windows and doors inside the truck was infectious. She giggled once, turned her face to the side window to hide her smile. He saw it anyway.

"If you're going to laugh every time you get angry, we're going to have a very fun next fifty years." Now she cut her eyes at him, but kept her mouth closed. "Maybe sixty."

"Just how old to you plan to get before you die?"

"As old as it takes to ensure we have an eternity together."

"Doesn't that happen the moment we say 'I do?'"

"I sure hope so," he said softly, smile fixed on his face, but thankfully not laughing anymore. "Okay, Elf. Let's get out of here."

"What about the rain?" she asked then looked out the window, gasped in shock. "When did it stop?"

"A few minutes ago. We've been sitting here for almost an hour, baby."

"Yeah, but… the storm was supposed to last most of the night."

Aaron shrugged his shoulders at her bafflement. "Maybe God decided to clear it out early, kinda like He cleared the way for our future."

Ally liked that scenario so she agreed. "Yeah. Maybe." She grinned over at him, reached for his hand and added, "Let's go home."

September 25, 2015

I will not pester him. I will not pester him. No matter how anxious I get, I am not *going to pester him.* Ally repeated the mantra over and over in her head, hoped that maybe she'd be able to listen to it. But with every passing day that she saw Aaron, spent time with him, and he didn't ask her to marry him again, she got more and more nervous.

What if he'd changed his mind? What if her Daddy had said no? Had he even asked her Dad yet? *He said he was going to. Of course he's going to. We've just been busy, Allyson. Take a chill pill.*

And that was true. They'd been swamped at the ranch trying to get ready for their first hunters for black bear and mountain goat seasons, both of which were already underway. There were other seasons, too. But bear and goat had always been Marx Ranch and Game's specialty, so that's where their focus stayed.

Like now.

Ally rode Trixie down the fence line, checked for breaks or holes that needed to be mended, marked those spots in her notebook. The sun was high in the sky and not a single cloud marred the pale blue canvas overhead. She paused in her forward motion to look up and admire the beauty. She found herself doing this more often these days, ever since the rainstorm night. She constantly noticed her surroundings. She hadn't done this since she was just a young and impressionable teenager who thought the world was her oyster.

Then she'd gone off to college and woken up to the harsh truths of life and her daydreams had turned into reality. And the reality was that not everything in life was big and beautiful. And, sometimes, you just had to drag through the days because that was what was expected.

Ever since her divorce, Ally had done nothing to make the time pass, other than her job here at the ranch. She hadn't had a life, not really. But now that she had one on the horizon with Aaron, it seemed all she could do was stop and smell the roses. She didn't want to let life pass her by in a blur. She wanted to embrace each and every moment with Aaron by her side.

So stop obsessing over when he's going to ask you again. Pledge firmly in place, she laid her hands forward, ready to let Trixie continue on. But before she gave her mare a kick, the ever-present man behind her cleared his throat. Her head dropped down to her chest and she heaved out a heavy breath. "What is it Jack?"

"What? Oh, nothing," he mumbled in response.

Ally turned in her saddle, stared at the older man behind her who'd been a longtime friend of her father's and a constant figure in her life since she was just a little girl, like a long-lost uncle. He wasn't as tall as her Daddy–not many people were–but he still stood over six-feet tall. His black hair was speckled with gray at the temples and his dark green eyes had faded over the years to an almost mossy-gray that were always glossy behind the glasses he'd started wearing several years ago as his eyesight faded. Those eyes wouldn't meet hers just now, instead looked all around as if the trees and dirt and birds were the most fascinating things he'd ever seen. "'Nothing' my butt. Something's on your mind, so why don't you just spit it out?"

He sighed and hung his head for a second before he looked up at her. His eyes held a note of something almost like uneasiness, the corners wilted like a dying flower. "I've just been wondering," he began, "if anyone has thought to talk to Ben or his family about what happened."

Why hadn't I thought of that? Ally wondered to herself. It made perfect sense. Ben had been so upset when she'd divorced him, even yelled at her as she'd walked out of the courtroom that "They weren't over!" and added something to the effect of her not being able to undo what God had joined. She'd never taken those parting words seriously, had always assumed that Ben would move on and forget about her and what they'd had. What *he'd* destroyed.

But what if she'd been wrong? Would Ben really stoop so low as to fire shots at her and her new boyfriend? It's been three years since they divorced. Could he still harbor those resentful feelings? Even after all this time? She wasn't sure, but she realized the need to at least check on it.

"I don't know, Jack. But I'll tell Daddy, see what he says and what he thinks we should do."

"No, don't do that."

"Why? It begs to be checked out."

"Yeah. But why don't you let me look into it first? If something happens and I'm wrong, the last thing Dave needs is to be in a war with the Willis family."

"What makes you think he'd end up in a war?" she asked. Jack lowered his head, gave her a look from over the top of his glasses that spoke more than a thousand words. She gave a humorless laugh.

"You're right. If Daddy suspected Ben had something to do with this, he'd go in like a bat out of hell and worry about the consequences later."

"Exactly," Jack agreed. "And he doesn't need that. Not with hunting season here. He needs all the paying customers he can get. If Dave starts a war with old man Willis, you can bet your ass he'll make sure you father loses every single one of the hunters scheduled to come here. And with seventy percent of your income coming from hunters, y'all can't afford that."

"I know. But I don't think you should be the one to talk to Ben or his parents about this. It's my problem, I'll do it."

"And have your Dad come after me for letting you? No way, I don't think so! I'll do it, and I'll let you know what they say."

"But____" Ally started to argue.

"No buts, Allyson. You're not going to move me on this." She stared at Jack, at the square set of his shoulders that were still strong, at the clench of his jaw, the steely look in his eyes that were no longer uneasy but bright and determined. And she knew he was right, there'd be no budging him. So she nodded her assent. "Good. Now let's finish this fence and head on back to the house. Your Mom's making her famed shepherd's pie for dinner and invited me to stay. I'm getting hungry."

October 8, 2015

"Punkin'? Come in here for a minute, would you?" Ally's Dad called from the dining room.

"Coming, Daddy." She rinsed off the last plate from dinner, placed it in the dishwasher, closed it and started the cycle. She dried off her hands with a towel and hung it back on the oven door, grabbed her tea from the counter and took a quick sip.

"Today, Allyson!"

"Yes sir!" she said and then to herself, "Geez, someone's impatient tonight." She walked into the dining room, saw her father still at his place at the head of the table with Momma to his left and Aaron to his right. No big deal, normally. Except that now they all had a serious look on their faces. Something was off and the hairs on the back of her neck rose in alarm. "What's going on?"

"Sit down, honey. We'd like to talk with you." This from her mother.

Ally moved her gaze over the three people in front of her, tried to gauge the situation. Momma put on a sweet smile, which effectively hid what was really inside her brain. Daddy held his face in a scowl. And Aaron wouldn't meet her eyes, just looked at the table and the linen napkin he wrung between his hands. *This is not good,* she thought. Even though every muscle in her body wanted to turn and run, she took a deep breath and sat down.

For several minutes there was silence between them all, the only sound the air conditioner that whirred loudly when it kicked on. Then it, too, became silent as it regulated and leveled out. *Whatever, I'm not going to be the one to break the silence. They called me in here, they can make the first move.*

Despite her promise to herself, when the silence reached the ten-minute mark, she almost gave in. Almost. Luckily, her Dad saved her.

"There's been some talk, Punkin'." Still she remained quiet, just crossed her arms over her chest and stared at her father, watched him fidget. "About a lot that's been going on around here, you know?" Lips sealed, Ally gave a small nod to say she heard and that he should go on. He huffed out a breath. "Either one of you want to help me out here?" he asked Aaron and Momma.

Ally saw Aaron shake his head from the corner of her eye. Momma gave Daddy's forearm a squeeze and an indulgent smile. "What your father is trying to say is that we've been talking about a lot. And we've come to a decision."

"Who's 'we' exactly?"

"Well, your father and me." Her Mom cut her eyes quickly and added, "And Aaron."

"I figured. Come to a decision about what?"

"About you. About the future and what needs to happen."

"Last time I did what *you* thought was best, I ended up divorced."

"Allyson Marx!" her Daddy scolded and that was all it took.

"I'm sorry," she whispered when her Mom sucked in a quick breath, hurt evident. "That wasn't fair. What happened was my fault and I know it. You did what any loving mother would have done to try to protect her child. Please forgive me Momma. That was disrespectful."

"It's okay, honey. I understand. But," she paused, glanced at her Dad who gave Mom an encouraging nod, "this isn't just about protecting you. It's about what really is best for you and your future. And Aaron agrees."

Ally looked to her left, silently pleaded with Aaron to look at her and give her some sign of what this was all about. He stubbornly kept his face down, the napkin discarded, his fingernails apparently now more interesting.

Ally scowled at him, but looked back at her Mom when she continued.

"It was his idea actually. And your father and I couldn't have been happier when he brought it up."

"Why don't you quit beating around the bush and just tell me what *y'all* have decided is best for me?"

"Okay. Aaron has asked____" her Momma stopped talking abruptly when the mudroom door slammed open and they all heard a loud thud on the floor.

Aimee Martin

All four of them were up from the table in an instant and headed in that direction. Daddy was the first one to reach the mudroom and whatever he saw had him cursing. Then he dropped to his knees beside a crumpled form on the floor. With Daddy's big shoulders out of the way, the rest of them were able to see what he'd seen.

It was Jack.

•••••

If Aaron didn't know any better, he'd think this might have been a sign from God that he and Allyson weren't meant to be.

But he did know better. And he knew that when two people were in love and willing to spread that love in the name of God, Satan would do whatever it took to squash that happiness. To bring out the hate and evil and anger instead. Somewhere in his gut, he had a feeling this was a move on that enemy's part because they'd been just about ready to set the plan in motion.

Then this had happened.

There'll be time to analyze it all later, Aar. Right now we've got to help Jack.

He knelt on the other side of the man, made a move to help Big Dave lift him. They paused when Suzi said, "Don't move him. Not yet. Just keep him awake. I'm going to call an ambulance."

Ally ran in with a down blanket, threw it across the prone man on the ground. Jack flinched when the heavy material landed on him but didn't complain. He shivered uncontrollably and Aaron figured–judging from the amount of blood that seeped from a gash on his forehead and poured from a slash he'd spotted on Jack's belly before the blanket had covered it–that the man was going into shock. Bruises marred his face and his lower jaw was so swollen, Aar knew he wouldn't be eating any solid food for a while.

Dave reached down and grabbed Jack's hand and Jack hissed in pain. They noticed three of his fingers at odd angles, the digits obviously broken. "Shit," Dave exclaimed. "Is anything else broken, Jack?"

"Don't. Kn-know," he stuttered. "Every… thing… hurts."

"Who did this to you? Did you see who it was?" Dave asked. Jack cut his eyes at Ally and they seemed to have some quick, silent conversation. Ally shook her head no but her eyes widened, like she knew what was going on in Jack's mind. Aar looked back at the hurt man just in time to catch the small shrug of his shoulders. He squinted his eyes back at Ally, but she avoided his gaze like the plague. "Jack, come on. Stay with me. I can't let you go to sleep, buddy," Dave said when Jack closed his eyes. They popped back open, looked wild and confused before he refocused on his friend.

"Paramedics are on their way," Suzi said as she ran back into the small room, a bottle of water in her hand. "Here," she said and held the bottle up to Jack's lips. He tried to sip from the upturned bottle but it dribbled down his chin and he choked. Suzi lifted it and used her apron to wipe off his face. "Sorry, bad idea I guess." Jack gave Suzi a little smile then groaned when he tried to reach for her hand.

"It's the… thought… that counts, Suz," he murmured.

"Don't try to talk anymore, Jack. Just rest. The ambulance will be here soon."

Ally, who'd been quiet since that silent exchange between her and Jack, finally spoke up. "I'll go outside and watch for them." Then she hurried out the door that still stood open from Jack's harsh entrance.

Aaron watched her run outside, down and off the porch, and stop by the closest gate to the house. He could just make out her silhouette from the light that hung from the power line twenty feet above her head. Could see her wrap her arms around her middle as if she were hurt or cold. *Or scared,* Aar thought but didn't say aloud.

"Why don't you go out there with her, Aaron? Suzi and I will stay here with Jack. Allyson shouldn't be alone." Aaron peeked back at Dave and hoped the look he gave the older man was clear. Dave gave a nod of his head, understanding what Aar silently pled with him. "I know. It's time to get her out here."

"I couldn't agree more, sir." His grim tone matched Big Dave's. Then, after he gave Jack one more gentle pat to the shoulder, stood and headed outside.

To his woman.

The gravel crunched under his feet and Ally looked over her shoulder to watch his approach, but didn't make a move to embrace him as he thought she would. When he reached her, he wrapped his arms around her and pulled her into his chest, a feat in and of itself since she refused to move her arms from their position around her middle. He laid his cheek on the top of her head, rocked her slowly back and forth.

The wind blew around them, ruffled the hem of her shirt and it tickled the underside of his forearms. She shivered slightly and he sensed that she forced herself to stop, to appear strong.

"You don't have to do that, baby."

"I don't know what you're talking about."

"Don't play coy with me. Not right now." He lifted his head and tucked a finger under her chin, raised her face to him so he could see into her eyes. "You don't have to act strong and unaffected. I know you're not, and that's okay."

"It shouldn't be. I should be tougher than that."

"Why? Because that's what everyone expects of you? I'm pretty sure you'll get a pass in this instance."

"But it's my fault."

"No, Ally, it's not."

"It is, Aaron. If I wouldn't have agreed to his stupid idea, this never would have happened!" she exclaimed then shut her mouth quickly, like she'd just let the cat out of the bag and couldn't figure out how to get it back in.

"I think it's time you tell me what was going on with you and Jack in there."

So she did. And Aaron's gut clenched in dread with every word. Just to think that this has been her ex-husband all this time and they didn't see it had Aaron feeling both foolish and overprotective all at once. So much could have been prevented. So many sleepless nights and worry. *Doesn't matter. Now we know, and we can notify the police and put this whole mess behind us.* And he told Ally the same, but she was skeptical.

"I don't know Aaron. I don't think he'll give up that easily."

"Can't say that I blame him." Ally jerked back, looked stricken that Aaron would say something like that. "I wouldn't give you up easy, either," he explained. "And I won't. And I'm going to protect you, no matter what. And that means you have to cooperate with me, okay?"

Ally looked suspicious, but agreed. "Alright. And how do you plan to do that, city boy?"

He smiled, kissed her forehead. "I'm taking you out of here. Out of Montana."

"Under whose authority?"

"Mine."

"I can't just up and leave, Aar. Season has already started and Daddy is gonna____"

"Your Dad agrees with me," Aaron interrupted. "And haven't you noticed there've been no hunters?"

"Yeah," she wrinkled her brow, "now that you mention it. What's going on?"

"Your Dad cancelled the hunts until we could get this situation figured out. No," he added, "don't start in on me. It was *his* idea."

Just then the flashing blue and red lights from the ambulance could be seen as it barreled down the dirt road. Luckily there was no blaring siren since there weren't any other cars to contend with. Aaron released Ally, grabbed the gate and held it open for the bus to drive through. They stopped for a second and Ally spoke to them through their open window.

"Hey Bill, Tom. Momma and Daddy are with him, right in there," she pointed to the open door of the house where the light from inside spilled out onto the porch and yard. "He's pretty messed up. You guys take care of him, okay?"

"We've got it, Ally," the big, bald man with the nametag that read 'Bill' said. Then from Tom, "Don't worry. He's in good hands. And the doc is already waiting at the county hospital for him. We'll keep you updated." Then they drove up the way and braked at the house.

Aaron and Ally watched them as they piled out of the ambulance, grabbed the stretcher from the back. Tom hauled a large blue bag on top of the stretcher, filled with all kinds of medical supplies, Aar guessed, and they pushed everything inside. When they were out of sight, Ally turned back to Aaron. She cocked out her hip and set her hand on that bone, and the look of annoyance on her face overtook any worry she'd had for Jack.

"So just where is it, exactly, that you think you're taking me?"

"Pack your bags, Elf. We're going to Texas."

Chapter 18

*"My beloved spake, and said unto me, Rise up, my
love, my fair one, and come away."*
Song of Solomon 2:10

October 9, 2015

As soon as Bill and Tom left last night, Jack safely
strapped onto the gurney in the back of the ambulance,
Momma and Daddy loaded up in Daddy's red pickup to
follow them. Ally tried to get in with them–*She wanted to
stay with Jack, too, dammit!*–but her desire had quickly been
vetoed.

"Not this time, Punkin'. You and Aaron need to get back
in the house, now, and make arrangements to get on out of
here."

"But Daddy____" she tried to argue only to have her
father cut her off.

"Not buts. You'll do as you're told, Allyson. Once this mess clears over, you can come back home."

"What about Jack?" she asked as tears clogged her throat.

"Don't worry, honey. The doc will take good care of him. And we'll keep you updated on his progress." This from her mother. Ally nodded her head at her parents when she realized there was no way she'd win the argument. Not with them and Aaron all on the same side.

"Yes ma'am."

As soon as the dust from the truck settled, Aaron placed his hand on Ally's lower back, steered her back inside. She quickly packed a bag while Aaron booked them two tickets on the first flight out of West Yellowstone. Then they headed to the bunkhouse to gather all Aaron's belongings, too. Once they had everything they needed, he bent to where she sat on the edge of the bed, gave her a quick hug and whispered into her hair, "Come on, love. Time to get up and get away from here." He ushered her to his rental truck and drove them the hour and a half to the airport. Where they spent the night in uncomfortable chairs with nothing but the sound of airplanes flying over to drown out the turmoil that'd taken over Ally's brain.

Hours later, they finally landed in Houston. Weary, and in desperate need of a shower, Ally followed Aaron to the parking garage where his rig waited. Parked at the end of the lot in between a motorcycle and a white sedan, sat his shiny Ford pickup. Ally climbed into the tall, champagne-colored truck–with the help of running boards–leaned her head back on the headrest and fell asleep before they made it out of the garage and into the sunshine.

When they finally pulled into Lake Shores, Ally barely took the time to reacquaint herself with her surroundings when Aaron pulled into the driveway of an older, but well-kept home. In the dusk, the color of the stone looked like bone, almost off-white, but darker. Aaron got out of his truck, walked around and opened her door, stood there while he waited for her to get out. She dragged her tired body down and out of the truck, swayed a little on her weak legs when her feet hit the pavement. Aaron let go of the door, wrapped an arm around her shoulders to steady her as he guided her up the walkway and three steps onto the porch.

He stuck his key in the lock, pushed the door wide and said, "Home, sweet home." Too tired to respond, Ally just smiled at him and started over the threshold. She stopped abruptly, turned back to the truck.

"The bags..." she trailed off.

"They can wait. Let's get you inside. I'll show you where the bathroom is so you can get cleaned up. I'll come back for the bags then." Aaron led the way upstairs and down a short hallway to a closed door. He paused, closed his eyes and took a deep breath before he finally opened the door.

Ally understood why as soon as the room came into view.

Judging from the size of the room, this had to be the master. *The place where he walked in on his wife.* She tried to ease his discomfort, told him they could go somewhere else. But he refused, said it was high time he started making new memories in his house. Ally tried to lighten the mood, teased him about using the situation as a way to get into her pants. And Aaron had thought she was serious, too. Until she started laughing and told him, "I'm kidding Aaron. I know you wouldn't do that."

He released a heavy breath, but smiled at her and led her into the room, past the large king-sized bed, into a bathroom on the far side of the room. He got out a towel for her, showed her where he kept bathing supplies. "The shower's there," he pointed to the glass enclosed space located on the wall opposite them, "or you can use the tub, if you'd rather." He angled his head toward the bathtub that sat cattycornered to the shower. "I'm going to get our bags. Holler at me if you need anything."

Once he left, Ally stripped down and eyed the bathtub. It was styled after an old-timey tub from a western movie, erected from slats of wood that were held in place by two wide strips of steel that circled around the tub. But it had been modernized by the stainless steel all on the inside. It was large enough for two and looked like Heaven for her exhausted body, but Ally was afraid she'd fall back asleep in there, so she opted for the shower instead. After quickly washing her hair with Aaron's shampoo that smelled of peppermint, and soaping her body–twice–with a bar of soap she found on the shelf inside the shower, she rinsed off and got out, dried her hair and body as best as her weak arms would let her, and walked into the bedroom.

She tried not to snoop, but since her bag was still downstairs, she looked through the drawers of a dark wood dresser until she found an old Houston Astros t-shirt of Aaron's. She put it on, laughed when it fell down past her knees, and climbed into his bed. She had just snuggled under the white duvet when he walked back in, her suitcase in tow. He paused in the doorway, and if Ally wasn't mistaken, breathed a little faster when he saw her in his bed. He swallowed thickly and Ally saw the way his Adam's apple bobbed up and down, even from across the room. Without breaking eye contact, he walked to the foot of the bed, set her case down on the round, white leather stool there.

"I'm going to sleep in the guestroom. It's just down the hall, on the other side of that open bonus room you saw when we first came up the stairs."

Ally nodded her head, continued to stare into his eyes that gleamed azure in the lamp light. He walked over to the side of the bed, bent down and kissed her on her forehead. Ally closed her eyes at the touch of his lips to her skin, realized how shaken up she was when her breath hitched. So when he tried to stand and walk away, Ally latched onto his hand, held him still until he looked back down at her.

"Don't go. Please," she whispered into the quietness. She watched the war wage in his eyes. The fight between risking a promise he'd made and saying "To hell with it" obvious as he tilted his head and chewed on his lower lip. "I'm scared, Aar. And I really don't want to be alone right now."

"What if something happens?" he argued and she knew what he was afraid of. What if he couldn't hold on to his promise of not making love to her?

"It won't. I trust you, Aaron."

He closed his eyes at her words, took a deep breath. When he opened them, Ally saw the resignation there.

He stripped off his shirt, and she made no pretense about not watching as his abs and chest came into view, the muscles rippling under his skin like a sleek panther. His pants came next, and he walked over to the dresser, pulled out a pair of cotton pajama bottoms and slipped them on over his boxers.

When he got back to the bed, he stared down at her for a full minute before he flicked his wrist, wanting her to scoot over. She did so and he climbed in behind her. After he turned off the lamp beside the bed, he wrapped his arms around her and pulled her back into his chest. Ally released a pent up breath, finally feeling calm and protected again as she laid her head on his bicep and twined her fingers with his, rested them next to her heart.

Please God, she prayed, *Please don't take this away from me. Please understand that I need some physical security right now as well as Your faithful security. I promise nothing will happen. Just let Aaron keep his arms around me for the night.*

She didn't get an answer from God, not directly. But a feeling of rightness and peace settled inside her heart and soul and she took that as a sign that they were okay. Right before she fell back into unconsciousness, she heard Aaron whisper in her ear.

"I love you, Elf. With all that I am."

And she went to sleep with a smile on her face.

•••••

October 10, 2015

Aaron woke slowly and snuggled closer to the woman in his arms. *Wait... woman? Shit!* he thought, *I'm in bed with Allyson!* His eyes popped open but he took care not to move a muscle so he wouldn't wake Ally. He glanced down, saw how peaceful she slept, released a small breath and closed his eyes briefly, relieved she was still here and safe. When he opened his eyes, he looked down at the woman in his arms again. At the woman he loved.

With her eyes closed, her lashes laid across her cheeks like little crescent moons, dark against her fair skin. The apples of her cheeks–that were pale and ashen yesterday– now had a healthy glow since she'd gotten some rest. Her bow of a mouth that was naturally pink was open slightly. He could feel small puffs of air come from between her lips and they tickled the hair on his wrist that she'd clutched tightly against her chest last night. And never let go of while they slept.

He tried not to think of how wonderful she felt nestled into the form of his body, how perfect.

He had been nervous when she asked him the night before to stay with her. And he'd almost told her no, it wasn't a good idea. Until he'd looked into her eyes, seen the fear there. Still, he almost fought it. But when her breath hitched–a sign she was trying desperately to hold in the tears–he'd given up. He didn't think she'd realized how loud that one, tortured sound was. And he wasn't about to tell. But it was that small noise that sealed the deal for him.

She needed comfort, and he'd be damned if he wouldn't be the one to give it to her.

When he thought of why she needed that comfort in the first place, he swore he saw red. Knowing that someone had gone so far as to beat Jack to a pulp, all to make a point to him and Ally, had him ready to go to war. Problem was, he didn't know who to go to war with.

It was time he talked to Ted, see if the other man had found anything since he'd shown up in Montana.

Aaron hadn't told Ally yet, but Ted had flown in and driven to Rosy Camp a little over a week ago, as soon as the older man had closed his open cases. They met once in person, at the bed and breakfast where Ted had rented a room. Aaron had given him the details of what all had happened, and what their theories were.

Which, unfortunately, weren't much help. Ted promised he'd do his best to see what he could dig up and that he'd be in touch if he found anything.

Aaron hadn't heard a peep since.

But that would change today. Because this entire situation just got a lot more dangerous.

Right as he was about to slip quietly out of bed, he felt Ally stir in his arms. He stilled, angled his head down and softly kissed the side of her neck. "Good morning, beautiful," he murmured and then, because he couldn't help himself, hummed the melody of the song with the same name by Steve Holy.

She sighed and smiled against his bicep, kissed him there once and said, "Morning. And to answer your question, my night was wonderful."

"I didn't ask you that."

"You did according to the song."

"True. So is all I get a lousy "Morning"?" She nodded and kept her face turned away. "How about something a little more substantial," he said and turned her over onto her back. He stayed to her side, bent his elbow and propped his head on his hand. She smiled up at him, but turned her face away when he lowered his for a kiss. He jerked back, confused. "What's the matter? Can't I get a little sugar?" She shook her head no. "Why?"

Now she covered her mouth with her hand, spoke through the cracks of her fingers. "Morning breath." He hadn't expected that. He laughed and she scowled up at him. "It's not funny. Morning breath is a serious issue."

"Not for me."

"Well it is for me. In fact, it's a deal breaker."

"Fine," he huffed, "you can go brush your teeth first. But I want a proper kiss as soon as you're done." She agreed and moved to get out of bed, which left her mouth unprotected. Aaron swooped in and kissed her. But because he wasn't a total jerk, he didn't try to open her sweet lips for something more. Just kept it light, and pulled back almost as fast as he'd gone in. He grinned down at her shocked face, dropped the smile when she squinted her eyes at him, and he flashed back to the time she'd slapped him. "Now, Elf. Don't go doing something you're gonna regret later."

"Oh, I am not going to regret it. Not one bit." Then *she* shocked *him*. Ally rose up on her elbows, laid her lips on the side of his neck. If that wasn't bad enough, she opened her mouth, licked a small trail to the center of his throat, stopped when she reached his Adam's apple. He swallowed when he felt her give an open-mouth kiss right there. "I've wanted to do that since last night," she murmured against her skin.

Then she bit him.

And while he was busy rubbing the spot and saying "Ow!" she jumped out of bed and ran for the bathroom. She stopped in the doorway, turned back to look at him with a smirk. "Nope. Definitely no regrets." Then she slammed the door closed. Aaron sat there in bed, stunned for a minute, before he finally burst out laughing. "I heard that!" she hollered from the other side of the door.

Instead of answering, he just shook his head, got out of bed and, still laughing, walked into his closet. After staring at the box on the shelf for a full minute, he smiled, pocketed it and headed downstairs to make some coffee.

Ten minutes later, Aaron stood at the kitchen bar, steaming cup of Joe in hand, when Ally walked down. He looked up when he heard her feet on the wooden stairs, froze as he watched her toned, bare legs make their way to him. He was still staring at those long, beautiful extremities when they came to a stop in front of him.

It wasn't until Ally cleared her throat and said, "Excuse me, my eyes are up here," that he snapped out of it. But just to give her a hard time, he kept his gaze down when he answered.

"I know they are. But your legs are much more inviting this morning."

She slapped him on the chest.

"I'm kidding," he laughed and rubbed the spot where her hand had just connected with his skin. "Would you like some coffee?"

"Please." She propped herself up on one of the wrought iron barstools and crossed her legs, which put them even more on display. Aaron suspected she did it just to tease him now, but he didn't say a word. "Thank you," she said when he passed over her mug.

After she'd taken a sip and set the cup on the counter, he placed his hands on either side of her body, caged her in. "Now about that kiss..." he drawled right before he dove in and took her lips in a searing kiss. She responded immediately, wrapped her arms around his lower back, ran the tips of her fingers up and down his skin. He loved it when she did that and groaned in response.

He palmed the back of her head with one hand, pulled her tight into his chest with the other in between her shoulder blades. His callused hands rasped against the soft cotton of his shirt she wore and he spoke against her lips, "I love this shirt on you." He kissed the side of her mouth, worked slowly over to her ear and whispered, "Makes me feel possessive, like I'm marking you." She shivered and he smiled, ran his lips down the soft column of her throat, licked her pounding pulse. Anything he could think of to keep her occupied while he moved his hand from her back, past her hips, down into his pocket. "I can think of another way to mark you," he muttered and she froze. *Perfect.*

He leaned away from her, saw her wide eyes and open mouth and bit back a smile. "Tit for tat, huh? I bit you, so now you're gonna bite me?"

"That's not exactly what I had in mind," he said and slowly dropped down to one knee. Her hand flew to her mouth and she gasped when he pulled out the small, black velvet box that had seen better days. And when he popped the lid open, her gaze dropped to the antique round diamond encircled with tiny sapphires that had belonged to his great-grandmother. A ring that no one–not his mother or Brin or Jess–had ever worn. Tears glistened in her eyes, rolled down her cheeks when she looked back at his face. But this time, he knew those tears were of happiness. He'd give anything in the world to see that smile, those shimmering and beautiful eyes, a thousand times over the rest of their lives.

"Before you say something that's only going to hurt my ego, let me start by saying that I talked to your parents."

"You did?" she whispered.

"Yes. I wouldn't be here, on my knees, if I hadn't."

"Technically you're only on one knee."

"Are you gonna keep being a smartass and ruin the moment? Or are you going to be quiet and let me ask you to marry me?" She giggled, ran a finger across her lips as if to say they were zipped closed. "Thank you." Then he took a deep breath, hung his head and laughed. "My God, Ally. I love you so much. I wanted this time to be perfect and I feel like it's ruined now."

Now it was her turn to laugh. "It's not ruined, babe. It is perfect. Because this is *us*. This is how we are and who we are."

He looked back up, saw the joy and love in her smiling eyes and knew she was right. And he told her so. "You're right. We don't need some storybook beginning, do we?" She shook her head, scooted off the stool and knelt in front of him. "Or corny words of commitment?"

"No."

"Or clichéd promises?"

"That's not what's important. Not to me. But you know what is." This last she whispered, as if she *hoped* he knew but wasn't entirely certain.

"Yes, I do." He laid his forehead against hers, closed his eyes and reached for her left hand. When he slipped the ring on her finger, he said quietly, "As God as my witness, I will never forsake you. I will never deceive you or betray you. And I will never, as long as I live, stop loving you." She sighed against his lips but stayed quiet. "Will you marry me, Allyson?"

She smiled, laid her mouth on his and he tasted her salty tears. "Yes."

Aaron caught her up in a bear hug, tucked his face into the side of her neck. He might have lost a tear or two of his own, but he'd never tell a soul about that. Happiness radiated through him because he knew this was a God-given second chance. He knew they'd be blessed. That their marriage, their life together, would be nothing short of a miracle.

And Aaron would thank God for it for the rest of his life.

"I love you, Elf."

"I love you, too. Always, Aar." She squeezed him so tight he could feel her heart beating, right next to his. "I promise."

They stayed like that, wrapped in each other's arms while they knelt on the floor, for what felt like an eternity. Finally, Aaron's knees started aching and he pulled back, tucked

Ally's hair behind her ear. She grinned up at him and he felt the world tilt on its axis. Her smile alone made his life whole. He knew there wasn't a thing on this earth that would keep him from her. No enemy that could separate them. What he never felt with Jess, he felt with Ally. Ten-fold. A hundred-fold, even.

Which meant they needed to get this business of who was after them cleared up so they could move on with their lives.

He was about to ask Ally if she wanted to call her Mom and give her the news when his cell rang. He shrugged his shoulders at Ally and she gave him an indulgent smile. He hopped off the floor and retrieved his phone from the counter next to the coffee pot. He froze when he saw who was on the line, then faced Ally and answered quickly before the call disconnected.

"Ted."

•••••

When Ally heard who was on the phone, she got up off the floor, made her way back to the stool and her now-cold cup of coffee. She listened to Aaron's side of the conversation while she walked over to the microwave and put her coffee in for a minute to warm it up. With her back to Aaron, she lifted her hand and stared at her engagement ring.

My engagement ring. Wow… never thought I'd say that again.

But the more she looked at the beautiful ring, the more right it felt. The old diamond and sapphires sparkled under the glow of the kitchen lights like a million prisms dancing in the sun. She suspected the ring was very old, but didn't want to ask where it came from. If Aaron felt the need to tell her, she'd be happy to listen. If he didn't, oh well. It didn't matter.

All that mattered was they were getting married.

And the small matter of someone trying to kill them.

But even the threat on their lives couldn't dampen the way she felt right now. A smile broke out on her face and her cheeks ached but try as she might, she couldn't wipe the silly grin off her face. She was getting married. To Aaron. *Guess there really are second chances at love, after all. Thank you Lord.*

"Is he locked up?" Aaron said from behind her and Ally turned to send a questioning look his way. He stared into her eyes as he said, "Do they think it's him?" He paused for a second, then, "Okay. So what now? They're going to question him and just let him go? I mean… they can't do that." Ally frowned at the frustration in Aaron's voice and he walked over to her, threw his arm around her shoulders, kissed her temple when she leaned against his chest. "Yeah, I know, Ted. I just," he sighed, "I really want this to be over. No, don't worry, we're safe. Just keep me updated on what's going on. I appreciate this. More than words or a check could ever express." Aaron rubbed his hand up and down Ally's arm and she wrapped her arms around his waist to hold him close. "We will. And Ted? Be safe up there, yeah? Until we know for sure. Alright. We'll talk soon. Bye." Aaron tossed his phone on the counter and linked his other arm around Ally, held her close without a word for several minutes.

Finally, impatient, Ally asked, "What did he have to say?"

Aaron breathed out heavily and rested his chin on the top of Ally's head. "The sheriff picked up Ben." Ally jerked back and gasped. Aaron ran his hand down the length of her hair and with a sad smile added, "But they don't have anything on him. He's in for questioning right now. Unless some evidence pops up that point either the shooting or the beating to him, Ben will be released before the end of the day."

"Can they do that? Just release him without having another suspect?"

"That was my question, too. According to Ted, they don't have to have someone in custody at all times. If they get a suspect, they'll bring that person in. But they can't hold them forever. Eventually it comes to a "charge 'em or release 'em" situation. Ted said he'd keep us updated on what's going on."

"Has he found out anything else? During his investigating... process... stuff."

"Not really. He hasn't heard of anyone bragging about taking a shot at us or getting the jump on Jack. He heard about an alibi for Ben on both nights, but it was with some girl and he's not sure it'll hold up. He's gonna check it out this afternoon and let me know if it turns out valid." Ally gave a small "Humph" when Aaron mentioned the girl. "I take it you know who the woman is?"

"I'm not sure I'd call her a woman. But yeah, I know who it is."

When she didn't elaborate, Aaron prodded her to go on. "And?" She sighed but still didn't answer. "Allyson, this information might help Ted. It could be the key in finding out who's behind this. He needs all the support we can give him."

"Fine. Her name is Bess. Bess Holms. She's the one Ben was having an affair with after I miscarried. Last I heard, they were still together. Her family is desperate to marry her off to Ben. They want the name and prestige that comes with being attached to the Willis family."

"So he's been dating this girl for... how long?"

"I wouldn't call what they're doing 'dating,'" she answered and Aaron gave her a look. " He started seeing her before we got divorced, over three and a half years ago."

"Okay. And would she lie to cover for him?"

"I don't know. Maybe. Her parents, most definitely. They'll do whatever it takes to make sure nothing gets in th..." Ally trailed off as the wheels clicked into place. "That's it," she whispered.

"What? What's it baby? I need you to share your wisdom here, 'cause I have no idea what's going on in that head of yours."

"It was her parents. It makes perfect sense."

She broke away from Aaron, paced the kitchen while she ran over the scenario in her head and bounced her theory off Aaron.

"You see, they never thought Ben and I were over for good. I remember Mr. Holms got drunk one night at the bar in town and started running his mouth about how there was no way on God's green earth he'd let his daughter get humiliated like I had. About how if he ever heard that Ben was thinking of ditching Bess to come back to me, he'd see Ben in hell before he let that happen."

"Okay, but what would give him that idea now? Why would he think Ben was leaving Bess to come back to you?" Ally stopped on the other side of the kitchen, wrapped her arms around her stomach. She couldn't hide the worry on her face, not even when Aaron took in her expression and straightened, anger and possessiveness evident in his dark blue eyes. "Ally, why would he think that?"

"Because Ben sent me some notes a while back. Telling me it was high time I got my butt back where it belonged, by his side on the Willis ranch."

Aimee Martin

Chapter 19

"He that loveth not knoweth not God; for God is love."
I John 4:8

"What do you mean he sent you some notes? And why am I just now hearing about this? Dammit, Allyson! If you'd told me about those letters before, maybe we could have prevented this from happening!"

"Don't you dare yell at me or blame me for this!" she hollered back at him. "How was I supposed to know it would go this far? How was I supposed to know that the Holms family would find out about the notes and come after me for it? *If* it's even them."

Aaron couldn't decide whom he was madder at. Allyson, for not telling him about Ben contacting her. Or Ben, for being brazen enough to send those letters in the first place. "It's not a matter of whether or not you'd have known it would come to this. It's a matter of you not trusting me enough to share this little tidbit of information."

"Trust has nothing to do with it, Aaron, and you know it. Of course, I trust you. But those letters... he sent them before you even showed up in Montana. And once you were there, I was a little preoccupied with *you* to give them a second thought." She was obviously furious. Her chest heaved with every angry word and her pale skin flushed with red. "And besides, do you really think if I'd have remembered and told you, it would have stopped some psychopath from doing what he's done?"

"No," Aaron admitted and breathed out heavily. He ducked his head ran a hand along his brow as he felt the wind leave his sails. "No, I don't think it would've stopped him. Still, it would have been nice to know."

He saw her feet approach him, stop right in front of him. Then he felt her cool hand on his wrist as she pulled his hand away from his face. She wasn't angry anymore, and instead wore a nonjudgmental smile. "You mean like how you told me Ted was in Rosy Camp?"

"There you go," he said quietly, "making me feel like an idiot again."

"I'm not trying to make you feel like an idiot, Aar. But you have to stop acting like one." He laughed despite her little jab. "This relationship is a two-way street. Give and take. I'm not the kind of woman to just sit back and let her man make decisions for her. I have a voice, and an opinion.

And I'll be the first to admit they're not always smart. But that doesn't mean they shouldn't have a chance to be heard. Same as yours. I'm sorry I didn't tell you about the letters."

"I'm sorry I didn't tell you about Ted. And I know what kind of woman you are. Strong, independent, willful... beautiful. I love every part of you. That's what scares me most of all. I just found you, Elf."

His last words came out choked and he crushed Ally against his chest, hoped that maybe if he held her tight enough, the rest of the world would cease to exist. They'd stay protected in their own little bubble and never have to worry about threats fighting against them.

"I can't lose you."

Ally twined her arms around Aaron's neck and he reached up, held her hands in place on the back of his head and rested his forehead on hers with his eyes closed. "You won't, Aaron."

"Do you promise?"

"I promise." He nodded, leaned in and laid his lips on hers. She kissed him back once, twice, then pulled away. "This is supposed to be a happy day. We're engaged. Can we not let this troublemaker, whoever it is, spoil our happiness?"

"You're right. Okay," he said and blew out a breath, stood up straight. "Let's get ready and go see my parents. They're going to be thrilled to have another daughter-in-law."

"Are you sure? I mean, the last time you gave them one it didn't turn out so well."

Aaron smiled as he remembered his mother's reaction when he'd told her about Jess. "Oh yeah, I'm sure. Let's just say that my mother has no lasting good impressions from Jessica. You, however, she's gonna love. Just like I do."

Ally stepped out of his embrace, backed away toward to the stairs and with a teasing grin said, "Well, I hope not *just* like you do. That would be awkward."

Aaron laughed as she ran the rest of the way up the stairs. When he heard the shower turn on, he grabbed his cell and typed out a quick text to Ted, let the other man know the information Ally had just shared with him. Ted replied that he'd look into and get back with him. That done, he called his Mom and told her that he and Ally would be over later.

"Oh, Aaron, I can't wait to meet the woman that's kept you from your family for the last three months."

"Mom," he warned.

"Don't you 'Mom' me, Aaron Lambert. Besides, I don't mean anything bad by it. From what I remember of her at Alex's wedding, she was very pretty and sweet. Granted, I didn't get to chat with her much. But that'll change today. And," she added, "if she's even half as important to you as Alex has let on, then I'm sure I'll like her just fine."

"You'll love her, Mother."

"Do you?"

"Yes. She's my whole world. What I feel for her… what I feel in my heart when I look at Allyson, is what I see in Dad's eyes when he looks at you."

His Mom was quiet on the other end of the phone for a minute. When he heard her sniffle, he smiled, knew she understood just how serious he was. Then she said, "I'm so pleased to hear that, son. You deserve this. You deserve a chance to be happy."

"Thanks, Momma. That means the world coming from you."

"Okay, we'll see in a little while. I'll have lunch ready at one, so don't be late."

"Yes ma'am. We'll see you soon."

By the time he hung up the phone, the shower had shut off. Aaron made his way upstairs, knocked on the closed bedroom door once and waited until he heard Ally say, "Come in," before he opened the door. He stopped when he crossed the threshold, struck by how beautiful she was.

How lucky he was that she'd agreed to marry him.

She stood on the other side of the room, next to the dresser, and looked into the large oval mirror above the drawers as she applied some shiny stuff to her lips. Her hair was still a little damp and curled around the ends as they flowed to the middle of her back. She wore a navy blouse and a pair of white linen shorts which showed off her legs. He tilted his head, followed her legs from thigh to ankle and back up again.

When his gaze caught on hers looking back at him through the mirror, he scowled.

"Are you trying to torture me?"

"Whatever do you mean?" she asked innocently. He didn't buy that naïve act for one minute.

"We're going to have lunch with my parents and your legs are on full display." He stalked over to her, stopped when his chest touched her back. She batted her eyelashes at him, still stuck on this coy game.

Well, two can play here, Elf.

He leaned down, kissed her bare shoulder, watched her eyes flutter closed the instant his lips met her skin, warm from the shower. Then he ran his hand up her smooth leg, and when he reached her waist, gripped her tightly. "How do you expect me to keep my hands to myself when you've got one of your most tempting attributes open to my gaze?"

"Would you rather I wear a parka?" she asked, breathless when he wound his hand around until it was flat on her stomach. He used his palm to keep her still as he nibbled the spot right behind her ear. She shivered.

"Never."

"Then don't complain." He bit her neck, just how he knew drove her crazy, for her smart response. "And don't start something you can't finish, my fiancé."

Now he turned her around and when her back hit the dresser, dove in and kissed her hard. "I can't yet. But I will. Soon."

"Hopefully sooner rather than later."

•••••

Ally would be lying if she said she wasn't nervous about meeting Aaron's parents. *You've already met them, Ally. Just think of this as a... refresher course.* True, she'd met them at Mel and Alex's wedding. But that was months ago and the meet had been brief. And, most importantly, she'd met them as a friend of their new daughter-in-law.

Now she was meeting them as a soon-to-be daughter-in-law. *No pressure,* she thought as Aaron pulled up in front of a gray brick house with a bright red door. He walked around the truck and opened her door, waited while she looked around. "It seems to me there are a lot more cars here than what two people need," she said as she took his hand and climbed down from the truck. She pointedly looked at the black, dark silver, blue and red trucks parked along the sidewalk and the sedan in the driveway. "Does your Dad have four trucks?"

Aaron glanced at the rigs as if he had just noticed them, smiled and shook his head with a laugh. "Nope. The black one belongs to my brother and that red one is Jaxson's. Hate to break it to you, Elf, but it looks as if the whole gang is here."

"What about the other two?" They walked slowly to the front door hand in hand, basked in the bright, warm sun as it beat down on their backs.

"The silver truck is my Dad's and the blue one is Blake's. He's a close family friend and the one who convinced me to leave Lake Shores for a while." Aaron gave a little shake of their clasped hands then said, "So, indirectly, I guess Blake is the one responsible for us being together." The door opened when they were ten feet away and Ally spotted three women as they fought for the front position. She saw Mel and smiled. Her smile faltered when she noticed the other two women–Aaron's Mom and sister–coming down the sidewalk. Aaron leaned over and whispered in her ear, "Relax."

"Easy for you to say," she mumbled from the side of her mouth. Then, right before the women descended on them, added, "Don't forget how nervous you were when you met my parents."

Aaron chuckled and ducked his head. "Hey Mom, Brin. This is Allyson Marx." He winked at her over the tops of their heads since they'd worked their way in between them. "My fiancé." As soon as the word left his mouth, the women in his family gasped and he turned and made a beeline for the house. *Coward!*

"Well, Allyson. It's so nice to see you again."

"It's nice to see you, too, Mrs. Lambert."

"Oh please, call me Tina. Do you remember Brinley?"

Ally smiled at Aaron's sister, whom she'd met briefly at the wedding. Even if she hadn't recalled, she'd know Brinley Lambert Mathews anywhere. She was one of Ally's favorite actresses. Ally was well acquainted with Aaron's little sister. Brinley had not been involved with her career much lately. Not since she met the handsome man she now called her husband and had a baby. It had been all over the news for several weeks until the paparazzi found some other poor soul to harass. The tall woman with strawberry-blond hair and green eyes looked happier to be living out life as a wife and mother than she ever did on the big screen.

"Nice to see you again, Brinley."

"Oh, you, too! I'm so thrilled to get to know you. And I can't wait to welcome you properly into our family."

"Really? Even though Aar just kinda threw that on y'all?"

"Of course, honey!" This from Tina. "I know a good woman when I see one. And I know when my son is happy. And you, darling girl, have made him very happy."

Ally blushed at the compliments and said, "Thank you. That means so much." Tina smiled and gave her a hug while Brinley let out a little squeal from their side. "He's made me happy, too."

"I know he has, sweetie. It's as plain as the nose on my face. Now come on, Let's go inside and have some lunch and you can tell us all about how my son handled Montana."

October 17, 2015

Ally sat on the back deck at Aaron's home, drank a glass of white wine while she watched the sun set in the horizon. The sky had morphed into deep shades of red and orange and looked like a hibiscus flower. The weather was warm, a bit more humid than she was used to. But the breeze that blew in from the south–"That's the direction of the beach," Aaron had told her earlier–helped keep the temperature bearable. She propped her feet up on the cedar railing that lined the deck, which was as long as the entire house, and wiggled her toes, freshly painted a bright red.

Ally had gone to the salon in town today with Mel, Brin and Tina for a pedicure, manicure and to have her hair done. While the four of them drank mimosas, Ally took the time to get to know her future in-laws better and spend time with her best friend. It was great, even though said best friend finagled Ally into listening to a pitch about why she should move here and work at the newspaper. She smiled when she remembered the hopeful looks that had crossed Tina and Brin's faces. It was obvious they were a close-knit family and they'd give anything to have Aaron closer.

Truth be told, she was actually considering it. Why not do something she loved? Live in a home with the man she loved? She'd been staying with her parents and helping them out at the ranch for so long, she almost forgot what it felt like to live life for *her*. The more time she spent here in Texas, the more she realized how staying in Montana for her parents' sake was actually hurting them all. Hurting their relationship.

Because Ally knew resignation had become a factor in her everyday life.

She didn't want to feel resigned to stay in Rosy Camp because she had no other future. If she stayed, she wanted it to be because she felt right there. Unfortunately, she didn't feel that anymore. What felt right was Aaron, Lake Shores and maybe a job at her best friend's newspaper.

Her place was here.

Problem was, how would she break the new to her parents? Would they understand? Or would they resent her for leaving?

It doesn't matter if they can't understand why you need to be by Aaron's side, Ally. This is your life. And it's time you start living it.

And she would, just as soon as they got this stalker business taken care of.

With her wine glass set against her chest, the cool condensation like a balm to her heated skin, she closed her eyes and let the last of the sun's rays disappear beneath the horizon. When she felt the sun vanish fully, she sensed someone watching her. She opened her eyes and stared into the woods about twenty yards away that backed up to Aaron's house. But all she could see were tall oak and pecan and cypress trees. Shadows snaked from beneath the branches and they gave Ally the creeps, as if they were long and evil fingers reaching out to grab hold of her. She heard a rustle of branches and looked in the direction it came from. But all she saw was a flock of robins as they flew off, presumably back to their nests for the night.

Through narrowed eyes, Ally kept her gaze on the woods, certain she'd not imagined it. *Someone's out there*, she thought.

Then a hand clamped down on her shoulder and Ally jumped and screamed.

The wine glass dropped from her hand, shattered on the wooden deck into a hundred tiny pieces. A wet spot spread on the wood and Ally had a vision of blood, with Aaron next to it. She lifted terrified eyes and let out a small shriek.

Aaron stared at her as if she were a wild animal in need of a gentle hand. "Allyson, baby, what's wrong?"

She didn't answer, just jumped into his arms. He caught her up easily, wrapped a hand under her knees and kept one around her back. He walked to a bench that was built into the rail and sat down, pulled Ally onto his lap. She buried her face in his neck, breathed in his masculine scent and tried to tell herself she had only imagined it. Aaron was here, she was safe and nothing was wrong.

"Ally, tell me what happened."

She shook her head against his skin, wrapped her arms around his neck. He didn't push her for an answer. Not yet. Just squeezed her tighter and rocked her back and forth. Ally trailed a hand down Aaron's chest, rested her palm right over his heart.

She knew it wasn't out of the ordinary, she often felt his chest and teased him about how she loved the way his pecs danced under her touch.

But right now, she just needed to be sure that his heart was beating. That the premonition she'd just had was nothing more than a sick trick her mind had played on her.

The solid thud against her hand reassured her and she sighed in relief. With her eyes closed tightly, she felt a tear slip out of the corner of her lid. It landed on his shirt, right under her cheek, and the material grew wet. Aaron lifted her face with a finger under chin, saw her tears, and asked again, "You're scaring me, Ally. What's wrong?"

"I felt... I thought that someone..." she struggled to get the words out. She closed her eyes once more, took a deep breath and tried again. "I had a weird feeling. Like someone was watching me." Aaron's whole body stiffened. His arms tightened around her body as he looked around them, his eyes focused.

Without looking back at her, he asked, "Where? When was this?"

"Out there," she pointed in the direction where the robins had fled. "And it was right before you came out. That's why I freaked when you put your hand on my shoulder." He started to lift her off his lap. She clutched him harder. "Where are you going?"

"Just stay here. I'm gonna go check it out, okay?"

"No!"

"Ally, I need to see if there really is someone out there. Go get the phone and be ready to call nine-one-one."

"Aaron, no! It was nothing. I'm just on edge, that's all. We haven't heard from Ted in several days. Not since he told us Ben's alibi checked out and the sheriff had released him and that they didn't have any other suspects right now."

"Which is a load of crap."

"Maybe. But they have no cause to pick up Mr. Holms yet. We just have to be patient and have faith that Ted will find something."

"That doesn't mean someone wasn't out there, Ally."

"No, it doesn't. But it makes more sense that I'd be imagining things than it does thinking someone followed us down here from Rosy Camp. Over seventeen-hundred miles away." Aaron cut his eyes at her, clearly not convinced. "Please, Aar. Just stay here and hold me."

He blew out a heavy breath, unhappiness evident, but wrapped his arms around her again. "What else happened?"

"What do you mean?"

"When you dropped your wine glass, you stared at the broken bits like they were snakes getting ready to strike. What was that all about?"

She bit her lip, unsure whether or not she should tell him what she'd seen in that spilled wine. *He's gonna think you're crazy, Allyson. Don't do it.* But she knew, crazy or not, she had to tell him.

"When I looked at that wine as it leaked over the wood, it wasn't *wine* I saw. It was blood." Aaron glanced over to where the liquid had begun to seep through the cracks of the deck and looked back at her. Not like she was crazy, but like he was curious. "And I saw you… lying next to it. I don't know if was some sort of premonition from God or just the devil playing tricks with my mind. But that's what I saw.

And it scared me."

Her last words came out on a choked sob and she swallowed to hold the tears in.

Aaron cupped her cheek, ran his thumb along her jaw and stared into her eyes. His baby blues did what nothing else had been able to since he'd come out. They calmed her. Reassured her.

"I'm right here, Elf. And I'm fine."

"I know that. But what if it'd been real, Aaron? What if you really had been lying there, dying, and we hadn't even had a chance to start our life together?"

"What are you saying, Allyson? I'm not sure I understand."

"Don't be obtuse. Of course you understand."

"Humor me, then."

"I'm saying I don't want to wait any longer than necessary. I'm saying I want to get married. Next week, sooner if it's possible." Aaron's eyes widened and Ally thought that maybe he'd told the truth. Maybe he really hadn't known that was what she was going to say. "You do still want to marry me, right?" she asked, worried that maybe the reason he looked so shocked was because he had doubts.

"Yes," he answered quickly, "of course I want to marry you. But… what about a big wedding and reception and all that? Don't you want that?"

"I've had that, Aaron. And frankly, it's overrated. All I want now, is you."

His eyes bounced back and forth as he stared into hers, scrutinized to see if she was serious. Ally had never been surer of anything in her life.

Then he smiled. Ally let out a laugh of relief and joy. *Thank God.*

"Okay, then. Let's get married."

•••••

October 22, 2015

Aaron walked into the closet in his bedroom and hung his new suit up. *I can't believe I'm going to wear a suit for my wedding.* Ally hadn't been kidding when she told him she didn't want anything fancy. They'd picked out the navy sports coat and matching pants at the boutique in town. Aaron tried to talk Ally into letting him wear a tux, but she refused. And when he asked about a wedding dress, she told him not to worry about her dress. Just don't expect to see her walking down the aisle in some fluffy, princess gown.

"You'll be beautiful no matter what you wear," he told her, to which she replied, "And you'll be handsome no matter what you wear."

Ally's parents were due in any time on their flight from Montana. After his and Ally's conversation on the deck the other night, she immediately called her Mom and told her the news. Of course, Suzi already knew he was going to propose and couldn't have been happier about seeing her daughter walk down the aisle. "For good this time," she'd told Aaron when he'd asked for Ally's hand in marriage.

When Aaron talked to Big Dave on the phone to give him directions from Houston down to Lake Shores–because Dave insisted on renting a car–the older man questioned the speed of the wedding. He even went so far as to ask if they had gotten themselves in the same situation that prompted Ally's first marriage.

"No sir. I promise, Dave, I haven't touched your daughter. Not like that. Like a husband and wife. But Ally… she knows what she wants and when she wants it. She wants to get married now, and I'll do anything to make her happy."

"Well, I do know how headstrong my Punkin' can be, so I can't say that I blame you for giving in to her requests."

"More like a demand," Aaron clarified and Big Dave laughed.

"Alright, then. Jack was released from the hospital a few days ago and he seems to be healing up nicely He's got a sister from Bozeman who came out to help take care of him so Suzi and I aren't really needed. I'll talk to Jerry about keeping an eye on things so we can get down there."

Here he was, five days after that conversation, getting ready to welcome the man and woman who were about to become his in-laws, into his house. His and Ally's house, if he could talk her into living there.

And he was nervous.

Not about the wedding. When he thought about his upcoming marriage, he felt a peace in his soul that could only be explained by knowing, beyond a shadow of doubt, that God was on his side. And He was, right there next to Aaron and Ally and the love that grew between them every day. No, he wasn't anxious about spending the rest of his life with Ally.

He was nervous about what his future in-laws would say about where he lived. About what they would think of his new job, working alongside Jax and Alex and Blake at the Burnt Aggie Ranch, something he hadn't even shared with Ally yet. He worried whether or not Suzi and Dave could trust in him to protect her.

He worried that he wouldn't be able to protect her.

He walked into the bathroom and over to the sink, splashed some cool water on his face. He grabbed the towel that hung on the ring next to the sink and stared at his reflection in the mirror as droplets of water ran down his face, landed on the marble countertop. *Don't think like that, Aar. You will protect her, with God's help. With God's love. With your last breath.*

It was enough. It had to be enough. Aaron would make sure of it.

As he wiped off his face and hung the towel back up, he heard the front door open and close. He walked from the bedroom and down the short hallway, stood at the rail in the bonus room that looked down into the living room and watched his woman stroll into the kitchen, hands weighed down with sacks of groceries from the store. She hummed along to a tune only she heard, then broke out in song and the words from the music flew from her lips in a sweet melody. Words he'd never heard before, but was transfixed by when she sung them in a soft, yet controlled, voice. The lyrics were laced with emotion and he couldn't help but feel the power behind them.

"Take my hand and I will pull you through," she sang tenderly. She sounded like an angel, and Aaron fell even more in love. *"The light is gone but I am still here with you."* As if finally sensing his gaze, she looked up toward the landing where he stood, smiled as she continued to sing, *"You are so far away..."* she trailed off and he knew what she saw when she looked at him.

His gaze was intense, focused on her–only her– as he made his way down the stairs, through the living room, into the kitchen. He stopped when he reached her, grabbed her right hand in his left, rested his free hand on her lower back. He swayed to the music she provided, right there in the kitchen.

"Aaron, what are you____"

"Shh," he cut her off. "Don't stop."

She nodded and kept singing, softly relaying words that clutched at his heart and laid it bare for her. *"Can you feel me, feel my reach. Oh honey, take it easy. Honey, just be."* She kept on, all the way until the words had ended. But

Aaron didn't let her go. Just kept swaying as the song played silently, in his own head now.

"What was that?" he asked.

"A song called *The Reach*, by Miranda Lee Richards."

"It was beautiful. Why didn't you tell me you could sing?"

"You never asked," she said and then quieter added, "Momma sings. Wonderfully. I guess I got it from her. But ever since David, she hasn't done it very much. Neither have I for that matter. Singing in our house, it was always a happy time. Something to spread the love and joy throughout the rooms. When he died, that kind-of went by the wayside. But now," she paused, looked up at him, "all I have is love and joy inside me. And the music… well, it's like I can't hold it in anymore. As if it's been locked up inside for so long, that now there's nothing that can keep it back. Nothing to keep me back.

"Music and singing are like windows into my soul."

"I promise, Ally, I'll spend the rest of my life making sure you always feel the desire to sing." She grinned up at him and Aaron bent down, kissed her upturned lips. Then murmured against her mouth, "As long as you promise to always sing to *me*." She nodded but didn't say a word.

So Aaron spun her around the kitchen, one arm locked around her waist and the other cupping the back of her head, with his lips sealed tightly to hers.

He didn't care if he ran into the counter or the fridge or straight out the back door. All he cared about was keeping her in his arms and kissing her while the world outside passed them by.

Until he heard the throat clear from the direction of the front door.

"You think you can keep that to yourselves until tomorrow? You know... when you're married?" Dave called from the entryway, a scowl on his face. Suzi stood next to him, her hands clasped in front of her smiling face as she fought off tears. Aaron could see it from here. She reached over and slapped Dave on the arm, turned back to Aaron and Ally.

"Leave them alone Davey." *Davey?* Aaron thought with a smile. *That's a new one.* "They're just dancing," Suzi continued. "Once upon a time you used to do the same thing with me." Dave's eyes widened and he quickly looked down at Suzi.

"You're not supposed to tell anyone that," he tried to mumble but his deep voice carried enough that Aaron and Ally heard it. They stopped dancing, looked at one another and laughed. Then he turned to the older man with a smirk in place.

"Your secret's safe with me... Davey."

Aimee Martin

Chapter 20

"And Adam said, This is now bone of my bones, and flesh of my flesh: she shall be called Woman, because she was taken out of Man."
Genesis 2:23

October 23, 2015

Ally stood in the bathroom at Aaron's house and carefully applied her cosmetics while Mel looked on from her place on top of the counter a few feet away. Ally was a natural kind of girl who rarely bothered with make-up. But today she acquiesced. After all, it was her wedding day. A pale pink eye shadow adorned her lids, lined with a charcoal liner and mascara that Mel told her made her eyes seem large and round and inviting. Soft plum blush added a healthy glow to her cheeks. And on her mouth, she brushed a gloss that Mel called "mauve bliss" across her lips.

Finished, she set the gloss down and stared at her reflection.

She chose to leave her hair down for the ceremony; she knew Aaron liked it that way. Mel helped her curl the ends and they laid in soft waves down her back and framed the contours of her face. The cream-colored silk robe she wore covered her white lace bustier and matching underthings. When she thought about what Aaron would say when he saw those underthings, Ally smiled, and felt her face heat underneath her makeup.

"I know that look," Mel from the other side of the bathroom. Ally glanced over to her best friend and shrugged her shoulders, as if that were all the answer she needed. "That's the look of a woman who can't wait for her wedding night. I know," she went on as she hopped off the counter and made her way to stand right behind Ally, looked over her shoulder at their reflection in the mirror, "because it wasn't so long ago that I had that same look in my eyes."

"I can't believe I'm here," Ally whispered and reached up a hand, laid it on Mel's that rested on the sleeve of her robe. "After Ben, I thought… that was it for me. I had my chance, and it was over the minute he strayed."

"But…" Mel trailed off and let Ally finish the sentence.

"Yeah. But… but then Aaron came along and now I know what a woman is supposed to feel like when she's getting married. I know where that term "blushing bride" comes from. I understand why so many women look forward to this day. I get it. Because I feel all those things, Mel. All of them, and more."

"That's the way it's supposed to be," came a voice from the doorway and Ally turned, spied her mother, clad in a navy dress covered in sequins that sparkled like stars when the light hit them just right.

"You trying to outshine the bride, Momma?" Ally teased. Mel stepped back as Ally's mother shook her head and walked into the bathroom, reached for Ally's hand with a tear in her eye.

"I should have known it wasn't right. And I never should have made you go through with that wedding to Ben. But at the time, we thought it was for the best, your Dad and I. We thought you'd be taken care of. Oh, honey… we didn't know that____"

"It's okay, Mom. I understand why. And I don't blame you or Daddy for any of it. None of us knew who Ben really was. The way he acted, the things he did, the promises he broke… those are all on him. And I refuse to lose one more night of sleep or moment of happiness because of that two-timing jerk." Suzi continued to look at her skeptically and Ally tried to reassure her once more. "Honestly, Momma. If it had not been for Ben and our mistakes–because I was involved in them, too–I never would have ended up back in Montana. Aaron never would have come to spend the summer with us and he and I never would have fallen in love and ended up here. That old adage about how everything happens for a reason? I wholeheartedly believe it. Now more than ever. So no more tears or doubts. And definitely no more regrets. I don't have any, and you shouldn't either."

Her mother finally sighed and cracked a smile. "When did you get so wise?"

"Just a little something I picked up on this crazy road called life. With the help of a wonderful mother, of course."

Suzi gave a short laugh and then with a sniffle and clap of her hands, said, "Okay, then. Let's get this show on the road. The rest of the women are downstairs putting food in the fridge and setting out chairs. Aaron and the men will be here soon and I suspect he's going to want to see his bride. It won't do to have you half ready."

Ally retrieved her dress from the closet and hung it on the hook on the back of the bathroom door, unzipped the bag and watched as the material flowed out from its confines. The two women on either side of her each breathed a quiet "Oh" when she removed the dress from the garment bag. Their reactions had her thinking again of Aaron and what he would say when he saw her.

And as Ally slid the chiffon material up her body, she said a silent prayer that he wouldn't do *too* much talking.

•••••

Aaron trailed behind his Dad, Dave, Jax, Alex and Blake on their way to the front door of his house, hoped that maybe if he walked slow enough, he could prolong this memory and make it last a lifetime. The anticipation of seeing Ally. The eagerness to join his life with hers. The yearning to join his *body* with hers. He never wanted to forget how he felt right now, how full his heart was. In those times of struggle that he knew would come—*What marriage didn't have struggles?*—he wanted to recall these feelings and remember that he was going into this marriage with both eyes open, with his soul whole. He was going into this marriage with the knowledge that *this* time, he and Ally had God's blessing.

With a deep breath, he walked over the threshold.

And straight into a scene from some historic western movie. All of his living room furniture had been removed and in its place was wood. A lot of wood.

His kitchen bar had been transformed into a saloon style bar-top, complete with sheets of oak laid up against the walls underneath the counter, and across the granite top, to make it look an old nineteenth century bar. Navy blue vases sat on each end of the bar and held small bouquets of lavender and pale blue hydrangeas. Directly across from where he stood at the front door, more sheets of oak were laid out as a sort of upraised stage. A small stone podium stood off to the side with a bible on top.

To the right of the room, in front of the fireplace, was a black piano. *Where the heck did they get a piano?* On top of the piano was another vase with the same flowers as those on the bar, only bigger. A large, gold, gilded mirror hung above the fireplace mantle and the reflection of the piano–that was polished to a high shine–glowed in the framed glass.

He wandered through the room in awe as he looked from the musical instrument and refocused his attention back on the center of the room. Wooden folding chairs were set up in two rows, Aaron assumed for their families to sit in for the ceremony. He stopped in the middle of the room and turned in a circle, still unsure if he'd come to the right house or not.

"Hey, Aar! Get your head out of the clouds, get over here and have a beer!" Blake hollered at him from where he stood at the new "saloon" bar. Aaron walked over, joined Blake and the rest of the men as they raised frosted mugs of light beer for a toast. "To Aaron and Allyson… may they live happily ever after." There was a chorus of "Cheers" and as they all lifted their mugs to their lips, Blake added, "And have lots and lots of practice making babies!"

Beer spewed from the mouths of every man there and Dave slammed his mug on the counter, glared at Blake. Blake had the good grace to look a little scared and Aaron couldn't help but to smirk and think to himself, *Yeah, I know how you feel buddy.*

"I know we aren't real acquainted with each other yet, so I'm not gonna pound you into the floor," Dave said in a low voice to Blake. "But could you please keep the quips about my daughter and her soon-to-be husband and their… bedroom engagements to a minimum? And by minimum, I mean nonexistent."

"Y-yes sir, Mr. Marx, sir. I didn't mean any disrespect by it. I'm sorry. It won't happen again." Dave gave Blake a long pointed stare, followed by a mumbled "Humph," and short nod of his head. Blake cut his eyes at Aaron and it took all Aaron had to not bust out laughing at the look on his friend's face, with his wide eyes and crinkled up nose as he mouthed "What the hell?" to Aaron.

Aaron just shrugged his shoulders and took a sip of his beer.

Twenty minutes later, Aaron's Mom came in and said it was time for everyone to get into place. There weren't any formal processions for the families, since it was mainly *just* family. With the exception being Blake and the woman they'd hired to tend the bar for them. Aaron went and stood by the podium, raised his eyebrows at his mother to make sure he was in the right place. She smiled at him and nodded her head, then linked her hand with Aaron's Dad, who sat to her left. Jax and Brin sat behind them with Aaron's niece, baby Sarah, snuggled in her Daddy's arms. Alex and Mel took up the two seats next to them.

On the other side of the aisle, Suzi sat in the front, an empty chair next to her for Dave. Blake sat behind her, with another empty seat beside him that had been reserved for Ally's brother, Danny. But Dave told Aaron this morning that Danny decided to stay home to help Jerry out with the first round of hunters that Dave had allowed to come up for the weekend. Aaron bit back a smile when their bartender walked up and took that empty chair. Blake looked over at the newcomer, did a double take, then scowled and faced forward again, arms crossed over his chest. *He's not fooling anyone,* Aaron thought as he watched Blake lean farther away from his neighbor.

Then the music started and Aaron stopped worrying about everyone in attendance. He looked up at the staircase and froze when he caught sight of Ally.

She stood at the top of the landing, looked down at him with a shy smile that broke into a shocked grin as she hooked her hand in Dave's arm. His eyes ran up and down the length of her in appreciation. Her long hair was curled and laid around her shoulders, just like he loved. Her makeup was light, but her hazel eyes were pronounced and focused on him with a barely reserved heat he knew matched his own.

Her off-white dress left her shoulders bare and tied back around her neck, the design leaving a classy V in front, on her chest. The material wasn't fitted, but flowed freely down her body and swayed with each step she took and Aaron thought she'd never looked more beautiful. Her dress came down to her mid shin and he spotted a pair of brown cowgirl boots on her feet with navy blue flowers sown into the leather in a vine-like pattern. He smiled as he thought to himself, *Then she must love my surprise.*

They traipsed down the staircase slowly as the melody of a Carrie Underwood song softly played from his living room's surround sound system. His breath wedged in his throat when *she* sang the lyrics, her eyes on him the whole time. *She's gotten me hooked on music, that's for sure.* He listened to the words, placed his hand over his heart and fought to not cry as he let the music, her voice, soothe his soul.

"Darling look at me, I've fallen like a fool for you. Darling can't you see, I'd do anything you want me to. I tell myself I'm in too deep, then I fall a little farther. Every time I look at you."

By the time she'd sung the last line, she and Dave stood in front of him, and the older man handed Ally off to Aaron. Ally reached up, ran her finger along his cheek and wiped away a tear that escaped, despite his best efforts to keep them at bay. Then she tipped her finger at the brim of the silver-belly Stetson cowboy hat he wore. "Nice hat," she whispered.

"Thought you might like that."

Ally wiggled her eyebrows at him. "Oh yeah. You better hold on to that for the rest of the night."

"Yes ma'am, O Mighty Queen of Permission." He used his teasing nickname that had stuck since the night she told him she loved him.

"And don't you forget it."

The minister–Reverend Pierce–began the ceremony, a not-so-subtle que for Aaron and Ally to quit their banter. They obeyed, turned toward the older man as he began with a prayer of blessing on their marriage. Before Aaron realized it, Ally placed a ring on his finger, promised to love him and be faithful to him and not to call him city boy. "As much," she added with a wink.

Aaron slid an identical, smaller white gold band on Ally's finger, repeated the same vows she had. Then included his own pledge. "I promise to never let you get on a horse that's not ready to be ridden." She laughed and started to argue but he stopped her and went on. "And to always let you catch the bigger fish."

She shook her head at him but didn't try to speak anymore.

Then the Reverend announced them husband and wife and gave him the only go-ahead he'd looked forward to since he woke up this morning.

"You may kiss the bride."

Aaron tilted his hat up, leaned down to kiss his *wife*. When she spoke up again, he could only chuckle at how Ally-like her response was.

"Why can't *I* kiss the *groom*?"

"You can," Aaron said, an inch away from her lips, "if you'll hurry. Or else I'll take the option away from you."

"Well, we can't have that now, can we?"

Then she threw her arms around Aaron's neck and locked her lips onto his. He captured her around the waist, lifted her feet off the ground and tilted his head, kissed her back harder, deeper, showing her that he was the one in charge. No matter how often he let her think she was. She moaned quietly into their kiss and Aaron knew that was her submission, from a wife to her husband, like the bible states. Not in the sexual way most people assume it is. But in the way that he–Aaron–was the protector and the provider and the keeper of Ally's love. And that submission was something he'd cherish for the rest of his life and never take for granted.

He could have gone on kissing her for the rest of the night. But the hoots and hollers from his left let him know that their small and intimate crowd had gotten restless. He lifted his head, stared down into the smiling face of his bride and said, "Guess we better stop, huh?"

"For now." The underlying promise in her voice had him praying for the night's end.

Quickly.

•••••

Ally sat on a stool at the makeshift saloon bar, ran her fingers around the stem of her wine glass and looked over the people who talked and ate in the living room of Aaron's home. *Their* home. Only a dozen people attended their wedding, twelve of their family and closest friends that meant the world to her and Aaron.

This, she thought as she drank the last sip of her wine, *is what I always wanted. Thank You God for giving me a second chance. Thank You for giving me Aaron.*

"Can I get you a refill?" came a feminine voice to her left. Ally turned to the woman who stood behind the bar. Kellina McDonald was very tall, close to six-foot Ally guessed, with long, curly, rich auburn hair, porcelain skin and eyes the color of the ocean. She was beautiful. She was also the daughter of the owner of The Bar here in Lake Shores, Jim McDonald, whom Ally hadn't had the pleasure of meeting. Kellina waited with the bottle of Sauvignon Blanc in her hand.

"Yes, please." She held out her glass and, when the other woman finished filling it said, "Thank you."

"My pleasure. And congratulations."

"Thanks. I know we don't know each other very well but I really appreciate you coming out to do this."

"Are you kidding? I got to be witness to one of the most laid back and gorgeous weddings ever. And… I get to give Blake a hard time for the rest of the night. Both of those put this night in the win category for me."

Ally chuckled at the other woman's jab at Aaron's friend and just knew she and Kellina would become fast friends. She lifted her glass in a mock salute. "Cheers to that."

Just then, Blake walked up the other end of the bar, hopped onto the top and tried to grab a beer from the barrel filled with ice and bottles just behind the counter. Kellina winked at Ally and headed in his direction. She watched for a minute as he quickly took his place back on the floor, then scowl at Kellina when she sweetly smiled at him and handed him the beer he sought. She saw his lips move quickly before he turned and walked off. She giggled at the scene, then sucked in a quick breath when she felt a set of warm lips on her neck.

Ally closed her eyes and breathed deep, took in the scent of Aaron's woodsy cologne and sighed when his hands wrapped around her waist to pull her back into his chest. She rested her fingers on top of his, linked them together, tilted her head more to the side as he worked his damp lips up the column of her neck. When he reached her ear, he gave a tender nip to her lobe and whispered, "Is it time to kick these people out of our house yet?"

"Now?" she asked. "We haven't even had cake."

"I could just have you for dessert." He gave an open mouth kiss to the spot behind her ear and Ally couldn't hold in the shiver that racked her body. He chuckled against her skin. "See? You think it's a good idea, too."

"Maybe. But we haven't danced yet, either." She turned her face to look at him. "And I refuse to end our wedding without a dance... Husband."

He leaned in, mumbled against her lips, "Mmm, I like the way that sounds coming out of your mouth."

"What? Refusing to end our wedding?" she asked, being purposefully ignorant.

"*Husband*," he emphasized. "I could go to bed happy every night for the rest of our lives as long as you keep saying that."

Ally hopped off her stool, grabbed Aaron's hands and pulled him in the direction of their oak dance floor. "It's a deal. Now dance with me, husband." Aaron beamed at her, lifted his head and gave a slight nod. If Ally hadn't been paying close attention, she'd have missed it. "What was that?"

"What?" he asked, now taking a turn at acting dense. Before she could ask her question again, she heard the piano come to life as someone played the keys with a lightness that she knew was surprising to Aaron. As they took their place in the middle of the floor, Aaron pulled her close with an arm around her lower back and took her hand in his other. Ally wrapped her free arm around his neck, toyed with the hair at the nape of his neck. "You never told me your Dad played the piano."

"He doesn't like to spread that little morsel of information around. Says it makes him look less intimidating and that's not something he wants to give up."

Aaron glanced in the direction of where her father sat running his fingers deftly over the keys, tapping out the tune to the song they'd chosen to dance to.

"I don't think it's possible for him to be anything other than intimidating," he said. Ally laughed and then hummed along to the tune of *Unchained Melody* by the Righteous Brothers.

Aaron bent his head, whispered in her ear, "You have my love, baby. Always."

Before she could respond, a voice broke out in the second chorus and Ally froze. She looked up at Aaron, scared to peak behind her and find that it was some sort of trick. But he nodded at her, told her simply "Look." So she did. And burst into tears.

Her mother was there with her father. She sat on top of the piano, her navy-sequined dress dangling from her bare feet, her hands behind her on the piano. And she was singing. *Momma's singing!* she thought as those tears ran in steady streams down her face. Her Mom smiled over at her, the lyrics flowing from her mouth like an angel singing one of David's Psalms. Momma blew a kiss in Ally's direction, twirled her finger to get Ally to keep dancing, looked back at their small crowd and never missed a beat.

Aaron turned her back around, caught her up in his arms and swayed around the oak floor.

"You did this."

"Yes."

"But… how?"

"I just asked her. And she said yes." He bent forward, kissed the tip of her nose, rested his forehead on hers. "Nothing is impossible when it comes to us and our future, Elf."

Ally wrapped her trembling hands on either side of Aaron's face, held his cheeks while she kissed his lips and breathed, "Thank you." She kissed him again. "Thank you so much. This is the best wedding present ever."

"I'm not done yet, love," he promised and suddenly Ally couldn't wait for everyone to leave either.

As her Daddy tapped out the last chords of the song, and her Momma held onto that final note until the sound of the piano had finished bouncing off the walls, Ally said to Aaron, "Then let's get this show on the road."

Since they'd opted for an informal wedding, there wasn't any music while they cut their cake, a chocolate sheet cake Tina made that was her grandmother's recipe. Nor was there a song for her to toss her bouquet. She did walk over and hand it to Kellina though and teased, "Since you're the only single woman here, I'm just gonna leave this with you."

Kellina replied, "And here I thought we were going to be friends."

Aaron tried to do the same with the garter Ally took off in the bathroom and gave him. But when he approached the man he wanted to pass it off to, Blake held up his hands in tight fists and threatened, "If you give me that thing, I will punch you in the face. I don't care if it is your wedding day." Aaron held his hands up in surrender. But when Blake turned his back to talk to Jax, Aaron slipped it inside his coat pocket.

They'd originally planned to skip out on the father-daughter and mother-son dances. But when their Moms got hold of that information, Aaron and Ally had been quickly vetoed. Ally watched while Aaron swung Tina around the floor in a Texas Two-Step to The Band Perry's *Mother Like*

Mine. When it was her turn, she met her Daddy on the floor and curled her hands around his shoulders. His protective arms circled around her waist and he hummed along to a song by Heartland that was borderline cliché, but Ally didn't care.

"I know you did, Daddy," she said softly as he hummed the line that said, "*I loved her first.*"

"I always will, Punkin'. And for what it's worth," he added, "I think you got a good one in Aaron. He might have taken his sweet time getting to you. But I guess it's better late than never."

Ally laughed "He wasn't late, Daddy. We were just waiting on God to set us up at the right time."

"I know, Allyson. I'm so happy for you. Even though you are moving almost two thousand miles away."

Ally looked up at her father in surprise. "Who told you?"

His lips tilted to the side and he gave her a look. "No one had to. It's the right thing to do."

"Thank you, Daddy." She went on her tiptoes and when he bent down lower, hugged him tight around his neck. "For everything."

"May I cut in?"

Ally and her Dad both looked over to see Aaron with his hand out while he waited for his turn. Her Daddy handed her over willingly, clapped Aaron on the shoulder once and walked to stand behind her Mom.

"Last dance," Ally said.

"Thank God," Aaron replied and took her in his arms while Van Morrison sang about there not being any past, only the future and the here and the now. "I will you know. Hold these days and these moments and *you* in my heart."

"I know." Ally kissed the side of Aaron's neck and spoke against his skin. "Now get these people out of here."

"Yes ma'am."

"We heard that!" Alex yelled from the other side of the dance floor.

Aaron wrapped his arm around Ally and she buried her face in his chest, laughed into his jacket when he answered, "Then I suggest you listen to my wife." He bent down and picked Ally up with an arm under her knees and the other across her back. She kept her face hidden, wrapped her hands around his neck and held on as he ran to the stairs. He stopped when he got to the landing and added the parting words, "Thank you all for coming. We love you and will see you tomorrow. Good night!" Then he walked into their bedroom and kicked the door shut on the snickers that came from the living room.

They stood in the middle of the room for several minutes, stared into each other's eyes until they heard Alex holler once more, "Everyone's gone and I'm locking the door. Don't do anything I wouldn't do!" Then the front door shut and Ally thought, *We're finally alone.*

Aaron released his hold on her legs and Ally slowly set them back on the ground. She didn't miss the way he licked his lips as her body slid down his or the way desire raged in his gaze as he looked at her. She ran her hands down his chest, slipped them inside the lapels of his jacket and pushed the material off his shoulders. Aaron slung his arms back, tossed the jacket onto the ground and brought his hands up to her face.

Lightly, he ran his fingertips down her cheeks, neck, chest. Ally closed her eyes at the feather soft touch. Her heart raced in anticipation and her breath sped up while she waited for what he would do next. Then she felt his hands inch up her exposed back, his callused palms rough and wonderful on her heated skin.

Her eyes popped open when she felt him release the catch that held her dress together behind her neck. She was entranced by his blue eyes, couldn't look away. Not even when she felt him bring the two side of her halter dress around and down so that the chiffon material fell and pooled at her feet.

She stood in only her wedding day lingerie, fidgeted as she waited for Aaron to look down. To give some hint that he was happy with what he saw. To say anything.

But he did none of those things.

Just backed her up until her knees hit the bed and leaned forward into her until she was forced to lay back. Aaron followed her down, his large, warm body covered hers and her hands immediately wrapped around his back. He bent his elbows on either side of her head, ran his fingers through her hair. "I feel like I've waited my whole life for this," he admitted.

"Me too."

"I want it to be perfect."

"It will be, Aar."

"Hang on a sec," he said and hopped off the bed. He walked to his dresser where his cell phone sat, punched some buttons on it for a minute before Ally heard the music.

"You're turning into quite the music aficionado."

He turned back around, shoved his hands into the pockets of his slacks and leaned back on the dresser as he now took the opportunity to stare at her. Ally knew how she must look. Laid out on the bed in her lacy bustier and panties, hair wild around her, skin flushed with her need for him. And it was a need.

She held her hands out for him and he stalked over to her, unbuttoned his shirt and pants along the way. And when Adele sang about making her feel his love, he came down on top of her.

He kissed her, probed at her lips with the tip of his tongue and when she opened for him, turned his head and kissed her deeper. Ally trembled and locked her arms around him, tried to get closer. Vaguely she felt his hands skim down her sides to rest on the material that separated them. Then there was no separation, only them, skin to skin. Aaron leaned back and gazed into her eyes when he said, "This is forever, Elf. There is no going back."

"Never." As she became flesh of his flesh, Ally closed her eyes, whispered a final plea. "Love me, Aaron."

"Always."

Aimee Martin

Chapter 21

"There is no peace, saith my God, to the wicked."
Isaiah 57:21

You cheating, little bi... he cut off his thought before he could finish it. Took a deep breath to calm his anger and keep from storming into that house and ringing her pretty, slender neck. And putting a bullet in that Aaron guy's head.

Oh yes, he knew all about the other man in her life now. He never went into a mission without all the facts, so almost a week ago–after he'd spied on her on the back porch–he'd broken into the house the couple was in now, looked through multiple drawers in an office upstairs until he'd found what he was looking for.

Did she know her new man had been married before? Did she know he didn't have a job? That he'd quit to go trekking all over Montana for a woman that didn't belong to him. Did she know Aaron hadn't been able to keep his last wife satisfied? *Probably not*, he guessed. Or else why would she have tied herself to him?

He couldn't believe they had actually gotten married. Even after all the hell he'd raised to keep it from happening. He had tried to do it the easy way. He'd tried to scare them apart. Then he had roughed up that old man who was asking questions that didn't need to be asked and hoped that would be enough. If anything, all it seemed to do was bring them closer together.

Well, enough was enough.

He knew the *happy couple* was leaving day after tomorrow and headed back to Montana. For how long, he wasn't sure. But all he needed was one day. Just a few hours to do what he needed to and then it'd be finished.

It was too bad, really, that he'd have to kill her now, too.

If only she'd have kept her legs closed. If only she wouldn't have gotten married to that piece of crap and slept with him. If only... then I could have let her live.

But she had. And now she would die. They both would.

He smiled despite the fact that he was watching his woman have sex with another man. He smiled because he knew that soon, very soon, he'd be able to cure the itch that had been in his finger for the last four months. Soon, he'd be able to put his Glock right up next to their heads and pull the trigger and finally breathe easy again.

And his Glock was definitely in the lineup. No far away rifle shot would do. Not now. Now he wanted, needed, to be up close and personal. Now he'd watch from only a foot away as the light went out of both of their eyes.

Bet they won't be too happy and in love then.

He couldn't wait.

Aimee Martin

Chapter 22

"Deliver the poor and needy: rid them out of the hand of the wicked."
Psalms 82:4

October 25, 2015

Aaron leaned back in the seat on the airplane, held Ally's hand tight in his, ran his thumb along the two rings that now adorned her finger. He peeked at his wife from beneath his lashes. Her eyes were closed and she squeezed his hand hard when the plane began to descend with a slight jerk. He held in a chuckle, still surprised that she hadn't confessed to him sooner how terrified she was of flying.

When they'd flown down to Texas several weeks ago, she'd taken some headache medicine and slept for the entire flight. Now, he suspected it had been a ploy to knock her out so she wouldn't have had to face the fear. So this morning, as they walked up to the gangway in Houston some five hours ago, he asked her if she wanted to take some Motrin again. She was adamant that, no, she didn't want to pass out this time around.

"We're starting our honeymoon," she said, "and I don't want to miss a thing." Then she quickly put her hand over Aaron's mouth when he opened his lips to sing. *She knows me too well. Already.* "And do *not* start singing Aerosmith. I beg you."

He laughed under her hand, wrapped his fingers around hers and gave a kiss to the center of her palm. "Alright," he said when he removed her hand from his mouth. "But next time, all bets are off."

"Fair enough."

Then they boarded the plane and Ally clutched him tight–hand, arm, leg, whatever she could grab onto–and hadn't let him go since. With the exception of when he had to go to the tiny bathroom. When he returned from that little venture, he sat down and immediately went into a complaint about the size of the restroom. "They really need to consider designing airplane bathrooms for the larger-than-average man." He looked over at Ally, saw how ghost white she was, and pulled her into his chest, murmured sweet nothings in her ear to get her mind off the fact that they were thirty-thousand feet in the air.

That was almost three hours ago. His arm was asleep, his hand felt as if it had a hundred needles in it. And his butt ached from not moving positions since then either. But he'd take the pain over Ally's fright any day.

The plane screeched when the wheels first hit the pavement, gave a little bounce and then hit again and Aaron could see Ally fight to hold in a whimper. Their speed decreased and, as the plane taxied down the landing strip to the parking lanes, Ally released a pent-up breath and asked, "Is it over?"

Aaron waited until she cracked open an eye and peered at him. Then, "No, Elf. It's just beginning."

Two hours later, they pulled onto the county road off Route Seventy-Eight. Five miles and they'd be at the dirt driveway of Marx Ranch and Game.

But two miles into their bumpy drive, Aaron stopped and hung a right to a barely noticeable cut-off and put the rental truck in park. Ally looked at the locked gate in front of them then over to Aaron with a question in her eyes. "What are we stopping for? And how did you know about the back entrance?"

"I told you I wasn't done with the wedding presents," he said by way of an answer. She gave him a look, the desire for an explanation plain on her face. "Fine, spoil my surprises. I set this up with your Dad. You didn't really think we were going to skip the honeymoon, did you?"

"Oh. Well... I don't know. I just thought that with hunting season we'd..." she stopped, gave a short laugh. "I guess I didn't give it much thought, after all."

"Well I did. And we're not here to work." Aaron hopped out of the truck, walked to the gate and found the key for the lock hidden in the hollow of a pine tree next to it. *Small towns,* he thought as he reached for the key and unlocked the gate. *Gotta love 'em.* He hopped back in the truck, and as he drove over the cattle guard added, "We're here to play."

With Ally's help, Aaron found the clearing Dave told him about. They pulled through the copse of trees, out into a meadow filled with white buttercups and sandcherry shrubs. A small pond sat to the left of the clearing. And to the right, stood a cabin, nestled back in a group of spruce trees.

The little house was nothing fancy, but built of logs and mortar with a green tin roof. An old and worn-down porch wrapped around the front and sides and a couple rocking chairs that had seen better days sat off in one corner. The front door was open and Aaron could just make out a flame burning inside, through the screen door. Smoke rose from the grey brick chimney and Aaron knew Dave must have lit the fire earlier, just as he said he would.

Aaron got out of the truck, grabbed their suitcases from the backseat and walked around to open Ally's door for her.

"You really are full of secrets, aren't you?" Ally said softly. She eyed the smoke that curled through the sky like a corkscrew, a gracious smile on her lips. She pulled her gaze away from the smoke and back to him. When she saw him staring at her, she licked those lips and suddenly Aaron didn't care about their luggage anymore. All he cared about was her. His wife. And all the things he wanted to do with her, experience with her. "Aaron?" she said his name as a question as she stepped out of the truck and stood in front of him, hesitant still, even after all they'd shared over the last thirty-six hours.

Aaron, on the other hand, wasn't hesitant at all. He knew exactly what he wanted. Her. And he wanted it now.

"Oh yeah, wife."

He bent down and fastened his arms around her waist, lifted. She wrapped her legs around his hips and her arms around his shoulders. Her chest heaved as she became restless in his arms. Aar didn't waste another second. He kicked the truck door closed with his boot, briskly walked to the cabin. He supported Ally with one arm while he bent down and opened the screen door, walked inside, shut the weathered pine door behind him.

He spun and laid her back against the door, kissed her hungrily. She matched him thrust for thrust with his tongue, tugged on the ends of his hair. It burned, but he loved it. Loved that she was as wound up as he was. He trailed his lips down the side of her neck, sucked on that sweet spot behind her ear.

"Aaron," she said breathlessly, "the bed. It's over there." She nodded her head in the direction of the bed on the opposite wall.

Aaron turned and walked over, never gave the rest of the cabin a second glance as he laid Ally down on top of the hunter green, down comforter and covered her body with his. They kissed and struggled to remove the layers of clothing that separated them. But finally, finally, the garments in their way disappeared. Aaron rolled over to his back, brought Ally with him and she sat up, stared down at him with hunger in her eyes.

But there was something else, too. Something that meant far more than the desire that he knew matched his.

He saw the love. And it was a greater turn-on than the sexiest lingerie.

He reached up, ran the tips of his fingers lightly down the column of her throat, rested his left hand over her heart, relished the way it picked up speed at his touch. She closed her eyes and threw back her head, covered his hand with her own. Aaron's gaze locked on their wedding bands, the way the crossed over each other, intertwined even on separate hands. That was them, their love, their future. They would always be linked.

He looked back up at her flushed face and neck, her plump and wet lips. And knew he'd never tire of seeing her like this. Unrestrained. Heart, soul and body laid bare before him, for him. *Thank You Lord for making her mine.*

"You're beautiful."

She opened her eyes, leaned down over him and brought her lips to his. Her long chestnut hair fell in a curtain around them, engulfed his senses with her sweet, honeysuckle scent. He kissed her slowly, the frantic need from before tamped down with his wish to show her the sweetest love.

And when she settled right where they both needed her to, a sigh escaped her lips, right onto his, as if she were breathing life into him. A lone tear seeped from the corner of her eye and Aaron understood why without asking. Their passion had become so strong that it evoked the same diehard intimacy inside of him.

He'd never live without this.

Never live without her.

As Aaron moved with his wife, inside his wife, he promised, "I'm yours, Allyson. Forever."

•••••

November 10, 2015

Ally sat on the porch, pulled the black-and-white checkered wool blanket tighter around her shoulders with one hand, lifted her steaming cup of coffee to her mouth with the other. She let the warmth from the Columbian roast invade her senses, wake up her body and mind as she watched the sun while it rose in the east.

There really wasn't anything like a Montana sky, and this morning's view didn't let her down. Directly on top of the horizon, a deep red and orange covered the tops of the mountains like a blanket. A purple as dark as the strongest wine blended with the denim dawn, laid across that red-orange blanket as if it were an ocean fighting for a way under the covers.

A small flock of wood ducks flew in from the north, settled in the pond across the clearing from her. She smiled when she spotted the males and females, the way they danced around each other in the water. It was breeding season for them right now. They'd be leaving soon, headed south before the winter got too bad. But not before they laid their eggs, hatched their babies and carted them south, too. Ally loved this time of year. Seeing all the new life from the spring and summer come together as a unit to protect one another was a primal instinct imbedded deep inside an animal's soul. It was an instinct Ally appreciated and had craved for many years.

But not anymore. Now she had her own protector. *Go ahead, Ally,* she told herself, *Call him an animal, too.* Her cheeks flushed as she realized how true a statement that was, even now, two and a half weeks after they'd gotten married. Her body ached in a wonderful way from her husband and his insatiable desire to be with her. Not that she would complain about it. Never had she felt so needed and loved.

Never had she felt so complete.

Ally wasn't sure what she'd done in her life to ever deserve Aaron. But she'd spend the rest of her days thanking God for bringing him to her.

It seemed like just yesterday when he'd barreled down the county road and almost slammed his rental truck into hers.

She chuckled as she remembered waving a crowbar around, silently threatening to hit him over the head with it. *Oh my, what a fool I was.*

"Want to share what's so funny?" the object of her thoughts said as he walked outside to join her. A pair of low-slung plaid cotton pants covered his legs, highlighted the deep V cut into his hips and waist. Ally ran her eyes up, over his muscled abs and chest, across his strong shoulders that rippled when he lifted his coffee mug for a drink. Then the screen door slammed closed behind him and she jerked out of her reverie, almost spilled her own coffee. "Too much caffeine already?"

"Ugh, not possible." He chuckled and set his mug down on a small table next to her rocker, pulled on a long-sleeve t-shirt. He lifted her effortlessly and sat down with her snuggled in his lap. She reached a hand out, traced the scruff on his jawline, leaned in and kissed the prickly hairs. "Good morning, Mr. Lambert."

He captured her chin between his thumb and forefinger, kissed her long and hard, moaned into her mouth, "Mmm, good morning, Mrs. Lambert. Why didn't you wake me?"

"You looked so peaceful. Plus you were snoring like the dead. I figured you could use the rest."

"Well if someone wouldn't have kept me up half the night, maybe I wouldn't be so tired." Ally scoffed, tried to wriggle out of his hold but he tightened his arms around her waist, buried his face in her hair and laughed. "I'm kidding.

Seriously, I didn't mean it. Will you stop?" he asked as Ally continued to fight. "You're gonna knock us into the table and spill the coffee."

"It might just serve you right," she argued but sat still. *She had no desire to get burned. Plus she really needed the caffeine this morning.* "If you're going to complain, I'll just let you sleep on that little pull-out sofa tonight."

"No you won't."

"Says who?"

"Says me." He nuzzled his nose farther into her hair, breathed deeply. "Who would keep you warm if you kicked me out of bed?"

"It's not that cold."

"This from the woman wrapped up in a wool blanket." He reached over, picked up his mug, and downed a good portion of his coffee. Then, "Besides, there's a front moving in tonight. A big one, if your weatherman is to be believed. He's predicting a *lot* of snow."

"Already? Gah, this winter's going to be brutal if it's starting already."

"Yeah," Aaron agreed and rested his chin on Ally's shoulder, watched the same ducks Ally had watched before he came out. His face was pensive, almost as if he was unsure or worried. He didn't say it, but Ally thought she knew why.

Well, he's going to have to wait a little longer til he gets that bit of information. I've already got the surprise all planned out and a little sad face is not going to get me off track.

But as they sat there and his expression didn't change, Ally decided there was one way to brighten his mood.

She stood up suddenly, turned around and faced him. He looked up at her with raised eyebrows, curiosity evident. She didn't answer, just opened her blanket wide, gave him a quick glimpse of her lavender camisole and matching panties, then sat back down on his lap and wrapped the blanket around them both. Aaron's hands went to her waist, slipped under her camisole and rubbed her cool skin on either side of her spine.

A tingle spread up her back and she asked, "Ever made love during a Montana sunrise?"

November 11, 2015

Ally woke with a start when something hit the window. She glanced down beside her, saw Aaron's spot in the bed was empty, the covers thrown aside haphazardly, as if he'd gotten out of bed in a hurry. She crawled out from under the covers and shivered with the cold. The weatherman had indeed been right, and the snow fell last night with a vengeance. Ally guessed they had at least eight inches before they turned in around midnight.

She grabbed that same wool blanket that had protected them from the chill yesterday morning, wrapped it around her shoulders and slipped her bare feet into a pair of Uggs. She walked toward the bathroom at the back of the cabin, peeked inside to see if Aaron was there, even though she knew it was unlikely since the light was off. *Nothing,* she thought with a frown. She headed into the main living quarters and stood in what passed as the living and dining room, spun in a circle and wondered where in the world he'd run off to.

She grabbed a glass from the kitchen counter, filled it with water from the faucet and drank deeply, then checked the time on the clock on the microwave. *It's six o'clock in the morning. Where could he be?*

Ally noticed the fire had died down–only a handful of red embers glowed beneath a pile of ashes–and thought maybe Aaron had gone to gather more wood from the pile on the side of the cabin. She headed to the door, stopped dead in her tracks when another crash came on the window. The hair on the back of her neck stood on end, goose bumps rose on her skin. It had nothing to do with the cold.

She paused when she placed her hand on the knob and the cold of the metal seeped farther into her bones. With a deep breath, she opened the door. It flew out of her hands with a gust of wind and snow blew inside. The entire clearing looked like a winter wonderland, only it was still fall. At least a foot of snow covered the ground and cabin and rose halfway up the tires of the truck. *It's a good thing we hadn't planned on leaving for a few days,* Ally mused as the took a hesitant step onto the porch. *It'll be at least forty-eight hours before we can get that truck out of here.*

As she stepped outside of the cabin completely, something caught her eye from her peripheral vision and she turned to her left with a jerk.

And screamed.

•••••

"Hello Allyson."

Aaron stood perfectly still, afraid that the smallest distraction would set the man off. And that was the last thing Aar needed, since said man currently held a gun to the side of his head and had Aaron in a chokehold. He tried to reassure Ally with his eyes, to let her know that he was alright. But really, how could she not worry? Some lunatic held him at gunpoint. If that wasn't cause to bring about worry and fear, Aaron didn't know what was.

Then his wife surprised him when she frowned in confusion and said, "Chris?"

"Ally, do you know this gu____"

"You shut up!" Chris angled his face at Aaron and jabbed the barrel of the gun harder into Aaron's temple for good measure. Aaron obeyed, but threw his own confused look in Ally's direction. She wouldn't look at him, wouldn't even acknowledge him. Just kept her focus on the man with the gun.

The man caught Aaron off guard earlier when Aar came out to get some wood for the fire. Right as Aaron bent to pick up a log, the crazed man dove at him from behind the trees, hit him in the stomach with his shoulder and took him to the ground. Not expecting an attack, the man had the advantage and was able to put the gun in Aaron's face before he could react. Aaron took one look at the man's wild brown eyes and knew he was dealing with an unstable person. An unstable person who had a plan, if the backpack slung over his left shoulder, the rifle that hung from a strap over his right shoulder and the black fatigues he wore were any indication. His light brown hair was closely cropped to his head, like a military cut, and there was a scar that ran through his upper lip and gave the man a sinister look. Without even asking, Aar knew this was the man that had hounded he and Ally for the last several months.

When he spoke, spittle flew from his lips and landed on Aaron's cheek, but Aar didn't flinch. "And you," he looked back at Ally, "I can't believe you. After all we had. After all I did. You just threw it all away and for what? This guy?" Aaron's throat constricted as the arm around his neck tightened. "He can't be worth it."

Ally didn't answer him. She seemed strangely calm, but Aaron saw the vein in her neck pounding like a jackhammer. She struggled to keep her face impassive and her breathing normal.

"What are you doing here, Chris?"

"I'm here for you. I've been here, for over five years. But you just kept messing stuff up. It's all messed up now and there's not a thing I can do to fix it!"

"Sure there is, Chris," she said and took a small step toward them. "Just let Aaron go. Then you and I can go inside, have some coffee and talk." Another step.

"Don't you come near us! Not anymore, not now!" She stopped and held her hands up in obedience when Chris tightened his finger on the trigger. Aaron swallowed thickly. "Good. That's good. I won't be rushed, Allyson."

"Rushed into what, Chris?"

He tilted his head at Ally and an evil grin spread across his face. Aaron saw his head give a little twitch and got the sense that the man holding him might have been hearing voices, like one of those people who suffered from schizophrenia. Aaron again tried to get Ally's attention, but she either didn't see his hand moving below his waist or just ignored it.

He knew they were probably only going to get one time to take this guy down and get out unscathed. He and Chris were about the same height, but Aaron had a good thirty pounds of muscle on Chris, thanks to all his work at the ranch this summer.

All Aar would need is one shot.

"I won't be rushed into the killing. I've planned this for a long time now. Killing takes patience, you know. Patience and skill."

"Who are you going to kill, Chris?" Ally asked and Aaron heard the quiver in her voice, the first sign she'd shown that she was scared. Aar prayed Chris had missed it.

"Why, you my dear. And of course your new *husband*," he hissed the word like it was full of venom and again spit landed on Aaron's cheek. "I've spent a long time clearing the way for this. Even had to kill that brother of yours when he caught me in your room one night. Of course, you were off in San Diego. I was only there to get some information, anything that would help me get to your heart. Then he walked in and ruined the whole thing and I had no choice but to get rid of him. It was easier than I thought to make it look like a suicide."

Aaron waited for the terror that he knew was coming, the scream that he was sure was bubbling up to the surface of Ally's throat. She'd wondered for years what had happened to her brother. Now she knew and it wasn't going to be an easy pill to swallow.

"You… *you* killed David?" Her strained whisper had his blood boiling with the need to put this piece of trash behind him down.

"Yes, yes, I killed him. But that was years ago and it's not important anymore. What is important is that you gave yourself to this man," he yanked on Aaron's neck again, "and now I have to kill you both. I can't very well have tainted goods, now can I? The question is… who to shoot first?" Chris moved the gun from Aaron's temple, shoved it up and under his chin and said, "Him?" Ally screamed 'No', made to lunge for Chris. She came up short when Chris swung his arm in her direction and the butt of the gun hit her on the side of the face. She fell back a step, her tiny hand covered the spot Chris had just hit. Aaron watched blood seep from in between her fingers and saw red. "Or you?"

Aaron knew this was the best chance he was going to get. He couldn't mess it up. One wrong step and that gun would go off. And it was aimed right at Ally's chest. *Please God,* he prayed as he took a deep breath, *Please let us live through this. Please keep her safe.*

Then he moved.

Aaron slammed his elbow back into Chris's gut as hard as he could. The man doubled over and wheezed out a harsh breath, tried to whip his gun hand back around at Aaron. Aar grabbed that wrist, slammed it down hard over his knee. The bone cracked and the man screamed, fell to the ground with a thud. Aaron kicked the gun away, sat down on the man's waist and punched him in the face. A cut opened up on Chris's temple, but it wasn't enough. Not after he'd hurt Ally.

So Aaron hit him again. And again. Everything around him faded to black and all he could focus on, all he could see or hear, was the man lying on the ground underneath him, bleeding and howling by Aaron's hands. Then something broke through the haze.

A faint call. His name, spoken by that feminine voice that he knew so well. The voice that made his heart stop when it sang and his soul swell to fullness when it said 'I love you.' He felt the yank just as he pulled his right arm back, ready to let loose another blow to Chris. It was an insistent force trying to keep him away from the target of his obsession. But neither the voice nor the pull could stop him. They weren't strong enough on their own.

But the hands that grabbed his face and the lips that sealed onto his and the eyes that implored with him to snap out of it were.

The fight left Aaron and he let out a deep breath, wrapped his arms around Ally and pulled her tight against his chest as he scooted away from Chris, closer to the door. She released his mouth and tucked her face next to his neck. He felt a tremor roll through her body and her tears on his throat and they nearly broke him.

"Ally, I'm so sorry baby. I'm sorry I did that. Please don't be afraid of me." She jerked back, looked at him with wide eyes as if she'd been slapped. "Please." His last word was a strangled murmur, pain and emotion clogged his voice.

"Aaron," she whispered and ran her hands down the sides of his face, rested them on his chest, right over his pounding heart. "Aar, honey, I could never be afraid of you."

"Are you sure?" She nodded in answer. "That wasn't me, baby. I don't know…. I don't understand what came over me. I was just so afraid that he was gonna hurt you. I'm so sorry."

"Stop saying that. You have *nothing* to apologize for. Aaron, you saved us. You saved me."

"But at what cost?" Ally shook her head, obviously puzzled at what he meant. "I've done a bad thing, Elf. This is one of the greatest sins."

"Aaron, you didn't kill him."

"No. But," he glanced down at the passed out form to his left, shuddered and looked back at Ally, "I would have. If you wouldn't have stopped me, I'm afraid I would have."

"Aaron, sweetie, if you wouldn't have done what you did, I guarantee he *would* have killed us. The important thing here is that you did stop."

"I didn't want to."

"So ask for forgiveness."

"Do you really think it's that easy?"

"I know it is. That's what Jesus died for, remember? For our sins."

"I love you Allyson." He hugged her tight again, buried his face in her hair and let the tears flow. "I love you so damn much."

"I love you too, Aaron."

"Come on," he said, stood with Ally in his arms, headed inside. "Let's go call the sheriff."

"What about him?" Ally looked over Aaron's shoulder at Chris, still dead to the world. He debated just leaving the man there in the cold, but worried that Chris would wake up and take off before the sheriff showed up if he did.

"There's some rope under the sink. First, I'm going to get you inside. Then I'll take care of him."

Aimee Martin

Chapter 23

"For where your treasure is, there will your heart be also."
Luke 12:34

It was almost two hours before the sheriff made it out to the cabin. Once he got there, he immediately took Chris into custody, read him his rights and placed him in the back of the sheriff department's four-wheel drive Bronco. He'd come back to check on her and Aaron and take their statements. And to try to calm down Big Dave, who paced the small confines of the cabin in angry strides.

Daddy had shown up an hour before the sheriff, cursing the whole time about the snowdrifts blocking the trails and making it harder for him to get there. Then he caught sight of Chris tied to the toilet. Ally thought Aaron was tough to control but she guessed she'd never really seen her Daddy this enraged. It took her and Aaron both to keep him back and then Aaron threatening to tie *him* down too before he finally relented. He pulled up a chair from the small dining room, parked it right in front of Chris, crossed his large arms over his chest, and didn't budge until the sheriff showed up.

Aaron called Ted, too, and the investigator made his entrance right after the sheriff had loaded Chris into the truck. He took a long look at the front porch where blood stained the snow, then regarded Aaron with an air of respect. He walked over and took a seat in the chair next to the couch where Ally and Aaron sat, Aar's arm around Ally's shoulders. She tucked her head under his chin, asked Ted if she could get him anything.

He shook his head no, said with a sigh, "I've been trying to get a hold of you. I found out about this guy two days ago."

"Yeah, what's his story?" Aaron asked as his gaze bounced back and forth between Ally and Ted.

Ted turned a questioning look at Ally and answered with a question of his own. "You don't know?"

"Oh cut me some slack, here. It's not as if I've been sitting around eating bon-bons. I haven't exactly had a chance to fill him in yet," Ally defended, pointed a finger at Aaron.

She turned to him on the couch and told him what she knew.

Which wasn't much.

"I don't know a lot about who he is. Not anymore. But once upon a time, he and I had a class together in college.

And Mel, she was there, too. Anyway, Chris was always asking me out, trying to get me to leave Ben and be with him instead. I played it off at first, very nicely but firmly told him no. Then he got more insistent, started asking me multiple times a day. He even showed up at our dorm room once. Please don't tell Mel that," she directed to Ted, "because she'd have a conniption. Anyway. So, I thought I'd made my point clear when I threatened to call the cops that day and slammed the door in his face. But in class about a week later, he hit the last straw. He got down on one knee, pledged his undying love for me. Said he'd move the ends of the earth if only I'd give him a chance."

"Why didn't you go ahead and tell the police? Get a restraining order or something?" Aaron asked.

"Because I thought I'd handled it. I thought he was just some immature kid who needed to be told strongly."

"Is that what you did?" This from Ted.

Ally nodded her head slightly and said, "In a way, yes. I told him I had a video of him snoring and drooling with his hand in his pants in the library and that I'd share it with the whole school and keep him from getting any more dates, ever, if he wouldn't leave me alone."

Aaron and Ted both laughed then Aaron spoke, "Well he left you alone, right?"

"For a while. But now look at what's happened?"

"Yeah, okay. So here's where I come in," Ted entered the conversation. "And this took some digging. I started out asking around about your ex-husband because he seemed like the obvious choice. When that turned into a dead end, I back-tracked to every person you'd had contact with in the last five years, then back into college. It really helped that the only people you saw on a regular basis these last five years were your family," he said to Ally. "So that left college. Turns out, you're not the first woman he tried to bully into dating him. Happened to another girl from the community college he went to before transferring to San Diego State. She *did* get the restraining order."

Aaron cut his eyes at Ally and she slapped him in the stomach. "Oh shut up."

"I didn't say anything."

"No, but you were thinking it. Go on Ted."

"So, once I found out about this guy, I started following his whereabouts since college. Call it a gut feeling, but I've learned to never ignore them," he said with a pointed look at Aaron. "Turns out I was right."

"He killed David," Ally butted in and told her father who still sat in the chair that faced the bathroom, even though Chris wasn't in there anymore. Her Daddy turned quickly to look at her, swallowed and nodded his head.

"I knew it," he said softly. "We knew it, didn't we, Punkin'?"

"Yeah Daddy, we knew it. And now he'll go to prison for it. Now David's murder will be solved and his name will be restored and he can rest in peace."

"He'd be proud of you, Elf," Aaron said and leaned down to kiss her forehead. Ally closed her eyes at the contact, thanked God for keeping them safe.

"He'd be proud to call you family," she told Aaron and felt him smile against her skin.

"So am I," her Daddy added and she and Aaron both looked up to see her Dad standing over them. His large shadow covered them in darkness, but Ally knew that was fleeting.

Never again would she live her life in the dark.

"I know I told you this already," her father went on, "but I'm positive you're the right man for my daughter. And I'm proud to call you son. Damn proud."

"You didn't tell me that," Aaron teased and her Dad cut his eyes at Ally's husband.

"Well, I told your wife and that's good enough. Now don't make me regret it."

Aaron set Ally away from him, stood up and faced her father, seriousness etched on his features. "I won't, sir. Til my last breath, I'll protect her. You have my word."

Daddy nodded his head at Aaron then surprised her when he pulled Aaron in for a hug. Aaron's eyes widened and he glanced down at her with a "What do I do now?" question on his face. Ally held in a giggle, shrugged her shoulders at her husband. Then stood up and wrapped her arms around the two most important men in her life. They each wrapped an arm around her and the three of them stayed like that for several minutes. Finally, Aaron broke into their sentimental position.

"Not that I'm not thoroughly enjoying this moment, but it's getting a little uncomfortable embracing my father-in-law for more than the standard few seconds." Ally laughed and stepped back just in time for Daddy to shove Aaron aside. He fell back onto the couch with a snicker. "You know I love you, Dave."

"Whatever," Daddy mumbled. Then, "I'm going to go on home, tell your Momma what happened. She's probably worn a hole in the carpet with worry by now."

Ally nodded her head in agreement and said, "Give her a hug and kiss for me." She wrapped her arms around her father once more. "And thank you Daddy for coming to our rescue."

He rubbed her back as he spoke but Ally knew he looked at Aaron as the words came out. "You don't need my rescuing anymore, Punkin'." Ally peeked over at Aaron in time to catch his smile and nod at her Dad. "Now go be with your husband." He released her, shook Ted's hand and walked out the door without a backward glance.

"He's quite intimidating, isn't he?" Ted asked as he stared at the spot her Dad had just vacated.

"Nah," Aaron answered, "you should see him play the pi____"

Ally leaned down and slammed her hand over Aaron's mouth and warned, "Don't even think about it." He smiled under her palm, kissed her once there and bowed his head surrender.

Then his smile vanished.

The teasing glint in his eyes changed, morphed into something she was fast becoming acquainted with. The initial shock from the night had worn off. The adrenaline from their encounter with Chris was still there, but now Ally felt it redirected toward Aaron. The need to feel one another, be with one another—make sure they were both here and alive and okay—overwhelmed Ally the more she stared into his eyes that reflected the same thing.

Aaron stood from the couch, closed his arms around her waist stared into her eyes, blue to hazel.

She vaguely heard Ted mutter something in the background like, "That's my hint to leave." But she couldn't focus on that. She could only focus on Aaron and the way he looked at her and the hunger she knew matched her own.

She opened her mouth to tell him how much she wanted, needed him. He didn't let her. He crushed his mouth down on hers and lifted her off the ground, made his way to the bed. They fell onto the mattress together, never breaking contact.

"I need you, Elf," he whispered against her lips.

There was desperation in his eyes, in the way his hands gripped her hips, in the way his forehead rested hard on hers. Then a shudder rolled through his body when Ally rose on her elbows, closed the small distance that separated their lips and answered him.

"Then have me."

•••••

November 19, 2015

It had been a little over a week since everything went down with Chris. After some of the snow melted, Aaron and Ally had gone to the sheriff's station and given their statements. The district attorney for Carbon County filed formal charges on the man including attempted murder, conspiracy to commit murder, assault with a deadly weapon, along with a whole other gamut of charges. Aaron didn't know what they all included, and he didn't care. All he cared about was that the D.A. told him and Ally that Christopher Anders wouldn't be getting out of prison in this lifetime. She took their statements and the state's charges to the judge, and he agreed that no bail should be set for fear that Chris would flee. Now he sat in a cold cell on a cold cot with cold food to hold him off until his day in court.

It might make him a bad Christian, but Aaron hoped the man rotted in jail. *No you don't, Aar,* he thought to himself as he threw the last pair of socks into his suitcase and sat down on the bed next to it. *Everyone should get a second chance. I hope he'll get the help he needs and become a whole man again someday.* And he did. He prayed that Chris would find his way to God and seek forgiveness for his sins, just as

FOREVER TREASURED

Aaron had, and be able to live a long and happy and faithful life. It's what everyone deserved. Lord knew he and Ally were given that second chance. And he wouldn't spend a single day taking it for granted. Except for today.

He was packing to leave, to head back to Texas and start his new job at his brother-in-law's ranch, The Burnt Aggie. He was getting ready to leave his new wife and it was killing him.

Just then, the beautiful woman who took up all of his thoughts nowadays walked into the bunkhouse where they'd been staying for the last few days since there weren't any hunters scheduled until tomorrow, and called out to him, "Aaron? You in here, babe?"

"Back here!" he hollered and stood from the bed when she walked through the door.

She took his breath away every time he saw her. In form-fitting jeans, a red and gray flannel shirt tucked into those jeans that showed off her shapely derriere, and a black, felt cowboy hat pulled low on her head, she looked like the perfect little ranch woman. She looked like *his* ranch woman. And it broke his heart that it'd be two weeks before he could get back up here and see her again.

But Aar couldn't let her see it. Let her see the depression that threatened to overtake his soul. He didn't want her to feel guilty just because she had a job to do. He understood why she needed to stay here through hunting season. It was just too late for Dave to find a replacement for her.

That didn't make it any easier to leave, though.

"Hey," she said softly as she walked over to where he stood and placed her hands on his hips. "Why so gloom?" Aaron tried to smile, he really did. But it felt more like a grimace and he knew Ally saw it when her smile turned into a frown. "Aar, what's wrong babe?"

"I can't do this," he admitted and then went on quickly when he felt her tense up in alarm, "Not *this* as in *us*. I mean I can't leave." Her shoulders dropped and her grin came back.

"Yes, you can, Aaron. You have to. Jax is expecting you."

"But I don't want to. I don't want to leave you."

He circled his arms around her waist, placed his hands on that backside that teased him at every turn, frowned when he felt something hard in her back pocket. He pulled the object from her pocket, felt that it was a box and asked, "What's this?"

Then gave Ally a strange look when he brought it around and set his eyes on it.

"Well this is awkward. I thought it was women who always dreamed of getting a little, blue box." He held the small Tiffany box up in front of Ally's face and caught the smirk before she had a chance to straighten with a forced scowl. Something was wrong. "What are you up to, Allyson?"

"I got you a present."

"I see that. Why?"

She shrugged her shoulders and said, "Consider it a going away gift." He slumped as he felt the breath knock out of him again. "Just open it before you have a fit."

"Fine," he muttered and tore the black ribbon from the box.

When he lifted the lid, he stared at its contents in confusion. He gently lifted the card that had **Allyson Lambert** written in bold letters across the top out of the box, raised his eyebrows in Ally's direction, waited for an explanation. She gave him an indulgent smile but didn't say a word. So he asked again, "What is this?"

"Did you look at it?"

"Yeah, it's a business card. So what? Why are you giving me a card with your name on it?"

She sighed and rolled her eyes. "Did you read what's *underneath* my name?" He slowly shook his head no and she prodded, "Go on. Read it." So he did.

And the card fell out of his hand.

He quickly picked it up, read it again, looked at Ally for clarification. His mouth hung open and his hands shook as he waited. She never said a word, just stared into his eyes with that smirk back in place. He asked, "Are you serious? Is this for real?" She bit her lips and nodded. "Are you sure?" Again she nodded. He looked at the card again, needing the words in print to sink into his brain so that they'd be real.

Allyson Lambert

Co-Owner

The Lake Shores Weekly
Public Relations & Sales Representative
A picture of a horse head with a horseshoe around its neck sat in the upper right hand corner of the card. And in the bottom left hand corner, was a cell number. With a Lake Shores area code.

"When did you... How did you..." he stuttered, his heart skipping beats just like his words. He took a deep breath and tried again. "I'm not sure I understand. I thought we'd talked about this and you were going to wait til hunting season was over."

"No. *You* talked about it. I just never agreed or disagreed. Never said anything, in fact. When you asked me to marry you, I talked to my brother Danny. He was more than happy to take my place as right hand man to Daddy. And he has a friend who's worked a few seasons here in the past. That's why he wasn't at the wedding. He stayed here to help get his friend more acquainted with the ranch while the first hunters were out."

"What about Dave? What does he think about this? I can't imagine he's too happy about having his top guide leave to move across the country."

"He knows. And he understands. Honestly, if I wouldn't have made this decision on my own, I'm fairly sure he would have pushed it himself. Daddy is old school, Aaron. He believes a husband and wife's places are beside each other." She leaned in, brought her lips within an inch of his. It took all of Aaron's willpower to not crush her against him. "And so do I. So take me home, Mr. Lambert. Take me home to Texas."

"Yes ma'am," he said, "But first..." he didn't finish his sentence. Instead showed her with his body how happy she'd just made him.

I've got to be the luckiest man on the planet, he thought to himself as his wife moved her body over his. She sat up and flung her hat across the room and her hair flowed down to cover her bare chest and belly. He ran his fingers along her soft skin, sat up and kissed her throat when she began to move, and amended, *Make that the luckiest man in the universe.*

November 20, 2015

Aaron set the last of Ally's boxes into the back seat of the truck and closed the door with a loud click. Ally stood next to the bed, her arms hooked over the side with her chin on her forearms while she stared off toward the hillside where the two of them had first kissed. It might have taken him months to come to grips with it and accept it, but he'd known that day that he loved her.

He watched her now as the bright sun streaked through her hair, highlighted some blonde strands mixed in with the chestnut that he'd never noticed before. He ran his palm down the back of her hair, delighted in the knowledge that they'd have the rest of their lives to learn everything about each other. She smiled at his touch, turned her face so her cheek rested on her arms.

"Whatcha thinking about, love?"

"Nothing," she responded. "Just grateful that you took a chance and kissed me that day."

"Even if it did get me slapped."

She stood up from her perch against the truck, set her hand on her cocked out hip. "Are you ever going to let me live that down?"

"Nope." She took a step toward him, placed her hands on his stomach, ran her fingers up over his chest and he couldn't help the involuntary flex. "Maybe someday," he corrected. She smiled that impish grin he loved so much, lifted her lips to his throat and kissed his Adam's apple. It bobbed under her lips and she smiled against his skin, did it again. "More than likely, yes," he squeaked out. She trailed her lips up the side of his neck, nipped at his ear, licked the sting away.

Then whispered, "And what about now, tough guy?" Another light lick. "You gonna let it go now?" Instead of answering, he wrapped his hands in her hair, tilted her head back and attacked her lips. He kissed her hard, hungrily, already anticipating the moment they'd stop driving for the day and find a nice hotel room to spend the night in. When he broke away, and their breaths both came out hard and rushed, she said, "Good. Grudges aren't healthy for a marriage. Besides, I slapped you *before* you kissed me."

She laughed and slipped from his arms, ran to the back of the truck. He started after her, stopped when he heard Dave holler from the direction of the barn. He looked at Ally on the other side of the truck, eyebrows raised in question. She shrugged her shoulders and met him at the bed of the truck. They walked over toward the barn hand in hand. And both came up short when they reached the drive in front of the structure that held the Marx's horses.

Aar was about to ask Ally if she knew anything about this. When he heard her gasp and looked over to see her hand fly to her mouth, he knew she was just as surprised as he was.

Big Dave walked out of the barn, his beefy arm slung over Suzi's shoulders as she smiled and wiped away a few tears from her cheeks.

They stopped next to the trailer and Dave reached a hand through the slat, pet Tuff along the neck once, then gave Aaron and Ally a hard look before he asked Aar, "I assume you know how to pull a trailer?"

"Yes sir. Why?"

"Because I don't have time to take it down there myself. How else are you gonna get these horses down to Texas?"

"Daddy," Ally spoke to Dave but kept her eyes on the trailer where Tuff and Fury stood, hitched inside, waiting to go, "what's going on? What is this?"

"What's it look like, Punkin'?"

"It looks like you loaded up two of your best horses into a trailer." He nodded his head. "But… why?"

Aimee Martin

Now he sighed, lowered his head and gave it a shake. Suzi giggled beside him, walked out from under his arm and headed to where Aaron and Ally stood. "This is your wedding present," she said and laid a palm on each of their cheeks like the loving mother she was.

"No," Ally uttered at the same time Aaron said, "It's too much."

"Not to me," Dave stated. "Knowing y'all have a couple of good horses down there in Texas is worth more than any amount of money. Plus, every time you ride, you'll think of us."

"Daddy, we'll think of you anyway."

"Probably. So picture it like this. Every time you ride, it'll be like I'm there, watching over you." Ally choked up, ran to Dave and he caught her up in his arms. Aaron wrapped his own around his mother-in-law, choked up himself. Until Dave added to him, "But if you mess up Tuff, I'll hunt you down."

Aaron laughed, stopped quickly when he saw the fierce look Dave gave him. But couldn't help the small smile that crept up his lips. He walked over to Dave, held out his hand. Dave took it in a firm hold and Aaron said, "Thank you, Dave. We'll take good care of them."

"We promise," Ally agreed.

"I wouldn't have given them to you if I didn't have every faith in you." Dave turned, walked in the direction of the truck to pull it over so they could get it hooked up. Aaron watched him, thought he heard the older man sniff, but chose to keep it to himself. Sometimes, a man's masculinity needed to stay protected.

Ally walked over to Aaron, rested her head on his shoulder. Suzi watched her husband for a minute, then turned to them and said with a wink, "Yes he would have. I'd have made sure of it."

•••••

December 18, 2016

Ally sat at her desk, chewed on her lower lip as she checked the time on her computer. Again.

Five-thirty. She huffed out an impatient breath and scolded herself, *Jeez, get a grip Ally. It's only been five minutes since the last time you checked. You're gonna set yourself into a panic at this rate.*

She rose from her desk, walked to the mini fridge that sat in the corner, grabbed a small bottle of water. She twisted off the top, took a drink and jerked when she heard the door to the office slammed closed. Water dripped down her chin and fell onto her chest. She wiped it off with the back of her hand right as Aaron rushed through the door. She froze when she saw the paper that hung loosely from his hand. She looked up into his face, tried to gauge his reaction, but he gave nothing away.

He gently closed the office door behind him and asked, "Is Mel gone?"

"Yes," she whispered, "She left about an hour ago."

"Before closing time?" He stalked over to her slowly like a predator closing in on its prey. She nodded and he held up the paper. "Is it true?" Her voice chose that instant to leave her so again she nodded.

His shoulders rose and fell on a deep breath and he threw the paper on the ground. He took the bottle of water she clutched in her trembling hands, set it on the refrigerator, picked her up around the waist and carried her over to her desk. When he set her down on top, he lifted the hem of her green blouse, just high enough to expose her navel.

Then he took her breath away.

Getting down onto his knees in front of her, he placed his hand on her belly. Ally marveled at the contrast of his sun-kissed hand on her pale stomach, then forgot all about tans when he leaned forward and placed his lips on her belly, right below her belly button. He kissed her again there, off to the left side. Then again on the right. Once more right over the center of her lower abdomen, then he stood before her and Ally's breath caught in her throat when she saw his eyes.

They were glossed over as he held back tears. Ally knew it, because she was doing the same thing.

"Really?" he asked, his voice clogged.

"Yes." He closed his eyes, rested his forehead against hers. "You're not mad?" Because that's what she'd worried about more than anything. They had only been married for eight weeks.

"No," he said emphatically. "I'm thrilled. Ecstatic. Overjoyed."

"Okay, okay. I get it," she said on a laugh at his penchant for always using more descriptions than necessary.

He lifted his head from hers, cupped her cheeks in his hands. "I'm *blessed*."

Ally covered one of his hands with one of hers, linked their fingers, placed her other hand on her belly. On their baby. "*We're* blessed, Aaron. All three of us."

"Thank you, Ally, for giving me the life I'd only ever dreamt of. I promise I'll never take it for granted. I'll treasure you and this baby like the gifts from God that you are. Both of you."

Ally lifted her mouth to Aaron's, laid her lips on his.

"I know, Aaron. I know we'll be forever treasured with you."

"Always, Elf. Always."

Aimee Martin

Epilogue

"Two are better than one: because they have a good reward for their labour."
Ecclesiastes 4:9

February 14, 2016

Aaron walked up the steps to the house, smiled at the new welcome mat Ally had ordered at Christmas. *'The Lamberts'* was written across the middle and three different sizes of footprints sat below their name.

As he stared at the smallest set that signified their baby, he couldn't believe that this was where his life had ended up.

Thank God he wasn't in charge of his future.

Otherwise, Aaron wasn't sure he'd have made it here, with Ally and a baby on the way and a life that fairytales were made of.

Good grief, I sound like a woman again.

It was true. But as Aaron unlocked the door, walked inside to the smell of fresh bread baking, he realized how much he didn't care. He'd always heard women found it endearing when a man showed his romantic side. And since Ally had gotten pregnant, he found he enjoyed showing that side, too. Of course, it hadn't hurt that he'd basically been forced to do *something* during those first couple months.

Right after she'd broken the news to him by putting a 'Wanted: Father for Baby Lambert' ad in the paper, Ally had been sicker than a dog.

Every day, Aaron came home from work at the ranch and helped out around the house as much as possible. He cooked, cleaned, held her hair when she was bent over the toilet. And his favorite, he rubbed her belly when she would settle in bed. Both because she said it made her nausea feel better, and because he could stare in wonder at that part of her body where a piece of him grew.

Turns out, he was ready to be a father after all. He just had to wait for God to bring him the woman He meant for Aaron to be with.

Thinking of the mother of his child–and it was his child, even if it was still in the womb–he walked into the kitchen where she'd placed the freshly baked bread on a cooling rack on the bar. Since the sickness had eased, Ally had turned into quite the baker. 'Nesting' was what she called it. He didn't care what the name for it was, just so long as she kept the goodies coming.

He reached over and was just about to tear a piece of the bread off when he heard her call from the living room, "You're gonna end up gaining more weight than me if you don't stop that."

Aar froze, his hand inches from the bread. He looked up and saw her seated in the big recliner in the living room, her hand on her expanding belly. The sun lowered behind her outside and Aaron swore a halo formed over the top of her head. Her skin shimmered in the glow from the fire to her left and made her look just like the little imp he always claimed her to be. *Well, she is my Elf.*

"Maybe if you'd stop baking, then I wouldn't have to worry about it."

"I can't help it," she defended herself. "I get the craving, I have to fix it. Pregnancy cravings don't go away. Not until you have whatever it is that you're craving."

"I'll have to take your word for it," he said, broke off a small piece of the bread and headed in her direction. He leaned down to kiss her while he chewed then said, "It'd help my expanding beltline if you'd eat more than just the first bite of the cakes and cookies and brownies and *bread* before you decided you didn't want it anymore. Thereby leaving me to finish it off."

She tugged on his belt, ran her hand on his still-flat stomach that twitched under her fingers. "I think you're fine." She slipped her hand behind him, just inside the waistband of his jeans and added, "*Just* fine."

"You're just trying to get in my pants."

"Yes, yes I am."

Aaron stood up straight, lifted his pregnant wife off the chair, brought her hands to his lips. He kissed each palm, moved to the tips of her fingers, nipped at each pinky and said, "Who am I to keep a pregnant woman from her cravings?" He walked backwards, pulled her in the direction of the stairs. He let her go up first and placed his hands on her upper thighs, ran his thumbs along the crease that separated her legs and butt. She glanced over her shoulder at him with a raised eyebrow. "What?" he asked innocently. "I'm just helping you up the stairs."

"MmHmm," she murmured but didn't make him move his hands.

When they reached their room, he made to take off her dark purple sweater that clung to her curves and showed off her already full belly. She stopped him with a hand on his wrist. He gave her a sheepish grin. "I know, I know. You probably want me to go shower, huh?"

"Are you kidding? You smell like horses and man." She wrapped her arms around him, tickled the small of his back. "Two of my favorite things."

"Are these a few of your favorite things?"

"Yes. But you won't hear me singing about it." He gave an exaggerated pout and she laughed, tugged on his stuck-out lip with her teeth. "I just need to use the restroom. Get on the bed and wait for me. I'll be right back."

She pulled away, held his hand until hers wouldn't reach anymore and her fingers slipped from his grip. As soon as she'd closed the bathroom door, he toed off his boots and yanked his jeans down. He undid the buttons of his flannel shirt, then got impatient and pulled it over the back of his head, tossed it onto the floor with his jeans and socks. He started to pull the blanket back but decided against it. She might not mind that he smelled like a well-worked man, but he did. *I do have to sleep there later,* he mused and reclined back on the mattress.

Just as he settled himself against the headboard, the bathroom door opened. He stopped fidgeting with the pillows and gawked at his wife.

She wore a white silk robe that was so thin it was almost sheer, swung the belt in a circle in front of her. The slit from the robe was open and her leg was propped out, bent at the knee. Aaron wanted to kiss his way up her leg, from ankle to thigh, just to get to his Elf. He wanted to leave the robe where it was so that as he moved over her, it would continue to show him glimpses of what lay beneath, teasing him to the point of sweet agony.

But he didn't do any of those things.

Instead, he stared at her through hooded eyes as she pushed off the doorframe, slowly walked over to his side of the bed. "See something you like, big guy?" He let his gaze travel over her face, down the sides of her neck and chest, past her belly, to her knee that she'd placed up on the side of the bed. Then jerked his head back up to her belly when he registered what he just saw.

Slowly, he pulled the two sides of her robe apart, revealed not one, but two set of footprints painted onto her belly.

"Think you can handle three of us?"

Dumbfounded, but feeling completely fortunate at the same time, Aaron grinned up at his wife, his Elf. "Oh yeah."

"Then let the fun begin."

****Get ready for the conclusion in the
Lake Shores Series
Coming in December****

LOVE THE LAKE SHORES SERIES?
Be sure to pick up your copies of the first
two stories...

Forever Home
Forever Grateful

About the Author

Aimee Martin, an International Best Seller, brings you the next book in her Lake Shores Series, **Forever Treasured**. Her first two novels, *Forever Home* and *Forever Grateful*, have sold digital copies in more than a dozen countries including Spain, Japan, France, Australia and many throughout the United Kingdom.

Aimee, from the Texas Hill Country, is a stay at home mother, wife and nurse. She lives with her husband, three children and many animals. When she's not living the life of a wife and mother, she can be found reading and writing. **Forever Treasured** is her third novel of a four part series of stand-alone novels.

Connect with her on Facebook, Twitter, Instagram and Goodreads.